THE CASE OF THE KAR
THE MASKED MAN OF CAIRO

BOOK FOUR

By Sean McLachlan

Copyright 2020 Sean McLachlan, all rights reserved

Cover design courtesy Andrés Alonso-Herrero

This Book is sold subject to the condition that it shall not, by way of trade or otherwise, be lent, re-sold, duplicated, hired out, or otherwise circulated without the publisher's prior written consent in any form of binding or cover other than that in which it is published and without similar condition including this condition being imposed on the subsequent purchaser.

For Almudena, my wife
And Julián, my son

THE CASE OF THE KARNAK KILLER

THE MASKED MAN OF CAIRO

CHAPTER ONE

Cairo, Winter 1919

Despite two days of meticulous caution, Sir Augustus Wall found himself trapped.

The affair had started ominously, with an invitation from Sir Thomas Russell to lunch at Shepheard's Hotel. While Augustus had neither esteem nor liking for Cairo's chief of police, he did have use for him. Both men were interested in the subject of murder, and Augustus was especially interested in solving murders that Sir Thomas could not. Because of this, Augustus was in the habit of leaving his antiquities shop in Cairo's medieval district two or three mornings a week to have breakfast with Sir Thomas. It gave him a chance to hear of police investigations that never got mentioned in the papers.

This particular invitation, however, made Augustus hesitate. Firstly, it was for lunch, not breakfast, and it was on a Sunday, which the police chief generally took off. Thus the invitation had the unpleasant hint of being a social affair.

And here he thought that he and the chief of police had reached an understanding. Augustus was not interested in social affairs. It was bad enough that he had to speak to his customers. He did not want to extend that habit any further than he must. A lunch at Cairo's most popular and exclusive hotel might involve other people. It might even (horrors!) include Sir Thomas's sister Cordelia.

That was a danger to be averted at all costs.

So Augustus sent an apologetic message via the Friday morning post saying that other affairs would keep him busy.

By evening post came the reply that this would be a great disappointment to Sir Thomas and his guest, the noted American criminologist Kent Lowell.

Oh.

Augustus's first impulse was to make up an excuse to annul his earlier excuse and accept the invitation after all. A criminologist, even an American criminologist, would be a worthy lunch companion. Augustus had heard of Mr. Lowell. He had been instrumental in breaking up an opium smuggling ring in New York City and a white slave trade racket in Chicago. He could learn much from such a man.

But caution made him hesitate. This could be a ruse. The American might be bait to lure him into a lunch with Cordelia. While he and Sir Thomas had an unspoken agreement that Cordelia's romantic overtures toward him were unwanted by everyone but Cordelia, women were wily and persistent creatures and Sir Thomas might have acceded to her pressure just to get some peace in his house.

So he telephoned Shepheard's and asked to speak with the maitre d'. The man, a hardworking Greek, knew Augustus well and didn't think twice about his excuse that there had been a muddle in the lunch arrangements and that Augustus needed to know for how many the table had been reserved.

"Three, Sir Augustus. Sir Thomas, a Mr. Lowell who is staying at our hotel, and yourself."

That satisfied him and he sent a card to Sir Thomas thanking him for his invitation and accepting.

It was only after arriving at the dining room for Sunday lunch that he realized he had made the tactical blunder of underestimating his enemy—for next to Sir Thomas's table was a table filled with women, including Cordelia and her Aunt Pearl. And the chairs were arranged in such a way that Cordelia sat precisely opposite the only empty chair at the men's table.

Augustus suppressed a groan. Briefly he considered flight, but he had never retreated in the war and he would not retreat now. If caution had lost to guile, rudeness would prevail over persistence.

He felt tempted to pull off the mask hiding the war wound on one half of his face. That would overcome Cordelia's girlish notions of him in a heartbeat. It would also clear the room and put their American guest off his lunch, so with regret he discarded the idea. There were limits to even his misanthropy.

Instead he didn't give the women's table so much as a second glance as he strode up, shook Sir Thomas's hand as the police chief rose, and turned to the stout, cigar-smoking and powerfully built man in the dreadful yellow suit who could only have been Mr. Lowell.

"Good to meet you, Augustus," Mr. Lowell said, clapping him on the shoulder as if they were old school chums on their fifth round. "Tom here has been telling me all about you."

"Has he now?"

Lowell exhaled a cloud of acrid cigar smoke and they sat down. Out of the corner of his eye he spotted Cordelia looking at him and half raising her hand in a little wave. He maintained eye contact with the American.

"Sure has. Sounds like you get into plenty of fun here in darkest Africa. Hey boy!" Lowell clapped his hands at an Egyptian waiter in a fez. "The menu. Pronto!" He turned back to Augustus. "Yeah, he says you helped solve a number of murders here in town, even saved his sister from a gang of anarchists."

Augustus cringed. It was just the invitation into the conversation that Cordelia needed.

She did not miss the chance.

"Oh, Augustus acted such the hero!" she called from the next table. "He's very clever, and tracked down the Apache gang with only the smallest of clues. Then he burst into their hiding place like d'Artagnan and defeated them all."

This time Augustus did groan. He looked over at the women's table to see an entire covey of them smiling at him. Several of them were of marriageable age, no doubt here on the annual "fishing fleet" of unattached women looking for husbands.

The only one at the ladies' table not smiling was Aunt Pearl. A red-nosed woman in her fifties, she had chosen spinsterhood over fishing and did not approve of her niece's fondness for Augustus. He appreciated having at least one ally in the feminine camp.

Sir Thomas was an ally as well. With an irritated look he said, "Sadly the ringleader got away. Pity you couldn't catch him."

If that criticism was supposed to dampen his sister's ardor, it failed.

"Oh, but Augustus was too busy. There were so many in the gang that stood and fought while the leader slunk away. Augustus was thinking of my safety."

"It was a most disagreeable episode," Aunt Pearl rumbled, taking a long sip of her gin and tonic.

"Indeed," Sir Thomas coughed. "And we're much indebted to you."

Augustus noticed that the chief of police and his sister both omitted the fact that Sir Thomas himself had been kidnapped by the gang. Everyone involved in the case had thought it best to cover up that little detail. There was still unrest from the independence movement, and knowing that the chief of Cairo's police had been a successful target might prompt others to try the same.

"I will always be indebted to you," Cordelia said, giving him a look that was supposed to melt his heart.

Silly girl, Augustus thought, *one cannot melt stone.*

"You were well on the way to saving yourself when I intervened," he said.

"Really?" Lowell said, looking at Cordelia with appreciation.

Augustus had a sudden hope. Was this help from an unexpected quarter?

"Oh, yes. She broke free of her bonds and was fighting off her abductors with a parasol in such a display of dexterity I began to wonder if they had started teaching fencing at girl's finishing schools."

Cordelia laughed. "Really, Augustus, you're such a flatterer. It was your servant boy who untied me, and I wasn't fighting the gang, but their pet baboons."

"Not much of a difference in this part of the world," Lowell chortled. He was openly eyeing Cordelia now. "You mean to say you actually fought a pack of baboons? I hear they're plenty fierce."

"Miss Russell," Augustus said, emphasizing the *Miss*, "is a most valiant woman. She knows Cairo quite well too."

"Is that a fact?" Lowell said, not taking his eyes off of Cordelia. "Perhaps you can act as tour guide."

Game, set, and match?

Just as Cordelia looked like she was about to say something accommodating, her brother had to blunder in and ruin it all.

"It's all over, in any case. Now if the ladies will excuse us, I and Mr. Lowell wish to speak with Sir Augustus. Waiter, we will have our lunch at the Long Bar." In a lower voice he added to Augustus. "There might be some work for you that will involve your talents."

The men withdrew, not without a final look from Lowell to Cordelia, and a final look from Cordelia to Augustus that he was careful not to return.

Augustus was of two minds about The Long Bar at Shepheard's Hotel. In its favor, it allowed only men, but the fact that it was one of the most popular bars in the city meant that it was crowded. Tourists and members of Cairo's European community were laughing far too loudly as they finished their second or third drink before lunch. But one could still find a bit of privacy. Even in the middle of the day the large room with its teak and marble bar, its wainscoting, and its scattering of little round tables was kept dark in order to lend an air of aloofness from the outside world. The shutters always remained closed to the African sun, and the door to the hotel foyer had frosted glass to keep curious eyes from looking in. Sir Thomas found the most isolated table he could and the three men huddled around it.

Gratefully Augustus relaxed, safe for the moment from Cordelia. Sir Thomas didn't approve of his sister's obsession any more than Aunt Pearl, and this talk of some "work" aroused his interest.

"That's right, Tom," Lowell said, keeping his voice low. "The truth is, I'm not here on a sightseeing trip. I've been hired by Charles Beechcroft of New York to look into the theft of some valuable jewels. Beechcroft made his fortune in real estate and he's worth a bundle. He came to Egypt during the 1913 season with his wife and teenage daughter and took one of Thomas Cook's paddle steamers up the Nile. Everything went fine until they stayed at the Winter Palace in Luxor. One evening they came back from dinner to find the safe in their suite had been opened. Someone had learned the combination, opened it, and took a wad of cash as well as jewelry worth more than $25,000."

"Someone at the hotel?" Augustus asked.

"You'd think so, but it couldn't have been. The safe was one of the new kind they're putting in hotel rooms these days, with a combination you can set. Clever mechanical gizmo. You flick a little lever each time you turn to a number and it remembers that as the combination. In order to make a new combination you have to open the safe first and then repeat the process. So none of the hotel staff knew the combination."

"Who did?"

"Only the family."

"So someone must have gotten it from one of them," Sir Thomas said.

"Right you are, Tom."

This case interested Augustus so much he forgot to be irritated by the man not using his and Sir Thomas's titles.

"Any suspects?" Augustus asked.

"There was a mesmerist working on the boat. Goes by the name of Alaeddin Bey."

Augustus smiled as he lit a cigarette. "Aladdin? If he's trying to hint at magical powers with that stage name, he's about as subtle as an artillery barrage."

"No, *Alaeddin*. It's the Turkish pronunciation. Claims to be Turkish but we think that's a dodge. Anyway, this joker travels up and down the Nile entertaining tourists, doing performances on the boats and in the hotels. Quite handsome and popular with the ladies. Beechcroft's daughter started spending time with him and even volunteered to act as his assistant for some of his shows on board the steamboat. Her parents didn't think anything of it, but now they believe he mesmerized her and got her to reveal the combination to the lock. I've done some footwork and found that plenty of American tourists who had contact with Alaeddin Bey lost money or jewels too."

"Looks like he's our man," Augustus said. "Why hasn't he been arrested?"

Lowell made a face. "Well, it's not so simple. He's a slippery character and most of the valuables that went missing were taken from ship's quarters, which are easy to break into, or the victims were pickpocketed. Most of the marks didn't even suspect the mesmerist until I found out they had all been traveling with him. And the Beechcrofts couldn't make a complaint because some … private papers also went missing from the safe."

"Compromising papers?" Augustus asked.

Lowell nodded. "Afraid so. They hired me to check it out, but then the war intervened and I couldn't even get here until now."

"Six years after the fact," Augustus mused. "The trail must have gone cold."

"Not quite. I wired Tom here and he confirmed that after a break during the war, Alaeddin Bey is traveling the Nile again. He isn't employed by Thomas Cook or any of the hotels. He travels on his own money."

"Or rather, other people's money," Sir Thomas added.

"True enough. We know he's going to board the *Arabia*, one of Thomas Cook's fleet, in a few days."

The police chief turned to Augustus. "This is why we wanted you to come today. Since this is a private matter and they haven't made a formal complaint, my hands are tied. But there's nothing stopping you from giving some assistance."

"That's right," the American said. "Tom here has told me all about you and you sound like just the kind of guy I need. You know the country like the back of your hand and you even speak the local lingo. Now the Beechcrofts made a lot in steel and coal shares in the last war and don't mind paying top dollar. I'm authorized to offer you—"

"Perhaps we can discuss this after lunch," Augustus said. This man wanted to discuss specific amounts in public? How gauche. Augustus suspected the fellow didn't even know what "gauche" meant. He probably thought it was some sort of French soup.

"Suit yourself," Lowell said, leaning back and puffing on his cigar.

Sir Thomas gave Augustus a sympathetic glance and suggested they order.

"Sounds good," Lowell said. "How is this place? I'm not going to get a case of Pharaoh's Revenge, am I?"

"No chance of that," Augustus said.

"I know this is short notice," Lowell said, "but I'll make it worth your while."

"Sir Augustus is a good man," the police chief said. "He'll be of great help to you. He's been of help to His Majesty's government on more than one occasion. He even helped stop an international incident in the Western Desert not too long ago." He turned to Augustus. "I appreciate you keeping mum about the whole Bahariya affair."

"You are quite right not letting that sort of thing be widely known."

Augustus had had quite enough of fighting the Senussi. News of a major attack on a British base would only rally people to their cause.

"The good major was quite disappointed that there was no opportunity to mention you in dispatches," Sir Thomas said.

"That's quite all right. I would have only asked you to censor it, and the major was so helpful to me. I wouldn't want to snub him."

Sir Thomas raised a theatric eyebrow. "Kind words for someone? You are a man transformed, Sir Augustus. There was discussion of a letter of commendation, signed by General Allenby."

"No."

"Then accept my thanks. If that whole show had gone badly, my job would have become considerably more difficult."

Lowell looked between the two men with growing appreciation. "So, you like to help but you don't want the limelight, eh? That's just what we need."

Augustus looked around. "Speaking of the limelight, aren't we running the risk of being spotted here? If your mesmerist hears of us speaking with the chief of police, he'll be on his guard."

"He's been banned from Shepheard's," Sir Thomas said. "The management suspected him of robbing the customers. They didn't have enough proof to press charges, so they trumped up some excuse to eject him from the premises."

"Well, let's hope he doesn't have any spies," Augustus said.

"We've investigated him and he appears to work alone, except for one or two paid men on the boats."

Lowell jabbed his cigar in Augustus's direction. "I usually work alone too, but I'm a long way from home and I need a man I can count on. As I said, there's some embarrassing information in those papers. I'd like a man who knows how to keep quiet."

"You can count on my discretion. So there has been no attempt at blackmail?"

"None. Either the man didn't know the value of the papers, or he's waiting his chance. The war broke out shortly after the Beechcrofts got back to America, so Alaeddin Bey might not have thought it was a good time. Money transfers between the United States and foreign nations came under stricter scrutiny. Now that things are settling down again, he might make his move."

Augustus wondered at this. Information that could be used as blackmail often did not have a very long shelf life, and waiting six years, even with a war disrupting communication, seemed an overly extended period. Lowell wasn't being forthcoming about what was in those papers, so Augustus would just have to take that part of the case on trust.

"There are two native assistants I generally take along on such cases."

Faisal may be especially useful in this, Augustus thought. *Perhaps it takes a pickpocket to catch a pickpocket.*

"No problem," Lowell said. "Bring whoever you think can help. The people at Thomas Cook tell me tourism still hasn't recovered from the war and so there are plenty of spots on board. The plan is we watch Alaeddin Bey, maybe get into his confidence, and see if we can catch him in the act."

"One of my assistants works in my antiquities shop. Shall I telephone him and have him come over?"

"Sure thing."

Augustus made the call to Moustafa, who was with a customer and promised to come as soon as he could. They had their lunch and once it was over, the police chief suggested a walk in the garden.

As they exited the Long Bar, Sir Thomas pulled Augustus a little to the side and said in a low voice, "Sorry about my sister, old chap. She came unannounced."

"Like now," Augustus said. Cordelia and Aunt Pearl approached. He and the police chief put on smiles.

"I hope you gentlemen don't mind if we walk with you," Cordelia said.

Sir Thomas looked embarrassed. "Actually—"

Lowell grinned. "Why of course not! I'm always happy to have the company of two lovely ladies."

Cordelia looked as flattered as Aunt Pearl looked unimpressed. They walked out into the garden, a vast shady space enclosed by a high wall. Little gravel paths wound through clumps of trees and flowerbeds bursting with color.

"You might be interested in the story of this hotel, Mr. Lowell," Augustus said.

"You can call me Kent, buddy."

"Um, yes. Shepheard's has a long history. It was the first proper hotel in the country. There was a smaller hotel here before this one that was once the palace of Princess Zeineb, daughter of the great Pasha Mohamed Ali. General Kleber used it as his headquarters after Napoleon left him to his own devices and scuttled back to France before the Royal Navy arrived."

"Hardly seems fair to General Kleber," the American detective said.

"It was worse than that. See that tree over there by the office of the managing director? An assassin stabbed him to death there."

"An interesting criminal case," Sir Thomas said. "The assassin was a

Syrian student named Soleyman El-Halaby. The French caught him quickly enough and executed him. The Frogs tend to go native in warmer climes and they certainly went native with dear old Soleyman's execution. They cut off his right arm and burned it, and then impaled the poor fellow in a public square."

"Poor bugger," Augustus said under his breath. Sir Thomas, if he heard, pretended not to, and continued.

"After he had died several hours later, they removed his head, defleshed it, and sent the skull to the medical school in Paris."

"Thomas, must you always tell these grisly tales?" Cordelia said.

"Hardly a fitting subject of conversation for a young lady," Aunt Pearl sniffed.

"Oh, I'm used to it," Cordelia said and laughed. "I've been hearing them all my life. But that doesn't mean I *want* to hear it. So why did they send his head to Paris?"

"Just his skull, Cordelia," Sir Thomas corrected.

"Members of law enforcement must be precise in these matters," Augustus said.

"Phenology was quite the rage back then, you see. It's the study of—"

"The bumps on the skull in order to determine personality. Yes, I know, Thomas."

Sir Thomas turned to Augustus. "Cordelia is enchanted with all the pseudosciences."

Yet another reason to avoid her, he thought.

"I've been reading up on mesmerism lately," Lowell admitted.

Cordelia's eyes lit up. "A fascinating subject!"

"As I was saying," Sir Thomas went on. "His skull was used to teach medical students. Apparently it had quite pronounced bumps related to crime and fanaticism."

"How intriguing! I can see that skull as if it was right here in my hand," Cordelia enthused. "No doubt it flared above the ears. This is the portion of the brain associated with acquisitiveness. One often sees it in businessmen, but if it gets overly developed it makes the person go beyond the bonds of the law. The frontal lobe would have been poorly developed, the eyes often being quite close together. This shows a lack of critical faculties and a tendency toward obsessiveness."

Good Lord. Augustus wondered if he could vault the fence and make good his escape.

"Didn't President Roosevelt stay here when he visited before the war?" Lowell asked.

"He did," Sir Thomas said, looking grateful for the change of subject.

"You were already in Egyptian service, were you not?" Augustus asked.

"Yes, but posted in the provinces. I had quite the junior position then. I didn't meet him. I heard something he said, though, that's stayed with me ever since."

"Which was?"

"After surveying how we were managing the protectorate, he said, 'Rule, or get out.'"

Augustus smiled. *Words of wisdom from an American. Will wonders never cease?*

The little group took a turn around the garden as Augustus grew increasingly impatient. He wanted to hear more about the case, but with the ladies present that was impossible.

Salvation appeared in the form of Moustafa entering the garden. The hefty Soudanese was dressed in a spotless white djellaba and matching turban. Augustus suspected he felt uncomfortable and out of place in a garden full of Europeans, but he didn't show any discomfort as he strolled up to them.

"Good afternoon, ladies and gentlemen," he said, greeting the men first and then bowing to the ladies.

Kent Lowell waved him away, his cigar smoke tracing circles in the air. "That's all right, boy, we don't need anything. We'll call you if we need you."

Augustus cleared his throat as Moustafa's face darkened. For someone as dark as Moustafa, that required quite a lot of simmering rage. Before the fellow could erupt in one of his strings of creative curses, Augustus said, "This is my assistant, Moustafa Ghani."

Detective Lowell looked him up and down. "Oh, I see. The muscle to back up the brains, eh? Looks like your master might be taking you on a boat trip aboard the *Arabia*. You'll get to see a bit of the world."

Moustafa didn't reply. Augustus suspected that he couldn't come up with anything he could say in front of the ladies, or the chief of police.

At least he provided Augustus a chance to get away from Cordelia.

"Righto," he said, clapping his hands together. "We have some business to discuss. Shall we retire to your room, Mr. Lowell?"

They did, and once there the American detective spoke more freely. Augustus explained about Moustafa's, Faisal's, and his own particular talents. Lowell seemed satisfied and named a sum so high it made Augustus feel embarrassed. Lowell then went on to detail what he called their "plan of attack."

"This guy is a slippery character and we haven't learned much about his real identity. He's resourceful, and I wouldn't be surprised if he cottons onto me being a private detective. That's all right because he'll get cautious around me and never suspect you. I'll be the distraction. You can tell everyone that you and your assistant are going down to Luxor to buy antiquities for your shop. That kid you mentioned can act as your servant. He'll make a good spy because no one will suspect him. Back in my early days I was a hotel detective, and I used the shoeshine boys as my eyes and ears. It's amazing what someone will let slip in front of them."

"Faisal has proven himself useful in that regard on more than one occasion," Augustus said, ignoring Moustafa's grumble.

"That's great. I've already booked on the *Arabia*. You'll have to buy your own tickets so you don't look like you're with me. Here's something for expenses." Lowell handed him a thick envelope. "Thanks for doing this on such short notice. It's a long trip down the river and you'll have to close your shop."

"That's quite all right," Augustus said. "Christmas is drawing perilously close and this trip gives me the perfect excuse to say no to all sorts of unwelcome invitations."

Lowell belted out a laugh. "Tom warned me you were a bit of a recluse. That's all right. You're good at what you do and that's all that matters."

Augustus put the envelope in the inside pocket of his jacket and rose. "This should be a most welcome distraction. Now if you'll excuse me I have a number of affairs I need to put in order."

Lowell rose and shook hands with him.

That was the last time Augustus saw him alive.

CHAPTER TWO

As they rose to leave, Mr. Lowell turned to Moustafa and said, "I wonder if I could borrow you for the rest of the day. I wanted to get some business done with the locals and having one on my side would help."

Moustafa turned to Mr. Wall, who nodded, and stayed as his boss left. Moustafa would have rather gone with him. He didn't like this man with his swagger and his showy ways with money, but he knew Mr. Wall would be generous with his share of the payment, and with five children at home, money was always welcome. The prospect of going up the river to see the antiquities was an added thrill. He hadn't visited those sites for years, and there had been many important excavations in the intervening time.

But being stuck on a boat with Faisal for several days? It would take all his self-control not to throw him overboard!

"So how can I help, Mr. Lowell?" he asked in the politest voice possible.

"This afternoon I need to do some shopping for the trip and I don't want to get ripped off. You'll help me get proper prices. And once the sun goes down, you and I need to take a little walk to the bad side of town."

Moustafa got wary. "I'm not familiar with that district, Mr. Lowell."

The American waved his hand in a dismissive gesture. "Oh, sure you are. I'm not saying you participate, but the police chief tells me your boss is a real fire eater. He's been all around this burg, high and low, and from what Tom tells me, you go wherever he goes."

"I suppose that is true enough, sir."

"This is for the case. From what I hear, when Alaeddin Bey is in Cairo he acts as sort of a fixer for tourists, getting them what they really came here for, if you know what I mean."

Moustafa nodded. He knew what Mr. Lowell meant. For all too many of the male Europeans, and even some of the females, a trip to Egypt was more about exploring what they thought of as the "sensuality of the Orient" rather than a study of its ancient heritage.

"There's a high-end brothel he takes them to not far from the hotel. My client was a bit vague on the details so I had to ask the tobacconist down the street. Didn't want to tell me. Acted all superior until I slipped him a bit of baksheesh. He gave me the lowdown. It's in some neighborhood called Eshbeka or Uzbeka or … "

"Ezbekiyya?" That was the neighborhood they were already in.

Mr. Lowell snapped his fingers. "That's it. Anyway, it's right around the corner from the fish market. Quiet little place with columns on either side of the door."

"And you think he will be there?"

"He might be. He might not be. I have a good description of the man, so I'm hoping that if he's there, he'll remember me when I'm on the boat later. That will mark me out as the kind of tourist Alaeddin Bey likes. If he's not there, I'll make sure the girls know I'm sailing on the *Arabia*."

"So you are going to … patronize this establishment?"

Mr. Lowell did not show the least bit of shame as he gave Moustafa a grin. "I don't usually mix business and pleasure, but it's for the sake of the case. Now I'll need a man backing me up in case they decide to roll me. You look like you can handle yourself in a scrap and—"

"I do not want to do this."

Mr. Lowell looked confused. "What?"

"I do not want to enter a house of prostitution. I did once for a case and felt soiled."

Mr. Lowell chuckled. "All right, all right. I've heard about baksheesh." He pulled a wad of money out of his pocket.

"It's not about the money, sir."

"Of course it isn't. It never is, is it? But take it anyway." He pressed a wad into Moustafa's hand. Moustafa was about to object when Mr. Lowell interrupted him. "This is for the case, remember. We're setting up Alaeddin Bey to target me. That gets him close without us having to be obvious about it, see?"

"But Mr. Wall wanted us to pretend we didn't know each other."

"I know, I know. This works better. It makes me a mark, and makes you a possible ally. Alaeddin Bey will think you're going behind your master's back."

"I see."

The problem was, Moustafa did see. Whatever this man lacked in moral fiber, he certainly did have a sharp mind. Then something occurred to him.

"So how do you know of this place?"

Mr. Lowell looked uncomfortable. "The chief says you can be trusted, that you know when to keep your mouth shut?"

"I do."

"Those papers that were stolen were medical papers. The Beechcrofts stayed at this hotel for a couple of weeks before going down the Nile, seeing the sights and enjoying high society. Well, Mr. Beechcroft likes low society too, and Alaeddin Bey took him to this place we're going to. Mr. Beechcroft caught something. He was treated by a doctor who knows that the Hippocratic Oath means you keep your trap shut. No trouble with that guy. The problem is, my client needed continuing treatment, so the doctor had to write out a medical report that he gave to Mr. Beechcroft to pass on to his physician back home. My client sealed it in an envelope bearing the address of his accountant. That way his family wouldn't suspect anything and take a peek. The envelope went missing along with everything else in the safe."

Moustafa wanted to sink through the floor with embarrassment. Such things should never be discussed. If people lived according to God's dictates, they would never need to be discussed.

"And you're going to consort with these same women?"

"Oh, there's a way to protect yourself. You probably don't have them here in Egypt, but a smart traveler always brings a good supply of—"

Moustafa clapped his hands over his ears. "God protect me from unclean speech!"

Mr. Lowell looked at him like he was an imbecile. "Knowing this might come in handy someday."

Moustafa looked him in the eye. He thought Mr. Lowell actually flinched a little.

"My wife is a virtuous woman, and I am a faithful husband. I have no need for such things."

"Well, sure. But if you have enough kids already you can—"

"I do not wish to speak of this."

Mr. Lowell chuckled again. He had a habit of chuckling at things that were not funny. Moustafa wondered if it was a national trait. "All right, buddy, but this is one situation where ignorance is definitely not bliss."

They found the place easily enough. After dark, the area around the fish market—a damp, low district close to the Nile—was rife with fallen women. Moustafa had never been there and had always turned away from conversation regarding it, so he was surprised to see how many European women were seated at the windows of the shabby houses, red candles illuminating their tainted wares. He had assumed they would be Egyptian, like the women who infested that belly dancing bar he had been forced to go to on a previous case.

The neighborhood was one of narrow streets with inadequate gas lighting, lending an atmosphere of gloom. The stone buildings with their cracked facades and peeling plaster had most of their windows open, a woman in each. A few were closed, and as Moustafa watched, a man appeared at one of them, a European gentleman in a nice suit. The woman, unattractive and tired looking even in this poor light, closed the shutters. Moustafa sent up a prayer to God for forgiveness for seeing such a thing.

The streets were crowded with men of all races and nationalities, strolling along smoking while casually studying the merchandise. The relaxed air of the place appalled him. These men, most of whom were probably cheating on unsuspecting wives, acted no differently than if they were passing through a street of Jewish tailors considering the purchase of a new suit. The only off note were crowds of drunken Australian soldiers, loudly braying in their strange accents as they staggered from one window to another to leer at the women within.

Moustafa tensed as one of these groups went by, arm and arm and singing a crude song. The smell of liquor wafted in their wake. There had been tens of thousands of Australians in Egypt during the war, and they hadn't yet all been demobilized. Thousands of them remained stuck on guard duty in remote posts or wasted away in dusty camps on the edge of the city, longing to see home. Every chance they got, they came into town to let off steam.

They caused trouble everywhere they went, beating up shopkeepers and smashing property for the sheer joy of smashing it. They had taken an eager hand in suppressing the independence demonstrations as well, firing on crowds even before being given the order.

Amongst all the Europeans and Australians were a fair number of Egyptians. Some were obviously customers, while others were pimps making whispered negotiations with the men who frequented this place. Some were simple street vendors. A chorus of shouts from behind made Moustafa and Mr. Lowell turn. The group of soldiers that had passed them had stopped at a melon stand and were arguing with the vendor over price.

"No! No! Four piastres!" said the vendor, a skinny old man in a drab, patched djellaba. He held up four fingers to emphasize his point.

"It's two piastres, you bloody Gippo!" one of the soldiers bellowed.

"No! Four!"

The Australian swore, took a melon, and threw it on the pavement, where it broke open with a splat. The vendor shouted in protest, but that only egged the soldiers on. They each grabbed a melon and tossed it on ground. Laughing, they worked faster and faster, and before long all the melons were broken in a big, fragmented heap.

All except for one. The lead man, the one who had been shouting at the vendor, tucked it under his arm. He walked up to the vendor, who was trembling with either fear or rage, and pulled out a knife.

Moustafa balled his fists. If that foreigner attacked the vendor, he would intervene, even if it meant his life.

But the soldier did not attack. Instead, a slow smile crept across his face. With a sudden jerk that made the vendor flinch, he jabbed his knife into the melon. In a few deft movements he opened up the melon and cut several big slices.

"Hey, good one Bill. Give some here."

"Wait a minute, pal. Got to give a bit to our Gippo friend." Bill stuck his knife into a piece and offered it to the vendor. "Go on, open up." Bill opened his mouth wide to demonstrate. The vendor hesitated a moment, then obeyed. Bill stuffed the piece of melon into his mouth and they all laughed.

They kept laughing all the way down the street and into one of the brothels.

Mr. Lowell shook his head. "Are they always like that?"

"Far too often."

"Come on, let's get off the street. It's this way, I think."

They found it after a couple of minutes. The building looked somewhat better than the others. The facade had been kept up, and the shutters were all freshly painted instead of being faded and splintered. Unusually, they were all shut, and for a moment the two men hesitated, unsure if they had the right place. The columns flanking the front door reassured them. It was the only building on the street that had them and they lent a certain veneer of dignity.

"All right," Mr. Lowell said in a low voice. "I'm a tourist and you're my native fixer, got it?"

"Very well," Moustafa said with a sigh.

Moustafa went up to the door and knocked. The instant his fist rapped against the wood, a slit opened in the door and a suspicious set of eyes studied him.

"There's nothing here for you. Go away."

Mr. Lowell cleared his throat and stepped into view. While the doorman had spoken in Arabic, his dismissive tone had been clearly understandable to the detective.

The doorman's tone, and language, immediately changed.

"Ah, welcome to Egypt, sir," the doorman said in English as he opened up. "You are welcome. Please come in."

"Thank you," Mr. Lowell said. He jerked a thumb in Moustafa's direction. "This is my friend. He's showing me around Cairo."

The doorman, a burly fellow with the light features of a Circassian, bowed.

"This way."

The Circassian led them down a short, carpeted hallway and into a side room. A woman immediately appeared with tea and the doorman stepped out into the hallway, lighting a cigarette and remaining in view. The woman was not, as Moustafa expected, some young, scantily clad houri like he had seen in the belly dancing bar (God save him from the memory!) but rather a stocky, scowling madam who dressed respectably and had an air of authority. She served the tea and sat beside Mr. Lowell.

"Welcome," she said in English, only addressing the American. "How can we help you tonight?"

"I'm shipping out on the *Arabia* in a couple of days and I asked my assistant here to show me some of Cairo's famous nightlife."

"You have come to the right place. We have only the finest hostesses for the finest gentlemen. Where are you from?"

"America. I own some oil fields in Pennsylvania. Have you heard of Pennsylvania?"

"Oh yes, very famous city."

Mr. Lowell looked around as he sipped his tea. "Nice place you got here. Very homey and clean."

"We keep very clean here. No Egyptians are allowed. Only European gentlemen."

Moustafa didn't know whether to be insulted or complimented by that.

"Sounds good to me," Mr. Lowell said. "And where are the ladies?"

The madam rose. "Right this way, sir. Your servant can remain here."

Moustafa sipped his tea, which was excellent, and waited. The Circassian in the hallway neither stared at him nor ignored him. He merely smoked and, when a knock came at the door a few minutes later, gave Moustafa a look that told him he shouldn't move a muscle as he went to answer it.

The man who entered was an elderly Armenian who must have been a regular because the doorman greeted him by name and sent him right through before returning to his post in the hallway opposite the waiting room.

Moustafa decided he needed to play his part better. He forced himself to speak.

"You must treat him very well," Moustafa said. "He is giving me good tips, and if he is happy here he will want to come back when he returns from Luxor."

"He will be happy. Are you going with him to Luxor?"

"Yes. I am another man's ... servant," Moustafa practically had to spit out the word, "but I make some money on the side getting Europeans what they want."

The man nodded as if this was the most normal thing in the world. "You will not find a place like this in Luxor."

"No, probably not. And the Thomas Cook company frowns on this sort of thing. They want to keep a good reputation in Europe. Once he comes back to Cairo he will want some more fun."

"Don't worry. They all leave satisfied."

That seemed to be the end of the conversation. Moustafa couldn't tell if the man was disinterested or only pretending to be so.

After another half hour, Mr. Lowell returned, a smile on his flushed face.

"Well, all in a night's work," he chuckled. He turned to the doorman and gave him a fat tip. "Thanks a million. I'll see you in a few weeks."

"You are always welcome, sir."

They left the house of sin, Moustafa seething. It was obvious that Mr.

Lowell had played his part only too well.

There was a new argument on the street, some shouting by a group of men at the end of the dim little lane. Moustafa couldn't see clearly.

"That went well," Mr. Lowell said. "The girl was pumping me for information like crazy. Wanted to know all about me. I'm sure everything I said will make it to Alaeddin Bey. I could tell she wasn't just making small talk. We've got it all set up now."

The shouting grew louder. Moustafa turned and saw an angry crowd of Egyptians rushing their direction. Shutters began slamming shut all up and down the street. The customers strolling along the avenue scattered.

"Clean the filth from the streets!" someone shouted.

For a moment he thought it was a crowd from a nearby mosque, coming to rid the neighborhood of vice, but he spotted the melon seller leading them.

And then they caught their first European.

He was a portly man, with graying hair and a handlebar moustache. Too slow to get out of the way of the crowd, he pulled out his wallet and threw it at them, showering them with banknotes.

That slowed some of them, but the more determined ones, the melon seller leading the way, descended on the man.

"Foreigners out! Egypt for Egyptians!"

The man fell under a flurry of blows. Someone grabbed the gold watch from his waistcoat, but that was the only theft. All the other hands were fists, and pummeled him to the ground. Then the crowd started kicking him.

Moustafa grabbed Mr. Lowell. "We must go!"

They started to run for the end of the lane. They made it about halfway before a burly man in a black djellaba rushed out of an ally, shouted "Egypt for the Egyptians!" and plunged a knife in Mr. Lowell's chest.

Moustafa grabbed the man's knife arm just as he pulled back to make another thrust. The attacker struggled for a moment, realized he was losing the test of strength, and slammed a fist into Moustafa's face.

Moustafa grunted with pain and grabbed the man's knife arm with his other hand, ignoring a second punch as he twisted it back until the man yelped with pain and let the knife go. Moustafa shoved him away, kicked the knife across the street, and thumped the man in the face when he rushed him.

"There's another one!" the melon seller shouted.

Moustafa whirled around to see the crowd had swelled. They had finished with the older European gentleman and were advancing on him.

Mr. Lowell groaned at his feet. Blood flowed freely from his chest. His eyes fluttered open but did not fix on anything. Moustafa lifted him up and started to run.

He did not get far. Burdened by the American detective, he could not outrun the mob, which caught up with him before he made it to the end of the street. Mr. Lowell got torn from his grip and someone tripped him, making him fall to his knees.

"Beat the Nubian for working for such scum!" they shouted as they began to kick him.

Moustafa came up swinging, knocking down men left and right. Mr. Lowell had disappeared in the crowd. Moustafa fought desperately, but he was overwhelmed by numbers and found himself backing away. When a new pack of rioters appeared on the scene, bearing cobblestones and knives, he had no choice but to flee.

Bruised, disheveled, with his djellaba torn in several places, he ran three blocks before he found an English policeman to whom he poured out his story. The policeman blared a whistle to summon his comrades and within minutes they were back at the scene.

Too late. The rioters had left. All the buildings were shut up tight, and except for a couple of smashed shutters on the lower floors, they hadn't been touched.

The same couldn't be said for the two bodies lying on the street.

Moustafa went up to the American detective. He had been beaten almost beyond recognition. Moustafa knelt down and shook him lightly, hoping against hope, but no. Detective Kent Lowell was dead.

CHAPTER THREE

When the Englishman went on his usual evening stroll, Faisal sensed that something special was going on. He had gone to the big hotel for lunch instead of breakfast the other day, and then yesterday Moustafa had left the shop looking worried.

Faisal, as he often did, waited for the Englishman in the shadow of the alley across the street. The Englishman always went on his walks fairly late, long after most of the shops had closed and only the loungers at the Sultan El Moyyad Cafe sat smoking their water pipes and drinking tea. They watched the Englishman pass, as they watched everyone pass, but took no special notice of him. He had become a fixture in the neighborhood, only a bit more interesting than everyone else.

When Faisal saw him get out of sight of the cafe, tapping on the cobblestones with his cane in time to his steps, he hurried to catch up and fell in beside him.

"Good evening, Englishman," Faisal said in English. He had learned many words on the long ride through the Western Desert and was proud that he remembered some of them.

"Right on schedule, I see," the Englishman replied in Arabic.

"You can speak in English, you know. I speak it as well as you do," Faisal said in Arabic.

"Is that a fact," the Englishman said, not slackening his pace.

"How was your day?" Faisal asked in English. It was another of those phrases the English always said to each other.

The Englishman continued to speak in Arabic. He could be very stubborn sometimes.

"Quite interesting. In fact, the past couple of days have been fascinating."

Uh-oh.

"Has someone been murdered again?"

This time Faisal asked in Arabic. He didn't know the English word for "murder", which was surprising considering how much time he spent with the Englishman.

"Indeed. An American this time."

"One of the cowboys from the moving pictures?"

They had gone to see one of those once. Those cowboys could fire two guns at the same time while holding their horse's reins in their teeth, and jump from a cliff on to the top of a moving train, and make a funny loop out of a rope to throw around cows or bandits.

"No, it was a detective who got murdered."

"Oh." That made sense. Cowboys never got killed, at least not the good ones.

"So … you need my help." That meant money, which was good. It also meant danger, which wasn't so good.

"The murderer might know me, and if he knows me he will know Moustafa."

"Wouldn't he know me too?"

"Moustafa is seen with me more. You're more invisible."

Faisal made a face. Being invisible could be helpful sometimes, like when you wanted to follow someone or sneak somewhere. But it meant that people thought you didn't exist. That's how the Englishman could be sometimes. If nobody was being murdered, Faisal was invisible to the Englishman too. Then he didn't want to be disturbed on his evening walks. Oh, he'd give Faisal a piastre or two, but he would make it clear that he wanted to be alone.

Faisal was beginning to hate that.

"Would you fancy a boat ride up the Nile?" the Englishman asked.

"You mean on the police motorboat?" They had ridden that once.

"No, on one of the big steamboats."

Faisal cocked his head. He had seen those along the river. They were bigger than a row of houses, all bright white in the sun and with lots of Europeans on them doing what Europeans do. People said they were like hotels on the water, with bedrooms and restaurants and everything.

"Will they let me on?"

"They will if I tell them to, and if you dress and behave properly."

Faisal jumped and spun in the air.

"A boat ride!"

"All the way up the Nile."

Faisal stopped. "All the way?"

"Well, to Luxor."

Faisal had heard of Luxor. It was very far away. He supposed those big white boats with the paddles on the sides could make it. They weren't as fast as the police motorboats but they didn't have police on them so that made them nicer.

"Can't we go to Bahariya Oasis instead?"

"Sorry, I know you miss your friend, but the murderer went south, not west."

"Yes, there will be a murderer we have to deal with," Faisal said with a sigh. "There's always a murderer. And snakes, and scorpions, and gunfights, and djinn—"

The Englishman rapped his walking stick on the cobblestones.

"I have explained it until I've turned blue in the face. There is no such thing as djinn! They are in your imagination."

"Am I imagining the murderer, snakes, scorpions, and gunfights?"

"Well … no."

"I didn't think so."

"I wouldn't want to put you in danger if you don't want to go."

"Do you need me to go?"

"Yes."

"A lot?"

"Yes, Faisal."

"You wouldn't be able to solve the murder without me, right?"

The Englishman rapped his cane against the cobblestones again. "If I've told you once, I've told you a thousand times that you're useful in these cases. Why do you always ask me that?"

Faisal smiled. "A piastre a day like last time?"

"Very well."

"And a moving picture when we get back?"

"They might even have them in Luxor."

Faisal hadn't thought of that. If he could get a moving picture in Luxor, he might be able to get a second one once they got back to Cairo.

"How is the food on the boats?"

"I'm surprised you didn't get to that sooner. Thomas Cook boats are famous for their cuisine."

That decided it.

"All right, Englishman, I'll solve the murder for you. When do we leave?"

"In a couple of days."

A couple of days? He had a lot to do! He had to talk to Mina and see what she wanted from Luxor. He had to make sure everything was in place in his shed on the roof. He had to figure out what to bring. And of course the Englishman would keep him busy spying on people and maybe breaking into houses.

He was about to ask for some money, because of course he would need money to get ready for the trip, when the Englishman handed him a bunch of coins.

Ten piastres!

"Now don't waste that. I want you to get your djellaba cleaned, the nice blue one, not those rags you have on now. And I want you cleaned up too. Go to a hammam if they'll take you and have a good bath. Borrow a comb and get out the worst of those lice. You need to be presentable or they won't let you on board."

"OK, Englishman. Do you need me to do anything right now?"

"No, I don't think so."

"How was the American detective murdered?"

"In an independence riot."

"The one next to the fish market? I heard about that. They killed an American and a Swiss man. Is Swiss in Europe?"

"It's called Switzerland, and yes."

"So you think this riot was a fake. They did it to hide murdering the American for some other reason."

The Englishman looked down at him and smiled. "You certainly are a clever boy."

Faisal jumped in the air and spun around. "I sure am!" Then his mood darkened. "Do you want me to look around there?"

"That's not the sort of neighborhood for you."

No it wasn't. Faisal had heard bad women worked in the fish market. Many people said his mother had worked there before she had abandoned him and his father, but that wasn't true. She had been a virtuous woman who had died giving birth to him.

"All right Englishman, I won't go."

He had been there once a couple of years ago, thinking he could beg among all the Europeans who went there after dark. While Europeans didn't give money to beggars very often, they gave a lot more than Egyptians when they did.

Faisal had only been ten when he had visited. Or nine. Or maybe eleven. No, probably ten. He wasn't sure when he was born and it didn't really matter. Anyway, he wasn't as smart as he was now. Now he was smart enough not to go to the fish market after dark.

He still remembered that night, although he didn't like to. It came in his nightmares sometimes.

The other street boys had warned Faisal not to go there, saying it was too dangerous, but Faisal had already begun breaking into houses and shops by that time, and he knew that the more danger you put yourself in, the bigger rewards you got. He had just broken into a sweet seller's shop because the fool hadn't put the lock on right, and he had come away with two big sacks of sugar. He sold one and earned enough money to eat for two days. The second sack he ate himself.

So ten-year-old Faisal (assuming he was really ten) felt pretty confident when he went to the fish market that night.

Right away he knew something was wrong.

People acted differently there. First off, there were no families, only men. He was the only boy there. There were women, but they weren't in the street. Instead they sat in windows with red candles lighting them. They didn't wear much, and none of them wore headscarves. He was surprised their husbands didn't beat them for showing themselves in public like that. They called out to the men, saying things he didn't understand. Well, he did a little, and it made him uncomfortable.

But he remembered why had had gone there and went up to a foreign man who was strolling from one window to another. Faisal stuck his hand out, trying to look hungry and sorrowful. That was hard to do when you've just eaten a handful of stolen sugar.

The man ignored him. That was all right. Faisal was used to being ignored. He went up to another European, who stood near a row of windows looking up at the women sitting there. Faisal stuck out his hand. The European looked down at him, frowned, and made a motion for him to go away.

"Please, sir, I'm hungry," Faisal said. He knew the foreigner probably didn't understand Arabic, but it was how you said it that mattered. They expected you to plead and whine.

The man made another motion with his hand, angrier this time, and Faisal moved on.

He only got a couple of steps before his way was blocked by another foreigner. This one looked like he had just arrived in Egypt. He had the red face and hands that all new Europeans had. It took some time before they turned brown like normal people. He smiled down at Faisal with one of those smiles you just knew was hiding something. Not a real smile at all.

Faisal took a step back. No one ever smiled at him when he was begging.

The man said something in English, and while Faisal couldn't understand it, he didn't like the tone. He spoke quietly, almost mumbling, but with force, like he was demanding something he didn't want to demand too loudly.

The last European, the one that had told him to go away, said a sharp word to the sunburned European and walked off. The sunburned foreigner frowned at the man and turned back to Faisal. Again he said something, more insistent this time, and pulled out a handful of money. Not coins—banknotes!

Faisal's eyes bugged …

… and he took another step back.

Faisal knew a jackal when he saw one. Living on the streets he had discovered there were a lot of bad people. He didn't know what this man was saying, or why he was holding out more money than Faisal had ever touched in his whole life, but he knew this man was a jackal.

"Hey!" one of the women sitting at the windows shouted. The sunburnt man jumped a little and hurried off, even though the woman had shouted at Faisal, not him. "Get out of here, you filthy tyke. We don't want competition from the likes of you."

"If you want to make money begging, you should dress poor and walk around the streets," Faisal replied.

"You little idiot, go home."

"I don't have one."

"Well, you won't find one here. Shove off."

"Hey, isn't that little Faisal?" another woman called. She sat two windows down. Faisal recognized her. During the day she sold cheap jewelry in one of the poorer markets where Faisal beg and stole. Her little stand with glass bracelets and rings of fake silver probably didn't make much money. Nobody in that market did. That must have been why she came here at night to beg from foreign men.

"Um, hello. How do you know my name?"

The woman grinned. She really shouldn't have grinned because she had more spaces than teeth. "I knew your mother."

"Really?" That was good news. Nobody ever admitted they knew Faisal's mother, or if they did they said bad things about her. Untrue things.

"Sure. She used to work here. Just across the street at that building there." Faisal turned and saw another building just like the others, with women sitting in windows lit by red candles.

"She worked as a cleaning lady," Faisal said. That must be it. "Keeping the hallways swept and buying candles when they ran out."

A chorus of female laughter made him cringe.

"You stupid boy! She was a window girl. See that window two from the right on the bottom floor? That was hers. She was popular. They used to call her—"

"Stop! All that's a lie! Why are you lying to me?"

Faisal picked up a stone from the street and threw it at her. It smashed into the bars of the window instead, making her yelp and jump back.

The women all started cursing at him, but Faisal wasn't listening anymore. He was running, running away from the doorman who was just coming out with murder on his face, and running from what they had said.

Because he had heard it all before. And he would hear it again, from so many people, from his drunken father to the fruit-seller on Ibn al-Nafis Street. Everyone said the same thing.

He hated that. Absolutely hated that. Why did everyone have to lie?

"You've gone silent all of a sudden," the Englishman said. They were still walking on the street, the Englishman's cane tapping in time with his steps.

"What's wrong with being silent? You always say I talk too much."

"No need to get snippy. What are you thinking about?"

"Nothing."

"I find that hard to believe. That lice-ridden head of yours is always full of notions and machinations. And worries. Are you having reservations about going up the river?"

"No."

"So what are you thinking about?"

"Nothing."

They walked in silence for a time. The street was quiet, with only a few people about. The Englishman said he liked this neighborhood because there were no Europeans and it was quiet at night.

"Englishman?" Faisal said after a while.

"What is it?"

"Do you … ever go to the fish market at night?"

"What an impertinent question! Certainly not."

"Good," Faisal said, nodding. "Because if you did I wouldn't talk to you. Never. Not ever."

CHAPTER FOUR

The following afternoon, Augustus had an awkward conversation with the chief of police. They sat in Sir Thomas Russell's office in the Citadel, not at Shepheard's.

"Sorry to make you come all this way," Sir Thomas said, "but as you can guess, I'm absolutely swamped with work. Whiskey?"

"Thank you."

Sir Thomas poured him a stiff one, and poured a stiffer one for himself.

"Now I suppose you've come up here to convince me there's something sinister in connection with the Lowell murder," the chief of police said.

"Well he did get killed the day we met with him, and just three days after arriving in Egypt."

"Simple bad luck. There's no indication it was anything other than a small-scale riot. The crowd burnt some Greek shops and roughed up a couple of Armenians as well, not to mention killing that Swiss fellow. Their embassy is up in arms. The incident was sparked because someone a block over got arrested for painting independence slogans on a wall. Some Egyptians tried to stop the arrest, and there was a tussle. You know how these things can spiral so quickly out of control."

"Moustafa tells me some Australians roughed up a melon seller."

Sir Thomas sighed. "Yes, I heard about that too. Those people need to get back to their sheep farms and leave us in peace."

"This could have all been staged."

"Perhaps, but how could they have known that Lowell and your man would have been there? If they had wanted to kill him, they could have sent someone into the hotel."

"Or waited for him to come out and follow him."

"With an entire riot packed up and ready for assembly?"

"These things can spark easily, as you say. Most of the rioters may have been unwitting bystanders drawn into the fray."

"That seems highly unlikely. Of the ones we arrested, most were known agitators, some of whom had already spent time behind bars. I guess I should have left them in for longer, but we're trying to strike a balance between firmness and tolerance. We don't want to be like the Ottomans. We are trying to extend to these people the guiding hand of civilization."

"Yes, we really showed them the guiding hand of civilization last March," Sir Augustus said dryly.

Sir Thomas frowned. "Now wait just one moment. We were responding to a riot."

"Ah, yes. A riot."

The commandant of police raised a hand.

"Now I know what you're going to say, that the early protests were peaceful, and you're correct. But surely you have been in this country long enough to have some insight into the Oriental mind. In groups they are dangerous and unpredictable. What can start as a collection of perfectly reasonable individuals can, at the least provocation, turn into a howling mob capable of any enormity, even its own self destruction."

"Yes, they don't take much provocation, these natives. A protest of union members in Manchester or Republicans in Belfast wouldn't be annoyed in the least by a few volleys of British rifle fire."

"Sarcasm is beneath you. We had to maintain order and I have no regrets. Where mistakes were made was in our handling of the war."

"You'll get no argument from me on that point."

Sir Thomas blushed a little, and could not help glancing at Sir Augustus' mask.

The chief of police quickly rallied.

"We did the Egyptians a disservice, I admit that freely. We squandered all the loyalty we have built up among the fellahin and city people. When we took Egypt from the Khedive and the Turk, we made countless improvements to infrastructure. We got rid of the hated conscription law, removed a great deal of corruption, and banned the flogging of the peasant class. That alone should have earned the fellahin's eternal gratitude. After a few short years, the farmer saw his crops increase, the shipping cost of those crops go down, and they enjoyed a freer and more dignified life. The city dwellers enjoyed public transport and a chance to send their children to European-run schools, with the opportunity of working in the Imperial civil service."

"That is all well and good, but what the Egyptians really want, and the Soudanese too, is self-rule."

Sir Thomas pointed a stern figure at him. "That is where you are wrong, and that is where they are wrong. The Egyptians only think they want self-rule, and most of the Soudanese are in such a state of ignorance the thought hasn't penetrated their thick skulls. No. The Egyptians want *just* rule, and that's where we slipped. You weren't here yet, so allow me to explain. During the war, most of the civil service was pressed into more urgent matters and many responsibilities devolved back on the village headman, who immediately got up to his old tricks. When we recruited for the Egyptian Labour Corps, without which we could have never launched the Palestine Campaign, it was the village headman who decided who should go. This led to all sorts of abuses. Anyone who couldn't pay a bribe, or who had a pretty wife or some nice land the headman coveted, found themselves conscripted. And then we needed to commandeer their camels and their donkeys. We paid more than the market price, but sticky fingers took much of that away, and what can a peasant do without his draft animals? Then we commandeered his grain and his cotton, and once again the sticky fingers—Egyptian fingers, Sir Augustus, not British ones—took much of that away. Our fault during the war wasn't keeping Egyptian a protectorate; our fault was not governing it. The Egyptians, and I daresay the Soudanese too, were happy as long as we ruled. When we stopped ruling, when they got a taste of rule by their own kind, that is when they rose up in anger. And the fools didn't go after corrupt Egyptians, but us. Mr. Lowell isn't the only innocent to have been killed. You know as well as I do that many civilians were caught up in the crisis. Dorothea herself nearly got attacked."

"Really?" Sir Augustus asked. He had only met Sir Thomas's wife fleetingly, and found her less irritating than her husband, and certainly less irritating than the usual run of colonial wives. She had spoken intelligently on Egyptology.

"Indeed. During the riots she was doing some volunteer typing at police headquarters and had to pass through a crowd of riff-raff alone in my motorcar. Not ten minutes later that same crowd stabbed one of my Egyptian detectives to death and did a dance around the body."

"That's terrible," Sir Augustus said, and meant it. There had been reports of European nurses being insulted in provincial hospitals, and more than a few European men had been killed in front of their families.

Sir Thomas smiled. "She's made of stern stuff, and came to the station every morning like clockwork to do her duty. But it only goes to show how common these incidents are. While the situation is not nearly as bad as it was in the spring, the country is still unsettled. I'm surprised the Thomas Cook company hasn't cancelled its trip up the river."

"We've been informed that we won't be stopping at some of the more remote sites and have received a partial refund. That's neither here nor there, since I'm not going for sightseeing in any case. I suppose you don't have any objection to me continuing with the work for which Mr. Lowell hired me?"

"Of course not. I've already sent a wire to the Beechcrofts about the affair, and I suspect that they will give you their full support. I'll tell you when I get a response. In the meantime, do be careful."

"I always am," Augustus said, removing his compact pistol from his jacket pocket and placing it on the desk.

"A fine automatic," Sir Thomas said, turning it over in his hands. "But I prefer a revolver. It's more reliable and has greater stopping power."

"Bullets stop most men no matter what their caliber."

"True enough, but it's best to be sure."

"I have a Lee-Enfield as well. That has more stopping power than one generally needs."

"You have more than that," said Sir Thomas in an exasperated voice. "Rifles and pistols and knives aplenty. I understand the need to go armed, but a private citizen doesn't require a personal arsenal."

Augustus managed not to smile. If the police chief thought a few rifles and pistols were the extent of his weapon collection, he was sorely mistaken.

"What else do you carry?" Augustus asked. "Surely you don't face down all the protests merely with a revolver?"

"Tact and a firm hand keep me from having to use weapons most of the time. You might take a lesson from that. I have a few rifles at home, of course. You know how keen I am on hunting. And my driver has a revolver. Across the back of his seat I hang a sawn-off twelve-bore shotgun. Right next to it I used to have a wonderful five-foot quarterstaff with a calf's knuckle joint tied with leather shrunk on to the end. It made an excellent club."

"What happened to it? Did you break it over the skull of an independence activist?"

Sir Thomas laughed. "If only! No, General Allenby was in my car one day and took a fancy to it. All but stole it."

"You should have arrested him."

"Well, he did ask for it, but what's a man to say? If it would have put me in an awkward position to say no, then I cannot really be considered to have said yes."

"True enough. Let's just hope that no more Australians decide to rough up any more melon sellers before I solve this case."

"The Australians have been a disciplinary nightmare ever since they got here. We've tried to hush that fact since they were so helpful to the war effort."

"You haven't hushed it up too well. The Egyptians constantly complain about them."

"I mean we've hushed it up in the press. It won't do to have that sort of thing straining international relations. And yes, they do cause trouble, but not as much trouble as the independence camp pretend." Sir Thomas chuckled, sipped his whiskey, and leaned closer to Augustus.

"Let me tell you a story about the riots. I'm sure you saw some of the marches where they bore their so-called martyrs aloft on biers and worked themselves into a frenzy."

"So-called martyrs?"

Sir Thomas raised a hand. "Just listen. It will amuse you. I was working at the Savoy, which we were using as HQ, when I heard the sound of an approaching protest. I went to the veranda and saw a large mob entering Opera Square. They were chanting independence slogans and at the front of the column several men carried a bier with the body of a young man on it.

"This got me in a fix. I only had a few British officers with me, the rest being Egyptians. With the Muslims being so touchy about funerals, I feared having my men try to intervene. I hoped that the funeral would simply pass. If they got up to any lawlessness, as they looked ready to do, then my men might be unwilling to stop them. And if my authority broke down in such a public manner, all our efforts would be lost.

"I arrayed my men on the veranda to block the mob from getting inside and awaited events. The crowd stopped in front of the Savoy and laid down the bier. The corpse was quite young and decently dressed, no doubt a student, and with a face white with death. After having presented us with evidence of British oppression, the crowd began beating their chests and jumping up and down like a pack of Zulus about to attack Rorke's Drift.

"Something had to be done. So I lit a cigarette to show my men I wasn't at all worried, even though the exact opposite was the truth. Looking at the body, I sensed something was a little off. I couldn't say what.

"Then I remembered a bit of advice a colleague had given me that he used in the Labban Red Light District when one of the ladies of the evening tried to evade questioning by pretending to faint. So, cupping my hand around my cigarette, I descended the steps as casually as I could. The crowd didn't stop me. They contented themselves with screaming in my face. My ears rang for an hour afterwards, I can tell you.

"I knelt down beside the body as if to pay my respects and ground the cigarette against its forearm.

"You should have seen the reaction I got! The so-called corpse leapt in the air, howling like a banshee. The flour he had used to whiten his face fell away and he regained his natural color. No one in the crowd saw my little trick with the cigarette, and they all started shouting at the student for giving the game away! It was easy enough to disperse them after that."

Augustus laughed. While his companion was an ass, he was a clever ass.

Not as clever as I am, Augustus thought. *And once again I'm going to show you who the cleverer man is. I'm going up the river and solving this crime.*

CHAPTER FIVE

Mr. Wall acted like a child being taken on a pleasure excursion. "The tickets are all arranged," he said as he cleaned the guns he had laid out on a table in his office. "The *Arabia* sails the day after tomorrow, and I had one of Sir Thomas's men check the passenger manifest to confirm Alaeddin Bey will be on it. We'll use Mr. Lowell's cover story of us going down to Luxor to buy antiquities. In fact, we'll buy some just for appearances. Faisal will pose as my servant."

It was midmorning. Moustafa had opened the shop as usual, his body a bit stiff from the beating he had received. Nur had fussed over him all the previous night, staying up late to soak his bruises with cool cloths and patch up his djellaba.

"We had a customer this morning," Moustafa said. "A Dutch tourist. He bought the Middle Kingdom statuette of Hathor and those Late Period painted mummy wrappings we got in last week."

"Oh, that's good," Mr. Wall said in an absentminded way. When he was on a case his shop became the least of his concerns, along with his personal safety. "Sold him real artifacts, eh?"

"Yes, he was polite and spoke most intelligently about the pyramids at Dashur. Most tourists never bother going to those. He explored the interiors of both the Red and Bent pyramids. The poor man got swarmed by bats in the Bent Pyramid but seemed to have enjoyed himself."

"Sounds like he deserves better than fakes. Good job." Mr. Wall produced a letter and some money. "I'd like you to post this at the telegraph office. Sir Thomas has already contacted Mr. Beechcroft but I want to send him a personal note assuring him that I will do everything I can to retrieve his papers. After that, buy three large water skins in case we need to go out into the desert. The ones we used on the Bahariya trip are a bit ragged. Close up shop before you go. I need to go buy some ammunition."

Moustafa nodded. That last item was one thing he could not buy for Mr. Wall. It was illegal for Egyptians and Soudanese to buy ammunition. The Europeans could buy as much as they wanted.

The telegraph office was an imposing stone edifice amid a cluster of British government buildings downtown. Moustafa ascended the steps to the great bronze doors, which stood open as Europeans and Egyptians scurried in and out.

Moustafa entered an echoing entrance hall, its high vaulted ceiling held up by Corinthian columns and painted with the figure of Britannia, a robed woman wielding a trident and a shield emblazoned with the Union Jack. A sign on the nearest pillar pointed him in the direction of the trans-Atlantic office.

A map on the wall made him pause. It showed all the telegraph lines in the world, the ones owned by British companies or the British government highlighted in red.

There were so many! From Cairo they went north to Europe, east into Palestine, and south deeper into Africa. He traced the line south as it followed the Nile, his heart doing a little jump as it came to Khartoum. But it did not stop there. The line continued down to Juba, and on to Kampala, Nairobi, and beyond, eventually reaching all the way to Pretoria.

Then he looked north, the lines going to Alexandria and under the Mediterranean to Italy and spreading out across Europe like a spider's web. Those lines were not marked in red. Instead, the British lines went underwater all the way to Gibraltar, then around Spain before reaching England. From there they fanned out across the Atlantic to reach Canada, several ports in the United States, and Latin America.

Moustafa stepped back and looked in awe at the whole picture—dozens and dozens of lines crossing every continent and every ocean and sea. Not all were British, but they were all, he realized with a clench of his stomach, European or North American. There were no African telegraph lines. There were telegraph lines in Africa, but they were not African. The same could be said of Asia and Latin America. That technological wonder, the miracle of laying a cable across the bottom of an ocean to communicate with Morse Code from one continent to another, was all in the hands of the white man. No black telegraph lines, no brown telegraph lines, no yellow telegraph lines, and no Muslim telegraph lines.

Shaking his head, Moustafa entered the trans-Atlantic office. A broad marble counter greeted him, staffed by several Egyptians. His heart rose. Going up to the only one who wasn't dealing with a customer, he handed over Mr. Wall's message.

"I need to send this to the United States. The recipient is written here."

The clerk looked at it. "A long message. It will be pricy. Your boss must have deep pockets."

Moustafa clenched his teeth. Why did this man assume he wasn't sending the message himself?

Immediately he felt foolish. Of course the man assumed that. Most of the customers here were white, except for an Egyptian wearing the uniform of the Continental Hotel.

He smiled at the clerk. "It must be interesting to know Morse Code and send messages across the ocean."

The clerk snorted. "I never even get inside the coding office. That's all done by the English."

"Oh."

The clerk studied him for a moment, a sympathetic smile on his lips. Glancing to his left and right, he leaned over the counter and whispered, "One day this office will be ours, brother. We'll both learn Morse Code and send messages wherever we want, eh? All over Africa, telling them to rise up."

Moustafa looked around nervously. That sort of talk could land you in jail.

"It will happen soon, my friend," Moustafa whispered. "But it must be done peacefully."

"Sure," the clerk replied, chuckling. "Peacefully."

A white manager walked by behind the counter. The clerk straitened.

"That will be 85 piastres, sir."

***

The conversation with the clerk followed him all day. Moustafa wanted Egypt to be free as much as anyone, but not at the cost of bloodshed. There had been too much already. But the English would not go on their own accord, so how could the Egyptians make them go?

Gradually, however, that larger question got pushed aside by his more personal troubles.

That evening as he returned by tram from the antiquities shop, Moustafa had a lot of thinking to do. His boss had caught himself up in yet another murder, and as usual had asked him to come along to help solve it.

And, as usual, he was of two minds.

If this case was anything like the previous cases, he would be in grave danger the entire time. He would also be taken far from home, and he'd have to endure that little brat who his boss thought was so useful.

On the other hand, he'd get to see Luxor again.

Ah, the great religious capital of ancient Egypt! He had seen it as a younger man, working his way up the Nile from Khartoum to Cairo. He had spent a season on the west bank of Thebes, excavating with the German archaeologist Georg Möller at Deir-el-Medina, the village for the workmen building the tombs in the Valley of the Kings and the Valley of the Queens. He had also helped Möller excavate the nearby Ptolemaic temple and some of the workers' tombs. On his days off, he explored the brilliantly painted pharaonic tombs and crossed the river to see the wonders of the temples of Luxor and Karnak.

That field season had always been close to his heart, and his mouth practically watered at the thought of returning. Yes, he was willing to face much danger to once again walk through Karnak's grand hypostele hall, or to delve into the deep tombs of the pharaohs of the New Kingdom.

But at the same time he felt guilty. Only a few months before, he had left Nur and their five children for several weeks chasing a murderer to Bahariya Oasis, deep in the Western Desert. To leave so soon, and again for such a long and indeterminate period, would be a hard thing for his family to take.

So it was with some trepidation that, after the last tram stop, he walked the final mile through Cairo's outskirts to the small house that was his own.

Nur stood in front, sprinkling some water on the road to keep down the dust. Her peach colored headscarf framed her brown face beautifully, and she looked so at peace going about her work in this friendly, quiet neighborhood far from the noise and trouble of the city. He could hear the squeals of his children playing behind the reed fence that enclosed the backyard. A few other neighbors were nearby. He nodded to Karim, an old man from across the street, who sat in the shadow of his house smoking a water pipe, and to Mohammed, a day laborer who was making his weary way down the street to a well-earned rest at home. There were several women in sight, but out of respect Moustafa did not acknowledge them.

Nur turned, spotted her husband, and her face broke into a smile. That smile faltered as he approached, and Moustafa knew that his face had betrayed him.

"That Christian is going to take you away from me again," Nur said. It was not a question.

"Up the river. Only for a little while."

Moustafa did not expect what Nur did next.

She let out a heart-rending wail and fell to the ground.

"Nur! Get a hold of yourself. It will only be for a few weeks."

"My dream! My dream! It's coming true!"

"What dream? Stop acting like this. All the neighbors are watching!"

"It's my dream!" Nur cried, rolling in the dust and tearing at her robes.

"Last night I dreamt I saw three feluccas sailing up the river, and only two came back! Now I know what it means. You and the Christian and that sewer rat you're always complaining about will sail up the river, and you will not return! How many times have you faced danger for that unbeliever? How many scars do you bear on your body from his foolishness? Only the other night you got beaten up and nearly killed! I always knew you would die for him some day, and now that day is coming! Oh, I'll be left alone to care for five children!"

Those five children had fallen silent, and were now peeking through the gaps in the reed fence, a row of ten astonished brown eyes watching the spectacle in the street.

Moustafa looked at them, then back at his wife, and his heart sank.

Because he knew he had been making the wrong decisions all this time.

CHAPTER SIX

The problem with money was that there never was enough of it.

Faisal thought he was rich with those ten piastres. He had it all planned out. He would buy some soap and wash his clothes. Then he'd bathe in the Nile to get clean enough to be allowed inside the hammam. They wouldn't let him in if they thought he was a street boy. Once he was clean, he'd buy a comb and get rid of some lice, then go to a barber and get a haircut, something he couldn't ever remember doing. He usually cut his hair with a piece of broken glass.

With whatever money was left over he'd buy some supplies for the trip. Sweets, mostly. You could never have enough of those and the Englishman couldn't be relied on to give him a regular supply. Maybe he should buy some other things too, but he would have to see how much money he had after all that.

He never got to find out, because just after he climbed down from the Englishman's house and crept out of the back alley onto Ibn al-Nafis Street, Hamza came running up to him.

Hamza was one of the other street boys. He was a bit older than Faisal, a tall, gangly boy with sunken cheeks and a cough that never went away.

"Faisal! Have you heard? Mehmed got beaten."

Mehmed was a ten-year-old Turkish boy. His mother was dead, and when his father got put in prison during the war he ended up on the streets. He wasn't very good as a street boy because he had grown up in a nice home and didn't know how to act. He was always getting caught or cheated.

"What happened?" Faisal asked.

"He was trying to steal some sugarcane from the market and the man caught him. He beat him with a length of cane. I saw the whole thing. The man shouted, 'If you like sugarcane so much, I'll make you wear it the rest of your life!' He beat him until Mehmed went limp. Then they dumped him on the side of the street and me and Mohammed and Abdul dragged him away."

"Where is he now?"

"In the house."

The "house" was a shack where Faisal used to sleep sometimes. Hidden in an alley stinking of garbage and cat piss, it was a terrible place but at least none of the bullies or human jackals that prowled the streets knew about it.

Hamza shifted from one foot to another, obviously anxious. "Can you help, Faisal?"

This happened sometimes. The other street boys knew he had money and food more often than everyone else, and they came to him with their problems. It got annoying to have beggars begging from him when he was a beggar sometimes too, but this was different. Someone was hurt.

"Let's go."

The two boys ran through the busy streets until they came to a shabby part of the neighborhood where the buildings closed in on narrow lanes and there were few people about. They climbed over some rubble from a half-collapsed building and entered a narrow alley between the ruins and another building that was once a grand home and now a tenement crammed with thirty families. The back wall, like the back wall of the Englishman's house, was blank, and so none of those loud, squabbling families knew of the little shack of stolen planks that leaned against that wall and sheltered a constantly changing group of street boys aged from eight to fourteen.

Faisal wrinkled his nose as he entered the alley. It sure did stink here. Did it always stink this bad? And was it always this dirty? It seemed to be worse than he remembered.

They came to the shack and pulled aside the filthy blanket that acted as a door. Faisal peered inside, waiting for his eyes to adjust to the dark.

He saw Mehmed lying face down on a pile of rags. His djellaba was off and Faisal could see the raised welts crisscrossing his back. Flies buzzed around him, landing on the bloody marks. Mehmed did not move. For a moment Faisal thought he was dead, but then he saw the slow rising and falling of his back as he breathed. Mehmed breathed shallowly, probably because it hurt to breathe, and didn't move because that hurt too. Faisal felt his mouth go dry. He had been beaten before, lots of times, but never like this.

"Where's everyone else?" Faisal whispered. For some reason he couldn't get the courage to speak in a normal voice.

"Off begging or stealing," Hamza said with a shrug. "We need to eat."

Faisal nodded. If you didn't scrounge and look for chances all day, you'd go to sleep hungry.

"He shouldn't be lying here with flies on him. The wounds will get dirty. Then he'll have pus and maybe get sick."

"What do we do?"

Faisal turned to him. "Get the cleanest bowl or bottle in here. Take it to the neighborhood fountain and clean it. And I mean *clean* it, Hamza. Then fill it with water and wash Mehmed's back. I'll go get Amira umm Dodi to look at him."

"The neighborhood healer? She costs money."

"I know," Faisal said, running out of the shack and down the alley.

He found Amira umm Dodi where she usually was, in a pair of small rooms in a nearby tenement that she shared with a crippled son and two small daughters. Her husband had been called up to go to the war in Europe and got killed by a German cannon. Now Amira umm Dodi supported her children by helping with births, mixing medicine, and bandaging injuries.

The front room acted as her little hospital. The door opened just as Faisal arrived. A young woman came out, looking embarrassed and clutching a small packet.

"I need your help!" Faisal blurted as he rushed in. "One of my friends has been hurt."

Amira umm Dodi was better than most adults in this neighborhood. She did not turn her back on the street boys.

The thin, bowed woman put down a mortar and pestle that she was using to mix up some herbs and studied him with tired eyes. "What happened?"

"He got beaten. He has horrible wounds all over his back."

"God preserve him. You boys live a rough life. Can you pay?"

Faisal did not feel insulted by this sudden question. Amira umm Dodi may have been sympathetic toward the street boys, but she was too poor to work for free.

"I have … five piastres."

The healer studied him. "If he is as badly beaten as you say, I will have to redress the wounds over the course of several days."

"Oh. Um, I have seven piastres."

"Eight."

Faisal sighed. "All right. Eight."

Amira umm Dodi gathered some things in a small bag and Faisal led her to the shack, having to help her over the ruins.

They found Mehmed lying where Faisal had left him. Hamza squatted next to him and they talked quietly.

"May God have mercy on him!" the healer said as she entered the shack, holding her nose. "Was this the boy the sugarcane vendor beat?"

"Yes," Faisal said.

"Then he deserved a beating, but not like this. Who washed his back?"

"I did," Hamza said.

"Good boy. I'll treat his wounds with this ointment I brought."

Amira umm Dodi pulled out a jar filled with a white cream. Mehmed hissed in pain as she dabbed it on the welts.

"Keep still. It will sting for a while. That's just the medicine working. Has he eaten anything?"

Hamza gave a shrug. "No one is back from begging yet. We have nothing here."

"If you want him to get better, he's going to need to eat and he's going to need to eat well." She looked down at Mehmed. "When's the last time you ate?"

"Yesterday."

Hamza turned to Faisal. The boys were always asking him for food. He could usually get some from the Englishman's house once the Englishman went to sleep. But it was daytime.

Faisal thought of the two piastres he had left.

"I'll get some food," Faisal said, then gave Hamza a hard look. "And if I hear you or anyone else takes any of it, you won't get any more from me ever."

Hamza nodded.

Amira umm Dodi finished putting on the cream and replaced the jar in her bag, covering Mehmed's back with a clean cloth. "Leave that on so the flies don't get in the wounds. I'll check on him tomorrow. In the meantime, feed him well and wash the wounds every few hours. He will be better in a few days."

That was a relief, but now Faisal had a new problem. If he spent his last two piastres on food, how was he going to get cleaned up?

First he had to get some soap. That was easy enough. After he had bought a bunch of bread and some falafel and vegetables for Mehmed, he went down to the river and walked along the bank until he found some women washing clothes where there were no men nearby. They were knee deep in the water, their robes fanning out around them like flowers as they scrubbed at some djellabas. More clothing hung on wooden poles stuck into the sand, spread out to dry in the sun. One woman came out of the water, set down a bar of soap and a scrubbing board, and started to hang up a man's djellaba. Probably her husband's.

That was just the chance Faisal needed. Without breaking stride, he walked past the woman, bent and picked up the soap, and tucked it in his pocket as he walked off. It was all done in a second.

After a few paces, he glanced over his shoulder. The woman was looking for her soap. She stopped, scratched her head, and looked around to see if anyone could have taken it.

Her eyes passed right over Faisal. Surely such a dirty street urchin couldn't have taken it!

Faisal giggled. He found a spot further down the river, not far from where some fishermen had docked their boat and were loading their catch onto a fish vendor's cart. Faisal stripped down, waded into the water, and gave his djellaba a good scrubbing. Then he gave himself a good scrubbing. When he came out he was almost as clean as if he had gone to a hammam.

The fishermen pushed off from shore and let out their sail. The fish vendor grasped the wooden handles of his heavily laden cart and struggled to push it over the sand.

"Do you need help?" Faisal said, coming up. "I'll help you get this onto the street for a fish. Just a little one."

"Get lost!" the man snapped, still struggling with the cart.

"Don't worry, I'm strong." Faisal grabbed the fish cart and yanked on it. It jerked backwards and he let out a cry and bent over like it had hit him in the shin. As the fish cascaded down, he opened up the neck of his djellaba and one popped right in. Fast as lightning he used his other hand to grab it before it fell out the bottom. Then he groaned and doubled over so the man couldn't see the bulge of the fish under his clothing.

"Serves you right, you little idiot," the fishmonger grumbled as he piled the catch back on the cart. The man stormed off, still muttering. Faisal grinned, stood up, and examined his catch. Not a bad fish. But it wasn't for eating, it was for trading.

First, he needed a comb. That was easy. He simply lounged around one of the stalls selling women's things in the market. The woman running it barely looked at him. It was the bread seller across the street who kept eyeing him. Obviously both women thought he was looking for his chance to steal a loaf. Neither of them noticed him slip a cheap comb in his pocket.

Once he had that, he snuck into a doorway where no one could see him and ran the comb through his hair. That wasn't so easy because his hair had so many knots in it. He did manage to get a lot of lice out, though. Once he had gotten as many as he could, he looked at the comb. It was nice. It was made of metal and was decorated with all sorts of spiral designs. Mina might like it. Well, maybe not with all those lice crawling on it. He tried to flick them off but some got stuck between the teeth of the comb and he couldn't get them out. He tried to use his fingernail but that only squished them. No, maybe this wasn't such a good gift for Mina. It would be a shame for it to go to waste, though.

Then Faisal hit on an idea. He could return it. That way he wouldn't have stolen it at all. As casually as he could, he walked by the dealer's stand and dropped it on the ground right next to the table. That way the woman would think she had dropped it herself. She could still sell it.

Oh, but what about the lice? He stopped and considered going back. No, those lice would get bored on the comb and scuttle away long before the woman sold it to someone else.

Proud of himself for doing a good deed, he went to the barber, a one-eyed man who was completely bald.

"I need a haircut," Faisal told him.

The barber put his hands on his hips. "You look like you needed a haircut a year ago. Do you have any money?"

"No, but I have this fish."

That evening Faisal—washed, partially deloused, and with a brand new haircut—sat in the Englishman's showroom, hidden away from the prying eyes of Ibn al-Nafis Street. The table was piled with good things to eat. Faisal knew this was a way the Englishman had to get him to say yes to whatever he asked, but he didn't mind. He had already decided to solve the mystery for him so the food was a bonus. Faisal was just stuffing something the Englishman called an éclair into his mouth when Moustafa showed up.

The fact that Moustafa didn't glare at him or tell him to sit up straight or stop eating like a half-starved hyena was Faisal's first clue that not everything was all right.

"Ah good, you've made it," the Englishman said. "Did you get everything I asked?"

"Yes, boss."

"Then sit down and have something to eat. Faisal might have overlooked a crumb or two."

Moustafa did not sit, which got Faisal doubly curious. What was going on?

The Englishman, as usual, did not notice the things right in front of him, and started talking.

"I've booked two cabins on the steamboat *Arabia*. It leaves the day after tomorrow and our man will be on it. I've also found a berth for Faisal in the servant's quarters below decks. That will give him a chance to mingle with the staff and see if any of them are in league with this mesmerist. Now what I'd like you to do is talk about how you are visiting one of your old digs down south. You mentioned being a foreman on a few so that should be easy enough for you to pull off. Talk about the rich finds they've had. Gold and jewels and that sort of thing. Perhaps that will attract him."

Moustafa took a deep breath. "I won't be going, boss."

The Englishman blinked. "What?"

Moustafa stood very stiff, and could not quite meet his eye. "I would like to hand in my notice. I cannot have these long separations from my family to go into danger. It is not fair to them."

Faisal could see the Englishman's hand gripping the arm of his chair so hard his knuckles went white. Moustafa must have seen it too because he quickly went on.

"I am very sorry, boss, but I have five children to consider, and my wife. She worries."

"Worries," the Englishman muttered with contempt.

Faisal looked from one adult to the other. Moustafa not coming? How could they make it through? They've always needed Moustafa.

"But you have a job here!" Faisal said. It was the only thing he could think of. Then he added in a quieter voice. "You need money for your family, right?"

To his surprise, Moustafa didn't shout at him or smack him. He only nodded and turned back to the Englishman. "Remember when we met Marcus Simaika during the Apache case? He offered me a job that day. I did not take it then because I did not think that anyone could get involved in more than two murders. Then you got involved in a third and I had to go to Bahariya Oasis. Now you are chasing a fourth. I cannot live this life, boss. Other people rely on me. I contacted Mr. Simaika and he says the offer is still good. I can start work at his Coptic Museum whenever I want. I will also help him with his collection of antiquities. It will involve some travel, but no danger. Nur understands this and has no objection."

"Nur?" the Englishman grumbled. "Who the devil is Nur?"

"His wife, you silly Englishman."

"I was asking him!" the Englishman snapped.

Faisal slumped. "Sorry."

Moustafa scowled, but for once he didn't scowl at Faisal, and that gave the boy an idea of what this was all about.

"I will arrange things at the shop before your departure," Moustafa went on, "and if you want me to run the shop until you get back, I am sure Mr. Simaika will understand."

"That won't be necessary." The Englishman's voice sounded sharp.

Faisal frowned at the Englishman. Faisal didn't want Moustafa to leave either, but there was no reason to get angry.

Moustafa placed the spare set of house keys on the table. "Then I best be going."

The Englishman went through the doorway to his desk and pulled out a little book, wrote something on one of the pages, and tore it out.

"Here is a month's pay," he said, handing the page to Moustafa.

Faisal gaped. He wasn't even going to give Moustafa money, just a little slip of paper?

Strangely, Moustafa seemed satisfied by this, put the page in his pocket, and held out his hand. The Englishman didn't look like he wanted to take it but he did.

Faisal waited for one of them to say something. Neither did. Moustafa turned, nodded to Faisal, and walked out.

Faisal stared at the Englishman, who went to a side table where there was a fancy glass bottle with a glass stopper filled with some liquid the color of amber. He poured himself a big glass of it. Faisal wrinkled his nose. It smelled of alcohol. He hated that smell.

And for a moment, he hated the Englishman too.

"You're just going to let him go?" Faisal demanded.

The Englishman stopped drinking, took the glass a little way from his lips and said, "It's his choice."

Then he started drinking again.

Faisal ran out of the house.

Moustafa was nearly to the end of Ibn al-Nafis street, walking fast. Faisal had to run to catch up with him.

"Wait!" Faisal grabbed onto his djellaba.

"What do you want?"

For a second Faisal didn't know what to say. He had expected Moustafa to shout at him.

"You can't just leave."

"I can and I will. I have people depending on me."

"Like the Englishman."

The old anger came back. "Bah! He only cares about himself."

"That's not true."

"Always running around trying to find murderers," Moustafa growled. "He just wants to prove he's still useful. He doesn't care who gets hurt in the process."

Faisal stamped his foot. Many of the shopkeepers were staring but he didn't care. "That's not true. He does it to help people. He saved Cordelia and he doesn't even like her. He saved Russell Pasha too, and he's always insulting him behind his back."

Moustafa waved away these words. "All so he can show he's better than he is. He lost more than his face to that German shell. He lost his mind too."

Faisal kicked him in the shin. "Take that back!"

Moustafa actually flinched from the kick, but didn't strike back at him. "He's mad, I tell you, and the quicker you and I get away from him, the better. Remember how he was screaming at us in the desert?"

Faisal did remember. The Englishman had said horrible things. "He didn't mean that. He was possessed by djinn."

"Stupid child. He was ..."

"Was what?"

Moustafa hesitated. "Nothing. Never mind." He jabbed a finger at Faisal. "But stay away from him."

Faisal looked up at him. "And do what?"

Be what I was before? Just another street boy who is no good to anybody?

"I don't know. Just stay away from him. Make something of yourself."

"I already have! I solve murders for him. I've saved his life. I'm even learning English." Faisal grabbed onto Moustafa again. "Don't go. I'll behave. I won't steal anything. OK, maybe if the Englishman wants me to, but only what it takes to solve the murder. Nothing else. And you can shout at me all you want. Come on back."

Faisal tugged at him, trying to lead him back to the house. Moustafa gently detached himself.

"You will regret staying with that madman."

"He's not mad! Look at everything he's given us."

"Goodbye Faisal." Moustafa turned away, hesitated for a moment, and turned back. Faisal was crying now. Moustafa put his hand under the boy's chin and made him look up at him. "You should leave. But you will probably stay because he gives you money and food and you are too lazy to work for yourself. You should get more than that. I know you have been having him teach you English. That is good. Keep doing that. Learn more from him too. You are an ignorant Little Infidel and you have much to learn. But if you stay, remember this—no matter what he teaches you, no matter how much time you spend with him, never forget that you are Egyptian."

CHAPTER SEVEN

Betrayed.
After all he had done for that man.
He had saved Moustafa from prison when he had been accused of stealing artifacts from an excavation. He had given him a job, lent him books, introduced him to scholars, and this was how he repaid him?

Augustus paced around his shop, hours after he should have opened. He would have to hire another assistant, but that could wait until later. The customers could wait too. To hell with them. Most of them were just gawping tourists who couldn't tell a sarcophagus from a shabti. One of his few pleasures in life was selling those idiots fakes.

A journey to the south to plan, a murder to solve, and here he was a man short!

The doorbell rang. Augustus ignored it.

Well, he could do just fine without him. He had telephoned Heinrich Schäfer, telling him what had happened and offering him the spare cabin he had already booked on the *Arabia*. The German scholar had jumped at the chance to see ancient Thebes once again.

"One can never see enough of the ruins around Luxor," Heinrich had said. "I've devoted many pages of my *Principles of Egyptian Art* to that wonderful collection of temples. But Augustus, you really mustn't be so cross with Moustafa. The man has family obligations."

Family obligations? Bah!

The doorbell rang again.

"Go away," Augustus muttered.

Heinrich would make a good travel companion, but wouldn't be much help in the case. Augustus would have to keep him out of danger. Hopefully there wouldn't be too much physical trouble, but considering how his previous cases had gone, that was a slim hope. The fact of the matter was he needed Moustafa, not only for his linguistic abilities and being able to mingle with the natives, but also his formidable strength and good aim. There was no way to replace such a man on such short notice.

The doorbell rang a third time, more persistently.

"Go away!" Augustus bellowed. He was about to go upstairs to escape from the annoying bell when a thought made him pause. Maybe this wasn't some irritating customer. What if this was Moustafa coming back to apologize? Or Faisal with some information he'd rooted out somewhere? He had best go check, and if it was a customer, he could get rid of him forthwith.

When he opened the door, all thoughts of Moustafa, Faisal, and even the case dropped away.

Jocelyn Montjoy stood on his doorstep.

For a moment Augustus could do nothing but stare in wonder.

There she stood, just as he remembered her. Jocelyn smiled broadly from a lovely face tanned and weathered by many months of desert travel. Despite being older than Augustus, she radiated youthful energy. She wore a pith helmet, a men's khaki shirt and matching trousers, and old army boots.

Jocelyn may have dressed and fought like a man, but she was every inch a woman. Every day since he had left Bahariya he had been hoping she would come to Cairo, and now here she was!

"Really, Augustus," she said and laughed that charming laugh of hers, "I've ridden ten days across the Western Desert and you're not going to invite me in?"

"Oh! Come in, by all means." He ushered her inside, his heart pounding.

"Do close the door, Augustus. The entire street is staring."

Once he closed the door, she planted a kiss on his lips.

"Oh Jocelyn, I'm so happy you're here." Augustus embraced her and kissed her back. After a moment he felt a fingertip press against his chest. He backed up as the finger kept up its pressure.

"Come now, Augustus, I may be a woman of the world, but don't get too familiar."

This comment would have crushed him if it hadn't been delivered with a warm smile and a brief follow-up kiss. Still, it left him flustered and baffled. She took his hand and walked into the showroom.

"So this is the famous antiquities shop. You have some fine pieces here. Is this the sarcophagus where you found the former chief of police of Paris?"

She rested her hand on the large stone sarcophagus, admiring the panther carved in low relief on the lid.

"It is indeed. The Apache gang put a second body in there too, among other tricks they played."

"Faisal told me all about it. I don't think he'll ever forgive you for seeing that severed head." She looked around. "Where is he?"

"How should I know?"

"Doesn't he live with you?"

"Of course not."

"Oh. And where is Moustafa?"

Augustus felt his mood darken. "He gave his notice."

Jocelyn looked shocked. "Whatever for?"

"We, or more precisely I, have been hired by an American detective to recover some stolen papers. The detective has since been killed in an independence riot, but we think he was murdered. Oh! I'm leaving for Luxor tomorrow!"

Augustus fell into despair. This woman had come all the way from Bahariya to see him, and now that she was here, he had to go down to Luxor.

"Why do you need to go to Luxor?"

"The thief is a mesmerist who works on the Thomas Cook steamboats fleecing passengers."

Jocelyn laughed. "Never a dull moment with you, Augustus. I would love a trip up the river."

Augustus blinked. "You … you mean you'll come?"

"Silly man," Jocelyn said, putting a hand on the good side of his face. "Of course I'll come."

The rest of the day was spent in frantic preparations. They rushed down to the Thomas Cook offices, where a tongue-tied clerk who couldn't stop staring at Jocelyn's trousers informed them there was an available cabin on the *Arabia*. They hurried around town buying what they needed for the expedition. Actually, it was mostly what Augustus needed. Jocelyn required very little.

"Should I get a dress for dinner?" Jocelyn asked as they passed a women's clothing store on the way back from the gun shop.

"Trousers suit you."

"Our stuffy fellow passengers may object," she said, following with a laugh that told how little she cared what those stuffy fellow passengers thought.

"You won't have time to get one tailored. Besides, women's dresses don't come with sufficient pockets to hold all that ammunition you just bought."

"You promised me an adventure when I came to Cairo, and your idea of adventure requires more ammunition than dresses."

That night after Jocelyn had left for her hotel, Faisal appeared at the door.

"Are you ready to go on the boat?" Augustus asked.

"Yes."

Faisal did not look as happy about that prospect as Augustus thought he would.

"What's the matter?"

"I wish Moustafa was going with us."

"Why? All he does is smack you around and shout at you."

"So do most people," Faisal said with a shrug. "He's also strong and can fight really well. We need him."

"Hopefully there won't be any fighting this time. I suspect this will be more a battle of wits. That's why Herr Schäfer will be coming."

Faisal brightened. "Your friend with the motorcar?"

"The same."

Faisal jumped up and spun around. "That's wonderful!"

"We won't be bringing the motorcar on board."

Faisal stopped. "Oh."

Sir Augustus smiled. "But we might have to hire one down in Luxor."

Faisal nodded. "I think that's a good idea. Yes, we will definitely need a motorcar." He paused. His face fell. "We need Moustafa too."

"Herr Schäfer can read hieroglyphs just as well as Moustafa can."

"Can he fight as well as Moustafa can?"

"No."

"I didn't think so."

"Hopefully there won't be any fighting."

"There's always fighting with you, Englishman. Does the other Englishman get into a lot of fighting too?"

"Who? Herr Schäfer? He's German."

Faisal's jaw dropped. "A German? They're your enemies!"

"Only some Germans, and not anymore. In any case, Herr Schäfer wasn't in the war."

"But he's—"

"A friend."

"So not all Germans are bad?"

"No nation is made up of only bad people, but every nation is made up of mostly bad people."

"Silly Englishman."

"You'll learn. We need to hire a couple of porters for tomorrow morning. Can you suggest someone from the neighborhood?"

"Oh yes! Mina's father."

"Who?"

"The man with the *fuul* stand. You sent him to a doctor for his back."

"Oh, yes. Him. Is his back up for it?"

"Sure. He's fine now. And if he hurts his back again, you can always send him to a doctor again."

Augustus examined his hand. "Funny. I thought I was made of flesh and blood but apparently I'm made of money."

"He can bring a strong friend for the heavier things," Faisal suggested.

"Oh, very well. Go tell him that he and his friend will get five piastres each and they need to be here at six in the morning."

"When?"

"After the dawn prayer," Augustus said, remembering that Cairo didn't need clocks when the muezzin belted out his song like clockwork five times a day.

"OK, Englishman. I'll be right back. Oh, what's for dinner?"

"Just go get the porters."

So the next morning Augustus hired a large open-topped motor cab, and piled in several steamer trunks packed with clothes, tools, and a small arsenal, as well as a passably cleaned up Faisal, the two workmen, and a young girl who looked equal parts terrified and excited at the prospect of her first motorcar ride. Faisal sat next to her, boasting that he knew how to drive.

"Come on Faisal," the girl said. "I believe you've ridden in motorcars before, but I'm not going to believe you know how to drive."

"I do! Englishman, tell Mina I know how to drive."

"He knows the rudiments."

The girl looked stunned.

"See? I told you! Here, I'll show you." Faisal tried to climb into the driver's seat.

"Over my dead body," the Egyptian driver said as he shoved him back into his place.

"A dead body with tire marks all over it," Augustus said.

The motor cab pulled out with a squeal of delight from the little girl and a shout of horror from her father. Soon they were speeding along one of Cairo's main avenues, the great stone banks and office buildings flying past, the motor cab weaving between donkey carts and other motorcars, to the docks on the Nile.

"Why don't we just drive to Luxor?" Mina asked.

"The boat's nicer," Faisal said.

"And the roads are terrible," the driver said.

"Can I go on the boat with you?" Mina asked.

"No," said her father, Augustus, and Faisal all at the same time.

"Why do only boys get to have fun?" Mina whined.

"I'll bring you something," Faisal said.

"I liked the camel bags," Mina said.

"So that's who they were for," Augustus said. It was odd to see that Faisal had a life outside of stealing and begging. He hadn't really suspected that before.

"I'll bring you something great."

"Like what?"

"Um, I don't know. What do they have in Luxor, Englishman?"

"The world's biggest temple."

"I don't want any pagan things," Mina said. "That's a sin, and they probably all have djinn in them anyway."

"More djinn," Augustus grumbled.

"The Englishman doesn't believe in djinn," Faisal explained.

"Is that why you call him silly all the time?"

"Mina!" barked her father.

They pulled off the road and onto an open stretch of sand next to the river. A gentle slope led to the docks. Past a frenzied crowd of porters, passengers, and vendors floated a grand white steamboat.

The *Arabia*, an enthusiastic brochure courtesy of Thomas Cook had informed him, was the jewel of the company's fleet. Measuring 236 feet long by 32 feet wide, its main deck boasted a dining room, library, games room, and smoking lounge. The upper deck had private cabins, and more modest cabins, supplied only with portholes, took up the lower deck.

The entire ship was painted in white, shining bright in the African sun. The flag of the Thomas Cook company—a blue pennant with the red letters "C&S" for "Cook and Son"—flew from the prow along with the Union Jack. A stream of European passengers made its way up the gangplank, accompanied by porters bent nearly double under the weight of large steamer trunks.

Mina's father and the other workman unloaded the motor cab while

Augustus took charge of the bag with the guns. In his other hand he gripped his sword cane and faked a slight limp in order to justify it. Faisal had a small bag of his own, a filthy canvas thing that he clutched protectively. Augustus didn't even want to guess what might be in it.

The workmen brought the trunks down to the pier, where they were taken by porters in Thomas Cook livery. Augustus paid everyone off, had to hurry Faisal along after he spent too long saying goodbye to Mina, and headed for the boat. Heinrich was leaning against the railing, wearing a bright yellow summer suit and wide-brimmed hat, idly smoking his pipe as he watched the crowd. Augustus waved to catch his attention and the German waved back.

"Show my servant to his quarters," Augustus told one of the porters.

"I'm not your servant, I'm your friend," Faisal objected.

"Don't talk back to your boss!" the porter said, smacking Faisal upside the head.

Perhaps we don't need Moustafa after all, Augustus thought, walking over to Heinrich.

"Good to see you, Heinrich."

"Good to see you too," he said, taking Augustus's hand. "I have two items of news for you, one good and one bad."

"I see. What are they?"

Heinrich lowered his voice. "The good news is that I've made the acquaintance of Alaeddin Bey. He was on the upper deck a few minutes ago holding forth on mesmerism, and as I have read some psychological studies related to that new science, I struck up a conversation with him. We're having drinks after we set sail."

"Good man. Mind your wallet. What's the bad news?"

Before Heinrich could reply, the bad news came along the deck.

Cordelia and Aunt Pearl.

Aunt Pearl looked surprised. Cordelia did not.

"Augustus!" Cordelia said with a smug smile. She was kitted out in a white sun dress, parasol, and hat and looked ready for a day in the country. "What a coincidence that we are traveling together."

"Coincidence nothing," Aunt Pearl harumphed. "She must have overheard your conversation at Shepheard's and booked us on the same boat."

You might have stopped her, Augustus almost said. The old spinster might have been an ally, but she wasn't a very effective one.

"Does your brother know you're here? This voyage might be dangerous."

Cordelia moved in closer—too close—and said in a low voice, "He believes the river will be safer than Cairo at the moment, so he agreed to us taking a boat. What I neglected to tell him was that I booked us on the *Arabia*. You're up to something, Augustus, and I want to be a part of it."

"Cordelia, this boat is most certainly not safer than Cairo. I'm here on a case."

"I am aware of that." She moved in closer, the brim of her large white sun hat nearly jabbing him in the face, its garland of fresh flowers filling his nostrils with their sweet smell. Augustus drew back, only making it half a step before his retreat was blocked by the railing. "I am also aware that you think I'm a silly, helpless girl. I am not, Augustus. I served throughout the war in France and saw my fair share of blood and danger. Our hospital was shelled on more than one occasion. And then I was swept up in the affair of the Apache gang."

"You intruded on that, just as you are intruding now, and you nearly got yourself killed."

"But I did not get killed, and I helped stop the gang."

"Really now, smacking a baboon with a parasol hardly counts as—"

Cordelia's eyes narrowed. Augustus looked for Aunt Pearl, but she had already stomped away in a huff. He looked back at the woman who relentlessly pursued him.

"You let your assistant come along on cases," she said. "You let that German academic. You even bring along a little beggar boy. But you won't bring me? Well, I'm here Augustus, and I'm going to prove to you that I'm just as useful as they are. I'm going to help you solve this case."

Augustus rallied.

"You will do nothing of the sort. I'm going to speak with the captain, I'm going gather your luggage, and I am going to get you off this boat."

Cordelia frowned. "You will do nothing of the sort. I am a free woman and I have just as much right to be on this boat as you do. My brother can do nothing." The loud shriek of a ship's whistle cut her off. The crewmen pulled the gangplank up and secured it to the side of the boat. She smiled. "In any case, it's too late."

CHAPTER EIGHT

Moustafa was almost shivering with nervousness and excitement as he stepped off the tram in the Coptic neighborhood of Cairo. It was his first day of work at Mr. Simaika's Coptic Museum. A new start for a man who had had many new starts.

It had all begun when he was sixteen and made the momentous decision to leave his village in the Soudan to find out what more there was in the world. At first he worked as a common laborer along the Nile, loading ships and tending fields. Then he had his first stroke of luck. He got a job on a German excavation filling buckets with sand and clearing away the foundations of ancient cities. Like most of his countrymen, he knew nothing about the past beyond a few stories of the Mahdi and the Prophet Mohammed. Soon, however, he learned that the Soudan had been home to a great ancient civilization. This fired his love of learning. One excavation led to another as dig directors noticed his quick mind and knack for languages.

Moustafa worked his way up the Nile and ended up in Cairo. Now a foreman, he helped run European excavations at Giza, Saqqara, and other sites until he was accused by his boss of theft. It turned out that the man's French assistant had been stealing the artifacts, but Moustafa had been so insulted by the accusation, and the lack of apology afterwards, that he quit.

And so he had fallen in with Mr. Wall. At first he seemed better than the usual European boss. While he never treated Moustafa quite like an equal, he did give him access to books, something his previous bosses rarely did. He also showed him a higher level of trust than he had ever enjoyed with any previous employer.

Moustafa had learned much from his time with Mr. Wall, but that time had to come to an end. There had been too many cutting remarks, too many times Mr. Wall had taken him for granted. And Nur was right. If he stuck with that madman, sooner or later he'd get himself killed. Already he bore several scars from fights he had gotten into for Mr. Wall's sake. Nur's dream had been silly superstition, perhaps even a ruse, but at its heart it contained pure truth. These adventures had to stop.

So now he was riding a tram with other respectable, educated people to work in a quiet, rewarding job. At the Coptic Museum there would be no murders to solve, no gunshots, no fanatics rushing at him with scimitars. Just peace.

A slight tinge of regret pulled at Moustafa's heart. He quashed it.

The Coptic Museum was housed in a converted home, a modest two-story stone structure with a garden. A few crude stone sculptures of saints and crosses were set between the bougainvillea and flowerbeds. While the early Christian carvings didn't approach the mastery of ancient Egyptian art, or later Islamic work, they had an immediacy to them. These had been the symbols of Egypt's first monotheistic religion, adorning monasteries and churches centuries before the birth of the prophet Mohammed. That made them hugely important both to the history of Egypt and the history of monotheistic faith.

The front door stood open. Moustafa squared his shoulders, climbed the steps, and entered the next phase of his life.

Mr. Simaika's secretary ushered him right into his office, a large room with windows overlooking the garden. One wall was lined with a bookshelf, another with a table adorned with various small artifacts. Behind an ornate Empire-style desk littered with papers sat his new boss.

The Coptic scholar wore a conservative suit of the finest cut, and a fat gold ring on his finger. He looked more like a banker or rich landowner who preferred city life, but Moustafa knew that Marcus Simaika was one of Egypt's finest scholars. And not only was he a man of learning, but one of action. He used his considerable wealth to travel around Egypt purchasing Coptic antiquities for his museum. Moustafa had already been promised a place on some of those trips.

Mr. Simaika greeted him with a handshake and a warm smile.

"I am so happy you have come to work for me. A man of your learning and linguistic talents will be wonderfully useful."

"Thank you, Mr. Simaika. I look forward to starting."

"And you will, but first I want to give you something." Mr. Simaika turned to his desk and retrieved two thick books, which he handed to Moustafa. "A Coptic grammar and a Coptic-English dictionary. A gift. You mentioned you wanted to learn Coptic. I'm sure you will have no trouble."

"Thank you very much, sir," Moustafa said, admiring the books. "I will get to work on these tonight. The best way to learn a language is to live in it, so I hope my new colleagues won't mind if I try as much as possible to speak to them in Coptic."

Mr. Simaika laughed and clapped him on the shoulder. "I expect nothing less. I presume you have visited my little museum?"

"Several times, sir."

"Well, you haven't seen the latest acquisitions from my most recent trip. Come."

His new boss led him across the front hall and into a room marked "Private." It turned out to be a storage room, bare of furniture and mostly taken up with wooden crates.

Mr. Simaika started opening them and bringing out an incredible collection of artifacts—fragments of carvings, old church plate, and textiles.

"Look at this," he said, opening a broad, flat box to reveal a tattered tunic. The material was shredded and threadbare. One sleeve was missing, but across the chest was a large round embroidery showing a swordsman on horseback fighting a griffin on a red background. The green of the griffin and the soldier's coat, and the yellow of the man's face and steed, remained remarkably bright. The entire scene was ringed with elaborate interweaving of flowers in red, yellow, and purple.

"This is incredible," Moustafa said.

"In the early Middle Ages, the Copts were the finest weavers in the world," Mr. Simaika said with obvious pride. "And like all advanced civilizations we were open to influences from abroad. This griffin, as you can see, is of Persian origin, not an Egyptian mythological beast at all."

"It does look Persian, yes."

"Sir Augustus has some Coptic textiles in his shop, I believe."

"Not as good as this," Moustafa conceded, his eyes still taking in the detailed scene.

"And much more expensive. I got this off an old family in Alexandria. It and a few other garments were tucked away in a storeroom on their estate. This is from the 6th century. Remarkable to think it's been kept all this time. Of course the 6th century is nothing to an Egyptologist, eh? Here's something a bit older, from the fourth century, the very beginnings of Christianity in Egypt."

With care he unpacked a terracotta flask. On the side was impressed the image of a haloed saint with his arms outstretched.

"Do you know what this is?" Mr. Simaika asked.

Moustafa flushed. "I'm afraid I don't, sir."

"It's a pilgrim's flask to commemorate a visit to the shrine of St. Menas, made not long after the holy man was martyred. I have several of these in my collection."

Then Mr. Simaika came to what Moustafa loved most of all—a stack of manuscripts.

"I got the flask and these books at the St. Menas monastery along the coast near El Alamein," Mr. Simaika said. "One is a Bible, and there are some hagiographical writings as well. Most interesting, though, is an account of a pilgrimage to Jerusalem from the year 1387. Considering how good you are with languages, you will be reading it yourself before long."

"I'm surprised the monastery wanted to part with them," Moustafa said, gazing at the old vellum pages with admiring eyes.

"They parted with them all too easily," Mr. Simaika scoffed. "I found them in an old box covered in dust forgotten in a back storage room. They were under a pile of rusty shovels. Lord knows how long they had been there. Sad to say, most of my people don't care one bit about their past. Even the religious houses neglect their artifacts and archives. That's why the Coptic Pope has given me permission to collect them. His Holiness Cyril V is a visionary. He knows that to build a nation one must make a firm foundation of the past."

"A wise man. If only more Muslim leaders felt the same."

"And more Coptic leaders! We have much work to do, Moustafa. In any society, learned men are in the minority, but in Egypt we are a minority of a minority. Most of our learned men imitate the West too much. They would rather read about Louis XIV than Akhenaten. They would rather read cheap French novels than the history of their own holy places. Of course there is much in the West that is good. I wear a suit, after all. I have a telephone. I ride on the train. But these are only superficial things, like using a Persian griffin to decorate a Christian tunic. We should not try to be Westerners any more than my ancestors tried to be Persians. We should be Egyptians, adopting what is good from the West and retaining what is good about our own nation."

"I am of the exact same frame of mind, sir."

Mr. Simaika smiled and nodded. "I know, and that is one of the many reasons I hired you. Despite working for Sir Augustus, you still wear a djellaba instead of a suit. And I bet you pray five times a day and never touch alcohol."

"Never, sir." Too many of his fellow Muslims had taken on drink as a vice.

Mr. Simaika flipped through the pages of the manuscript. "You are a good Muslim, just as I am a good Copt, and that is another reason I have hired you. You are, at present, the only Muslim working at the museum. I hope to hire more as we expand. We need to work together, people like you and I." His boss looked up from the manuscript to meet Moustafa's eye. "For it is people like you and I who will usher in a new era, an era of renewed Egyptian independence."

Moustafa's heart raced. "Yes, sir. Egypt has been occupied many times, but none of the occupiers have lasted for long."

Mr. Simaika set Moustafa to work cataloging the new acquisitions alongside a young Coptic man named Joseph. His new colleague taught him the cataloging system, and helped with the identification of various objects. As they went through the sculpture fragments and the icons and the battered old chalices, Moustafa realized just how little he knew about Coptic heritage. Joseph, a good ten years his junior and with barely a wisp of a beard, was acting more as a teacher than a coworker.

That didn't bother Moustafa at all. Joseph was patient, and didn't act superior about his education like many young scholars did. He seemed eager to share his knowledge. It was odd, but he reminded Moustafa a bit of Faisal. Of course it would be a horrible insult to the Copt to compare him with the Little Infidel. Joseph had none of his sloth or filth or devious habits, but he did have Faisal's energy and quick wit. Too bad Faisal would never rise to Joseph's level.

So they worked together all that long morning, Moustafa learning the cataloging system and many fascinating facts about Coptic history. During a break for tea, Joseph even taught him a few Coptic words and phrases, delighting in how quickly Moustafa picked them up. Other employees came in to meet him, and he surprised them by greeting them in their own language.

But all through that busy, exciting, and fulfilling workday, Moustafa felt something nagging at him, something that did not feel quite right. For a time, he thought it was guilt at letting Mr. Wall and Faisal go off the Luxor alone before he realized that he had already acknowledged that emotion and decided it didn't outweigh his commitment to his family. Then he wondered if it might be a case of nerves at being the only Muslim scholar at the museum. That couldn't be it either, because the Copts were very welcoming and obviously valued his abilities.

Then he hit on it.

The man who had killed Mr. Lowell had come out of a side alley. He had not been part of the mob. The alley was well ahead of the mob, almost at the entrance of the dead-end street where it connected to a busier street. It had been dark, a good place for someone to hide and await a target coming out of one of the bawdy houses and leaving for home.

And once he had killed Detective Lowell, he had run off. He hadn't stayed to attack Moustafa or search for more victims like the rest of the mob.

That man had not been a rioter; he had been an assassin.

Moustafa rubbed his eyes and sighed.

Joseph looked up from his work. "Tired?"

"No, um, a mere headache. It will pass."

"I'll go get us some tea. I could use one myself." Joseph got up and left the office. Moustafa barely heard him.

Now that he thought about it, he realized the truth had been simmering beneath his thoughts ever since that fatal night. The killer's movements had been too focused, too determined for someone killing in the heat of the moment. The question was—who sent him? Alaeddin Bey? The bawdy house? Some third party?

He should investigate that. No, he *must* investigate that. If the assassin was so aware of Lowell's movements as to know that he was coming to that neighborhood, surely he knew he was scheduled to sail on the same boat as Alaeddin Bey. And if he knew that, he may very well know that Mr. Wall and Faisal had gone on the *Arabia* too.

Those two were in danger and didn't know it.

CHAPTER NINE

Riding on a steamboat had to be the best thing ever, even better than riding in a motorcar.

For a moment when Cordelia and Aunt Pearl showed up, Faisal thought the trip would be ruined. He didn't get to see the Englishman's reaction because one of the ship's crew showed him where the servant's quarters were—down two flights of stairs into a little windowless space that was a bit smaller than his shed on the roof, but nice and snug with a real bed with sheets and a pillow and everything. Once Faisal had left his things, and made sure he had his charm against djinn around his neck, he went back up on deck to find the Englishman talking to Mr. Jocelyn.

Faisal stopped and stared. He hadn't expected the beardless Englishman to be here.

"Hello!" he said, bounding up. "Is Ahmed here?"

"Oh hello, Faisal. No, I'm afraid he's still in Bahariya."

"Oh." Faisal slumped. He couldn't stay disappointed for long, though, because he noticed Cordelia standing some way off, frowning at the two Englishmen, especially Mr. Jocelyn. Faisal didn't know why Cordelia didn't like Mr. Jocelyn, but if she was angry maybe she would stop chasing after his Englishman. It must have been that spell he had cast that made Mr. Jocelyn show up out of nowhere and make Cordelia angry. He had learned that spell from Khadija umm Mohammed, and her magic always worked.

He fiddled with the charm around his neck. It had protected them from desert djinn. He hoped it would protect them against water djinn.

"So are you looking forward to the boat ride?" Mr. Jocelyn asked him.

"Oh yes! As long as there aren't any severed heads in Luxor."

"Why would there be severed heads in Luxor, you silly boy?"

"There was a severed head earlier this year." His Englishman looked embarrassed.

"Oh yes, there was, wasn't there?" Mr. Jocelyn said. "Well, I can't imagine he'd be involved with a second severed head so soon after the first one."

"You don't know the Englishman like I do."

Suddenly, a loud shriek split the air. Faisal leapt up, then hit the deck, looking all around him. Some Europeans nearby looked at him and laughed.

"Get up, Faisal," his Englishman said. "That's only the steam whistle announcing our departure."

"Oh, right," Faisal said, standing up. "That."

"It went off just a minute ago. Didn't you hear it?"

"I was down below. I heard something but I thought it was just Aunt Pearl sneezing."

Now he realized he had heard those whistles before when he had watched the big boats leave the docks here at Bulaq. Never from so close, though. His ears were ringing almost as much as after those gunfights the Englishman liked so much. They were ringing so much he could feel it all through his body, as if a swarm of bees was buzzing inside of him.

Then he realized that wasn't a swarm of bees, but the engine of the steamboat. He ran over to the side where the great wheel was, like the wheel of one of the big mills on the edge of the city but even bigger. It was turning.

When he looked out over the railing he almost leapt in the air a second time. The boat was pulling away from the shore. The Europeans who had come to see their friends leave on the boat already looked small. But they still stood there waving as the Europeans on board waved back to them.

The Egyptians in the crowd were walking away, the porters to load other ships, and the vendors to sell their wares elsewhere. But three Egyptians stayed—Mina, her father, and his friend. They watched the ship in wonder. Mina had told him that they had never been to the Bulaq docks before.

Faisal jumped up and down, waving his hands in the air. "Hey, Mina! Look at me!"

"Don't make a fuss," a waiter in a Thomas Cook uniform snapped. "You'll disturb the guests."

"I'm a guest too."

"Know your place!" The waiter stormed off. Faisal stuck his tongue out at him, but he couldn't stay in a bad mood for more than a second. He turned back to Mina and waved. She hadn't spotted him. There were too many people on deck waving and he was too short.

Faisal rushed to a narrow set of stairs and went up to the top deck. There weren't as many people up there and he found an empty spot and waved again. Mina's father put a hand on her shoulder and pointed him out.

Faisal could hear her squeal of delight all the way out in the river. She waved.

"Look! I'm on a ship!"

The railing was getting in the way. She couldn't see him good enough. So Faisal clambered up the side of the ship, using one of the cabin's windows for handholds and footholds until he got to the flat top of the steamship. There he jumped up and down and waved both arms over his head. He could see Mina laughing and clapping her hands, and so Faisal jumped even more. Even Mina's father and his friend looked amused.

That only encouraged him. He did a cartwheel, then ran over to where the big smokestack from the engine belched out puffs of black smoke. It rose over him like a minaret. Wouldn't they be impressed if he climbed it? He grabbed it and yelped. It was hot! Blowing on his fingers, he ran along the length of the roof, waving to his friends on shore. He could hear them yelling to him and pointing. The yelling seemed really close. How could it sound so close?

Oh wait, that was because that waiter was the one yelling. He had climbed up on the roof and was chasing him. That's what Mina and her father had been pointing at!

Time to go. With a final wave he hopped off the roof onto the top deck, going to the opposite side of the ship from the shore where there would be no people, then vaulted over the railing, climbed down as much as he could, and dropped to the main deck.

And froze.

Because right in front of him was the strangest European he had ever seen.

At least he thought he was a European. He wore Turkish robes and a turban made of some strange silvery cloth. In the center of the turban was a ruby that was far too big to be real.

If this wasn't strange enough, his face was even stranger. It had European features but dark, like he had been in Egypt for a long time. He had heavy eyebrows and a broad, black moustache that came to points far past either side of his face.

The man had been at the door of one of the passenger's cabins. Maybe his own. Probably not. Not the way he spun around in shock as Faisal suddenly dropped in. The man tucked something into his baggy sleeve and fixed him with big, brown eyes that bulged a little from his face.

Those eyes were strange. They just seemed to get bigger to more they stared at you. Faisal shifted from one foot to the other.

"And who are you, young man?" he asked, leaning forward with his arms folded in front of him.

"No one."

"Everyone is someone." The man looked up at the sound of running feet above, then back at Faisal. "And I think you're a very interesting someone."

"Not really. Do you know where the bathroom is?"

The man smiled. "You are not hurrying to the bathroom. You are in a hurry to get away from whoever it is up there chasing you. Best be on your way. Don't worry, your secret is safe with me."

Your secret isn't safe with me, though. I'm going to tell the Englishman you're sneaking around picking locks.

"Bye."

Faisal ran off. He found the Englishman talking with Mr. Jocelyn and that German fellow.

"Do any of you have a cabin on the other side of the ship and a little way toward the back?" he asked.

"I'm on the upper deck," the Englishman said. "Jocelyn's cabin is just there and Heinrich took Moustafa's cabin on the lower deck. Why do you ask?"

"I think I found the man you're looking for. He was breaking into a cabin."

"Let's go," Augustus said. "If we can catch him in the act, we can solve this case early."

Mr. Jocelyn put a hand on his arm. "Let me go. He'll suspect me less. Faisal, did he spot you?"

"Yes."

"All right. I'll go alone."

"He's got a big turban with a fake ruby," Faisal said.

"That should make him easy to find."

Mr. Jocelyn came back a couple of minutes later. "He was at the back of the boat talking with some other passengers and is just coming this way."

Mr. Jocelyn said this while walking past. Faisal took the hint and moved away from his Englishman and the German. It would be best if they weren't all seen together. This turbaned man would figure out they were together soon enough, but that was no reason to tell him right from the start. The less a person you were trying to trick knew about you, the better.

Faisal went inside to get to the stairs leading down to the servants' quarters. He'd go to his little cabin and get out of sight for a while.

As he opened the door that led to the little corridor where the stairs were, another door opened and a foreign boy his age came out. He wore one of those funny blue and white suits that Faisal had seen the foreign sailors wear, but he was obviously not a member of the crew. His face was a bit red like all Europeans who were new to Egypt, and that made his blonde hair and blue eyes look even brighter. He looked rich, with a fresh, clean face and soft hands and a bit of a belly. He even smelled rich. The smell of soap wafted behind him as he passed Faisal without even looking at him.

And then the foreign boy went out on deck. Faisal stopped for a second to watch him go. Those were nice clothes. It would be fun to pretend to be a sailor all the time.

Shrugging, Faisal went down the flight of stairs to the lower deck where the lower passenger cabins were and waved to the German who was just opening the door to his room, and then went down a second flight of stairs to the crew's quarters. The hallway here was narrower, and there were no windows because it was underwater. Faisal felt strange being underwater and being dry at the same time. It was kind of creepy, actually.

A Nubian passed by. He wore all white like the chefs in hotels. Faisal had never been in a hotel, but he'd seen chefs going to work.

"When's lunch?" Faisal asked.

"Lunch? I have to make brunch first."

"Brunch? What's brunch?"

"Hasn't your master taught you anything? It's the meal between breakfast and lunch."

Faisal blinked. There was a fourth meal in the day that he hadn't known about all this time?

"When do we get this brunch thing?"

"You don't! Only passengers get brunch."

Faisal almost told him that he was a passenger, but then he remembered he was pretending to be the Englishman's servant so they could solve the murder.

"So when do we eat?"

"Servants have to wait for lunch, and only after the passengers have eaten. Now go do your job. I have work to do."

The man walked off.

Brunch! He'd have to figure out a way to get some of that. Yes, riding on a steamship was definitely the best ever.

He went into his cabin, locked the door behind him, and looked around. It really was amazing. The room wasn't very big, and had no windows since it was underwater, but it had a nice bed, plus a washbasin with a towel and a bar of soap. That was good. He'd have to keep clean for this job and he didn't want to go through the trouble of stealing soap from one of the passengers. There was a shelf where he could put his things, and so he unpacked his bag. Inside was the ancient lamp Moustafa had given him, which he put on the shelf. Next to it he put the ripped tickets from the moving picture shows he'd gone to with the Englishman. This one was from the first moving picture he ever saw, the one with Charles Chaplin in the bakery. This one was for the moving picture with Buster Keaton when he was building a house and making such a mess of it. And this one was for the cowboy show. He was so happy when they finished one moving picture and then put on a second cowboy one. The Englishman hadn't told him they'd do that so it came as a big surprise.

Faisal looked at the shelf and smiled. Now the cabin felt like his little shed on the Englishman's roof.

He also unpacked his old djellaba, the filthy one he begged with, and tucked it out of sight under his bed. He might need that for a disguise.

Faisal blinked. A disguise?

He looked into a long mirror set into the wall. He was all cleaned up with his hair properly cut for the first time in forever, and wearing that blue djellaba Edmond had given him. That djellaba had been a disguise so he could sneak into the Citadel. On this trip he would be wearing it every day. So did that make it his regular djellaba instead of a disguise?

He bent down and pulled out his old djellaba from under the bed. Getting in front of the mirror again, he held it up in front of him and messed up his hair, imagining that his face and hands were dirty.

And he stared. Was the beggar Faisal the real Faisal, or a disguise? He put the filthy thing back under the bed, tidied his hair as much as the unruly stuff could be tidied, and looked at himself again. Was this real or a disguise? He was wearing these nice clothes because he needed to pretend to be the Englishman's servant, just like he had pretended to be a servant at the Citadel.

But I'm not the Englishman's servant, he told himself, *I'm his friend.*

Then why does he pay you? Why does he ignore you if no one is getting killed?

That's not true! Faisal almost shouted at himself. *Masters don't take their servants to the moving pictures.*

But nobody knows that. Everyone is going to treat you like his servant, until you get back to Cairo and then everyone will treat you like a beggar.

What if he had one of those nice sailor suits like that European boy? He tried to imagine himself in one. He'd look funny. He'd stand out in his neighborhood and wouldn't be able to sneak or steal, and certainly not beg. He'd look good, though. He was sure of that. Maybe the Englishman could buy him one and then everyone would know he was a passenger and he would be allowed to eat brunch.

But no, he had to pretend to be the Englishman's servant. Which made this nice blue djellaba and his new haircut and clean face a disguise.

Faisal sat down on the bed, hanging his head. So the real him was that filthy djellaba hidden under his bed.

No. That was him before he had met the Englishman, and it was him when he wanted to beg since no one could beg in a new, clean djellaba. If he had gone from that old thing to a new djellaba, why couldn't he go from a new djellaba to a sailor suit?

He should ask the Englishman for one once he had solved the murder for him.

Always remember that you are Egyptian.

Moustafa's words came back to him. Silly Nubian. Couldn't he be Egyptian in European clothes? And what was the big deal about being Egyptian anyway? Egyptians never trusted him. An Egyptian had beaten Mehmed. But those foreign soldiers at Bahariya Oasis had given him chocolate and let him climb all around an armored car.

Even in a sailor's suit they won't think you're one of them.

That was Faisal's own thought, although it could have been Moustafa talking.

Faisal turned away from the mirror and lay down, his mind cluttered with confusing thoughts and hopes it hurt to dream about.

CHAPTER TEN

Augustus sat at lunch while the passengers gabbled platitudes about the scenery that rolled by out the window. They had quickly left the city behind and were now headed south, upriver past little villages of mud brick homes set behind green fields. In the distance rose brown hills marking the start of the desert.

If it wasn't for the view out the plate glass windows, Augustus could have been sitting in an exclusive dining room in London. The burnished floors and wainscoting, the white tablecloth, the gleaming silverware, all conspired to make the passengers feel at home, and in the correct social set.

Augustus found the conversation to be polite, eager, and a tad guarded. It reminded him of when he had joined his regiment. Everyone wanted to get along but not reveal themselves too much or cause offensive among people who they would soon get to know all too well. They were stuck together on a boat for three days going to Luxor, then a week at that spot before returning to Cairo. So the conversation was more irritatingly superficial than usual for such a dull set of people.

The *Arabia* had set sail with only half of her passenger compliment, some forty people. The tourist industry, suspended during the recent war, had yet to recover before the independence riots dealt it another blow. He had heard from the steward that there had been some last-minute cancellations owing to the small riot that had killed the American detective. Augustus had overheard several of the men mentioning they had brought hunting rifles along, initially intending on bagging some game but now wondering if they might prove to be of more practical use.

The passengers were more or less what he expected, mostly well-to-do English. One could immediately tell who the highest on the social order was because the others deferred to him. It turned out he was a baronet from some dreary northern estate, here no doubt to refamiliarize himself with the properties of the sun. Heinrich was the only passenger from the Continent, although there was an Australian lieutenant on leave as well as an Irish couple who were ignored almost as much as Heinrich was. There was also an American woman, a Ms. Trasher, wearing a conservative brown dress and with her hair up in a tight bun, who insisted that everyone say grace before eating. At the head of the table sat the ship's captain, who spoke politely with anyone who addressed him but otherwise sat silent, no doubt long since weary of conversing with passengers.

Despite the inane chatter and the company of far too many strangers, Augustus was in a fine mood. The ladies, Cordelia and Aunt Pearl most of all, gave Jocelyn appalled stares while the men looked like they didn't know what to think. Jocelyn sat at Augustus's side talking intelligently about Egyptology. She was going to keep Cordelia away like one of Faisal's anti-djinn charms.

Heinrich sat a little further down the table talking with Alaeddin Bey. That oddball was getting even more looks than Jocelyn. Dressed in a ridiculous stage magician getup, the mesmerist, who was of uncertain nationality but most certainly not a Turk, chatted with Heinrich and two other male passengers in impeccable French.

The mesmerist was holding forth on the power of the mind over matter.

"The mind is the most powerful instrument in the universe. The Creator has given us the means to overcome all obstacles, obtain any goal, and understand any puzzle. It is all within our grasp. Sadly, most of us are stuck in the feeble trackways we have cut for ourselves and through which we go through life. We cannot get onto another path without assistance from outside. This is where hypnotism can help. Through the efforts of a skilled mesmerist, an individual can break out of their self-imposed limitations and achieve what they have always thought impossible."

Augustus studied him, trying to figure out where this fellow was from. His French bore no trace of an accent, but had that perfect, neutral mannerism of an astute student. A Frenchman from Paris or Lyon or Toulouse would have some sort of regional accent. This man had none. His face was rather dusky, with black hair and dark, prominent brown eyes, but with Caucasian features. Mixed blood?

"Freud and other psychologists have had some success using hypnotism in their therapies," Heinrich said.

Alaeddin Bey nodded, that fake ruby on the front of his turban sparkling as it caught the sunlight streaming through the window.

"I have trained many of the leading psychologists in Vienna, Berlin, and London," he said.

Augustus decided it was time to get into the conversation. Since Heinrich was taking the stance of the interested scientist, Augustus decided he'd take the role of skeptic.

"I saw a demonstration of hypnotism in London once before the war," he said, talking over another passenger. "It was quite the show. This fellow had members of the audience quacking like ducks and doing all manner of other silly behavior. I hope he paid those poor people well for putting on such an embarrassing act."

Alaeddin Bey's bulging eyes fixed on him. "Oh, you think it was all a trick?"

Augustus let out a derisive chuckle. Several of the other passengers were looking now. "Indeed. I went with a large group. When the hypnotist or mesmerist or necromancer or whatever you call him asked for volunteers, none of us were chosen. Neither were any of my other acquaintances in the audience. When I asked around among my fellows, they all said that those who made it on stage were entirely unknown to them."

"That man was no doubt a fraud," the hypnotist said.

"Really?" Augustus had not expected that answer.

"It is sad that this new science is so rife with fraudsters and cheats. The performer no doubt paid some actors to be part of his show. This is because he was incapable of putting someone under an actual hypnotic trance. Because the scientific and medical world does not accept us, even the serious mesmerists have to resort to some trappings of the stage." Alaeddin Bey gestured at his ridiculous outfit. "After all, here I am wearing an exaggerated version of my native dress when the educated of my country are now wearing suits and fezzes."

If you're Turkish, Augustus thought, *I'm the Prince of Wales.*

Augustus noted that Alaeddin Bey had switched to English and had raised his voice slightly. That made more of the conversations around the table go silent. The captain dug into his lunch, ignoring them all.

Jocelyn cut in, following the mesmerist's lead by addressing him in English. "I don't think Sir Augustus meant any offense, Alaeddin Bey. Obviously a man such as yourself isn't some cheap performer at a penny gaffe. But don't you find it frustrating to have to wrap your research in such trappings?"

Augustus resisted the urge to smile. While he knew little of mesmerism, he knew that a key part of the show was for the male performer to put handsome women under the influence. It added a bit of titillation.

"It is indeed a burden. But I press on. I've given demonstrations of the power of animal magnetism in all the capitals of Europe, but still I struggle under the twin yokes of doubt and mockery."

If you don't want mockery, take that bloody turban off.

"You use the terms hypnotism, mesmerism, and animal magnetism interchangeably," Jocelyn said. "I thought they were different things? I must confess not to know much about these matters."

There was a whisper and a chuckle at the other end of the table. Augustus glanced that direction and spotted the culprits from how they immediately concerned themselves with their Beef Wellington.

And Augustus saw what all those staid middle-class English people saw—the freaks all chatting together. The man with a mask, the woman in trousers, the unwelcome German, and the fake Turk talking nonsense.

I'll take any one of us over any ten of you, Augustus wanted to say to them. *Even Alaeddin Bey. He may be a thief and a fraud and may very well be a murderer, but at least he's an individual.*

That individual was still talking, and Augustus suppressed his rage to pay attention.

"I use those terms interchangeably because their definitions are somewhat fluid. Mesmerism is the older term, first coined in the early years of the last century, as was animal magnetism. Hypnosis is the more modern and more scientifically precise term, as it draws not upon the occultism of the previous century but the scientific progress of our own."

You should have been on the front. Then you'd have seen some scientific progress.

"So hypnotism has rejected occultism?" Jocelyn asked.

"No. While there is much nonsense in occult circles, there is much wisdom too. That is why I have not dispensed with the word mesmerism entirely. My technique is a fusion of occult wisdom and scientific principles."

Ms. Trasher scoffed and grumbled something to the Irish couple next to her, who frowned and nodded. The American Bible thumper and the Irish Catholics no doubt had a dim view of occultism.

Then Cordelia cut in, which was the last thing Augustus wanted. "Hasn't the term animal magnetism been surpassed by hypnotism? I thought that animal magnetism was based on the idea that there was a magnetic force between the subject and the mesmerist that could be manipulated."

Good Lord, she really has been reading up on this claptrap.

"I see you have been studying this topic," Alaeddin Bey said, fixing his bulging eyes on her. "That shows a keen mind. So many simply accept society's views without question, and I mean no disrespect to this gentleman," Alaeddin Bey gestured at Augustus. "He was open-minded enough to go to what had been billed as a scientific demonstration and was treated to cheap vaudeville. No wonder he doubts. But you have delved further, I see. Yes, the original idea of animal magnetism has been discredited. I use the term in a different manner. By using it I refer to the animalistic attraction between two individuals, as nature intended."

Cordelia blushed. Ms. Trasher put down her spoon on the edge of her bowl with a clank and glared.

The Australian lieutenant cleared his throat. "Moving on to more prosaic matters, I spoke with Mr. Cook at his office in Cairo the day before yesterday and he assured me that every measure will be taken to assure our safety. We will be only making one stop before Luxor, a brief stop at Assiout, a little more than halfway to Luxor."

"Assiout?" Heinrich said. "There's not much in the way of antiquities there."

"It's only a quick stop to drop me off," Ms. Trasher said. "I run an orphanage there. Mr. Cook is a Godly man and assists my work by allowing me free passage on his boats."

"Oh, I've read about you in the *Egyptian Gazette*," one of the Englishwomen said. "They say you're doing fine work."

"We currently have fifty boys and girls, and we plan to expand if we can find the funds."

"I've read about your organization too," the Australian said. "I'd be happy to make a donation. I've seen the conditions these street children live in. Dreadful. And their own people do nothing. But back to my original point. While Mr. Cook is doing all he can to keep us safe, we must also look to our own affairs. I have a Lee-Enfield in my cabin as well as a rifle with telescopic sight. The latter is for hunting, but it works just as well on a man. Who else brought weapons with them?"

The Baronet, the *Arabia's* captain, and several of the other Englishmen named a variety of firearms, either hunting rifles or small pistols for personal protection.

"I've brought a hunting rifle as well," Jocelyn said.

The Australian officer treated her to a condescending smile. "I don't think a little fowling piece will be of much use."

Some of the men chuckled.

"No, but a Winchester 94 firing .30-.30 rounds with the aid of a 1x50 sight would be."

What a woman.

The Australian took a moment to get his mouth in working order and said, "Well, um, yes. In steady and trained hands that would be of use."

Jocelyn only smiled.

Augustus did not share with the rest of the table. Instead he studied the waiters. They all wore the neutral expressions of the native servant class, making it impossible to discern what was going on underneath.

The officer turned to him.

"You have nothing?"

Augustus briefly considered lying, but figured this man was sharp enough to spot the bulge in his jacket pocket.

"I carry a compact automatic."

"You might need something larger. I'll lend you my Lee-Enfield. I'm sure you know how to use it."

Yes, this mask marks me out as a veteran to all and sundry. Thank you for bringing it up.

"That won't be necessary."

"I can't use two rifles at the same time, and I'd feel better if my spare was in capable hands."

"Oh, very well."

I'll put it next to the other two in my cabin.

The conversation drifted on to other things. Heinrich spoke with Alaeddin Bey, playing his part well, while Augustus kept to himself. He did not want to show too much interest.

After dessert, people began to leave, the men retiring to the smoking lounge and the ladies leaving to "freshen up," a female term Augustus had never entirely decoded. Alaeddin Bey headed for the smoking longue but was cut off by Cordelia who, under the disapproving gaze of Aunt Pearl, began to chatter away about hypnotism. The two moved to the main walkway on the side of the ship with Aunt Pearl a few steps behind.

"That might prove useful," Jocelyn said in a low voice, "or bring more trouble."

Augustus nodded.

A male passenger approached him. "I hear you are a dealer in antiquities."

"I am. In addition to having a holiday with two of my friends I will be purchasing some items down south."

The man grinned. "That's a stroke of luck. My *Baedeker's* warns there are many fakes about. I'm hoping you might help me once we're down there. I want the real thing for my mantelpiece. Nothing too pricey, just something to show that I've been."

"I'd be happy to be of assistance."

I'll be sure to find you the finest fake in Luxor.

Before the man could continue to bore him, all attention was taken by Faisal entering the dining room, sitting down at the table, and grabbing a piece of bread.

"What's that servant boy doing here?" one of the ladies snapped.

He wasn't there for long. A waiter yanked him out of his seat and smacked him upside the head.

"Hey!" Faisal protested. "It's lunchtime, isn't it?"

"In the servant's mess down below, you little idiot," the waiter said, opening the door to the main deck and tossing him out.

Augustus strode for the door. "I apologize for the behavior of my servant. He's newly hired and unaccustomed to riding on a boat."

He hurried out to find Faisal picking himself off the deck.

"I was told we ate after the passengers."

"Below decks, as the waiter said. Try to fit in." Augustus glanced around to make sure no one was close by who might speak Arabic. "Have you found out anything?"

"That magician is in cabin 42."

"Thank you. I would have found that out soon enough but it's good to know sooner rather than later."

They began to walk along the deck, past a few passengers standing around looking at the scenery. They were well out of Cairo now and only small villages were visible. A few feluccas plied the waters, their lateen sails looking like quill pens writing on the shimmering surface.

"Riding on board a ship is funny," Faisal said. "It's always shaking a little, like if you hum really loudly with your teeth clenched."

"That's the engine. Have you found out anything else about our suspect?"

"Not much. The staff talk about him a bit. He's been on the boat before, and on other Thomas Cook boats too."

"What do they think of him?"

"I'm not sure. They haven't said much. I'll keep listening, though. And I'll ask over lunch. I better get down there so I don't miss it."

"All right, but be subtle. Don't act too curious."

"Anyone would be curious about someone dressed like that. Why are you pretending you hurt your leg?"

"I've been shamming in order to have an excuse to carry my sword cane. We're dealing with a murderer, after all, or at least someone who commissions murders."

"You're not faking very well. You exaggerate too much. Here."

Faisal walked a short way down the deck, demonstrating a limp that would have easily gotten him a part as Richard III on the West End if it were not for his tender age and dusky skin.

"I'm impressed," Augustus said in all truth.

Faisal grinned. "Show it but don't show it too much. That way they believe it. You can also fake open sores with a mix of pomegranate juice and hummus. Want me to make some for you?"

"I think I'll be quite all right with a simple limp. I don't think your little mixture would stand up to a close inspection."

"It can't. But begging on the street you're lucky if they look at you at all." Faisal looked past him. "Hello."

Augustus turned to find Alaeddin Bey standing just behind him. How the Devil did he get there without his hearing? And how long had he been there?

"I was most pleased to make your acquaintance at lunch and would like to invite you to a demonstration of my hypnotic techniques after tea. We will meet in the library. I would like to show you, and some of the other intelligent passengers, how I can influence a subject and expand their mind."

"I'd be most interested. And who will be the subject?"

Alaeddin Bey smiled. "Why, Cordelia, of course."

CHAPTER ELEVEN

Moustafa did not get to act immediately. On the first day his new employers kept him late, and only afterwards did he have time to make some investigations. He had already told Nur he would be kept until the evening and let her assume it was because of his job. It pained him to lie by omission, but he didn't want her to worry about him.

He was sufficiently worried for himself.

Moustafa arrived at the fish market district just after dark. Not all the windows were yet open, and there were few men on the streets. That suited him fine, because he wanted to investigate the scene of the riot without any harassment from those fallen women or any glances from passersby.

He was wrong about the first assumption. Being one of the few men on the street, the women began calling out to him from the windows.

"Hello, Nubian. Want to be my first of the evening?"

"Would be nice to have someone who wasn't a tourist for a change. I'll give you a discount!"

"There's nothing down those alleys, Nubian. We're all up here!"

Moustafa flushed with shame and embarrassment at being the object of these entreaties. Didn't God command the faithful to avoid places of sin? He also commanded that you had to right wrongs, which sadly meant that Moustafa needed to be here.

At least the few men on the street ignored him. They were too busy staring at the sinners in the windows.

There was little evidence of the riot from just a few nights before. The blood and debris on the street had all been washed away and the shutters fixed. It was as if a howling mob had never slaughtered two people here.

They would have killed me too, Moustafa reminded himself, *if I hadn't run away.*

He still felt guilty about running. Of course there had been no way to save Detective Lowell. He would have only been killed in the attempt. But running away from a man he worked with, even a sinful man such as Mr. Lowell, did not sit well with him.

You ran away from Mr. Wall too.

Moustafa growled and dismissed the thought. He had lost enough blood for that man. He didn't owe him anything. And a man's first obligation is to his wife and children.

So why are you here?

That question haunted him. He had thought he had put all this nonsense in the past, and yet here he was helping with an investigation.

A man was murdered, he told himself. *Since you couldn't save him, you have an obligation to find him justice.*

Moustafa slowly walked along the street, looking for the alley from which the murderer had emerged. Given the chaos of that night, the explosion of violence, and the rush to escape, his memory was hazy. He had to walk the length of the street and back again twice—exciting the women in the windows to ever more shameful calls for his attention—before he finally found the correct one.

It was a narrow, dingy little space between two tall buildings. Not a place where anyone would normally stand, unless they were waiting to get up to some evil. Moustafa glanced down it as he passed, but the light from the street did not penetrate far. All he saw was a bit of strange graffiti near the entrance. Some sort of pictures. No doubt some obscene images some low individual had been too drunk to draw accurately. He did not look at them again.

He continued along the street, passing the spot where he now felt sure Mr. Lowell had met his end.

How could he enter the alley without attracting attention? The answer was that he couldn't. Briefly he considered returning in the daytime, but then the market would be open and there would be even more people around. Sighing, he turned around, went to the alley, and plunged inside.

One of the women called after him. "Hey, love. There's nothing down there."

"Maybe he's hoping to meet some handsome fellow down there," another teased.

"I need to, um, make water," he called over his shoulder.

Moustafa almost choked with shame. Why did he feel the need to justify himself to such a person? And he had just blithely lied. Lying was a sin even if one lied to a sinner.

"God forgive me," Moustafa muttered.

After the first few steps beyond the street, he could barely see five feet in front of him. Moustafa felt very alone, and very vulnerable. He did not have a weapon. Summoning his courage, he lit a match. Rats scuttled away at the sudden light.

He moved forward, glancing over his shoulder to make sure no one followed. The alley ended at a left turn, the wall in front of him a blank. Looking past the turn, he saw the alley ran behind a row of buildings that faced the street he had just left. A few doors, all shut tight, opened onto the alley. Heaps of empty bottles, refuse from old meals, and other trash littered the narrow space. From the smell he could tell why the prostitute had believed him about going to relieve himself. That was obviously one of the functions of this spot.

Moustafa moved down the alley, taking care not to step on the shards of broken glass. His match burnt down low and he lit another, the rasp of it igniting making him grit his teeth. It sounded far too loud in this silent place.

Before he had ducked into the alley, he had counted the number of buildings between it and the brothel he and Detective Lowell had visited.

He counted again now.

The back of that building looked little different than all the rest—a shut-tight door, a few small windows in the upper stories open a crack to let in the night air, and nothing else.

Except on the ground.

He didn't spot it at first amid all the filth. It was a rag, discarded near the door, with dark stains on it. Bending down low and bringing the match close, he thought it looked like blood.

The murderer, he realized. *He came from here and returned here, wiping his knife clean on a rag before tossing it aside.*

That told him two things.

Firstly, the brothel had sent him to kill Detective Lowell.

Secondly, they had sent an amateur. Who discards a bloodstained rag right next to their hideout?

Unless he wanted to shift blame. Maybe he isn't an amateur after all.

But if the brothel didn't send him, who would? Who else knew Detective Lowell was even here?

We could have been followed.

After working for Mr. Wall, he had become adept at spotting someone following him, but the street had been busy, and Moustafa had been distracted and nervous, looking for obvious threats rather than a subtle tail.

So why shift blame to the brothel? Was it just because that was where they had visited, or was there a deeper reason?

And what about the riot? Had that been faked? It didn't seem to have been. To do such a thing would have required the cooperation of those Australian soldiers as well as the people of this neighborhood. That stretched credibility.

After all you've been through with Mr. Wall and you concern yourself with credibility?

Moustafa looked around, unsure what to do next. He waved out the match and lit another.

Another close look around the area revealed nothing, so he picked up the rag and put it in his pocket. He tried the back door and found it locked.

What to do? It wasn't like the assassin was waiting around the scene of the crime days later for Moustafa to stumble upon, and the ladies in this house of sin, assuming they were in on the conspiracy, wouldn't tell him anything. He seemed to be at an impasse.

Then it hit him. Detective Lowell had said he had learned more details of the brothel from the tobacconist down the street from Shepheard's Hotel. There was only one shop he could have meant. Unlike most hotels, Shepheard's did not have a tobacconist on the premises at the moment. Mr. Wall had told him that the shop had gone vacant when the previous owner had died and there had been a fight over who would get the commission. The man's son by rights had the contract, but he couldn't afford the rent. He didn't want to sell his commission either, and there had been a big tussle as various tobacconists had stepped forward trying to get Shepheard's to break the contract and let them take over the empty shop. Mr. Wall had complained about it on more than one occasion. He was in the habit of stocking up on Woodbines when he went for his breakfasts with Sir Thomas Russell Pasha.

So for months now the guests at Shepheard's had to run the gauntlet of all the hucksters and salesmen crowding the front steps of the hotel and go to the tobacconist's down the street.

Was Alaeddin Bey using this shop as a lookout post? Shepheard's was the most popular hotel for well-heeled tourists in Cairo, and all of them would pass through the shop. It was a perfect place to examine the tourists for possible victims.

Or possible threats.

While it was a slim lead, Moustafa was accustomed to slim leads. He'd have to follow it up and see where it took him. He had found in this line of work that often a single thread could lead to a whole fabric of crime and corruption.

Perhaps he should tell Sir Thomas Russell Pasha. No, that man wouldn't listen to a Soudanese. Every time they met he referred to him as "Sir Augustus's servant" and then pretended he wasn't there.

He had seen how that man's mind worked. Sir Thomas Russell Pasha was intelligent enough to put down straightforward crime. Indeed, until the recent disturbances the streets had become considerably safer under his rule. It made Moustafa's teeth grind to admit it, but it was true.

But the man lacked imagination. He could not see beyond the obvious. Granted, the obvious was the correct answer nineteen times out of twenty, but Mr. Wall had a talent for attracting the twentieth. It was up to Mr. Wall to solve those cases. And yes, the Little Infidel as well.

And Moustafa.

With a groan he started to walk back out of the alley. Damn that man. He was miles away on the Nile and yet still managed to drag him into a case. It didn't matter that Moustafa had quit. Mr. Wall and Faisal were in danger. He had to help them as best he could.

And how was he supposed to do that when he had work tomorrow?

CHAPTER TWELVE

Faisal didn't find out much at lunch. The crew had just come off from three day's break in Cairo so they were all talking about the time they had spent with their family and friends. The food was good, though—hummus and tahini and vegetables and as much bread as you could eat. Too bad there wasn't any of that beef they had served upstairs. He felt tempted to ask for some but he didn't want to get smacked again.

The crew were all adults—Egyptians and Nubians and a Greek man who took care of the engine—except for one boy a little older than him named Rashid who made tea and shined shoes. He wore a uniform of red pantaloons, a white shirt, and a green vest embroidered with gold thread. Of course it wasn't real gold, but it looked nice. Even the servants were dressed well on this boat. Faisal sat next to him.

"This food is great," Faisal said. "Do we always eat this good?"

"This is nothing! Usually we get chicken too. Once a Frenchman bagged so many pigeons with his shotgun the passengers had more than they could eat and we got some of those too."

"I've eaten pigeon."

Stolen pigeon. A lot of people in Cairo kept pigeons on their rooftops. All you had to do was climb up there at night, sneak into the coop and wring the neck of one or two.

"Your master sure treats you nice."

"He's not … um, yes, he does. He even takes me to the moving pictures sometimes."

"Oh, come on," Rashid smiled and shook his head. "No master does that."

"He does!"

Rashid chuckled and grabbed another piece of bread. A couple of adults nearby smiled as if they didn't believe him either. Faisal decided to drop it. He was supposed to be a servant, after all.

"So where are you from?" Faisal asked Rashid.

"Helwan. That's a town just south of Cairo."

"I've heard of it." Until Rashid told him, he had no idea where it was.

"Which one is your master?"

"The Englishman with the mask."

"Oh, I've seen him. Why does he wear that?"

One of the waiters sitting opposite them cut in. "He lost his face in the war. I've seen that with another passenger when I was working on the *Ramesses*."

Rashid crinkled his nose. "Eeew. Did it make him crazy?"

Faisal paused. "No."

"He's crazy if he takes a little tyke like you to the moving pictures," the Greek mechanic said. Everyone laughed.

"He's not crazy!"

"Oh relax, we're only teasing," the waiter said. "Is this your first time out of Cairo?"

"No. I've been to Giza and even Bahariya Oasis."

"And the moving pictures," Rashid said. Everyone chuckled.

Faisal frowned. "The Englishman collects old things. He takes me along sometimes."

I could tell you that I help him solve murders and I've ridden in a motorcar, but you wouldn't believe that either.

"Well, someone has to shine his shoes while he mucks around with that stuff," Rashid said. "I've never understood why the foreigners waste their time wandering around old ruins."

"Why complain?" one of the cooks said. "It gives us a good job."

"It's good for Egyptians to understand their past," Faisal said, remembering what his friend Ahmed had told him in Bahariya.

"And what do you know of Egypt's past, little servant boy?" the cook asked.

"Lots! I even have a lamp from the Late Period. That's old. Really, really old. Older than the Romans even."

"This boy is full of stories," the cook said and laughed. He wagged a finger at Faisal. "It would be better for you to concentrate on your work instead of making up tall tales. An ancient lamp indeed. What's next? That you rub it and make a djinni come out?"

That got a round of laughter. Faisal blushed. Why did no one ever take him seriously?

Rashid elbowed him. "Don't pay any attention. We're just making fun of you because you're new, and because you're full of tall tales. We don't get many personal servants on board. The Europeans don't need them with us around. Some of the ladies bring chambermaids, but that's it."

"You never know what Europeans are going to do," Faisal said. "Who's that Turk? I didn't expect there to be a Turk on board."

"If he's a Turk, I'm the emperor of China," the cook muttered.

Abdelkarim, the waiter who had smacked Faisal earlier, glared at the cook and the man looked away. Then the waiter turned to Faisal. "Alaeddin Bey is a respectable gentleman and you will treat him the same as any other passenger. You'd be better off focusing on your work."

Faisal looked around. Several people looked uncomfortable and he knew he had hit on something.

Rashid cut in.

"Did you see what Mohammed the porter did at Bulaq this morning? He was carrying two steamer trunks, one on each shoulder—"

"Wow," Faisal said. "Sounds like he's strong."

"He is, and he likes to show off. It gets him good tips from the foreigners. Not this time, though. He was walking along and slipped on an orange peel. Whoopsie! He went face first right into the sand, the two steamer trunks landing on top of him. He got sand all over his face and a big bump on his head!"

Everyone laughed, and Faisal sensed the laughter was louder than normal because everyone wanted to break the mood his question had caused.

After that, everyone broke into little conversations about nothing. Faisal chatted with Rashid and bided his time. He had noticed a piece of paper pinned to the wall next to the door. It had a list of numbers next to it and writing next to each number. Although Faisal couldn't read, he could read numbers. That was useful for things like money.

Once they had finished and cleaned their plates in the kitchen, Faisal touched Rashid on the shoulder and pointed to the paper.

"What's that?"

"The passenger manifest. It shows which cabin each passenger is staying in."

"My Englishman is staying in cabin 30."

"Yes, and there he is, Sir Augustus Wall."

Faisal turned to him. "You can read?"

"I went to a Koranic school for a few years. Boring. We just sat in rows reciting all day. But at least I learned to read. That's useful. You should learn."

"My, um, master has a German friend. What cabin is he in?"

Rashid ran his finger down the list. "Heinrich Schäfer? That sounds German."

"Um, yes."

"Cabin 11."

"Wow, you really can read! Who's in this cabin?"

"Mr. and Mrs. O'Leary."

Faisal glanced to make sure the angry waiter wasn't around.

"And this one?" He asked, pointing to cabin 19.

"Lieutenant Arthur Hemsworth." Rashid laughed. "Yes, I really can read!"

Now for the trick. "And this one?" Faisal pointed to cabin 18, the one where he had seen Alaeddin Bey trying to break in.

"Ms. Lillian Trasher. She's an American and gets to ride for free."

"That must be nice."

"She runs an orphanage in Assiout that the boss Mr. Cook supports."

"Oh. Anyway, I better get back to my work."

"Me too. The passengers will be wanting tea, and I have a whole bunch of shoes to shine. Bulaq is very dirty. You better go shine your master's shoes too."

Faisal headed to the Englishman's cabin, and found him standing outside with Mr. Jocelyn. Faisal stood beside the cabin door and gave him a look that showed he needed to talk with him inside. Mr. Jocelyn understood too.

"I will see you later, Augustus," Mr. Jocelyn said, and moved away.

"He should come in too," Faisal said. "He needs to hear this."

"That wouldn't be respectable."

"Why not?"

"Because ... well, never mind." The Englishman took him inside the cabin. Faisal looked around. It had a little sitting room with two chairs and a table, and a bedroom and even its own bathroom.

"This is much nicer than my place."

"Of course it is."

"Can I stay here?"

"No. What did you want to speak with me about?" The Englishman sat down in one chair. Faisal sat down in the other.

"I caught Alaeddin Bey trying to pick the lock on cabin 18. Someone named Ms. Trasher is staying there. Is there a cowboy on board?"

"A cowboy?"

"Ms. Trasher is American."

"Not all Americans are cowboys," the Englishman said, "although most act like they are."

"Oh. She gets to ride for free."

"She does, and she's a friend of Mr. Cook himself." The Englishman rubbed his chin. "Now why would he want to break into her cabin, of all people? Surely there are richer passengers to pluck. The baronet, for example.

Or myself."

"Maybe she was collecting donations in Cairo."

The Englishman snapped his fingers and pointed at Faisal. "Clever boy! I bet she's got a packet of money in her cabin."

Faisal grinned. "That's why you need me on these trips. I'm useful. I'd be more useful if I stayed here."

"You're not staying here. You could be more useful finding out how Alaeddin Bey knew about Ms. Trasher."

"I think he's working with one of the waiters, Abdelkarim. He might be working with more people on the boat too."

"That would make sense, if he's a regular passenger on Thomas Cook boats. Try to find out more."

"I will, but first you need to teach me how to shine your shoes."

The Englishman blinked. "I beg your pardon?"

"I'm supposed to be your servant. I have to be seen working for you."

"Oh, right. I normally shine my own shoes. It's a habit I acquired while in the army. Weren't you ever a shoeshine boy?"

"No. They have to walk around the cafes all day and there are so many of them you hardly make any money."

"It is true they swarm around the cafes like Biblical locusts. Very well. Let me fetch my polishing kit."

The Englishman came back with a small box containing a rag and two colors of shoe polish. They moved the chairs together. Faisal already sort of knew how to do the job since he had known lots of shoeshine boys, and so the Englishman didn't have to spend much time showing him how to do it right. When the first shoe was done, he handed the second shoe to Faisal.

"Go outside with both shoes and shine them on the gangway. That way everyone will see you working for me. Good for appearances."

Faisal rose. "All right, Englishman."

He didn't really want to shine these shoes, because only servants did that, but he reminded himself that he was in disguise.

"Oh, Faisal."

Faisal stopped at the door. "Yes?"

"What do you think of the locks on these cabins? I'm sure you've already studied them."

"They're pretty good. That magician must be a good lockpick to think he can break in."

"Oh. That's disappointing. I was hoping to have you use your skills to gain access to a cabin or two."

"No problem, Englishman. I'll just go through the window. It's a simple latch. The windows are loose enough I can put a stiff wire through and unhook it. The magician would have done that himself but the windows are too small for him to fit through."

"Excellent. Now all we need is a stiff wire."

"I brought one."

"Smart lad."

Faisal grinned. "So whose cabin do you want me to break into?"

"Alaeddin Bey's. He's giving a demonstration in the library this afternoon. It should last an hour or so. That should give you plenty of time."

Faisal bit his lip. "Getting in won't be a problem, but getting in without being seen on this busy boat sure will be."

CHAPTER THIRTEEN

The library on the *Arabia* was a well-appointed little room with a few armchairs and a shelf of books filled with standard texts on Egyptology. A newspaper rack, supplied with yesterday's editions, stood to one side.

The chairs had been lined up in three rows in the center of the room. Two armchairs sat facing them.

The audience numbered about a dozen and consisted of Augustus and his friends, along with the baronet, the Australian officer, and several of the English men and women. The pious Irish couple had not been invited. Neither, apparently, had the rest of the passengers. Augustus wondered how Alaeddin Bey had chosen. It hadn't been based on gullibility. He had been invited, after all, and he recognized a couple of other scoffers in the room, most notably his fellow veteran.

The Australian, whose name Augustus had learned was Lieutenant Hemsworth, nodded a greeting and sat beside him. Augustus tried to hide his disappointment. This man was sharper than the bulk of this crowd. He did not want him making friends. The fellow might notice he was more than a simple tourist.

"This should be good for a chuckle," he whispered, making sure he did so loudly enough for those sitting nearby to hear.

"Wouldn't miss it for the world," Augustus said.

The Australian lowered his voice. "You know I overheard him inviting Ms. Trasher?"

"Did he now? How did she respond?"

"How do you think she responded?" Hemsworth replied with a laugh. "He'll make no convert out of her."

"And she'll make no convert out of him."

"True enough." Hemsworth looked around. "But where's the entertainment?"

A moment later, Alaeddin Bey entered with Cordelia. Aunt Pearl was not far behind, still looking angry even though her flushed face showed she had been having some of her regular constitutionals. A waiter closed the door. None of the *Arabia's* crew remained in the room.

The hypnotist moved to the front of the room and addressed the small crowd.

"Good afternoon, ladies and gentlemen. I wish to thank you for attending. I also wish the thank Cordelia Ruskin for agreeing to participate in this demonstration of the science of hypnotism."

Ruskin? If that had been a slip, Cordelia would have corrected him. Had she given him a false name? Why? And why would Aunt Pearl agree to such a deception?

He glanced at Aunt Pearl, who had sat down nearby. Heinrich caught his eye, sending him a silent question. Augustus checked Alaeddin Bey wasn't looking their way and gave a small shrug.

Then it hit him. *She's using a false name so Alaeddin Bey doesn't discover her relation to the chief of police. Blast! She's probably even registered as Ruskin so her brother can't trace her.*

This raised his estimate of Cordelia's intelligence considerably, and his annoyance with her even more so.

Without a word, Cordelia sat in one of the chairs facing the crowd. Silently Alaeddin Bey went to each of the windows and pulled down the blinds, blocking the view of the river and the slowly passing scene of villages and green, cultivated fields. As the blinds went down one by one, the chatter in the room subsided and everyone watched the hypnotist.

Even with the blinds shut, enough of the strong African sunlight filtered around them to provide the room with subdued illumination.

At last, Alaeddin Bey came to the front of the room and turned to the audience. He folded his hands before him and studied them for a moment.

"Greetings," he said at last. "I am honored to have such a collection of refined men and women interested in my noble science. Some of you doubt that hypnotism is anything more than chicanery and bluff. For that, I do not blame you. There are many stage magicians on the entertainment circuit who do nothing more than silly tricks involving actors. They give hypnotism a bad name. I feel it is my duty to change that, and Egypt is the perfect place in which to work. Here one is close to the roots of humanity. One can walk through the temples and tombs of one of man's greatest ancient civilizations, a civilization deeply rooted in magical wisdom. I have been a student of ancient Egypt for many years, and while I am not as knowledgeable of its art as some of us"—here he bowed to Heinrich—"I have delved more deeply than any man I know into its lost wisdom. The kind of hypnotism I do is not the tomfoolery one sees on the vaudeville stage, nor is it exactly like the modern hypnotic science as it is practiced by psychologists and medical doctors. No, this is a fusion of Western science and Eastern mysticism. It brings together the greatest of both civilizations to create a truly unique practice."

He turned to Cordelia and bowed. The young woman smiled and for a moment Augustus was taken aback. The smile she gave the hypnotist in return was a bit too warm, a bit too familiar. She never smiled at him like that.

What was her game? Surely Alaeddin Bey hadn't worked so quickly on this woman as to make her give her heart to him? The constant presence of Aunt Pearl, no matter what her stage of daily intoxication, would have stopped such a thing. Besides, they had only left Cairo a few hours ago. No, something else was going on.

"I introduce to you Miss Cordelia Ruskin, of Hampstead."

Lied about her borough too, Augustus thought.

"Miss Ruskin has a great interest in hypnotism, and has agreed to be my subject for this demonstration. We talked at length about the procedure during and after lunch. Now the doubters in the room may cry foul. They will say that I have conspired with Miss Ruskin to put on a show. This is a common technique of stage hypnotists, after all. So we will also have a second subject today, someone who I have not spoken with privately. I would, indeed, prefer someone who does not believe in the power of hypnotism. May I have a volunteer?"

The question was met with silence, broken a few moments later by a suppressed chuckle.

"I'll volunteer," Heinrich said.

"Ah, Herr Schäfer. I am afraid you know too much about the process to make a good subject. It is better to have a clear mind, one that has not been cluttered with facts about hypnotism." Alaeddin Bey looked around the room, his gaze settling on Augustus. "How about you, Sir Augustus?"

"Me?"

Everyone turned to look at him.

"Why not? Yes, you presented your doubts and objections to my science over lunch, but that does not disqualify you. You have a keen mind. I can see that clearly. I think you'd make an excellent subject."

What are you playing at? Have you started to suspect me already and you want to get me into your power? Well, you'll find my mind is stronger than yours.

"Come," Alaeddin Bey extended his hand. "It will cause no pain and you will not be in the slightest danger. Let me assure you that hypnotism works by the power of suggestion. One cannot be made to do anything one does not wish to do."

"So you're not going to make him bah like a sheep?" Lieutenant Hemsworth asked in his Australian drawl. That elicited a ripple of laughter.

Alaeddin Bey smiled. "Only if he wishes to," he said, bringing forth more laughter. Augustus flushed.

Nevertheless, he stood and walked over to the spare seat in front of the assembly. His mind was too strong to be affected by this showman, and he had the feeling that if he played along he might get more insight into the suspect's nature.

He sat, shifting in his seat as he saw all those eyes fixed upon him. People always stared, of course. They'd been staring ever since the war. Most at least had the courtesy to look away when he spotted them. The Egyptians would keep on staring, but that was different because the Egyptians stared at all foreigners. To the natives, his appearance wasn't all that much stranger that Cordelia's or Heinrich's.

But now he had an entire crowd of his countrymen staring at him. And they weren't staring at him because he was about to be the subject of a mesmerism show. He knew perfectly well why they were staring.

His hand tightened on the grip of his sword cane. He'd like to draw out the blade and poke out every one of those bugging, voyeuristic eyes.

Wait, not everyone was staring. As Alaeddin Bey droned on, his back to Augustus, he saw two people not looking at his mask. Aunt Pearl was glaring at her niece. Heinrich, too, was also looking at Cordelia, studying her intensely.

Augustus turned.

Cordelia was gazing at Alaeddin Bey with unabashed admiration and affection.

Good Lord. I wanted you to stop following me around like a puppy, but did you have to fixate on the worst possible person on this boat?

Alaeddin Bey finished his speech and turned. His eyes met Cordelia's. The girl flushed. The mesmerist gave her a warm smile. Augustus did not see Aunt Pearl's reaction. He could imagine it well enough.

"I am now prepared to begin. Are you ready, Miss Ruskin and Sir Augustus?"

"I am happy to be of assistance, Alaeddin," Cordelia effused.

First name basis already? Must you act so shamefully in front of all these people?

"And you, Sir Augustus?"

"Um, yes. Fire away."

"Nothing so dramatic as that, my good sir. Only a simple method of bringing into focus your unconscious mind and making it amenable to change."

The only thing that's going to change here is your legal status, my friend. Stealing and murdering is bad enough, but if you meddle with the chief of police's younger sister, you're going to get thrown into the darkest hole in all of Cairo.

"Now I would like you to both close your eyes. Get comfortable in your chair. Relax. This won't hurt you. On the contrary, it may very well help you. There will be no tricks, no show business, merely the application of certain scientific and mystical principles.

"Are you all settled? Good. Now relax. Take slow, deep breaths. That's right. Focus on my voice as you relax. All is calm now. Nothing to worry about. Just focus on my voice. Now I'm going to count backwards from ten, and as I do so you will find yourself getting ever more relaxed. Ten. Beginning to relax ... nine, getting more relaxed now ... eight, much more relaxed ..."

The calm, measured tones of Alaeddin Bey's voice soothed Augustus. The thought of everyone staring at him dropped from his mind.

"Listen to the sound of my voice. Seven ... more relaxed."

Augustus tensed, suddenly aware of this ridiculous position he was in, his eyes closed in front of a probable murderer while a bunch of strangers gaped at him.

"Relax."

Yes, relax. Play your part. He's not going to stab you in front of all these people.

But what's Cordelia's game? Why did she agree to this and why was she looking at him like a lovelorn schoolgirl? If she gets hurt there'll be hell to pay.

"Five ... even more relaxed."

What happened to six? Oh, calm yourself.

Augustus took a deep breath and willed his muscles to loosen, only to find they already had. Alaeddin Bey had a truly remarkable voice. He could put a man to sleep more efficaciously than opium.

"Four ... even more relaxed ... three ... fully relaxed now ... two ... floating effortlessly on a warm sea of relaxation and ... one. You are completely relaxed, the most relaxed you have ever been in your life. I want you to just enjoy this feeling for a time. Breathe into it. Yes, take deep breaths. That's right. For a moment simply sit and enjoy this state of complete relaxation."

Augustus found himself slumped in his chair, his hands resting on his lap, his chin on his chest as if he was taking a nap. A distant part of his mind realized that his posture looked rather embarrassing, but he found that he did not care. He couldn't even keep the worry in his mind for long. Thoughts just seemed to slide away as he listened to the soothing purr of the hypnotist's voice.

"Now Sir Augustus, I will start with you. Just sit there for a moment. No need to open your eyes or move. What I want you to do is to picture a happy time, perhaps when you were a child. Yes, remember when you were a child. Did you have a happy childhood, Augustus?"

"Yes."

His own voice sounded strangely distant in his ears.

"Then remember a time when you were a child. Picture it in your mind. Now step into that picture. Be there."

Augustus had been imagining the football pitch at his old school in Oxford. The image of the muddy field came to him with remarkable clarity, a memory almost twenty years old rising up in his mind as if he had been there the day before. When Alaeddin Bey told him to step into that picture, something remarkable happened.

He did step into it, and he was there.

It was a cold day in March, the early morning air sharp in his lungs. Augustus was thirteen, and the best striker in fourth form. Riley Dodgson was goalkeeper and famed for stopping tricky shots. He was also impulsive, and had foolishly challenged the best men from fifth form to a match. They were a year older—Ted Somers and Fredrick Unwin even had to shave once a week—but they had been slacking on the pitch of late. Augustus and his mates had been practicing hard all winter, come snow or sleet. So the fourth formers had a chance against them, but if they lost they'd be ribbed mercilessly by all the upperclassmen. Dodgson would get it the worst, and so would Augustus because Riley was his best mate.

It was Saturday morning just before the match. Everyone was warming up. The fifth formers were on their side of the field. Mr. Gainsborough stood in the center as referee. The pitch was surrounded by all the students and most of the staff. All the older boys had crowded around the fifth formers' end of the pitch to cheer, hoping they'd thrash the fourth formers as punishment for the unforgivable hubris of challenging their supremacy.

Mr. Gainsborough motioned for the team captains to come to the center of the pitch. Riley Dodgson was their captain because it had been his daft idea to challenge the older boys. Ted Somers, a hulking lad who had thrashed a third former just this past week for stepping on his foot by accident, was captain of the fifth formers.

The fourth form won the toss, and Riley chose to have the ball first. A wise move. The bigger boys would not tire so quickly, so the fourth form would need to score in the first half and play defensively in the second, hoping to keep any lead they might have gained.

But that's not what happened. The fifth formers bulled their way through the defense and scored an early goal. Riley blocked a couple of other attempts before the tide shifted late in the first half and the fourth formers got a chance. Jim Kennington fumbled a good opportunity, and Augustus got his legs cut out from under him when he got a go. The referee gave him a penalty kick.

Now was his chance. He readied himself, glancing twice at the right side of the goal, hoping the goalie would notice, and then kicked hard for the left.

The goalie called his bluff and dove straight for it, saving it easily.

The crowd groaned. Augustus felt like sinking all the way through the Earth and becoming a hermit in China.

As they feared, the second half was a desperate rearguard action to save them the humiliation of losing 2-0. Riley did a man's work stopping attempt after attempt. Thirty minutes in, Kennington managed to break away and head up the field, only to get an elbow in the face from Ted Somers.

That earned Somers a yellow card, and Kennington a bloody nose and a penalty kick.

And earned his team a miracle. The goalie missed by inches. The score was 1-1.

The fifth formers doubled down, bringing in a fresh striker and a fresh midfielder. Augustus and his mates didn't have any backup. None of the boys sitting on the bench, no matter how fresh they were, could compare to those already on the field.

So they panted through the next minutes, barely foiling several attacks. The game was now entirely played on the fourth formers' side of the pitch, and a goal against them appeared inevitable.

Then Augustus got his second chance. Kennington managed to break free and cross the center line for the first time in almost ten minutes. The fifth form defense concentrated on him, cutting him off and trying to trip him up without the referee seeing. Kennington broke away for just a moment, long enough to pass it ahead and to the right of Augustus, who looped around the defense, sprinted to gain some distance, and got the ball.

For a precious two seconds he was alone. The bigger boys would close in on him soon enough. He was at a bad angle, running for all he was worth, and the goalie was staring right at him.

Now or never. He let fly, aiming for the far top corner of the goal. The goalie sprang for it, stretching himself up as his gloved hands reached for the ball …

… and missed by a fraction of an inch.

Goal! The crowd erupted in cheering. The young lads, the fourth formers, the staff, even some of the older boys shouted in triumph at the excellent goal.

A moment later Augustus got buried in a heap of his classmates. Everyone was shouting gleefully into his face. They lifted him aloft, and he pumped his fist as the cheers rang in his ears.

Alaeddin Bey's calm voice pushed through the cheering.

"Now I want you to come back. I am going to count backwards from three, and when I am finished you will open your eyes."

The cheering faded a little, the image of that glorious day wavering.

"Three …"

Augustus smiled. He'd shown those older boys a thing or two.

"Two …"

All the boys in his form wanted someone to lead the team to victory, and he'd been the one.

"One …"

The image faded, the cheering returning to its place as a beloved memory.

"Open your eyes."

Augustus did as he was asked, and found himself standing in the middle of the room, one foot raised as if he was going to kick a football. Cordelia was not far off, bent over with her hand reaching for the floor as if she was going to pick up something, a mixture of surprise and delight on her face.

Augustus whirled on the audience. They were all staring! Some were even smiling. That, he knew, was only courtesy.

They really wanted to be laughing.

Laughing at him.

He turned to Alaeddin Bey, hatred boiling in his gut. The mesmerist treated him to a serene smile.

"Now, Sir Augustus, do you see there is something to my science?"

CHAPTER FOURTEEN

Work at the Coptic Museum was just as interesting on his second day as it had been on his first, but Moustafa had trouble focusing. He and Joseph finished recording the new acquisitions in the museum's catalogue, and then started setting up a new display room with a Copt named Abraam, an older man with a stoop who handled the artifacts as if they were made of the thinnest glass.

"These are irreplaceable," he told Moustafa. "Egypt's past must be kept in museums for all to enjoy, and must be taken care of only by those trained in the task."

Moustafa thought he heard in the old man's words a rebuke for his earlier job as a seller of antiquities. He felt tempted to tell him that he had sold only fakes to those who couldn't appreciate the real thing. Instead he listened to the man's instructions as he told him how to set up the displays.

Of course Moustafa knew all about displaying items for purchase, but displaying them behind glass as museum objects was a somewhat different skill.

"We don't necessarily display the most attractive items," Abraam explained. "Instead we display those that can teach the most about the past. For example, look at this wall painting I just put up. It comes from a ruined church Mr. Simaika visited in the Eastern Desert. As you can see, it's all cracked and faded. Most of it is missing. You can barely make out the images of Jesus flanked by two of his apostles. At least we think they are apostles. It's too fragmentary to tell. We have many nicer images of this kind, but none from the Eastern Desert. It is also early and of slightly different style than the ones we have collected from along the Nile. Thus it is a good example for teaching the development of early Coptic art."

Moustafa studied it. "I must admit I don't see the stylistic differences."

Joseph laughed and clapped him on the shoulder. "You've only been on the job one and a half days! You'll learn it all soon enough."

Moustafa shook his head. "No, one can never learn it all. That's the joy of it, and the frustration."

Abraam looked at him with an admiration that warmed Moustafa's heart. "It is always nice to meet a scholar from our part of the world. There are too few of them. Tell me, do you not feel a little uncomfortable handling Christian and pagan things?"

"No. These are part of Egypt and Nubia's past. One can be a devout Muslim, or a devout Christian, and still study these things. Just because I've read the myth of Osiris doesn't mean I believe in it."

The two Copts laughed.

"Well said, my friend," Abraam replied. "It's a shame more of our countrymen don't believe the same. They don't even value their own past. Many of the artifacts we have in this museum we've actually had to save from monasteries and private homes where they were treated as old junk."

"Mr. Simaika told me. Sadly, we Muslims do the same. Many of the medieval religious buildings are falling into disrepair. I used to work for someone who lives in the old Islamic quarter, and not far from his house was an Ayyubid mosque that was practically falling apart, abandoned to the pigeons. There was also a Tulunid madrasa, perhaps the oldest in the city, in the same state."

Joseph grimaced. "It is even worse with ancient artifacts. The early Christians defaced many of the old statues and bas-reliefs. There's a temple in down in Luxor called the Ramesseum where the early fathers built a chapel right in the back. It seems remarkable to build in such a place. I suppose since they had a ready-built stone building they didn't bother building a new one. Instead they just hacked off all the carvings, even toppled giant statues."

"I've been to the Ramesseum and seen that chapel," Moustafa said, but he was no longer listening. The mention of Luxor had got him thinking about the case again. He needed to go see that tobacconist down the street from Shepheard's Hotel. Detective Lowell had gone there to ask about the brothel behind the fish market. The owner of that shop may have been the only man to have known Lowell's intentions.

The more Moustafa thought about it—and he could think of little else throughout that long day—the more he became sure the shop owner was in on the crime. It seemed the perfect cover. Sir Thomas Russell Pasha had said Alaeddin Bey had been banned from the hotel, so having a lookout in a shop that all the hotel guests patronized was the next best thing.

Time seemed not to progress at all. Mercifully there wasn't a clock in the display area, but when he went back with Joseph to the cataloging room his seat directly faced a grandfather clock that ticked with agonizing slowness through the minutes.

Joseph caught his eye a few times. Finally, he asked, "Is there somewhere you need to be?"

"No, um, I was just thinking I won't be able to stay for tea today. I have to meet a friend right after work and it's a long tram ride."

"Must be quite a friend. If you watched a woman like you've been watching that clock, I would think you were in love."

Moustafa managed an awkward smile and kept his head bent over his work.

At last the day ended. Moustafa hurried out as quickly as dignity would allow.

The tobacco shop stood a few doors down from Shepheard's Hotel, close enough that he could hear the entreaties of the crowd of hucksters who stood in front of the hotel terrace, crying out for the Europeans' attention, practically begging them to buy cheap carpets, poorly made brass lamps, and fake antiquities. Some bowed low, crying out to the indifferent drinkers as their foreheads touched the ground. One vendor did a little dance, making his pile of cheap ceramic bowls clatter in a crude rhythm. Moustafa wrinkled his nose as if he had caught a whiff of foul odor. He never used to notice such things; now the whole spectacle struck him as distasteful in the extreme. Good Egyptians debasing themselves in the hope of a few piastres!

Yes, he had made the right choice to work for Mr. Simaika. While his old job had carried with it many benefits, he had still been working for a European. When he had told his neighbors and his friends at his favorite cafe that he now worked for an Egyptian, they looked at him differently. Yes, Mr. Simaika was a Copt, some felt obliged to point out, but at least he was a fellow countryman.

Now Moustafa had to deal with a very different sort of countryman. The tobacconist's was a narrow storefront bedecked with the signs of various brands of cigarettes and rolling tobacco. The displays blocked any view of the interior. Good. He did not want prying eyes.

Moustafa entered and inhaled the rich smells. Two others were in the shop, both European. Behind the counter stood an Egyptian in a clean white djellaba and a tarboush of fine material, perhaps imported from Fez itself. The store looked well-stocked and organized, with a humidor to one side and an array of products behind the counter. On a top shelf sat a row of gleaming brass sheeshas.

The two Europeans in front of him in line bought their foreign brands—one English and one French—and quickly departed, leaving him and the tobacconist alone.

"And how may I help you, my Soudanese friend?" the tobacconist asked in quite good English. An act of courtesy with the assumption that he could speak the language, or a deliberate slight with the assumption that he did not?

"You have a fine collection here," Moustafa replied in the same language, biding his time.

"Indeed. Are you looking for some good sheesha tobacco? We have some fine Lebanese brands just in."

"Actually I was looking for some cigarettes for an American friend. Do you carry Camel cigarettes?"

Moustafa was expecting to get a guarded reaction. Instead, the man didn't skip a beat. "Yes we do. We're getting more and more Americans since the war. They are travelling more than they used to, and further. The war has woken them up to the existence of the world beyond their borders."

The man pulled down a carton and held it so the image of the camel standing in front of a pyramid was visible.

"A complement, isn't it?" the tobacconist said. "Virginia tobacco using the images of Egypt, because they know our tobacco is better."

Moustafa gave him a level stare. "Our tobacco may be better, but our hospitality is often lacking. My friend—"

The sound of the door opening made him cut off. A European couple came in.

"You speak English?" the man said abruptly, getting between Moustafa and the tobacconist.

"I do, sir," the proprietor said, bowing a little.

"A carton of Benson and Hedges, then," he demanded. His wife looked around with a bored air.

The Egyptian served them and they hurried out. Then he turned to Moustafa with an apologetic smile.

"My apologies. You know how Europeans are, and with my business right next to a big hotel, I can't afford to offend them."

Moustafa glared at him. "You can afford to kill them, though."

The man stared at him blankly for a moment. His gaze flicked to the Camel cigarettes on the counter, and then he ducked down.

Moustafa knew he must be going for a weapon. He vaulted over the counter and slammed into him. They ended up in a heap on the floor, a cascade of American cigarettes following them.

A metallic clatter woke Moustafa up to the real danger. A revolver lay not far off. No doubt that was what the man had gone for, dropping it when Moustafa landed on him. He reached for it.

The tobacconist was quicker. He grasped the revolver and tried to turn the gun on Moustafa, who grabbed his arm and pushed it away just in time for the bullet to smash through the counter instead of his skull.

Moustafa smacked the man's arm against the floor. Then again. The third time the tobacconist cried out and let go of the revolver. Moustafa grabbed it and drove his knee into the man's back, putting all his considerable weight behind it.

"I give up! I give up!" the man cried.

Just then the door opened. Moustafa poked his head above the counter to see a confused-looking European standing there. He obviously hadn't noticed the shot thanks to the noise of the busy street outside, but once he had opened the door he must have heard the sounds of struggle and perhaps noticed the neat little hole in the counter.

"What do you want?" Moustafa asked in English.

"Are you, um, open?"

"Not to the likes of you. We don't serve foreigners here. Go back to your hotel."

The man gave him an outraged look and slammed the door. Moustafa felt a strange mixture of satisfaction and guilt.

But he had more important things to think about. He treated the man beneath him to a smack that knocked his head onto the floor with a loud clonk, got up, and hauled the tobacconist to his feet.

"I hope I have ruined your business," Moustafa told him. "Now if you don't want me to ruin the rest of your life, talk."

"I—I don't know—"

Moustafa slapped him upside the head like he would slap a disobedient child. Faisal, for example. He hadn't realized how much he missed doing that.

"I had to! I was forced!"

"Nonsense," Moustafa said, pushing him to the door. "Lock it. We don't want any more interruptions."

The man did as he was told. Moustafa stepped back, covering him with the gun.

"Talk."

"I didn't want to. They forced me," he pleaded.

"Who?"

The man's eyes shifted, looking for a way out. Moustafa cocked the revolver.

"Who?"

The tobacconist slumped.

"They'll kill me if they find out I spoke with you," he murmured. "They'll kill my family too. They'll make an example out of us."

Moustafa felt a tug of sympathy. Although this fellow was trying to get out of talking, what he said was no doubt true. He'd seen enough crime to know how these gangs worked.

"If you don't talk to me, they will probably kill a man and boy I know. You have to talk. You *will* talk. I'll do what I can to protect you."

The tobacconist shook his head. "It won't do any good."

"It will if I break up this gang. I've done it before. Talk."

"This is about the American detective?"

"Yes. Who else would it be about?"

The man studied him for a moment. To Moustafa's surprise, he saw sympathy in his eyes. "Oh, you have no idea what you're stepping into, do you? You should go back home to Nubia, my friend. Save yourself while there's still time. Although perhaps Nubia won't be far enough away. They have a long reach. A very long reach."

CHAPTER FIFTEEN

The window to the magician's cabin turned out to be just as easy to pick as Faisal thought it would. Passing by it casually as if he was heading somewhere else, he gave it a quick, expert look and saw the frame was a bit loose and the latch big and easy to hook and pull up. He had packed a thin sheet of bent metal and a stiff wire and a long piece of cord, thinking he might need them on this trip. The wire would do the trick in two seconds flat. The silly Englishman never thought about such things. You had to plan ahead on jobs like this, and the Englishman tended to rush in and get into trouble. It was Faisal's job to get him out of it.

But right now he had to worry more about himself. He walked along the gangway, pretending to idly look out at the view while really waiting for his chance.

That chance took a long time coming. Not all of the passengers had gone to see the magician's show. Some stood looking at the river, and waiters passed to and fro. The Greek mechanic passed by, stopped to examine the big paddle wheel on the side of the ship, then nodded in satisfaction before walking away.

Why did this ship have to be so busy? He couldn't hang around here all afternoon. It wasn't like a street in Cairo. He didn't really belong here. Sooner or later someone would tell him to move on. That suspicious waiter would look at him funny and ask what he was up to, or that mechanic would come back and say some nonsense about how he should be in his master's cabin shining his shoes or brushing his coat.

Well, he didn't even have any shoes to shine. After shining the second shoe outside the cabin, the Englishman had given him another pair of shoes to shine. He had taken his time so that as many people as possible saw him doing the work, but he didn't like it. Sure, he was playing a part, but sitting on the floor outside the cabin shining the Englishman's shoes made him feel like a servant, and he was not a servant. He'd have to talk to the Englishman about getting paid extra to shine shoes. Not much, just a little. Just so he felt better about it.

Then he spotted his chance. A pair of Europeans who had been watching the view turned and went inside, a waiter rounded the corner and disappeared, and for the moment he was alone.

Faisal rushed over to the magician's window, shoved the wire, which he had already bent into the right shape, into the window jamb and popped the latch.

Just then a door opened not far in front of him. Faisal turned, slipped the wire into his pocket, and strolled away as casually as he could, heart pounding. A European man in a white suit and a big white hat passed by him, smoking a stinky cigar, and stopped at the prow of the ship.

Faisal stopped too. The man paid no attention to him and had his back turned. Glancing back the way he had come, Faisal saw no one else around. The window was open a crack.

Should he risk it? The European didn't look like he was going to move any time soon. He just stood there, looking out at the river.

Go away, Faisal fumed. *Did you come all this way just to look at a river? Don't you have rivers where you're from?*

The man kept standing there, puffing at his cigar as the big smokestacks at the back of the boat puffed away too.

Faisal couldn't stay here much longer. Someone would come by who had been by before and wonder why he was spending so much time standing around doing nothing at one spot in the boat. If he was a European, he could get away with it. Europeans stood around staring at things all the time, especially Egyptian things. But no Egyptian would stand around looking at water pass by.

Making up his mind, he stepped to the window and, with a last look at the European in the white suit, pushed it open and pulled himself onto the windowsill and into the room as fast as he could.

He landed on the floor with a thump. Hoping nobody had heard him fall, he peeked out the window. No one. He couldn't see the European without sticking his head out the window and he didn't dare do that. He'd just have to hope the silly man hadn't seen anything. Probably not. The tourists were even sillier than your average European. It was like they were asleep on their feet. He closed the window except for a little crack that no one would notice unless they looked really closely.

Now to get to work. The magician's room looked just the same as the Englishman's. There was a front room with two chairs and a table. A book and a stack of newspapers sat on the table, along with a meerschaum pipe. The papers were in Arabic and some European language. Faisal couldn't read but the letters looked different so that's how he knew. The Englishman would probably be impressed he knew that. Faisal would have to tell him. There was nothing else in the room except a pair of slippers and a bottle of what looked like wine.

Faisal frowned at it. Didn't the magician say he was a Turk? The Turks were Muslim. He shouldn't have wine.

He shouldn't be killing people either, but he's doing that, Faisal thought. *Hurry up and have a look around and get out of here.*

Faisal peeked in the bathroom but saw nothing of interest except a paper envelope by the sink. That seemed strange. Who wrote letters in the bathroom? He opened the envelope and found a brown powder inside.

Was the magician sick? He didn't look sick. The Englishman would probably know what it was. He should take some of the powder. But how?

Faisal went back to the pile of newspapers and tore a little bit off the corner of one of the inside pages. The magician wouldn't notice it unless he turned to that page, and he'd think it had torn off by accident. He'd never think someone had snuck into his room and torn his newspaper. Faisal grinned. Who would do that?

He took a pinch of the powder and put it in the paper, folded the paper up, and put it in his pocket. Then he put the envelopes back exactly as he had found them. He was good at that. He wandered through the Englishman's house almost every night, and the Englishman never found anything out of place.

The sound of footsteps made Faisal bolt into the bedroom, looking for a place to hide. He tried to dive under the bed and ended up clonking his head against a steamer trunk. Before he could find somewhere else, a shadow passed across the light in the window.

Faisal moved behind the open door. If the magician stayed in the front room or the bathroom, he wouldn't be spotted. If he came into the bedroom, it was all over.

He tensed, waiting the sound of the cabin door opening.

Nothing.

Faisal peeked out, then ducked back as a woman passed by the window.

Great, it's busy again.

Faisal set about searching the bedroom. He didn't dare turn on the electric light. There was enough sunlight coming in from the window anyway. The magician hadn't drawn the curtains. While that exposed Faisal to view, since the inside was darker than the outside, someone would have to stop and peer in the window to spot him.

First he tried the little safe set into the wall, but of course it was locked. Then he rummaged through the closet and found lots of different clothes. He found a sparkling shiny red robe, a set of khaki clothes like the Europeans wore when they worked in the desert, a European-style suit, and a fez. In the chest of drawers, underneath a stack of socks and undergarments, he found a pistol and a box of bullets.

Faisal paused, a little shiver going through him. The Englishman said this man was a murderer. Had he murdered anyone with this pistol?

He looked around. Something was odd about this cabin. It didn't look like a place a magician would live. Except for a couple of funny bits of clothing, it could be the cabin of any European. The gun was a common thing to have, and even that powder could just be medicine. He had expected weird statues and talismans hanging from the ceiling. If it hadn't been broad daylight on a busy ship, Faisal would have never agreed to break into this cabin at all.

Faisal put everything back in place and gave the rest of the room a second look. Nothing. He considered pulling out the steamer trunk and searching inside, but it looked big and heavy and would probably make a lot of noise. He was also running out of time.

No one was in sight of the window when he peeked out the bedroom door. Crouching low so no one would spot him, he crept to the window and listened. He could hear two people talking in English. A brief peek out confirmed his worst suspicions. One of the English couples stood right outside the magician's window, chatting as they looked out over the Nile and the far shore.

Great. There was no way he could sneak out without them noticing, and foreigners talked forever. He'd seen them on the terrace at Shepheard's Hotel sitting around all morning. Blah blah blah. These two could stand there until the sun went down.

Maybe he should be bold, walk right out as if he belonged there. He could take some of the towels or something. To make it even more realistic, he could talk to them. What would be a good thing to say in English? Unfortunately, he didn't know the word for towels. How about, "You wants tea sir or madam?" Yes, that would work.

It might work too much. If they said yes, then he'd have to bring them tea, and pretty soon all the Europeans would be asking for tea and making him shine their shoes. Pretending to be one Englishman's servant was bad enough. Better just to wait.

But he couldn't wait long. The Englishman said he'd have an hour or more. Any time you had to sneak somewhere, you should always assume you had less time than you thought. And how long had he been at this already? He wasn't sure. Europeans were more concerned with things like hours and minutes than Egyptians. Faisal didn't even know how to read a clock. He usually judged time by the calls to prayer. That's all you really needed to know. But here on the river you couldn't hear the muezzin, so it was hard to tell how much time had passed.

Too much. He knew that for sure.

He crouched beneath the window, growing more and more annoyed as those two English people blabbered on. What were they talking about, anyway? "I see we're still going up the river." "Oh look, there's a palm tree." Stupid foreigners. They acted like they had never been on a river before.

Faisal tensed as he heard the footsteps of several people approaching. Had the magician finished his show? If everyone was getting out of that library, the walkways on the ship would fill up. He'd never get out of here.

He breathed a bit easier when the footsteps passed by and no more came for a couple of minutes. But each minute increased his danger.

The English couple stopped speaking. Faisal cocked his ear, waiting to hear them walk away.

Nothing. He dared another peek.

Ugh! Now they were kissing! How can decent people do that when someone was watching?

Oh, they didn't know anyone was watching. Faisal blushed and ducked back out of sight.

At last the man said something in English and the woman responded. He heard them walk away.

Now was his chance. He stood up, ready to climb out the window, when another couple strolled by.

If you start kissing, I'm going to throw a chamber pot at you.

Luckily they kept on going. Faisal waited a moment, listening for footsteps, then opened the window.

He dared a peek in both directions. Nobody!

Faisal didn't waste any time, he hopped onto the windowsill, vaulted out, landing softly on the deck in his bare feet. Quickly he shut the window and turned to stroll away as natural as you please. Silly Europeans, he fooled them all!

Someone whistled from the gangway just above him. Faisal spun around and looked up, his heart clenching.

Rashid leaned against the railing, looking down at him. The tea boy gave him a triumphant smile.

"Well, well, well. I knew there was something shifty about you. Faisal, you have broken into the wrong cabin."

Rashid nodded his head toward the nearby stairs.

"Come up here and we'll talk."

Faisal tried to think of an excuse to tell the older boy. There was nothing. He had been caught red-handed.

He summoned his courage as he climbed the steps. No one was near. It was the heat of the day and most of the foreigners had gone inside. He saw two foreigners on the far end of the upper deck, but they paid no attention to him and Rashid.

Nevertheless, Faisal kept his voice down.

"My Englishman will beat you if you tell on me."

"Not if I tell Abdelkarim."

That made Faisal pause. "So they work together. I knew it."

Rashid made a face and looked around. "You don't want to get involved with those two. They rob the passengers."

"And you do too?"

Rashid shook his head. "And get them angry at me? No, that's their territory. Sometimes they slip me a few piastres to keep me quiet. They do that with everyone except the mechanic, who is stays below and sees nothing, and the captain, who is either at the the helm or with the passengers."

Faisal nodded. That made sense. The captain and the mechanic were the only two Europeans who worked on the boat.

"Why are you telling me this?" Faisal asked.

"So you don't get yourself hurt, and so you don't mess everything up. Those tips come in handy, and this is a good job. If I don't play along, they'll figure out a way to get rid of me. I can't lose this job. There's nothing back in Helwan except for my older brother's farm. A boring village and beans and bread for dinner every night."

"Riding on a boat is nicer," Faisal agreed.

The murmur of many voices came from the lower deck. Faisal and Rashid leaned over the railing and saw everyone coming out of the library. He spotted the Englishman and his friends. If only he could be with them and not with this older boy who knew too much.

"You got out just in time," Rashid said. "What did you find in Alaeddin Pasha's cabin?"

"I didn't take anything."

"Nonsense."

Rashid's voice had grown harder. Faisal wondered who would beat who in a fight. Faisal was a good fighter, he had learned that on the streets quick enough, but Rashid was a farm boy. They were all strong. And he was at least a couple of years older.

"The safe was locked and there was no money lying around. No watch or ring or anything either." Faisal decided if he added something more interesting than that, Rashid would be more likely to believe him. "I found a gun in his bureau."

"I knew it! You better hope no one saw you go into his cabin, because you'll be in big trouble. You're an outsider. He'd kill you." Rashid took a step forward. "Now tell me, what else did you find?"

The hardness came back into the shoeshine boy's voice. Faisal could tell he didn't want to be involved, but he wasn't going to be cut out of any loot.

So Faisal did an old trick he had learned years ago. He turned out his pockets, pulling them so far out that the sides of his djellaba poked out like a pair of horns. He held onto the tips of the inside-out pockets. What Rashid couldn't see was that he had kept his thumb, hidden behind the rest of his fingers, stuck in the very bottom of the left pocket, jamming packet of powder inside. It would be hard for the shoeshine boy to notice, and he wasn't even looking because he got distracted by Faisal's lockpicking tools clattering onto the deck.

"Hide those, you idiot," Rashid said in a tense whisper.

Faisal had to try hard to stop himself from giggling. Country boys never knew any of the tricks. He scooped up his lockpicking tools and slipped them in his pocket before anyone else saw. Rashid looked at him like he was stupid. Faisal didn't mind. If someone thought you were stupid, it was easier to trick them and they were less suspicious of you in the first place.

"So now what?" Faisal asked.

"I won't say anything if you don't get up to any more tricks. But if you do …" Rashid stepped closer to him and held his fist up at Faisal's nose. It was a big fist, Faisal noticed. He'd obviously done a lot of farm work with it before joining the crew. It didn't look like the kind of fist he'd like to have hitting his face.

But the boy behind it wasn't nearly as clever as Faisal was.

Faisal trembled a little, and stood up straight as if he was trying to act brave.

"All right. I won't rob the passengers. Is it all right if I rob people on shore?"

"Do what you want on land. Just don't mess up what I have here. And don't cross Abdelkarim either. He doesn't like you."

Oh. That could be a problem.

"Why not?"

"Because you're an outsider, and he doesn't trust outsiders. He says you have shifty eyes."

Faisal blinked. Shifty eyes? Him? He'd never been told that in his life. People shouldn't make judgments of strangers like that!

"All right. I'll behave on the boat and do what I like on land."

He made to leave, but Rashid put a hand on his arm. His grip was tight. Strong.

"I don't like Abdelkarim, but if it comes down to it, I'll pick him over you. Watch your step, and watch your things."

"My things?"

"Abdelkarim has a master key to the crew and servants' deck. He swiped it from the captain and made a copy. I'd bet a thousand piastres he's already looked through your cabin, and if you make a wrong move, he'll probably come in at night and slit your throat."

CHAPTER SIXTEEN

The hypnosis session had left Augustus confused and unsettled. The images from his past had seemed so clear. The only other time the past came back so clearly was when he got to fighting and suddenly found himself back on the Western Front, or if he didn't have any opium before bed and his nightmares thrust him back to that horrid place.

This experience, on the other hand, had been entirely different. While it had not seemed as real—at no time had he stopped being aware of the year or where he was—the visual and emotional impact had been every bit as strong. He had really felt like he was thirteen again.

It had been wonderful. His entire life before the war had been wonderful, like some brilliant dream.

And now here he was, with half a face and a murder to solve.

Augustus stood at the prow of the ship with Heinrich and Jocelyn. Heinrich was in raptures.

"What a remarkable man he is! You should have seen yourself, Augustus. You were transformed! It's the happiest I've ever seen you."

Jocelyn smiled at that. Augustus caught her eye and shared the joke. She had seen him happier. But Heinrich had a point. No stranger could have such an effect on him.

"So you weren't shamming at all?" Jocelyn asked.

Augustus cleared his throat, feeling uneasy. "No. At first I planned to do so, just to allay any suspicions he might have. But once we started I found I didn't need to. Incredible that I'd put on such a ridiculous performance. I'd never normally do such a thing. I found that I didn't care. You know how when you're describing some event you're excited about and you start acting it out a bit? It was like that. We all do that, but not to the point of getting up in front of a room full of strangers."

"A hypnotist cannot make you do anything you don't want to do," Heinrich said. "You really wanted to go back to your youth and relive those days."

"Who doesn't? But we don't all go around kicking phantom footballs. I don't like that he was controlling me."

Jocelyn put a hand on his arm. "But if Heinrich is correct, he wasn't controlling you. You were allowing him to manipulate you."

"That's worse! Now I see why he's been so successful at thievery. He's got a talent for getting into one's confidence and putting one off their guard. Speaking of the low art of manipulation, what was Cordelia doing during all that? I must confess I forgot about her entirely."

"She was picking flowers," Jocelyn said. "She was a little girl at her auntie's house in the country."

"A little girl, eh? Why does that not surprise me?"

"Don't be so hard on her, Augustus," Jocelyn said. "She mentioned working as a nurse on the Western Front. Little girls are not capable of that."

Augustus ignored that comment and asked, "Where is she now?"

"Our mesmerist and a small crowd retired to the bar," Heinrich said.

"The bar, eh? Well at least Aunt Pearl will be there to watch over her."

"Don't be wicked, Augustus," Jocelyn chided.

Faisal appeared, looking nervous.

"I got into the magician's cabin and took a look around," he said. He kept his voice calm and natural. While surely none of the tourists gabbling nearby knew any Arabic, the boy obviously didn't want his tone to show that he had been up to something sneaky.

"Good boy," Augustus replied in the same language. "Did you find anything?"

Faisal grinned. "I did. But I can't show you here. Let's go to your cabin."

"Why don't we go find a quiet spot somewhere else?" Jocelyn said. "I want to see."

"Why can't you just come to the cabin?" Faisal asked.

"Silly boy," Jocelyn said. "This way."

Heinrich excused himself. "I'll go join the conversation in the bar. We'll meet later."

"All right," Augustus said. The scholar was proving useful. Pity he couldn't hold his own in a fight.

They searched around the ship until they found an empty sitting area with wicker chairs on the shady side of the boat. Faisal told of what he had found in the cabin, and produced a packet of powder.

"Well, well, well," Augustus said. "This is certainly interesting. I wonder what this could be. Jocelyn, do you have any idea?"

"I'm afraid not. I've never learned much beyond basic first aid and cures for my children's coughs. Why don't we ask Cordelia?"

"Cordelia? We don't want to get her involved!" Augustus exclaimed.

"Bad idea," Faisal agreed.

"She was trained as a nurse."

"So?" Faisal said. "Nurses don't know anything about powders."

"Sadly they do," Augustus grumbled, then perked up. "But Jocelyn, you have a medical bag and some training. Why can't you analyze them?"

"Cordelia was at the front. She has more training and far more practical experience."

Augustus slumped and turned to Faisal. "Go get her, will you?"

"Me? I can't speak to her."

"Well that's a damned inconvenience. I'll need to teach you more English." Augustus sighed. "Look, just go up to her and say, 'Sir Augustus wants to see you.' And try not to get hit by Aunt Pearl's parasol again."

"All right," Faisal moped as he trudged away.

Jocelyn chuckled. "I don't think he likes Cordelia much."

"The boy has some taste at least."

He turned back to Jocelyn, realizing that for the first time since they had boarded, he had her all to himself. For a moment he said nothing, simply staring into those kind eyes as she smiled back at him. He was about to tell her how happy he was that she had come along, that this trip would have been a lot less fun without her, but then he realized he didn't have to say any of these things. She understood.

So all Augustus did was to sidle a little closer and stand with her looking out over the glittering Nile and the Egyptian countryside with its lush fields and waving palms as the steamboat slowly chugged its way up the river.

He took a deep breath of air, made cool and moist by the water, so unlike the dust and smells of Cairo, or the biting aridity of the desert. Soothing, as was Jocelyn's company. And beneath that the crackle of excitement from being on another case and moving into the unknown. Augustus knew that Jocelyn felt the same, and that made her presence all the more enticing.

Then Faisal returned with Cordelia and Aunt Pearl, spoiling the moment.

"Not playing footie with your little mates again, are you?" Aunt Pearl said, her voice louder than necessary thanks to the gin Augustus could smell on her breath.

"Come now, Aunt Pearl," Cordelia chided. "He was in a hypnotic state. It was a most remarkable experience. You should try it."

"I am perfectly happy with my mental state, dear girl," the older woman said, sitting down in one of the wicker chairs with a grunt. She closed her eyes and within a moment appeared to have fallen asleep.

Cordelia turned to Augustus. "Your servant boy says you wanted to see me. At least that's what I think he was trying to say." At this she put a hand on Faisal's shoulder, who frowned and pulled away.

"Indeed. He broke into Alaeddin Bey's cabin and found this." Augustus showed her the packet of powder.

Cordelia looked confused. "Broke in?"

"It's one of his many talents. Picking pockets is another, so mind your things."

"Oh, I suppose he had to when he was living on the street. Now that he's living with you he needn't do that anymore."

Augustus grew impatient. "Could you just examine this, please?"

Cordelia studied the powder, sniffing it and wetting the tip of her finger, touching it, and bringing her finger to her tongue. Then she spat over the railing, apologizing to everyone and checking to make sure Aunt Pearl didn't notice such an unwomanly act. She needn't have worried. The older woman had started to snore.

Faisal tugged at his sleeve.

"How long is this going to take? It's almost dinner time."

"Never rush someone when they're doing an important job," he told the boy. "It's something I learned in the war."

"I had to rush when I did my job," Faisal grumbled.

Jocelyn pulled out some string from her pocket. "Come sit over here with me, Faisal. I'll show you a trick."

Cordelia visibly relaxed when Jocelyn moved away. She studied the powder for a while longer as Jocelyn showed Faisal how to play Cat's Cradle. Finally, Cordelia put the substance in her pocket.

"The powder is a soporific. I can't tell from a superficial examination just what's in it, but it appears to be one of the more common sleeping medications that you can find at any chemist's. If you are given a small dose it can make you weak-willed and easily fooled. It has a bit of a flavor, so if he wanted to drug someone he would have to add it to something with a strong flavor, port wine or a seasoned dish, for example."

"He does stage magic too, so I'm sure he's quite good at sleight of hand. Oh, and your brother says he's a pickpocket. Take care when you're around him."

Cordelia glanced at Faisal. "So we have two pickpockets on board. I wonder who is the better one?"

"That would be an interesting competition to witness. What else can you tell us about that powder?"

"I'm not so sure. I brought along my medicine bag, so how about I go back to my cabin and run some tests?"

"You have a medicine bag?"

"Of course. An old habit from my days in service. I go everywhere with it. I certainly would be remiss to not bring it when going on an adventure with you. From what my brother says you're always getting into trouble, and I don't think that is going to change in the presence of a lady."

The way she stressed the word "lady" made Augustus suspect she was throwing a barb at Jocelyn. Augustus's mood darkened.

"I think making that examination is an excellent idea. Thank you for your help. Jocelyn and I will remain here to discuss strategy."

The dismissive tone was not lost on Cordelia. She shot Jocelyn an acid look, which Jocelyn did not acknowledge at all, and stormed off.

"Mind your step with her," Jocelyn murmured in English as Faisal pulled on the string to make a different pattern, giggling with delight. "Hell hath no fury like a woman scorned."

"These are neat tricks, Jocelyn," Faisal said. "Do you know more?"

"Sure. Let me show you one called the Cup and Saucer."

"Cordelia is going to be a few minutes," Augustus declared. "I'm going to check on Heinrich. If I miss her, relay to me what she says."

"I'm sure she'd prefer speaking to you directly," Jocelyn replied. "Now move that string there, Faisal."

"Wow! It really looks like a cup and saucer. Hey Englishman, why didn't you ever show me these English tricks?"

"Must have slipped my mind," Augustus said.

Jocelyn switched to English. "You should really pay more attention to him, you know."

"Good Lord, no. He'll stick to me like a barnacle."

"Would that be so tragic? It wouldn't hurt you to have a bit more human contact. From what I've seen you have quite a few friends, Augustus, or at least people who could be friends if you let them. You should appreciate that more than you do."

Augustus cleared his throat. "I hardly think a thieving street boy is worthy friend material."

"Yes, friend might not be the right word in his case. Nor is it in mine," she treated him to a smile that warmed his heart. "But you have Heinrich, and those antiquities forgers you told me about, and the chief of police—"

"Sir Thomas? He's an ass."

"An ass you have breakfast with on a regular basis."

"So I can find cases."

"So you say." She switched back to Arabic to address Faisal. "Here, I'll show you another trick."

"I admit that he can be a source of good information at times," Augustus said.

"And you like to show him up at every opportunity, and yet you never reveal to him that you are showing him up. That's because you care about his feelings."

"Hardly!"

"He is your friend, Augustus. Even this little street boy has noticed that you claim to want to shut yourself away from the world and yet surround yourself with people."

"There doesn't seem to be much place on this planet where one can get away from them," Augustus grumbled. "In any case, I'm off to see Heinrich."

He left as Jocelyn showed Faisal another string trick.

CHAPTER SEVENTEEN

Moustafa waited, tense and alert, in a grimy little cafe across the street from the bar the tobacconist had told him about. Sitting at a rickety little table smoking a sheesha in order to have an excuse to remain for as long as he wanted, Moustafa scrutinized everything going on in the street.

The cafe was a run-down place, a single dreary stone room with a few tables and chairs. An oil lamp, its shade studded with dead flies, cast a feeble glow over two old men playing a desultory game of backgammon. Most of the customers sat outside, enjoying the cool of the night and seemingly impervious to the stink of the filthy street. A sullen man with a scar across his face served them bad tobacco and even worse tea.

At least there was no sin involved. That was more than could be said of the business across the street. Beyond the discarded refuse and animal droppings stood a low building with shuttered windows. From the ground floor came the sound of raucous laughter and clinking glasses. The door stood open, and every minute or two some wastrel stumbled out, only to be replaced by a new customer. In the two upper stories he could see light in only a few windows, shining feebly through the narrow slats of the shutters.

Moustafa stifled his irritation. Why did he always end up in such low dens of degradation? He thought he had gotten away from all that.

The tobacconist had told him of this bar. It was the meeting ground for a large criminal enterprise called the Invisible Scorpions. They had branches in a dozen cities and a hundred villages, running operations in extortion, smuggling, blackmail, theft and, if they were opposed, murder.

If the tobacconist was to be believed, it was the biggest criminal gang in the country. Moustafa wasn't sure how much of this was true. The tobacconist certainly believed it. The man was utterly terrified. But Moustafa knew criminals had a habit of exaggerating their prowess in order to intimidate others.

Whatever the truth of the matter, the Invisible Scorpions were organized and dangerous. The tobacconist had admitted that when the tobacco shop in Shepheard's Hotel had shut, the gang had seen an opportunity and made the poor fellow a proposal. He would act as a spy and a procurer, hinting to European customers that he could show them the pleasures of the East. Many foreign men, like Mr. Beechcroft and Mr. Lowell, came to Egypt looking for exotic adventure of the uncouth kind, and there was good money to be made in providing them with such things.

There was even better money to be made mugging or blackmailing them.

That was their main objective. They lured foreign or rich Egyptian men into houses of prostitution, then took their valuables. The men could not report the thefts to the police without a scandal.

So it was with all sin. It always begets trouble. Nothing ever remains truly hidden.

But they had not robbed Mr. Beechcroft. Moustafa considered this. The thieves must have recognized him from the society pages and seen a gold mine. They had followed him onto the boat, and that Alaeddin Bey had gotten into his confidence and robbed him. He would have surely been blackmailed if the war hadn't intervened.

The tobacconist claimed no knowledge of that case, and in that he was probably telling the truth. He had not been a part of the operation at that time. All he knew about Detective Lowell, or so he said, was that the Invisible Scorpions had told him to be on the watch for him and to try and lure him into the bordello. Then that foolish American had blundered into the trap by asking about it himself.

The assassin, the tobacconist assured him, would have left Cairo for a while. They always did after a murder in order to avoid trouble.

Moustafa felt it was more likely that he had gotten on the steamboat *Arabia*, or was following the boat south by train to intercept it somewhere in Upper Egypt.

And so here he sat, watching over a den of iniquity when he should be home with his family. "At least you're not in danger," Nur had said when he had told her he would work late again tonight. He had not told her what he was working on, and that half-lie shamed him.

Yes, he was in danger. Anyone could see this neighborhood was full of it.

He didn't even have a gun on him. He had left the tobacconist's gun at the shop so that man could protect himself if the gang decided to enact vengeance upon him. All the guns Moustafa was accustomed to using were in that madman's personal arsenal in a house he no longer had a key for.

I'm in more danger not working for him than I was when I did.

That gloomy thought didn't have time to run its course, for coming out of the bar with a small group of people, who did he see but a man he recognized as one of the waiters at Shepheard's Hotel.

Moustafa felt a coldness in the pit of his stomach. He'd wager a month's pay that this had been the man serving table when Detective Lowell, Sir Thomas Russell Pasha, and Mr. Wall had sat discussing the case. All three would have been intelligent enough not to speak in front of a member of staff, but their mere presence together damned them …

… and killed Detective Lowell.

Moustafa got up and paid, then headed down the street, trying not to look like he was in a hurry to catch up to the waiter and his friends.

There were five of them, all drunk and boisterous as they walked down the street arm in arm singing loud enough for their off-key voices to echo off the decrepit buildings. Moustafa wasn't sure how to handle this. He could not take on five men, even five drunk men. Strong men made the common mistake of thinking they could always beat smaller ones. A small man with sufficient training can easily win, like that French fellow who had fought so hard in a previous case. And a group of men could always take down even the biggest man if they were bold enough.

He had to find another way.

So he followed them for several blocks, keeping well back. They continued their singing and jokes, oblivious to his presence.

They came to a main street and two of the group said their slurred goodbyes sheared off, leaving the waiter and two others stumbling along. That evened up the odds a bit. Moustafa kept following.

With surprise, he could overcome the man's two friends and then threaten the waiter to make him talk. He needed a quiet spot, though, so no one cried out for the neighborhood watchman, and this street was too busy.

Moustafa bit his lip as the trio got onto an even busier street, one with a tramline. They followed it, obviously heading for a stop.

He paced them until they got to the next stop, and stood at the stop with them as if waiting for the tram as well.

No one else was at the stop. One of the drunks glanced his direction, but then the waiter started telling a crude joke and he turned back to listen.

Moustafa stood a little apart, looking across the street as if lost in his own thoughts.

The tram came and Moustafa moved as if to board, but at the last moment he checked himself. The waiter and one friend didn't move as the third man got on board.

"I'll see you at work tomorrow," the waiter said, waving.

"Assuming I wake up in time," said the man boarding the tram. All three laughed.

The doors shut and the tram clattered away.

The waiter and his remaining friend turned to Moustafa with a puzzled expression.

"Not getting on, brother?"

Moustafa glanced to the left and right. Plenty of people on the street, but no one too close. It was now or never.

He turned back to the drunks.

"Are you Muslims?"

The men laughed. "Well, we sure aren't Jews!"

Moustafa slugged the waiter's friend, who went down like a sack of oats.

He grabbed the waiter by the collar and hauled him to the nearest side street.

"It would be better for you if you were a Jew," Moustafa said, giving him a gut punch when he tried to resist. "God allows the Jews to drink."

"Who are you? Some sort of fundamentalist?" the waiter groaned.

"No, I'm the man you nearly got killed the other night."

There was a shout behind them. Moustafa hauled his captive along to the side street and out of sight of anyone close by. There wasn't much time. He threw the man against the nearest wall with a thud.

"Talk."

The waiter put on an innocent face. "About what?"

Moustafa slapped that false look of innocence right off his face.

"If this is about the cocaine, I told you I delivered it. There must be a problem on the other end."

Moustafa blinked. "Cocaine? No, I'm talking about the conversation you overheard between Sir Thomas Russell Pasha and the American detective, Mr. Lowell." Moustafa decided to leave his old boss out of it. Glancing around to make sure no one was coming for them, he added in a lower voice, "I'm talking about the Invisible Scorpions."

Even in the half light, Moustafa could see the man go pale.

"N-no. Don't make me talk about them!"

Moustafa glanced around again. A couple of people had moved to the entrance of the street and stood staring. He put his arm around the waiter.

"Pretend we're friends and walk with me. If you resist, I'll pop your head off like a cork, and blood will shoot out of your neck quicker than champagne."

Best to put it in terms this degenerate could understand.

Moustafa led him at a quick pace down the side street, away from the tram stop where his unconscious friend no doubt still lay. The two people at the entrance to the street watched them go, looking confused, but Moustafa did not hear anyone raise the alarm. Luckily this was a shopping district, with all the shops closed for the night. If they had been open for business, or if this had been a residential district, people would be more likely to get involved. As it was, many of those in view were probably on their own unsavory business.

The waiter stumbled. Moustafa kept a tight grip on his shoulder. The man's boozy breath wafted in Moustafa's face, making him curl his lip in disgust.

"What's the matter with you, don't you have any pride?" Moustafa grumbled.

They got to a quiet spot and stopped again. Moustafa glared at him, his hands balled into fists.

"Now tell me everything you know."

"They'll kill me if I do."

"I'll kill you if you don't."

The waiter's eyes narrowed, judging his chances. "No you won't. You're too high and mighty, with your lecture about Muslims not drinking. You're not the type to kill in cold blood. But they are. Oh, but they are."

Moustafa paused. The man had seen right through him. He could thump him a few good ones, but that wouldn't make him talk. Fear of the Invisible Scorpions would ensure his silence. This gang must be ruthless to have inspired such fear.

"You're right," Moustafa said at last, eliciting a drunken bark of a laugh from his captive. "I'm better than that. But I won't let you stay in your current position. I know Sir Thomas Russell Pasha, and I will tell him you are involved with the gang as their eyes and ears in Shepheard's Hotel. He will haul you off to the Citadel and you will lose your job. Oh, you might be able to resist British torture, but that would be a mistake. Because eventually they would let you go, and the Invisible Scorpions will be waiting for you. You will not be able to convince them you hadn't talked. They would kill you slowly trying to get a confession out of you, and you would have none to give. You know better than me how much they would make you suffer."

The man slumped.

"But what can I do?" he asked in a small voice.

"Tell me everything, and then get out of town. Run. You're a young man. Are you married? Do you have children?"

"No."

"Then it will be easier."

"But my brothers, my cousins! I can't leave them behind."

"If you disappear without telling them, they will be safe. The gang will think you were killed, or ran off for some other reason."

The waiter shook his head. "You don't know what they're like."

"This is your only other option. If you resist, I will haul you before the police. If you talk, I will let you go. Yes, your family might be in a little danger, but there is a man and boy in danger right now and I will not stand idly by while they get killed by your associates. Tell me everything, and make it the truth. If I find out you have lied, I will tell Sir Thomas Russell Pasha the reason for your disappearance. Then you will be hunted by the police as well as the Invisible Scorpions."

"You are ruining my life, Nubian!" he wailed.

"As you have ruined so many others. This is justice, and you have nobody to blame except for yourself. Talk."

The waiter hesitated. Moustafa felt tempted to give him a good swift punch to the stomach to loosen his tongue. He held back, though. This man was making the decision of his life.

After a moment, he made the right choice, at least for Mr. Wall and Faisal.

"They are a large gang of Egyptians, Nubians, and a few foreigners. I don't know who runs it, only that she is Egyptian."

"She?"

"Yes. She goes by the name of Sekhmet."

Moustafa felt a little chill. Sekhmet was one of the foulest of the ancient Egyptian goddesses—the bringer of plagues, the hot breath of the desert, the warlike conqueror. The ancients portrayed her with a lion's head, an appropriate metaphor for her fierceness and ravenous appetite for blood.

And for an Egyptian woman to take on the name of a pagan deity … she must be truly evil.

"Tell me more. If they're so big and powerful why haven't I heard of them before?"

A man strolled into view. Moustafa and the waiter fell silent and waited for him to pass. Once he was gone, Moustafa nudged his captive.

"Speak."

"They work in secret, with branches all over the country. They have spies in the other gangs, people in positions of influence who bend the gangs to their will. Many criminal organizations work for them without even knowing it."

"What do they do?"

He had asked the tobacconist that same question, but wanted to hear it from another and compare the answers. This waiter appeared to have closer ties to the organization than the tobacconist.

"Blackmail, extortion, theft. Their power runs along the Nile, and they are great rivals to the Bedouin tribes who control the smuggling and drugs trade coming through the desert. Sometimes they work with them, but they hate them too because they can't control them."

"What about the foreign gangs, like the Lebanese drug traders or the Greek smugglers? Or the French Apache?"

"The same thing. They work with them or fight them. Those foreign gangs have contacts and influence outside the country, but inside Egypt, and parts of Nubia too, the Invisible Scorpions rule. And they are far cleverer than the foreigners. The Bedouin and the Lebanese and the Greeks sometimes get arrested, and the Apache gang got wiped out by the police not so long ago."

Moustafa couldn't help but smile. He had had a hand in that.

"The police will break this gang like they broke the Apaches."

The waiter shook his head slowly. He seemed to have sobered up. "How can the police break up a gang they don't even suspect exists?"

"I will tell them."

"You will not live that long, Nubian. You are a fool to try to take them on."

Moustafa ignored that. He had been in danger before. "What goes on in that bar I saw you come out of?"

The waiter hesitated, then saw the warning look on Moustafa's face. "It's a meeting place for the servants of the Invisible Scorpions. I am not in the gang. I have only met gang members a few times. They got in touch two years ago because I work in the hotel. They offered me death or money. I chose money. I cannot get in touch with them, so don't ask me to. They only talk to their servants when they choose to. You go there, and if they want to give you a message they do so."

"So your four friends are servants of the Invisible Scorpions as well?"

"No, only me. We are allowed to bring the unsuspecting as an extra guise against police and rival gangs."

Moustafa wasn't sure he believed that, but it didn't really matter.

"I hear the Invisible Scorpions especially target foreigners."

"Anyone who has money. They have members or servants in all the places where money flows."

"Like the Thomas Cook steamboats?"

"I suppose. I am only a servant. I am told what to do and obey. They do not tell me of their operations. I only know what I know through rumors."

"So tell me exactly what happened on the day your eavesdropped on Detective Lowell and Sir Thomas Russell Pasha."

The waiter sighed. "I work the lunch and dinner shift, and I was surprised to see the police chief come in for lunch on a Sunday. He rarely does that. I decided there must be something special about this American visitor, and a strange Englishman with a mask who was with them. I hadn't seen the Englishman before, although I had heard he has ... is seen regularly with Sir Thomas Russell Pasha."

"You must have an agent on the breakfast shift since that's when they go to Shepheard's."

The waiter tensed and looked at his feet. "I don't know who that is."

Liar. "Go on."

"So I listened in as much as I could. They were very guarded when I approached, so I didn't hear much. But I could piece it together. The American detective had come to investigate some crime that had happened to another American. I didn't hear who. The concierge had mentioned Detective Lowell was boarding the *Arabia*. That was a boat I was told to keep a note of."

"Because you have an agent on board."

"I'm sure they do. I'm not told who that is."

"Alaeddin Bey, the mesmerist."

The waiter's brow furrowed. "Alaeddin Bey? He's not one of the Invisible Scorpions, or one of their servants. Of that I am sure."

Moustafa had not expected that. "Why?"

"Because he was ejected from the hotel. He had been dining there for some time, befriending the guests and even renting one of the meeting halls to do his shows. But a lot of the people who attended those shows lost their valuables. The hotel management suspected him of picking their pockets either during the show when he was in the habit of passing through the crowd, or afterwards when he would often sit in the lounge speaking with select people. The management couldn't prove it, though, so they trumped up a charge. They had a private detective pose as a guest and plant his wallet on Alaeddin Bey's person. He was then caught and ejected from the hotel."

"Why didn't Shepheard's Hotel go to the police?"

"Alaeddin Bey might have won in court if it was revealed his so-called victim was a plant. Besides, the hotel didn't want any scandal. If it were known that a pickpocket had been working there for nearly a year, the guests would go elsewhere."

"It's always about money," Moustafa grumbled. "So you're saying that if Alaeddin Bey was tied with the Invisible Scorpions he wouldn't have been kicked out?"

"As far as I know the management has no ties to the gang. The Invisible Scorpions work more subtly than that. But the staff was all warned well before the sting to keep an eye on Alaeddin Bey. I told my contact with the Invisible Scorpions about this development but he never told me to warn the mesmerist."

Moustafa thought for a moment. So Alaeddin Bey was not part of the gang? Then how did he fit in? Why would the Invisible Scorpions kill someone who was investigating a criminal with no ties to them, one who could even be seen as a rival?

Maybe because they wanted to keep the mesmerist alive so they could use him somehow. Maybe they had learned of the Beechcroft papers and wanted those.

He had no way of knowing for sure. He only knew he had to get down there.

Mr. Wall and Faisal were investigating the wrong man, and that left them open to the true danger.

CHAPTER EIGHTEEN

Faisal did not like how this trip was turning out at all. Not only had Rashid found out all about him, but now he had to worry about Abdelkarim breaking into his cabin and Cordelia taking away the Englishman.

That last part was the worst. While he had dealt with bullying boys and sneaky thieves all his life, he had no idea how to deal with a woman trying to take away his friend. And it was obvious she wanted to. You just had to see the way she looked at him.

He hoped that spell he had cast was still working. It seemed to be. The Englishman still avoided her as much as possible. But women had spells of their own, lots of them. He'd heard men talking about that. What if Cordelia cast a spell that was stronger than Khadija umm Mohammed's?

And now he had to go sneaking about the ship at night.

He had already spent some time in his cabin, checking to make sure nothing had been moved. If Abdelkarim had been snooping around in here, he sure had been careful. Then he had idled around deck as the sun set and the sky darkened, looking through the windows of the brightly lit dining room as all the foreigners sat eating nice food and drinking that wine they liked so much. Faisal didn't like the wine being there, so he ignored it and focused on all that wonderful food.

They were eating a big roast that he had heard was called a "turkey." The waiters served it with soup, bread, and lots of vegetables. It sure looked yummy. He studied how the foreigners ate it, so he could imitate them with his own knife and fork back home. He was still a bit clumsy with those, but they were really nice. Real silver and everything. He had swiped them the last time someone got murdered.

Oh, so that's how to cut into meat right! And they only bring a little bit to their mouth at a time, instead of tearing off a long strip with their fork and gnawing at both ends. His way was better because you could eat faster, but if he wanted to sit at a nice table with a white tablecloth and lots of food and silverware, he had to learn to eat right. That foreign boy with the blonde hair sat with all the adults just like one of them. They were even talking with him. Look, now he's laughing! That man in the uniform sitting next to him must have said something funny.

It would be nice to sit there like that, to eat good food and have adults tell you funny things.

And look how they eat their soup! They don't bring the bowl to their mouth and slurp it down. They take a spoon and—

A smack on the back of his head took him out of his thoughts. His forehead thumped against the glass, making some of the diners look up.

"Stop staring at the passengers," one of the waiters said. He was just bringing another bottle of wine from below. "Look, you left a nose print on the glass."

"That was from my forehead, and that was your fault," Faisal said, rubbing his forehead. Then he rubbed the back of his head because that hurt too.

"Get lost. Go shine your master's boots or something."

The waiter went inside. Faisal stuck his tongue out at him and left.

But he didn't go far, because he had to keep an eye on the magician. He went to the upper deck just about where Rashid had been spying on him. He found a place behind a lifeboat that hung on a pair of ropes. The lifeboat blocked the lights from the ship, casting a shadow that he could tuck into. Faisal waited.

After a while he heard the chatter and footsteps of the foreigners leaving the dining room. He peeked over the railing and saw several of them on the deck below. Some, he knew, would come up the stairs to the upper deck where he was. That didn't matter as long as they didn't bother him. Some went to the reading room in the front or the bar, while others returned to their cabins.

He spotted the magician chatting with Cordelia. Faisal frowned. The Englishman said she was acting nice to the magician to gain his confidence. Faisal wasn't sure that was true. What if Cordelia wanted to get Alaeddin Bey to cast a spell on the Englishman?

He'd have to watch her.

But right now he needed to keep his eye on Alaeddin Bey.

The magician said goodbye to Cordelia and walked along the deck to his cabin, but didn't enter. He stopped outside his door and pretended to look out over the dark water.

Pretended, because it was obvious that he was waiting. You can tell when someone isn't really doing what they're doing but waiting for something, because they stand a different way. Like Alaeddin Bey. He was making a show of looking out over the water, smiling and turning his head this way and that as if he had never seen the moon and stars hanging over palm trees before. And turning his head this way and that gave him a chance to keep an eye on everyone nearby.

The lower deck began to clear as the passengers all got to where they were going. A few had come up to the upper deck, including some who stood looking at the view, actually really looking at the view.

Then Faisal saw what Alaeddin Bey had been waiting for. Abdelkarim came along the lower deck carrying a tea service on a brass tray. Faisal stepped a bit back to make himself less visible. Abdelkarim stopped and spoke to Alaeddin Bey in a low voice for a moment, then rounded the back of the ship and stopped again. The magician followed, glancing over his shoulder to make sure no one was following, then making a few quick steps across the back of the boat to check to make sure no one was approaching from the other side. Faisal ducked out of sight and counted to three. The magician was a clever one, and wouldn't forget to glance up at the upper deck to make sure no one was up there either.

He was also in a hurry, so Faisal didn't have to stay out of sight for long.

When he peeked again, Alaeddin Bey had his back to him and was pouring some of the powder from that paper packet into the teapot. Faisal ducked out of sight again. He heard them speak a few words, far too quietly for him to make out, and then he heard one go each direction.

Faisal had a suspicion he knew where the crooked waiter was going. He was going to the opposite side of the ship, the side where that American woman with the orphanage had her cabin. The same cabin where he had spotted the magician trying to pick the lock.

Sure enough, when Faisal dared another peek, he saw Abdelkarim stop in front of Ms. Trasher's cabin door, balancing the tray with one hand and knocking on the other.

"Yes?" came a soft voice in English.

"Tea, madam."

The door opened and he recognized the American woman's voice. Knowing that Abdelkarim was busy talking with her, Faisal moved right over them and peeked over the railing.

Abdelkarim said something to Ms. Trasher and she stepped aside to let him in. Then he came out, smiled and said thank you when the American woman gave him a tip.

What a viper! He made that smile look so heartfelt, and he had handed her some drugged tea. That was some really good acting. Faisal wished he was that good.

A demanding voice in English right behind him made him turn around.

One of the passengers, a fat fellow he recognized from earlier that day with a sunburnt face that made him look like a tomato, was saying something to him. Faisal tried to move away but the man stopped him, and demanded louder this time. The fellow raised up a shoe and made motions of shining it. Faisal shook his head and the man snapped something in English at him. Cringing at the noise, Faisal looked behind him and down.

And saw what he feared the most. Abdelkarim was looking right up at him, a suspicious scowl on his face.

The tourist put a hand on Faisal's shoulder and said something else, obviously angry that Faisal hadn't immediately bowed and scraped and started shining his shoes.

"Shine your own shoes, you stupid foreigner!" he shouted, tearing himself away and running around the front of the ship to get away from him, Abdelkarim, and the magician.

Once he got there, he looked around, not sure where to go next. Ships were too small. You couldn't get away from people properly here. Back in the city there were millions of places to hide, and if things got really bad you just went to another neighborhood. What could he do here? Jump into the water and swim to shore? Yeah, he could probably do that, but then he'd have to walk back to Cairo and that would take forever.

He came to the lower deck. Abdelkarim popped out of a door and looked right at him. His heart in his throat, Faisal turned and walked the other direction, pretending there was nothing wrong.

Just then Cordelia came out of the library right in front of him. What luck!

He smiled up at her, took her hand, and said, "Hello."

"Oh, hello Faisal!" she said, all smiles.

What a dummy. Didn't she realize he couldn't stand her? Well, it didn't matter, not at the moment. For the first time ever, he was actually glad to see her. Abdelkarim wouldn't dare touch him in front of a passenger.

They walked along the deck for a moment, Cordelia speaking to him loudly and slowly like he was going to understand. As if he would suddenly know the meaning to English words just because she was saying them loudly and slowly. At least Abdelkarim couldn't grab him. Was he still lurking behind them somewhere? He didn't want to risk a look. Better to act all innocent. Having a nice djellaba and pretending to be the Englishman's servant helped with that. He could never get away with acting innocent back home.

A low thudding and chanting drifted over the water. Faisal tugged on Cordelia's hand and pointed to the shore, which was lit up by a bonfire the fellahin had made. The farmers were dancing around it, chanting some country song as one of them banged on a drum with the palm of his hand. It was one of those flat, circular drums you hold in one hand. The farmer stood right in front of the fire, his body just a black shape, and the fire made the drum look like a dark sun.

Faisal shuddered. He'd heard that the sun went black sometimes. Some of the old people talked about how it had happened long before Faisal was born, and it had brought famine with it. He remembered how they told of thin people staggering through the streets, too weak to walk straight, and how the rural police came to villages sometimes to find everything quiet, all the peasants having died and nothing left but flies and wild dogs feeding on the corpses.

Faisal gripped Cordelia's hand tighter. She misunderstood, thinking he was excited, and started babbling and smiling and pointing at the dancing fellahin.

The steamboat drew closer. Faisal tried to tell himself that it was just a bunch of fellahin dancing, the most normal thing in the world, but their song sounded creepy. He couldn't understand the words. The country dialect and the way they chanted made it so he could only understand one word in five. And the song had words in it he was sure weren't Arabic.

It was magic. It had to be. They were casting spells. That's why they sang by the river and not in their village.

Faisal shuddered again when he saw what the fire was lighting up.

Just on the other side of the field stood one of the ancient temples. He hadn't noticed before because he had been staring at the dancing men. The firelight cast their shadows onto a high stone wall made of huge blocks and a tall open doorway leading to darkness. On either side of the doorway stood giant stone djinn, at least they were stone for the moment. They stood with their arms at their sides, one foot in front of the other. Faisal suspected at any moment they'd put the other foot forward and start walking for the boat. They were tall enough to wade right out here and pluck him off the deck.

With his free hand he clutched the charm around his neck, wondering if it was powerful enough to stop djinn that big. This was an English ship filled with foreigners. Would that give him protection too? He hoped so. At least those djinn hadn't moved yet.

Then he remembered why he had made Cordelia stop by the railing. He wanted to peek from the corner of his eye to see what Abdelkarim was doing.

So now he did, and found Abdelkarim already gone.

He'll be back soon enough, or his magician friend. They'll put some of that powder in my tea, or lay a curse on me. Who knows? Maybe they sent an ibis to tell the fellahin to cast a spell on me from the shore. Magicians do that, even in ancient times they did it. One of those pagan gods had an ibis head, and he was always carrying a pen. That proves it.

Faisal's eyes were drawn back to the shore. They were passing it now, but the farmer with the drum was still between Faisal and the fire, holding up his drum to make a black circle as he hopped from one foot to the other in time with the drumbeat.

Thump ... thump ... thump ...

Hadn't he been on the other side of the bonfire? Had he moved when Faisal had looked away? Did he do it on purpose just so Faisal could still see him? Or maybe this was a vision only Faisal could see. Cordelia didn't seem frightened at all. No, she seemed happy.

That's because magic doesn't work on foreigners. She probably doesn't even realize they're casting magic.

Thump ... thump ... thump ...

The drum's pounding came at him over the water, sounding louder and louder. The farmer raised his drum higher and waggled it, as if making fun of the boy watching.

Faisal shook all over and tugged on Cordelia's hand.

"Sir Augustus," he said, pulling her along.

She asked something, looking at him with concern. Faisal realized he was sweating.

"Sir Augustus," he said again, and picked up the pace.

When the Englishman opened his cabin door he blinked with surprise to see Faisal and Cordelia on the other side, holding hands.

"Get rid of her," Faisal said.

"Gladly. I didn't want you to bring her here in the first place."

The Englishman and Cordelia spoke in English for a moment. Cordelia moved to leave, but Faisal was still clutching her hand. He let go and she bent down to tousle his hair and kiss him on the forehead.

Eeew. At least she was leaving now.

Faisal entered the cabin and slammed the door shut just before he burst into tears.

"What happened?" the Englishman asked.

"Rashid saw me and warned me they'd try to kill me and then the magician put powder in the woman's tea and Abdelkarim gave it to her and saw me and then the black sun saw me too and winked at me and the giant djinn are going to wade out here and grab me. They're going to kill me for sure!"

"Wait. What? You're not making any sense."

Faisal didn't make any sense for a long time. The Englishman sat him down and knelt beside him and talked to him in a soothing voice. Finally, he got the story from him.

"I'm sorry," Faisal said between sniffles. "I did everything wrong."

"No, you didn't. You've done very well. Cordelia tells me that powder puts people to sleep. They're obviously drugging Ms. Trasher so they can break into her cabin and rob her. I recall Ms. Trasher saying she likes her tea very sweet. She said that was her sole indulgence. That will hide the taste of the drug. Being a waiter, Abdelkarim will have noticed that. I bet they're after that money she raised in Cairo. You figured that out yourself."

"Oh, that's right," Faisal said as he wiped his eyes. "I did."

"Because you're a very clever boy."

Faisal managed a smile. "Now what do we do?"

"We'll have to stop them. If we catch them red-handed, we can have them arrested. But we have to do this carefully. Now Abdelkarim and this Rashid boy both saw you. That's bad, but they have no reason to suspect I'm investigating them. They probably just think you're a nosey boy looking to swipe something."

"Hey!"

"I'm not saying you're really a nosey boy who likes to swipe things." Faisal gave him a dubious look. The Englishman ignored it and went on. "But if they think that they'll be less suspicious of me. That gives us room to work with. I'll keep an eye on Ms. Trasher's cabin. I'll have Jocelyn check on her too. She could make an excuse for a social call."

"Jocelyn can't go into her cabin. Jocelyn's a man. Even foreigners don't do that."

"Um, right. I'm sure she—I mean he—will figure out something."

"Can I stay here tonight?" Faisal asked. When he saw the Englishman's reaction he added hurriedly, "Rashid said Abdelkarim has a key to the crew cabins and he'll come in and kill me for sure."

"Then I suppose you'll have to," the Englishman sighed.

"I'll be very quiet. I won't snore like Moustafa does. I'll sleep on the floor."

"All right. Better get your blankets and things from your own cabin."

"I don't want to go down there! The second I set foot below decks, Abdelkarim will slit my throat!"

"Oh, very well. I'll give you my blankets and I'll sleep in my overcoat. I certainly had to do that enough in the war."

Faisal looked around. "We'll have to block the door with these chairs. See how the door opens inward? If we put the chairs there, with a few things balanced on top, then they can't open it without making a lot of noise. We'll put the washbasin on top. That will make a big crash and wake us up."

"Clever, but we're not going to sleep yet."

"No?"

"No. We have a thief to catch."

CHAPTER NINETEEN

The boat was quiet. Nothing moved on the water and the only lights shone fore and aft to signal the boat's position, plus a few soft lights in the dining room and lounge, now both empty. At dinner the captain had explained that the next stretch of river had a few half-submerged sandbars that made navigation hazardous during the hours of darkness, so shortly after sunset, the *Arabia* had moored for the night. They had not docked at either of the two towns they had passed.

The captain had not needed to explain why. It was safer to moor in the open river.

Not so safe that the captain hadn't set a crewman on the roof of the upper deck to watch for approaching boats. Luckily, Ms. Trasher's cabin was two-thirds of the way to the back. In the dim light, and with the watchman looking out over the water and not back at the steamboat, if they took care and kept quiet, they should be all right.

Augustus sat completely still on the upper deck just above Ms. Trasher's cabin. Jocelyn stood further along on the upper deck, right next to the stairs. Faisal lay hidden in a lifeboat close to the watchman. Augustus had given the boy his lighter to signal if the watchman made a move toward the center of the deck. Faisal was under the tarpaulin that covered the lifeboat. Augustus had instructed him to lift up the canvas at the front and back of the lifeboat so he could watch the sentry and use the lighter as a signal if need be. The way the lifeboat was situated would keep the watchman from seeing the light if the boy shone it out the back.

Faisal had been delighted when Augustus showed him how to use it.

"You just flick this little thing and fire comes out! Can I keep it?"

"No. It's not a toy. Only use it if you need to signal."

Faisal kept flicking it on and off. "I'll be careful. But after we catch Abdelkarim, can't I keep it? I'm sure I'll have to signal you again sometime."

"No. It was very expensive."

"Please?"

"No."

"Pleasepleaseplease?"

"No! Now behave."

"I'll give you a piastre for it."

"It's worth considerably more than that."

"OK. Five piastres."

"Just sneak into the lifeboat and keep quiet!"

"But—"

"No."

Too bad Moustafa wasn't here. A good smack upside the head would have nipped that conversation in the bud.

So now they waited. And waited. It must have been midnight by now at least. He hoped Jocelyn and Faisal were keeping good vigil. They weren't accustomed to sentry duty like he was. Twice Faisal flicked his lighter to signal that the sentry was moving, and Augustus crept out of sight. He assumed Jocelyn did too, but he neither heard nor saw her. She had stalked game all across North Africa. It appeared that wonderful woman was now using those skills against thieves.

It felt like such a relief to be hiding here in the near-darkness waiting to spring the trap. The hypnotism show had shaken him badly. The memories had come on too strongly, grew too clear. He didn't like having his emotions manipulated so. He had never suspected he was so vulnerable to hypnotism. It was embarrassing and dangerous.

Lying in wait against an enemy? Now that was something he understood.

At last their patience was rewarded. Augustus spied a dark figure moving silently along the lower deck. It paused once, looking both fore and aft before continuing to Ms. Trasher's cabin door. If Abdelkarim had really spiked her tea with sleeping powder, the orphanage owner would be sound asleep by now. It would take quite a lot to rouse her, and this waiter moved like a professional.

To Augustus's surprise, a second figure appeared. It made some slight sounds as it moved, but approached silently enough. The two met in front of Ms. Trasher's door and, without speaking to one another, the second figure bent over the lock.

Augustus kept well back from the railing, only getting close enough to see the top of the thieves' heads. He wanted to wait until they were in the cabin with their hands on the money before he sprang. Caught red-handed, Alaeddin Bey would try to make a deal. He'd offer up the damning papers on Mr. Beechcroft and perhaps other victims. Sir Thomas would probably give him a light sentence and then banish him from Egypt. Everyone would be satisfied.

Especially Augustus, because he could spend the rest of his time floating down the Nile with Jocelyn as company. He could show her the wonders of Luxor and Karnak, and the tombs of the Valley of the Kings. He'd have her all to himself. No murderers, no pesky street boys (he'd fob the boy off with a pile of money and sweets), and no annoying customers.

Those delightful fantasies got cut off short as Augustus heard the soft click of the door unlocking.

Augustus withdrew a moment, fearful that the sound of the door unlocking would make Alaeddin Bey and Abdelkarim look around them.

Silence. Augustus peeked over the railing again. One figure had disappeared. The other moved toward the back of the ship.

Blast! He hadn't anticipated that. They didn't want to risk both men getting caught. Augustus couldn't risk making noise telling Jocelyn or Faisal to go after the one who had left, and he couldn't leave those two alone to face the burglar.

They'd only get to catch one.

One would have to be enough.

Augustus leaned over the railing and saw the cabin door was open a crack. The man had slipped inside and had all but closed the door behind him. No doubt he didn't close it entirely so as to avoid making any unnecessary noise and also to give him a quicker escape. A soft light appeared within. Augustus climbed onto the railing and signaled to Jocelyn. A slim figure detached from the shadows and moved down the steps with impressive silence.

Good. Whoever was inside the cabin would not hear her. She'd get to Ms. Trasher's door and then he'd …

A flickering light off to his right made him turn. Faisal was signaling with the lighter.

What a time for that sentry to move position!

Augustus swung off the railing, gritting his teeth as the heel of his shoe clanged against the metal, and withdrew back into the shadows.

If the sentry heard that, he gave no indication. His steady step thudded softly on the roof of the upper cabins as he moved down the length of the ship. He did not so much as pause at Augustus's position.

Surely the sentry must have heard him? Perhaps because he was focusing on the potential danger from the river, he did not care what sounds he heard from the ship itself. Or perhaps he had been paid not to.

The real question was—had the thief in Ms. Trasher's cabin heard him? No sound came from below.

The sentry's footsteps reached the far end of the ship and stopped. Good. If his previous pattern held true, he would remain there a good quarter of an hour.

Augustus stepped up to the railing again. A thud inside Ms. Trasher's cabin—as if from someone bumping into furniture—made him tense, but the sound was not repeated. He climbed on the railing, ready to pounce on the thief when he came out of the cabin.

A shadow moved along the lower deck. Augustus blinked in surprise when he recognized Jocelyn's trousered yet unmistakably feminine figure. She held up a warning hand to him.

What was she up to?

She walked along the deck, making no attempt at stealth, and came to the door.

"Ms. Trasher?" she called out in a soft voice.

What are you doing? You just warned the thief we're watching!

The cabin door creaked as she opened it.

"Ms. Trasher, are you all right?"

Jocelyn screamed and leapt back as the thief burst from the cabin. Augustus dropped from his perch on the railing and hit him with both feet, knocking him flat on the deck and out cold.

It was Abdelkarim.

The sound of movement from the adjoining cabin. A sleepy male voice called out, "What's going on?"

The question was repeated by Ms. Trasher, calling out in the dark in slurred, drugged syllables.

"Run," Jocelyn whispered. "It's best if they don't know you're involved."

Augustus jumped, grabbed the lower part of the deck above, and lifted himself up. He had just clambered over the railing when the cabin next to Ms. Trasher's opened.

"What happened?" Lieutenant Hemsworth's voice demanded.

Augustus did not stay to hear Jocelyn's answer. He could hear the thudding of the sentry's running feet. Augustus bolted in the other direction, grabbing Faisal as he appeared out of the shadows and yanking the boy along with him.

They rounded the upper deck as sounds of an increasing hubbub came from the other side of the ship. Augustus hustled Faisal to his cabin, unlocked and opened the door, and bundled the boy inside, easing the door shut and latching it as quietly as he could.

They stood there for a moment in the dark, breathing heavily. Even with the door shut they could hear the muffled sounds of shouting.

"Do you think anyone saw us?" Augustus asked in a whisper.

"I don't think so. Why did we abandon Jocelyn?"

"That was her idea."

"Her?"

"His. That was his idea. Since we could only catch Abdelkarim, she didn't want the rest of us involved. That way we can still move in on Alaeddin Bey."

"Clever. So Jocelyn will take credit for knocking him out."

"I suppose so." Augustus wondered how the passengers and crew would react to that.

Faisal giggled. "You landed on him just like that cowboy."

"What cowboy?"

"In the last moving picture we went to. Remember how the bandits were robbing the bank and the cowboy was on top of the bank and jumped off the roof and landed on them? Splat!"

"Oh yes, I had forgotten that."

"You can learn a lot from moving pictures."

"Indeed. They are the highest form of education."

They stood by the door for another minute. The shouts continued for a time before dying down.

"Now what?" Faisal whispered.

"Now you sneak back to the servants' quarters and go to bed."

"But you said I could stay here."

"With Abdelkarim nabbed, you don't have anything to worry about."

"What if he gave the key to Alaeddin Bey? Besides, your cabin is nicer."

"Oh, very well," Augustus grumbled. He opened the curtain a little to allow in some meagre illumination from the ship's lights. No one stirred on this side of the ship. Good. It appeared only Ms. Trasher's immediate neighbors had been awakened. He could claim ignorance of the entire affair.

"You sure Jocelyn will be all right?" Faisal asked, tearing the sheets off the bed and making a nest for himself on the floor.

"Abdelkarim was down for the count. If the sentry was planning any trouble, that would have been stopped by Lieutenant Hemsworth. He seems a game enough fellow. I heard stirrings in a couple of other cabins as well."

"Too bad we didn't catch the magician. You'll have to land on him tomorrow night."

"Or perhaps we'll catch him in a more circumspect way."

"Let's barricade the door like we planned."

"Very well."

They moved both chairs against the door and balanced the wash basin on top of one of the chairs, near the edge so if it got jarred the basin would fall on the floor.

Once they finished, Faisal lay down and Augustus moved to the small bathroom. His opium was in a small carrying case along with his straight razor, a jar of shaving soap, and a few other essentials. It was late, well beyond the hour when he usually had his nightly dose.

"Close the door if you're going to pee," Faisal told him as he nestled down on the floor.

"I, um, am just going to brush my teeth."

Augustus moved by feel. It was almost pitch black in the bathroom but he didn't want to turn on the light in case anyone saw it. He unclasped the carrying case and pulled out the little bottle of tincture of opium. Generally, he smoked it as that proved more efficacious, but he had bought tincture instead because he was stuck in close quarters on this ship.

"Shh," Faisal said, "I'm trying to sleep."

Too close quarters.

His entire body yearned for that opium, but he controlled himself and only took one drop. He needed to be able to awaken in case of trouble.

"What are you doing in there?"

"Go to bed."

"I'm already in bed."

"Then go to sleep."

"I'm trying to."

Where's Moustafa when I need him?

Augustus put away his opium, turned to leave, then remembered he was supposed to be in here brushing his teeth. He did so, then got into bed, covering himself with his overcoat as a blanket. The opium eased his muscles and gave a pleasant smoothness to his thoughts, removing the stress and negative associations that were the general background to his waking mind. It would keep his nightmares at bay too.

Worries of how to handle Alaeddin Bey fell aside. He would figure out a way to deal with him tomorrow.

Faisal giggled in the darkness. "Splat!"

***

Despite the partial success of the previous evening, Augustus did not awaken in a good mood. He had stayed up far into the night and that single drop of opium allowed him some rest and a respite from his nightmares, but not a good night's sleep.

At least he didn't wake up screaming from visions of the front. He had terrified the boy before with that, and it had been most embarrassing. So a semi-restful half-sleep was all he got.

Then Faisal had woken him early in the morning as he removed the barricade at their door.

"What are you doing?" Augustus had grumbled from beneath the overcoat he was using as a blanket. The blankets were scattered over the floor, no doubt now infested with lice.

"Getting breakfast. I missed dinner last night, you know."

"Oh, I didn't know."

"You could have asked," Faisal said, heading out the door. "Or at least kept some snacks in your cabin."

"There aren't any."

"I know. I checked."

Augustus grumbled, got up to lock the door behind him, grumbled again, got back in bed, and tried to sleep. The events of the previous night kept him from doing so.

What would Alaeddin Bey do next? And how best to catch him? If the fellow was smart, he'd play it calm and cool. He'd continue his chats with fellow passengers and perhaps even do another demonstration. But all the while, Augustus felt sure, he'd be trying to figure out who was onto him. He would not assume that Jocelyn had only happened upon the scene of the crime at such a late hour. Augustus knew, and no doubt the crafty mesmerist knew, that her cabin was en suite. There was no need for her to leave her quarters in the middle of the night.

Alaeddin Bey would also assume that being a woman, she hadn't been working alone. While Jocelyn was certainly capable of investigating the crime all by herself, most women—and indeed most men—were not.

And that would put Alaeddin Bey's suspicions squarely on himself, Faisal, and Heinrich.

He saw no way to avoid that.

Could he enlist the aid of some other member of the crew, perhaps? Too risky. Even the English captain, who had remained quite aloof during the entire trip, could be in on the game. What about one of the other passengers? Lieutenant Hemsworth was the only one Augustus would trust in anything more serious than a mild argument, but Australians tended to be bullheaded and overly direct. He'd more than likely give himself away.

Half an hour after Faisal left, the breakfast bell rang. So with insufficient sleep, and still no answers to his questions, he got up to eat.

He found the dining room already full. Ms. Trasher was speaking amicably to Jocelyn. Of course the entire breakfast room was abuzz with news of the previous night's attempted theft. He was assailed by half a dozen halfwits all wanting to be the first to tell him the juicy details. He feigned amazement and asked a waiter for a cup of coffee.

"Actually, make that a pot of coffee," he said. It was the Nubian one this morning. Faisal had told Augustus that he was probably all right. He hoped the boy was correct and he didn't get any soporific along with his coffee.

To his utter annoyance, he saw no spare space next to Jocelyn. Everyone had crowded around the two women in order to overhear their conversation. Even Cordelia was sitting right opposite. The mesmerist sat next to her, overly close, and acted as appalled as the rest of them. Jocelyn spotted Augustus and turned to the Englishman seated next to her, the same idiot who had asked his aid in buying antiquities.

"Would you mind terribly if I asked you to change seats?" she asked him. "I would like to sit next to Augustus."

In the space of two sentences, all Augustus's sleepiness and irritation vanished. Not only had she made room for him, but her dropping the 'sir' announced to everyone a level of familiarity that, while he knew he already enjoyed, he wanted to sing to the world.

Augustus sat gratefully, even remembering to thank the departing fool. Perhaps he'd help him get a real antiquity after all.

Ms. Trasher said good morning to him and added, "I was just thanking your friend once again for her heroic actions."

One of the other passengers laughed. "Raising the alarm was surely useful, but I'm waiting for the good lieutenant to admit that he knocked out that thieving native and not Ms. Montjoy."

Lieutenant Hemsworth grinned. "I've told you before. When I came out of my cabin, the waiter was already flat on the deck."

"So she's earned those trousers?" the passenger joked. Augustus resisted the urge to put him in a headlock and mash his face into his scrambled eggs.

"Plenty of the gals back home wear trousers. Can't do much sheep farming in a dress," the Australian drawled.

"We are not on a sheep farm, my good man," Ms. Trasher sniffed. "But despite the inappropriateness of her attire I am most grateful that she's a woman of action. She reminds me of some of the women I've met from out West," Ms. Trasher said.

"You mean in America?" Augustus asked. "I've only seen the West in moving picture shows."

Jocelyn arched an eyebrow. "I'm surprised you'd be interested in cowboy pictures."

"Um, I'm not really. Faisal likes them." He turned to Ms. Trasher to explain. "That's my, um, servant."

"Most moving pictures give a bad example to the young." The missionary sniffed.

"Oh. Are you from the West?" he asked, wanting to change the subject away from himself.

"No. I was born in Florida and grew up in Georgia."

"How did you come to live in Egypt running an orphanage?" Cordelia asked. "You're a long way from Florida and Georgia."

Ms. Trasher smiled. "I am indeed. It was the Lord's plan for me. I worked for a time in an orphanage in the United States and began to feel that might be my calling. But then I met a man, a quite Godly man. He proposed and I assented. I guessed that God wanted me to be a mother and homemaker like He wants most women to be. But shortly after his proposal I attended a speech by a missionary, a truly great man doing fine work in India. The Lord spoke to me, reminding me of my calling. Sadly, my fiancé did not share my enthusiasm and so I had to say farewell to him. I had heard of the great need in Africa, and so came here."

"Why did you pick Egypt?" Augustus asked.

Ms. Trasher laughed. Augustus was surprised to hear her laugh. He didn't think she did that much. "Because I don't speak French! I had to go to a British colony and Alexandria was the cheapest ticket I could find."

"I take it you didn't arrive with much in the way of funds?"

"No I did not. But the Lord provides."

"It's a good thing he provided some timely protection," Mrs. O'Leary said in her Irish brogue, obviously eager to get the conversation back on its previous subject.

Ms. Trasher ignored her. She had warmed to her subject. Augustus felt a sermon coming on but was nevertheless interested. Women who actually did something with their lives always interested him, even if they were prudish Americans. "I had met a pastor who works in Assiout, so that's where I went. I wasn't quite sure what exactly I'd do once I got there, but that was shown to me on the very first day. I had barely settled in to my new house when an Egyptian peasant came knocking. He said his neighbor was dying and that perhaps I could help. Well, I knew almost nothing about medicine back then but I promised to do what I could. So I went with my translator, Sela, who is still my right hand at the orphanage, and followed the man. He took me into a neighborhood of such filth and despair that it made me tremble to look upon it. It was a warren of little huts, the children all but naked, flies and animal droppings everywhere, and many of the adults broken down and ill, too weak to work."

"I've caught glimpses of such places in Cairo," Cordelia said, looking somber. "It made me feel that I had seen what Hell itself looks like."

Ms. Trasher shook her head gravely. "No. Hell is far worse. In Hell there is no hope. There is always hope in this world, no matter what your condition. The sick neighbor turned out to be a widow woman, living in a shack of reeds rife with vermin. Her only attendants were an aged mother and the woman's infant, a tiny starving girl that looked like nothing more than a bundle of sticks."

"Poor thing," Cordelia said.

Ms. Trasher shook her head. "There was no helping the woman. She was malnourished and had a terrible fever. We tried to make her as comfortable as possible but she died within the hour. I gave the grandmother some money for the burial and a decent meal and rose to leave. As I wondered aloud what would happen to the poor motherless infant, Sela said the old woman would most likely throw her granddaughter into the Nile. She had no means to care for her and a quick death would be more merciful."

"That's terrible!" Cordelia cried.

"Yet sadly common," Augustus said.

"It is the same in my country," Alaeddin Bey said.

And what country would that be? Augustus wondered.

"Indeed," Ms. Trasher said with a sigh. "I found that I couldn't leave this poor infant to her fate, and so I volunteered to take her. The grandmother assented quickly enough. The fellahin don't want to kill their children. It breaks their hearts, but they often have no choice. The girl is with me still at the orphanage. I named her Fareida and she's now a bright and happy nine-year-old who sings and plays and is quick on the loom. I have the children do weaving and other crafts to help support the orphanage, and to give them skills for when they are old enough to go out into the world."

"Augustus has taken in a waif as well," Cordelia said.

Ms. Trasher turned to him. "That little servant boy of yours?"

"Um, yes," Augustus said, shifting in his seat.

"He's been nothing but trouble this entire voyage," the missionary scolded. "You need to teach that boy some manners."

"That would qualify as one of the labors of Hercules."

"Nevertheless you must do it," Ms. Thrasher said, shaking a finger at him. "If he has been on the street for any length of time he has learned all manner of bad habits. I've known hundreds of these boys and girls. They spit, they steal, they speak the most degenerate filth. Those habits will only grow in him. You will find he starts stealing from you, and talking back. He will become willful."

"He's already willful."

"He will become more so."

This woman was beginning to irritate him. "Faisal is an individual and he is a certain way because that is how he needs to be to survive."

"That is true on the street, but he is no longer on the street. Now that he is in your care, in your house, you need to take him in hand. He may seem independent and streetwise, but he is still a child and he is now your responsibility."

Augustus realized that he could not argue with Ms. Trasher being, as he was, trapped in a lie. Everything the missionary said would be perfectly true if Faisal actually shared his home, and he couldn't reveal that that was not the case. More troublesome was having to reveal what kind of a boy Faisal was, and what he was capable of. He noted that while the rest of the table had returned to their own conversations, Alaeddin Bey was not speaking with anyone. His eyes were on his food, which he ate slowly, and Augustus had no doubt that he was taking in every detail of their conversation.

To his surprise, Cordelia came to his defense. "Oh, Faisal is much better than when I first met him a few months ago. He is clean and better dressed. He has even put on weight. He was so thin before. Augustus has worked wonders."

And there it was again, that admiring look. Even the presence of Jocelyn couldn't stop that look for long. Would this annoying girl never give up?

"I am glad to hear it," the missionary told her. "Since you are his friend perhaps you could help raise the boy."

Augustus's heart filled with horror until Cordelia answered, "Oh, Faisal doesn't like me. He frowns any time I enter the room."

Faisal has some sense at least.

"Work on him," Ms. Trasher said. "Show him some kindness to overcome the natural wariness he has developed on the streets. He could use a woman's care. No doubt he lost his mother, or she was a fallen woman. He needs a woman to look up to as a surrogate mother just as much as he needs a surrogate father."

Cordelia's face softened. "There was one time, just last night, where I think I broke through to him a little. We were on deck looking out at the shore. A crowd of fellahin were dancing around a bonfire, beating a drum and singing. Most picturesque, and yet something about it frightened the boy. He took my hand. That surprised me, because he never wants to come near me. He clutched it and made me bring him to Augustus."

Whatever is this woman talking about?

Cordelia turned to him. "He seemed very upset, and wouldn't let me go until I delivered him to your door."

Ms. Trasher raised her hand and smiled. "You see? The orphan seeks out adults to be parental figures. If he doesn't find good ones, he'll find bad ones."

Cordelia nodded. "Then we must do what we can to help him make the right choices."

The horror returned tenfold. Cordelia had found a new plan of attack. She would spoil Faisal in an attempt to earn the affection Augustus had been carefully denying her. Not only would that be highly annoying, but it would interfere with Faisal's work. How could he spy on Alaeddin Bey and the crew if he was being mothered?

He had to warn him.

Then some new trouble got heaped on the pile. Alaeddin Bey had finished his breakfast and turned to Cordelia.

"Shall we take a turn around the ship and enjoy the view?"

Cordelia smiled at him. "Most certainly, Alaeddin."

They rose and stepped out of the dining room. Through the window, Augustus could see the mesmerist offer her his arm, which she took, and they strolled out of view.

"How vulgar!" Mrs. O'Leary said. Ms. Trasher nodded.

Augustus supposed they were objecting because Alaeddin Bey was of another race—although it was still unclear which one—but that didn't bother Augustus in the least. What bothered him was that Cordelia's idea of investigating a murderer was to make puppy eyes at him. He recalled what Detective Lowell had said about the mesmerist's philandering.

If Alaeddin Bey meddled with Cordelia and Sir Thomas heard about it, the chief of police may very well blame him for not protecting her virtue.

CHAPTER TWENTY

Moustafa dreaded this conversation. He had delayed it for the entire work day, forcing his mind to focus on his job. But now the clock had struck five and he knew that within an hour Mr. Simaika would be heading home.

He excused himself from the cataloging room where he and Joseph had spent so many enjoyable hours, and walked the short distance down the hall to Mr. Simaika's office.

The door stood open as always unless his boss had an important meeting. Mr. Simaika sat at his desk writing a letter. Moustafa rapped lightly on the door. His boss looked up.

"Ah, Moustafa, come on in. Why the long face?"

A man who keeps his door open instead of hiding from the world. A man who notices my moods and actually cares about them. I am throwing away treasure.

Moustafa took a deep breath. "I am afraid I am going to have to hand in my notice, sir."

Mr. Simaika sat up. "What? Why?"

"I have … something to do. I need to go to Luxor. I will take the train tonight."

"Is a member of your family sick?" Realization dawned on the Coptic scholar's face. "No. This has something to do with Sir Augustus."

Moustafa sighed. "Yes, sir. I'm not going back to work for him. I love this job. It's just that he's … in trouble."

Mr. Simaika studied him for a moment. "I know a bit about Sir Augustus, and you. I did not hire you out of thin air, you know. I check on the backgrounds of all my prospective employees. Our work is too important not to. You and he do more than sell antiquities. I have heard you have links with the chief of police, and that you have helped him solve crimes. I have even heard rumors that you were in a gunfight."

"More than one gunfight, sir. Many more. Mr. Wall has a penchant for getting into danger. But we have stopped many foul criminals."

"And now you need to stop another."

Moustafa nodded. "A whole gang, sir. Mr. Wall doesn't know how much danger he is in. He's so overconfident that he could very well get himself killed. And he brought a boy with him, a thieving little street urchin who deserves a good thrashing every day of the week but certainly doesn't deserve to die."

"It sounds like they need your help. How long will this take?"

"I don't know. I cannot ask you to hold my job for me. From what I hear this is our worst adversary yet. I don't think we'll break up the entire gang just on this case. We might be fighting these thugs for a long time."

"So after you save them, you will continue to fight crime at the side of your old employer and this street urchin."

Moustafa looked at the floor. "They need me. They do not even respect me and yet I cannot fail them. Mr. Wall treats me like an underling. Faisal doesn't listen to me at all. But how can I abandon them to their fate? I did not ask for this sort of life. I don't want to hunt criminals and get into gunfights. I want to stay here and study. I want to learn Coptic and explore old monasteries and—"

Mr. Simaika laughed. "Oh, Moustafa. You understand so many things but you don't understand yourself. When will you realize you are not a scholar?"

Moustafa stiffened. "Mr. Simaika, I know you must be disappointed that I'm leaving, but that's no reason to—"

The Copt waved away his objection. "I am not insulting you, Moustafa. Of course you are very learned, and you have a bright future ahead of you with your Egyptological investigations, but your scholarship is only an excuse to indulge in your real self. You are an explorer and an adventurer. You told me that when you were barely out of boyhood you left your village in order to see the world. You were ignorant, and you did not go seeking scientific knowledge, but new things. New experiences. As soon as I heard you say Sir Augustus was in trouble again, and it would involve a trip to Luxor, I knew I had lost you. Go with God's speed."

Moustafa let out a breath of relief. "Thank you for understanding, Mr. Simaika."

"I understand now that you cannot be tied completely to any employer. You quit a very good job with Sir Augustus because you thought working for an Egyptian would give you more freedom. It didn't give you enough. What you really need to do is work for yourself, while keeping your obligation to your friends at the same time."

"Friends? I hardly think—"

"Friends, Moustafa. They are your friends, no matter how irritating you may find them. But you must be your own man too. You must be your own employer."

"I'm not sure how I would do that, sir."

"Sir," Mr. Simaika chuckled at the word. "Such a strong, intelligent man like you saying 'sir' sounds strange no matter who you say it to. Don't worry. God has something very interesting written for you. I suspect there will soon be a time when you will no longer have to say sir to anyone. Good luck."

Mr. Simaika stood and shook his hand.

"Thank you again, sir," Moustafa said.

He turned to leave.

"Oh, Moustafa."

He turned back.

"Yes?"

"Why do you call him Mr. Wall and not Sir Augustus? Why don't you use his proper title?"

Moustafa thought for a moment. He had never noticed he did that.

"I … don't know. It's not out of disrespect. I suppose it's because it's a foreign title. I don't see why an Egyptian should respect a title from a foreign country. One should respect the man, not the title."

"And he has never corrected you?"

Moustafa blinked. "Why, no. He hasn't."

Mr. Simaika smiled. "It sounds like he respects you more than you think."

Moustafa didn't reply. He nodded to his former boss and walked out of the Coptic Museum, giving it one last regretful look before he got to the street and picked up his pace.

Mr. Wall had told him that the boat was not due to stop until it reached Luxor. It would stay there a week for the tourists to visit the sites before heading back to Cairo. He knew no way to get a telegraph message to the ship. Would the Invisible Scorpions strike as they sailed up the river to Luxor?

Moustafa decided not. If Mr. Wall and Faisal were murdered en route, the police would stop anyone from leaving the boat at Luxor in order to investigate. The murderer would most likely strike once they got off the boat. It would be easier for the killer to escape into the town or the countryside.

Unless he dives off and swims for shore. He could be on the boat already, awaiting his chance.

There was nothing he could do about that. He'd have to hurry down to Luxor and be there when the *Arabia* docked. Luckily the train only took 18 hours. He'd get there in time to do some investigating before the *Arabia* showed up.

He went straight to the bank, withdrew a large portion of his slim savings, and headed to the ticket office and bought a ticket for a train leaving that evening.

As he walked away from the window, he felt guilt weigh him down like a hundred pounds of refuse. He had spent lavishly to leave his family behind in order to go into danger, and he hadn't even told Nur yet!

He had just enough time to speak with her, pack, and get back to catch the train.

Nur did not take it well.

She did not scream and shout, as he expected, and she did not roll on the ground and wail about her dreams, as he feared. Instead she looked at the floor as he explained, Moustafa keeping his voice low so the children in the yard wouldn't hear. The sounds of their playing came through the half-closed door.

When he was finished she simply nodded, moved over to their bed, lay down, and turned her face toward the wall.

Moustafa hurried through his packing. He was just about done when Fatima, his eldest child, appeared at the door. She was nine, and was already a great help to her mother around the house. She kept the smaller ones in line, as much as anyone could keep a crowd of small children in line.

"What's wrong?" she asked, staring at Nur lying in bed. "Is mother sick?"

Moustafa let out a sigh, stopped what he was doing, and went over to her.

"Is mother sick?" Fatima asked again.

"No, she's just upset."

Fatima saw the half-packed bag. "Are you going into the desert again?"

By now the other children had realized something was going on and had crowded in the door behind their older sister. Muhammed, the next oldest, came first, followed by Amira and Munirah, with little Bachir toddling behind. Five sets of innocent eyes stared at him.

"I need to go away for a little while. Up the river to Luxor."

Munirah burst out crying. Bachir toddled over to her and started tugging on her sleeve, laughing. Amira looked stunned, Muhammed turned away and Fatima just stood there, frowning.

"Again?" she asked.

"I need to help some people."

"I thought you worked for an Egyptian now," Fatima said.

"I ... did. It's just that my old employer needs my help. Just one more time. Only this once."

"Lying is a sin," Muhammed called from over his shoulder.

Moustafa almost rushed over and smacked him upside the head, but two things stopped him. First, he'd have to wade through all his other children to get to the boy, and secondly, his eldest son had hit upon something that may very well be true.

Moustafa took a deep breath to calm himself. "I do not want to go, and I do not want to work for Mr. Wall anymore. It's just that I have to go. It's too complicated to explain now."

His eldest son did not reply, and did not turn back to look at him.

Moustafa went over to Munirah, picked her up, and dried her tears. "Come now, don't cry. See how Bachir is reaching up for you? Your little brother wants to play. Now be a good girl and take care of him."

"Who's going to take care of mother?" Fatima asked.

"The neighbors will help. I won't be gone long." He glanced at the clock by the door, a selfish gift from Mr. Wall to make sure he got to work on time. "I have a train to catch."

"You're going on a train?" Munirah said through her sniffles. "Can I come too?"

"One day I'll take you all on a train. We'll go to Alexandria and see the sea. Won't that be fun?"

Munirah brightened. "Really? Promise?"

"I promise."

Bachir giggled and clapped, not knowing what his big sister was happy about but celebrating anyway. Amira smiled. Even Fatima's face softened.

Moustafa put down his daughter and finished his packing as well as he could with his children crowding around asking him questions about trains and Alexandria. Muhammed was not among them, and Nur kept her face to the wall.

"I have to go now," he said, putting a gentle hand on his wife's shoulder.

"Go then."

"Their lives are in danger."

"It will be you who will be killed."

He glanced at the clock.

"Then you better hug me goodbye."

She did, a flood of tears wetting his djellaba. After a long time she let him go, and he went out to say goodbye to his children. The smaller ones were all excited about the trip to Alexandria. Fatima put on a brave face. Even Muhammed came out of his sulk in the far corner of the yard.

"If you have a duty to your friends then you should fulfill it," the boy said, echoing something Moustafa had once said at the dinner table. "But come back soon."

"I will," Moustafa said, hoping that was true.

At last he said his final goodbyes and hurried down the street to catch the tram. His children waved from behind the fence, Bachir sitting on Fatima's shoulders so he could see.

Curse that man for taking me away from all this.

He made the train with seconds to spare. Settling into his second-class seat, a hard wooden bench in a compartment crowded with Egyptians and Soudanese, he stared out the window at the activity of the train station.

I'll send them a telegram from Luxor to say that I have arrived safely. Nur can get one of the Koran reciters in the mosque to read it for her. That will cheer her up, and the novelty will be great fun for the children.

As soon as he thought of the idea, he began to worry.

Both men I interrogated said the Invisible Scorpions are everywhere. What if they have agents in the telegraph office? Perhaps they know about me. They could trace the telegram and find my family.

A coldness spread through Moustafa's chest. In all the adventures he had been on with Mr. Wall and Faisal, he had never considered that his own family might be at risk. The possibility had seemed so remote. Now it looked like a looming threat.

He wondered just how much of a reach this gang had. Was it just the panicked assumptions of two frightened underlings who themselves admitted they didn't know much about the Invisible Scorpions' operation? Or did they really have agents in every city and town in Egypt?

They certainly had monitored Detective Lowell effectively. They had that killer waiting for him.

He still wondered about that riot. Had that just been coincidence? It had helped the killer achieve his aim, but really it had not been necessary. The man could have probably rushed out of the alley and stabbed the American before Moustafa could have intervened. He had the element of surprise.

But why leave the bloody cloth in such an obvious place?

The Invisible Scorpions had certainly put agents on the Thomas Cook boats, and that was the largest travel company in the country. They also had agents in the country's most famous and popular hotel. Where else did they have people?

Moustafa looked around at his fellow passengers. That sleepy businessman in the cheap Western suit sitting opposite him. Could he be an agent of the Invisible Scorpions? What about that strong fellow across the aisle in the dirty djellaba? He had been looking at Moustafa and turned away when Moustafa noticed. Could he be a killer? Or even that middle-aged man with his wife and daughter. Could he have a gun in his pocket?

I better not send that telegram.

The whistle screeched, the engine huffed, and the train pulled out of the station, headed for Luxor.

Night fell, and the regular clattering of the tracks and rocking of the carriage eventually lulled Moustafa to sleep. He had brief flashes of disturbing dream—a gunshot echoing amid giant stone pillars, a felucca sinking in the Nile, and Nur's weeping face.

He shook himself awake, blearily looking around the cabin, lit only by a dim bulb at either end. Most people were asleep, except for that big man in the dirty clothes he had caught staring at him before. Now he sat there, looking at nothing. But he seemed tense, as if he had been up to no good. Had the man been watching Moustafa as he slept, perhaps awaiting his chance?

Moustafa pretended to go back asleep, every now and then cracking open one eye to spy on the man across the aisle. He did not look at Moustafa.

Or at least Moustafa did not catch him doing so.

It had been a long day full of stress and sadness. Despite Moustafa's suspicions, sleep pulled him under once more …

… only for him to be jolted awake by the screeching of brakes and being flung into the lap of the older man seated opposite him.

Moustafa tumbled to the floor along with two other passengers. The entire cabin was in an uproar, everyone crying out in pain or asking what was going on. A baby wailed.

Climbing over his fellow passengers, Moustafa stumbled to a window, yanked it open, and stuck his head out into the cool night air. An engineer ran past, a lantern in his hand.

"What's going on?" Moustafa asked.

"The track's torn up," the engineer called over his shoulder, not slowing down. "It must have been the independence protestors."

More lights appeared as crewmembers spread out around the train. They had stopped in an open stretch of desert. He could see little beyond. A moist breeze from the west brought the scent of cultivation. They weren't far from the green line.

The lights in the carriage abruptly switched off. Craning his neck out the window, Moustafa saw the lights in the other carriages switch off one by one.

A moment later the door to the carriage opened.

"Keep calm everyone," someone called. He presumed the man to be a conductor. "We have been delayed by a torn up track. For your own safety stay in your seats and do not turn on any lights."

Several British soldiers ran alongside the train, rifles in hand, their equipment clattering. Moustafa stared. Where had they come from? Had they been riding along as guards? Their officer barked an order and the men spread out, disappearing into the night.

A long hour passed, with Moustafa peering out the window at nothing, alert for the sound of shots. Then the conductor walked along the length of the train.

"Ladies and gentlemen, we apologize for the trouble, but the track is too damaged to repair tonight. For the safety of the passengers and crew, we are returning to Cairo. Your tickets will be refunded."

Moustafa groaned. He would not make it to Luxor in time.

CHAPTER TWENTY-ONE

Faisal felt a bit better now. Abdelkarim had been sent on shore at the next town. Among his things they had found the staff deck key he had copied from the captain's key, so Faisal was safe in his cabin again. He knew Alaeddin Bey could pick locks, but he'd look suspicious going down to the crew deck and wouldn't want to do that now that he was on his guard.

The magician still worried Faisal. He had more tricks up his sleeve, that was for sure. If he was smart, he wouldn't try any more crimes on this trip. He'd be sure to try and figure out who caught Abdelkarim, though. No way would he think Jocelyn was acting alone. He was too clever to be fooled.

But for the moment the sun was shining, they were passing along a nice stretch of green farmland, and some local fellahin had rowed out to sell them sweets and nuts and freshly caught fish. The Englishman had been so happy with how well Faisal had done the previous night that he'd bought him some sweets and peanuts.

He'd already finished the sweets, and now he was working on a big packet of nuts wrapped in old newspaper. The strange vision of the darkened sun had slipped from his memory.

Faisal stood by the railing, munching on the nuts and looking out across the river. This was nicer than the desert, open like the desert but green too, with the fields of the fellahin lining each bank and the palm trees waving in the wind. The air was fresh too, not filled with cooking smells and the stink of rotting garbage and cat's piss. He could get used to this. Maybe he could convince the Englishman to find more people murdered on the river.

The foreign boy in the sailor's suit came to the railing near him. The boy's blonde hair blew in the wind, and his bright blue eyes eagerly looked out across the river. Faisal could tell this foreign boy liked the view as much as he did.

"Hello," Faisal said in English.

The boy looked at him, frowned, and looked away.

Maybe he doesn't speak English, Faisal thought. *Some foreigners don't.*

He waved to get the boy's attention, then pointed to a village of mudbrick huts by the riverbank, their roofs made of papyrus reeds. Faisal grinned.

The boy clucked his tongue and looked away again.

What's the matter with him? Oh, I didn't offer him any nuts. Here I am eating in front of him and he's probably hungry.

Faisal held out the bag of nuts.

"Want some?" he asked in English.

The boy's response came in English, but it was so angry and quick Faisal couldn't understand any of it. He smacked Faisal's hand, sending the nuts overboard and into the water.

Faisal slugged him.

What happened next caught Faisal by surprise. The boy fell flat on his back, blood spurting from his nose, and started squalling like a baby. He didn't jump up and hit Faisal back, or try to kick him in the shins, or even swear at him, he just lay on the deck moving his arms and legs like an upturned beetle, crying, "Mother! Mother!"

A foreign woman ran over, shrieking, followed closely by two waiters.

"You little piece of trash!" the bigger one said. "I'll teach you to hit the passengers!"

"I'm a passenger too!" Faisal said. He was already running when he said it, because the look on the waiters' faces told him that nothing he said would matter.

Faisal ran right between a circle of foreign men drinking whiskey. That slowed down the waiters who had to apologize and wait for the men to move aside. The delay gave Faisal just the edge he needed, and he ran to one of the doors, entered, passed through the room where the foreigners sat reading, and to the other side of the ship.

But the waiters knew the ship better. While one followed him through the room with the books, another popped out of another door a few steps further along the ship, cutting him off. Faisal ran up the stairs to the upper deck with them hot on his heels.

Once he got to the top, Faisal grabbed hold of one of the lamps attached to the side of the cabin and used it to haul himself onto the cabin roof.

From there he scampered along the length of the cabins, keeping low so they couldn't see him. Of course one of those baboons would get on the cabins soon too, so once he was far enough along, he peeked over, saw no one was looking, and dropped down onto the walkway, then dropped back down to the main deck.

He jumped as he saw a European man just on the other side of the window, his face hidden behind a newspaper. If the man heard him, he didn't bother to see what the noise was and kept reading.

"Silly foreigner," Faisal chuckled, then looked over the side of the boat. Aha! He had guessed correctly. The German's cabin was just below him. Good thing the porthole was open.

A shout and the sound of running feet made him hurry.

Faisal let himself down the side of the boat and just managed to get his foot inside the porthole of the German's cabin. Now came the tricky bit. There were no handholds or footholds. His fingers gripped the edge of the railing, and his foot barely reached the rim of the porthole. He was stretched to his limit. Below him, the water raced past. If he fell, he'd be swept away, maybe even swept under the boat. He'd drown for sure.

He tried to figure his way out of this mess. Climbing back up was a bad idea. Those men would beat him.

He'd have to rely on his reflexes. Taking a deep breath, he let go.

For a moment, he didn't fall. His foot began to slip from the rim of the porthole but slowed him down enough that he could bend his leg and, when his foot finally slipped out, he grabbed at the rim of the porthole where his foot had just been.

Faisal gasped as his body fell and his arms were almost pulled from his sockets, but he managed to keep his grip. He hung there for a moment, his feet almost touching the water, and then pulled himself up.

The first thing he saw when he stuck his head in the porthole was the German sitting in a comfortable chair, smoking his pipe with a book on his lap. The German was watching him.

Taking another puff of his pipe, he let out a cloud of smoke.

"Hello," the German said in English. Faisal didn't realize the Germans spoke English in Germany.

"Hello," Faisal said.

Faisal lifted himself inside, grunting and squeezing. This porthole sure was small. Why did they make them so small? He should talk with Mr. Cook.

Or maybe it was the Englishman's fault. Faisal had been gaining weight. He had always been skinny, but lately he had stopped being able to count his ribs. The Englishman shouldn't keep such nice things in his pantry if he wanted Faisal to do lots of climbing and squeezing through small spaces.

With a final effort, Faisal pulled himself through with an audible pop and landed in a heap on the floor. The German still sat there smoking and watching him. His eyes strayed to the porthole as there came the sound of shouting and running feet.

"He must be somewhere!" someone said. "He can't have disappeared into thin air."

As Faisal picked himself off the floor, the German said something in English he didn't understand. He still hadn't learned enough English. Faisal pointed up toward the deck and made a face. The German nodded and motioned to a seat opposite him. In between was a small table with a pile of books and a tin box.

Faisal sat. The tin box had a picture painted on it of strange houses all covered with white stuff. The ground was covered with the same white, as were the trees, which for some reason didn't have leaves.

"Hungry?" the German asked. Faisal knew that word.

"Yes, please."

The German smiled and opened the tin. Inside was a bunch of little chocolates, each wrapped in paper. Faisal's eyes went wide.

The German went back to his reading and smoking. Faisal took a chocolate. The German took a chocolate.

Faisal had eaten chocolate before, but they had been the Egyptian-made chocolates. While those were good, they were nothing like this. The flavor seemed to take Faisal over, like suddenly every part of him was made of delicious sweetness.

But like so many good things in Faisal's life, it was gone too soon. The flavor lingered, and he knew the memory would last forever, but the chocolate had melted away.

Faisal looked at the German. He was still reading. The chocolate box lay open, the chocolates arranged in tidy rows except for the two missing spots.

Faisal kept looking at the German. After a long wait, because it always took Europeans a long time to notice anything, the German looked over the top of his book and noticed Faisal watching him. The German smiled and gestured to the box of chocolates.

"Thank you," Faisal said. He was good at saying that. Moustafa was always shouting at him to say it all the time, even when he was getting something he deserved.

Faisal popped another chocolate in his mouth, moaning and lying back on the chair as that wonderful taste overwhelmed him. After a minute the German took one too. He read for a little bit, then looked over his book and raised his eyebrows.

Faisal didn't need any more invitation than that. He took another chocolate. The German took one too.

They sat like that in silence until the chocolates were gone. Faisal looked sorrowfully at the empty box. He should really speak to the Germans about making bigger boxes.

Then the German asked something else. The only word Faisal understood was "lunch." He nodded eagerly. The German pulled the bell cord and motioned for Faisal to move from the little sitting room to the bedroom. Faisal hid behind the door as the waiter came. The German said some things to the waiter and Faisal was able to pick out the words "chicken" and "tea."

Faisal perked up. His friend Ahmed had been right. Learning English sure was helpful. The German motioned for him to come out and said something. All Faisal understood was "wait." Wait for lunch, he hoped.

They sat back down and the German packed his pipe, lit it, and got back to his reading.

Faisal fidgeted. Now that the chocolates were gone he had nothing to do. The shouting had stopped up on deck, so he might be able to sneak out, but he didn't want to miss lunch. The Englishman was always busy so there was no guarantee Faisal would get lunch from him. If he tried to get lunch at the crew dining room he'd only end up with a beating. And there was no point taking the risk of stealing food if food was already on its way. That would be wasteful.

He looked around. The German sure had brought a lot of books with him. There were books on the table, books on a shelf on the wall, and he had seen books in the bedroom too.

The German looked up and asked something. Faisal shrugged. With a smile, the German pulled a book out of the pile and handed it to him.

"I can't read, you silly German." Faisal said that in Arabic. He didn't know the words in English.

The German said something back at him. Faisal groaned. This was getting frustrating. That food better come soon.

His host gestured for him to open the book. With shrug, Faisal did as he was asked.

Oh! Pictures. Well, that wasn't so bad. Here was a big one of a man with a club hitting a bunch of little men. At first he thought they were children, but when he looked closer he saw they were soldiers with spears and swords. Must be a giant. That would make sense.

The German leaned over and pointed at the giant.

"Pharaoh," he said. Then he pointed at the little men. "Libyans."

Faisal nodded. He understood that much. The pharaohs were the sultans of old Egypt. He didn't know they were giants. Unless the Libyans were small back then. He had met Libyans and they were normal size now.

The German took the book from him, opened it to a page, and handed it back.

This picture showed a big building with no roof. Tall stone pillars stood in long rows, a whole bunch of them like the pillars in the big mosques, except these pillars were covered with the old picture writing.

"Karnak," the German said, tapping the picture. "In Luxor."

Faisal thought for a moment and put some of his English words together. "We … go … here?"

"Yes."

Faisal looked at the picture again. He noticed there were a few Egyptians sitting at the bottom of pillars, tiny compared to the huge stone columns. This must have been the palace of one of those pharaoh giants.

The book had lots of pictures. When he got done, he picked up another book from the stack, but that one didn't have pictures. The German got up and fetched another book with more pictures.

"Thank you," Faisal said.

"You're welcome."

Too bad the German didn't speak Arabic. He seemed nice.

A knock at the door made Faisal leap out of his chair and retreat to the bedroom. Through the crack where the door met the wall he watched a waiter come in with a little wheeled cart. It was the waiter who had accused Faisal of telling tales when he said the Englishman took him to moving picture shows. Faisal moved away from the crack in case the waiter looked up and saw him. The German said something in English and laughed. The door closed.

Suddenly the cabin was filled with the wonderful smell of roast chicken. Faisal's stomach grumbled.

"You can come out of hiding now, Faisal," someone called out in Arabic. That was the Englishman's voice!

"How did you know I was here?" he asked as he walked into the sitting room. On the table were two big plates simply heaped with chicken. Potatoes and vegetables too. Faisal licked his lips and sat down. The German started arranging the cutlery.

"I saw a serving for two coming to Heinrich's cabin. It wasn't too difficult to deduce why. Have you been here this whole time?"

"Yes. We've been discussing Egyptology."

"Have you now?"

"He showed me some pictures of that Karnak place. That sure was a big palace the giant pharaoh had. How tall was he? Twenty feet? Thirty?"

"It's, um, not known with precision."

"Are you staying for lunch?" Faisal asked.

"I've already eaten."

"Good. There isn't enough for you anyway," Faisal replied, digging in with his knife and fork.

"There was a commotion up on deck," the Englishman said.

"Really?" Faisal said, stuffing some chicken in his mouth.

"Yes. Mrs. Herbert is very upset because she says some Arab boy punched her son."

"You can't trust these Arab boys," Faisal said around a hunk of chicken. "Very rude."

"And they never admit when they've done something bad. Why did you hit him?"

Faisal put on an innocent face. "Why do you think it was me?"

"Because she said the boy wasn't wearing a Thomas Cook uniform, and you are the only Egyptian boy on board who isn't."

Faisal glanced at the German. The Englishman was having this conversation in Arabic because Faisal didn't understand enough English to follow along, but it also meant that the German didn't understand. That could come in handy. Several years on the streets had taught Faisal that the less someone knew about you, the better.

"He hit me first."

"Why would he do that?"

"I offered him some peanuts."

"That makes no sense."

Faisal shrugged. "I know. I've given up trying to figure out Europeans."

The Englishman stamped his foot, making the German look up curiously.

"Look, we're trying to investigate a murder here. I can't have you going about thumping the passengers."

"But he hit me first!"

"Nonsense. Now sooner or later you'll have to face punishment. The moment you step out of Heinrich's cabin they'll catch you."

"I'll just stay here. They'll think I jumped overboard."

"You can't stay here for the rest of the trip."

Faisal looked around at all the food and the books with pictures and even spotted what looked like another tin of chocolates on the shelf.

"Why not?"

"Because you can't, that's why. Now finish your lunch and we'll go apologize to Mrs. Herbert and her son. I suspect I'll have to spank you in order to satisfy them."

Faisal put his fork down. "Englishman, that's not going to happen."

"Don't talk back." He turned and spoke to the German for a moment in English that went too quickly for Faisal to understand. The German laughed and nodded. What? The German was betraying him too?

Faisal was about to leap out the porthole when the Englishman picked up a book.

"We'll use a trick I always used in boarding school. Stick this under your djellaba. I'll hit the book and you won't feel a thing. Just make sure to shout and moan like you're really getting hit."

Faisal raised his eyebrows. "Were you bad at school?"

"I was an unholy terror. That's probably why I haven't let Moustafa strangle you."

"So what did you do?"

"It doesn't matter what. Now come on and let's get this over with."

Faisal giggled. "I'll come if you tell me what you did."

"Quit messing about."

"No story, no fake spanking."

"If you don't get out of that chair this instant I'll let one of the waiters do the honors."

Faisal hesitated, then smiled. "No you won't. You always threaten that but you won't. Come on, tell me just one little thing you did."

"Well if you must know, I had a run-in with my maths professor. I never liked sums, and struggled in the class. Once when I was a little older than you are now he told me I was stupid. Said it right in front of the entire class. Well, my adolescent sense of honor couldn't abide that, so I slipped a laxative into his tea."

"What's a laxative?"

"A medicine that makes you need the toilet so much you're liable to burst. And he did. Right in front of the class."

Faisal howled with laughter. It took him a minute to get a hold of himself. "Did they whip you for that?"

"Ten of the best with a birch rod."

"Ouch. Did you do it again?"

The Englishman tried not to smile. "Well, I never got caught again."

Faisal turned to the German, who had been watching all this and trying to figure out what was going on. Faisal pointed to the Englishman and said, "He very bad."

The book worked just as good as the Englishman said it would. Faisal leaned over a table in one of the public rooms while that stupid boy and his mother, plus a few other foreigners, looked on. Faisal howled and screamed as the Englishman's cane smacked down on the book. He had to try hard not to laugh at how easily the foreigners were fooled, and at how silly that stupid boy looked with red bits of cotton stuffed up both nostrils. His only worry was that the Englishman's cane would become unstuck and the sword would come out. That might get him in trouble.

When it was over, the foreigners all stuck their noses in the air as they liked to do and left the room. The last to leave the room was the stupid boy, who turned back at the door and stuck his tongue out at him. Faisal gave him a smile, which made the stupid boy look confused.

Alone in the room now, Faisal allowed himself a giggle. That turned into a chuckle, which turned into a loud laugh that brought tears to his eyes and made him double over.

Faisal was still laughing when he noticed Alaeddin Bey watching him through the window. The magician had a slight smile on his lips. His gaze was not unkind. It was more calculating.

And that made Faisal stop laughing, duck out of the door, and hurry down to the doubtful safety of his cabin.

CHAPTER TWENTY-TWO

At least Ms. Trasher was getting off the boat and could inspire no more trouble. In the early afternoon they approached the docks at Assiout, where she had set up her orphanage many years before.

Assiout was a small city of low whitewashed homes and a few mosques. From the river, Augustus could see no major buildings. Much of the settlement was inland to conserve farmland, and only a small portion of the city reached through the green belt of cultivation to meet the river.

Augustus stood with Lieutenant Hemsworth and a few of the other men on deck as the *Arabia* docked. Each man had a rifle hidden under a blanket or coat on the wicker deck chairs beside them. Jocelyn stood with them, hiding her own rifle just like the men. That got her odd looks.

Amusing, Augustus thought. *And here I thought the lads were finally getting used to her.*

"What do you think?" Lieutenant Hemsworth drawled as he scanned the shore. The docks had the usual crowd of porters, fishermen, and loungers. Augustus spotted the harbormaster, an Englishman in civil uniform. Beside him stood half a dozen soldiers, all white as well.

"I see no native police," Augustus said. "it appears they can't be trusted to guard such a sensitive spot."

"But the Gippos don't seem excited today."

"Don't call them that."

Lieutenant Hemsworth gave him a curious look, and then, obviously deciding not to address the issue, went on. "The crowd doesn't look larger than expected."

"That's something at least."

The baronet stood nearby, scanning the shore with a pair of binoculars. "I don't see anyone hiding in the fields, but we must remain on our guard. There have been a few incidents in Assiout."

"Not against my orphanage or my wards," Ms. Trasher said, appearing in deck with her bags. "Thank you for your donation, Lieutenant Hemsworth."

"You are most welcome, madam."

At dinner the night before, the Australian officer had made a show of giving her a couple of pounds, a significant portion of a month's pay for a man his rank. Soon the man's slouch hat was going around the table. Augustus had felt obligated to put some money in as well, although saving her from theft had surely counted as a donation.

To his surprise, he had pulled a fiver out of his wallet and put that in. He thought that overly generous and yet felt better after doing so.

The *Arabia* pulled into the dock, crewmen fore and aft tossing ropes to the ready hands on shore. Within a minute the steamboat thudded against the dock and the gangplank came down.

Ms. Trasher turned to Augustus and extended her hand. He took it.

"It appears you gentlemen have been overcautious."

"I believe the American term is 'better safe than sorry'?"

The missionary smiled. "Indeed." She had not let go of his hand. "Take care of that boy of yours."

"He's not—"

"Make sure he is safe and well cared for."

She withdrew her hand, turned, and went down the gangplank. Two men at the foot of the gangplank, one an Englishman in the uniform of the telegraph office and an Egyptian carrying a suitcase, let her pass before coming on board. The Englishman, of course, came first.

"Is there a Sir Augustus Wall on board?" the man asked on a loud voice, looking around.

Augustus stepped forward. "Here I am."

"Telegram for you, sir."

Augustus took it, but didn't read it. Instead he looked over the man's shoulder at the Egyptian, who was speaking with the captain.

"Who's he?" Augustus asked the telegram man. "We're not supposed to be taking on passengers."

"Local official from the Ministry of Agriculture. He got wind that the *Arabia* was docking here and asked permission from his superior to take the boat down to Luxor."

"And how would he have heard that?"

"All of Assiout knows by now, sir. Ms. Trasher is famous here."

"But why does this chap need to come on our ship?" Augustus asked, still looking at the man, who had produced a letter that the captain was reading.

"Some sort of official business. Not sure of the details, sir. I just run the telegraph office."

"I appreciate your coming down and not sending a boy."

"It seemed important, sir."

Augustus glanced down. The return address was from Sir Thomas Russell Pasha.

"What does the telegram say?" Jocelyn asked. Moving in deliciously close and looking over his shoulder. "Something about the case, no doubt."

"Sir Thomas must have checked with Thomas Cook and learned we were stopping here. Let's find a quiet place to take a look, shall we?"

Before they could do so, Mrs. O'Leary walked up, a look of concern stamped on her face.

"Sir Augustus, you are well traveled. Do you think Ms. Trasher will be all right by herself in Assiout?"

"Oh, I suspect the authorities will keep an eye on her."

"Such a service she does for those darling children," The Irishwoman's face clouded. "Who's that who came on board?"

"Some Egyptian official."

"Well, I hope he won't be dining with us!"

Augustus and Jocelyn took their leave and moved to the opposite side of the ship. The *Arabia* was already pulling away and there was no more need for him to stand guard duty.

He tore open the letter and read.

"How remarkable!" he cried. "I've never seen anything like it."

"What?"

"It really is quite extraordinary. I can't think of another time this has happened to me. Good luck such as this never comes my way."

"What? Do tell."

He waved the sheet of paper. "Mr. Beechcroft answered Sir Thomas's undersea cable. He has approved of our joining the case, as I knew he would, and even increased the reward money."

"To how much?"

Augustus pointed at the figure.

"Goodness," Jocelyn whispered.

"Less split four ways, but still a handsome sum."

"Four ways?"

"You, Faisal, and Heinrich are helping. It would be mean to keep it all for myself."

"Oh, I don't need it."

"Nevertheless you'll have your share. I suspect Heinrich will go out and buy another library's worth of books."

"We have to solve the case first."

"We're halfway there. Although now Alaeddin Bey is on his guard."

Jocelyn thought a moment. "It should be shared five ways."

"What do you mean?"

"Cordelia."

Augustus grunted.

"She's been of some assistance," Jocelyn insisted.

"I suppose."

Jocelyn put a hand on his cheek. "You should not fault her for having good taste in men."

Augustus flushed. He took her hand and kissed it.

"Thank you," he said. "I just wish she wouldn't be so single-minded about it. Her brother has introduced her to no end of suitable bachelors."

"Who she has no interest in. What will you do with Faisal's share?"

"What do you mean?"

"Well, you can't just give it to him."

"No, I suppose not. He'll kill himself with sweets."

"You'll have to put it in some sort of trust, and spend some on his upkeep and education."

"Education?" Augustus chuckled. "Can you see him sitting in a madrasa? Or one of the Jesuit institutions? Pity the poor teachers!"

"True enough," Jocelyn said with a smile. "You have to think of these things, though."

Augustus didn't see why it was up to him to think of these things. "Let's not get ahead of ourselves. We haven't solved the case yet."

"Have you ever failed to solve a case?"

Augustus laughed. "Actually no. Once or twice the perpetrator has managed to get away, though. That happened when I broke up a gang of French anarchists called the Apaches. We nabbed the lot, but the leader gave us the slip."

"Is that when you saved Cordelia?"

Augustus cleared his throat. "Ahem. Well, yes."

As if summoned by magic, that infernal woman appeared. To his surprise, she did not come up to him, but to Lieutenant Hemsworth, who stood not far off.

"Alaeddin Bey will be hosting another demonstration of mesmerism in the library in an hour and hopes that the guests from last time will rejoin him." She said this in a loud enough voice for Augustus and Jocelyn to hear.

"I'll try to make it, madam," the lieutenant said with a slight bow.

Cordelia headed inside without even looking at them.

"Perhaps she's finally been scared off," Augustus said in a low voice.

"Or wishes to appear so. I think she's cleverer than you give her credit for."

"I may even grant you that bit of charity. Through Heinrich she has given me a harmless powder identical in appearance to the soporific Alaeddin Bey used on Ms. Trasher."

Jocelyn smiled. "And you're going to have Faisal make the switch?"

"Who better?"

"He's already been adding up the moving picture shows you owe him. I think he might have some innate mathematical talent."

"He does have a head for sums when they are in his favor. But this second demonstration of mesmerism is an interesting development. I wonder what Alaeddin Bey is up to?"

"I suggest we go and find out."

"Where's Faisal? This is a good chance for him to sneak into Alaeddin Bey's cabin."

"I haven't seen him since that fake spanking you administered."

"Hmm. Go check with Heinrich. I suspect he's in the library. I'll check around the boat and we'll meet back here in ten minutes."

A quick search produced nothing.

"He must be in the servants' quarters," Jocelyn said.

"He was afraid to go below."

"Something must have made him more afraid to stay up here."

Augustus summoned a waiter. "Go knock on my servant boy's door and tell him I want him."

The waiter bowed and returned a minute later. "He was in his cabin, sir, but he started screaming at me, thinking I was a djinn and warning me he had a charm that would banish me to the City of Brass."

"Tell him if he doesn't get up here I'll spank him so hard he'll wish he was there too."

That produced the desired result. Within less than two minutes Faisal appeared.

"I was only being careful," the boy said when Augustus remonstrated with him.

"Alaeddin Bey will be giving another demonstration soon. I have something for you to do."

"All right."

"Here's a packet of powder that Cordelia has prepared. It's identical in appearance to the one Alaeddin Bey is using to drug his victims. I want you to sneak into the cabin and switch them."

"What do I do with the real stuff?" Faisal asked, putting the packet in his pocket.

"Throw it away, or give it to the first one of us you meet."

"Even Cordelia?"

"Yes. Actually she would be the best because Alaeddin Bey doesn't suspect her."

"I can't just switch the packets. The paper is different. The one the magician's powder is in is a thicker paper than this. It's like wrapping paper. This is writing paper."

Jocelyn chuckled. "I didn't realize you were an expert on paper."

Faisal shrugged. "You have to notice every detail if you want people to be fooled."

"Augustus was just saying what a clever boy you are. I suggest you put it in the toilet."

Faisal shook his head. "Then I'd have to flush it. That makes more noise than a fat man with stomach trouble. I'll pour it down the sink and then run the water just a little bit to wash the basin clean. If the tap is on a little bit, it hardly makes any noise. Then I'll take the piece of paper and throw it over the side of the boat."

"Excellent," Augustus said. "Now go make yourself scarce until our mesmerist friend calls us into the library."

***

The library was prepared as before—the curtains drawn, two chairs facing the audience, and the same guests invited to see the demonstration. To Augustus's great irritation, the same test subjects were brought to the fore. He and Cordelia sat facing the leering audience once more.

Even more irritating, to the point of nausea, was seeing how Cordelia fawned over Alaeddin Bey. They stood, far too close together, whispering in low voices and staring into one another's eyes. More than one member of the audience looked on with open disapproval.

At least Aunt Pearl wasn't there to see such scandalous behavior. She had had too many constitutionals at lunch and was sleeping it off.

Finally, Cordelia took her seat. Alaeddin Bey came to the forefront and addressed the audience.

"Ladies and gentlemen, thank you for coming again. Our journey has not been an uneventful one. Sadly, a member of the ship's staff was caught trying to break into a passenger's cabin. Thankfully, Ms. Montjoy and Lieutenant Hemsworth reacted quickly and our missionary friend came to no harm."

No thanks to you, you sneaky fraud.

"Now I sincerely hope that the rest of our journey will be a pleasanter one. The captain announced at lunch that tomorrow we will reach Luxor, our destination. There we will check into the Winter Palace Hotel and enjoy a relaxing stay seeing the mystical epicenter of ancient Egypt. The great temple at Karnak, dedicated to Amun-Re and with smaller temples to a myriad of other gods and goddesses, is the largest sacred structure in the history of the world. It is a place filled with ancient magic and wisdom. To prepare you for visiting such a place, I wish to introduce you to some of that ancient knowledge."

If I didn't know you were so dangerous, Augustus thought, *I'd probably die from laughing.*

Alaeddin Bey turned to his two subjects and indicated them with a flourish.

"Here we have two intelligent, sober individuals. I have no doubt that if they had been on hand to help poor Ms. Trasher, they would have leapt at the chance."

Augustus only just managed to keep himself from bursting out laughing. A moment later he grew more serious. Was that reference to leaping a malicious hint that Alaeddin Bey knew what had happened?

"You have gotten to know Cordelia and Sir Augustus, if I may be so familiar to use your given names ..." *You're certainly getting far too familiar with Cordelia*, Augustus thought, "... and you know them to be level-headed, worldly individuals who have seen much of life. Both served on the Western Front, so sadly they have seen too much of life."

Augustus stiffened. Everyone could see his injury. Pointing it out was going too far.

"Life has been hard for them, as it has to a greater or lesser extent on all of us. This can lead one to focus on the negative. When my own country lost its empire last year, after a disastrous decision to come in on the wrong side of the Great European War, I was left without my national pride and without my home. I was born in a region of the Ottoman Empire that is now no longer ruled by the Turks, and where Turks are no longer welcome. I have been made homeless, and yet here I am having intelligent conversation with veterans who helped in its destruction. I have no hate in my heart, because I have looked at the good side of things."

Easy for you to say. You probably fled Constantinople or wherever you're from with the police hot on your trail.

Augustus controlled himself. This was an unusual direction Alaeddin Bey was taking, and Augustus was curious to see how it would play out.

The mesmerist went on.

"It would be easy to focus on the negative. So for this session I would like our subjects to concentrate on something positive. Sit back comfortably in your chairs, Cordelia and Sir Augustus. Close your eyes. Relax. I'm going to count backwards from ten ..."

Augustus settled himself in the chair and forced himself to relax. As before, Alaeddin Bey's calm, susurrating voice made it easy to do so. Once again, all his muscles' habitual tension eased away and he found himself being carried along.

Briefly he wondered why he was so susceptible to hypnotism. He had assumed that only weak minds such as Cordelia's could go under so easily. He'd have to talk to Heinrich about it.

Before Alaeddin Bey had counted backwards another two numbers, all thoughts of that riddle, all thoughts of Cordelia or Heinrich, all thoughts of his embarrassing position, had been smoothed away by that compelling voice.

"… and one. You are now completely relaxed. Sit there for a moment, savoring this feeling. What you will do now will not hurt you, even though you have avoided it for some time. It is time to conquer fear, mankind's worst enemy. I want you to think of a time before the war when you were happy, a time—" Here there came a sound from the crowd and Alaeddin Bey paused for a moment, almost breaking the spell, but then he resumed and Augustus was carried away on that voice again. "—a time before the war when you were happy. Think of a specific time that did not come again. Do not vocalize it. Do not act it out. It is for your own personal introspection only. Think of a time, a wonderful time that the war broke off."

Alaeddin Bey paused again. This time it did not disrupt Augustus's concentration. He was already moving into the past.

Before the war everything seemed brighter. While no longer a youth, Augustus was still a young man, full of vitality and optimism. He had a promising job, a modest amount of inherited wealth, and the eye of the most beautiful woman in Oxford.

Emily Haverfield was the daughter of his favorite professor. Augustus had read classics and archaeology at Oxford, and had stayed in touch with his professor after graduating. It was only after graduation, when Augustus had risen from promising student to young protégé, that Professor Haverfield had him around for tea.

And that's when he had met Emily.

While it had not been love at first sight as the poets drearily drone on about, there had certainly been a good mutual first impression. Most women bored Augustus, confined as they were to domestic duties and concerns. He wanted a woman who excited his mind as much as his heart, and until he met Emily he had never met such a person.

Emily, on her part, had noticed that among all her many admirers at that first tea party, Augustus was the only one actually listening to what she said. Soon they were politely disagreeing about certain interpretations of neo-Platonism, conversing in Latin as smoothly as they could have in

English. One by one the other admirers dropped out, most due to poor Latin and the rest from their ignorance of the subject. He was told later that Professor Haverfield and his wife stood to one side during the entire conversation, smiling. Neither Augustus nor Emily noticed.

This was followed by more visits, and walks in the park with Mrs. Haverfield trailing at a discreet distance. Being still relatively young, Augustus did not realize that these were the happiest days of his life. Happier days had been promised.

A part of his mind realized he was sitting on the edge of his chair in the library of the steamboat *Arabia*, smiling and acting as if he was attentively listening to Emily's every word. As before, he did not think this strange, and did not care what the audience thought. His mind was too detached from everything for that to matter.

As if from a great distance, he heard Alaeddin Bey's voice intone, "Those were good times. Times you should treasure. No matter what happened afterwards, those times are a part of you that should not be dismissed, should not be diminished by what came after. Think of what changed. Do not act it out. It is for you alone."

Augustus heard the shell but never felt the explosion. He had been hunkered in a muddy crater with some of his friends when the shrill whine of an approaching shell told him it was going to hit close.

The next thing he remembered was the bleary haze of the hospital. Drugged with painkillers, he lay more dead than alive for many days before he fully realized what had happened to him.

The deaths of his friends he could accept. They hadn't been the first. Even his injury, horrifying as it was, he could learn to live with.

It was the rejection that cut him the deepest.

In the hospital in France he received regular letters from Emily. While he had not told her the nature of his injury, she knew it to be serious. No doubt she thought he had lost a leg or a hand. Back home the streets were full of mutilated men. Emily made it plain that no matter what it was, she was there for him.

Until he came home without a face.

The pained expression, the immediate distance that grew between them, the fumbled excuses and evasions—it made him wish that German shell had been a bit more lethal.

Emily hadn't been the only traitor. Everyone acted pained around him, as if walking on a floor of thin glass. Invitations to the club or dinner dried up. Servants were overly formal. Even family members managed not to talk about the one thing everyone was thinking about. Thank God the war ended quickly and he could get out of England. Get away from all those people who pretended their attitudes toward him hadn't changed.

Alaeddin Bey's voice cut through the misery.

"The war broke many precious things, my friends. I should know. My country has been shattered. Millions dead. No one felt the war as harshly as the Turks. But one must move on. We must turn foes into friends. It is the only way to struggle toward the light. To become whole once again, we must let go of the past and move forward. The war is over. It left an evil legacy, but it is not a legacy we must accept. Foes can become friends. Wrongs can be forgiven."

Easy for you to say.

The trance wavered, almost broke, but Augustus found himself slipping back into that easy, passive nature of the hypnotic state. It felt comfortable there.

"Now I will count to three. When I get to three, you will come out of the trance. You will remember my instruction to make good on what went wrong before. You will remember to put it behind you and move on, and to come to the aid of those who you think have wronged you. One. You will soon return to your normal state of being, and yet be forever changed. Two. All bitterness and suspicion gone. There are no enemies here. At my next word you will come out of the trance. Three."

Augustus's eyes snapped open. Everyone in the audience immediately looked away from him as he did so.

They had been staring, as usual. They thought he had been reliving his injury. They had been right and they had been wrong. He had been reliving the injury that resulted from his injury.

Augustus flushed a deep scarlet and, forgetting that he was supposed to walk with a limp, leapt from his chair and hurried out of the library.

It was either that or run Alaeddin Bey through with his sword cane.

CHAPTER TWENTY-THREE

Twelve hours after leaving Cairo, Moustafa found himself back where he had started. The officials at the train station had no idea when the next train would go out.

"Twenty-four hours at least," was all they would say.

Moustafa paced around the waiting hall. The southern line was the only one to be cut, and trains were still going north to the Delta and northeast to Port Said. Their departing whistles seemed to mock him.

What to do? He could send a telegram to Luxor warning Mr. Wall, but by then it would probably be too late, and he didn't want to alert the Invisible Scorpions he was on the case. That would expose Nur and the children to danger. If he got on a boat, he would travel no faster than the *Arabia*, and probably considerably slower. Most passenger vessels for Egyptians stopped at every city and town.

A motorcar! He could find Herr Schäfer, tell him the trouble, and the scholar was sure to drive him down to Luxor.

He made his way as fast as he could to Herr Schäfer's house, only to have his supercilious servant inform him that he had sailed on the *Arabia* and the motorcar was in for servicing.

Next he headed to the telegraph office. At the very least he could warn his old boss, assuming he and any of his companions were still alive. He had to word the message carefully, though, in case the Invisible Scorpions had an agent there and were on the lookout for any telegrams to Mr. Wall.

Then he hit on it. He could use a false name! But then how would Mr. Wall know it was him? Taharqa, the great pharaoh of the Nubian dynasty! Mr. Wall would see through that in an instant.

As he made his way to the telegraph office, he found himself smiling at the joke. His pulse was racing from the excitement of being back on the trail of a murderer.

"God forgive me," he muttered. "I like this too much."

At the telegraph office he was served by the same Egyptian as before.

"Back so soon, brother?" the man asked.

"Yes, I have another message to send, this time for myself."

"I wish all customers were Egyptian," he said. "Or do you wish for Nubia to be its own country?"

"I haven't decided. Separate from the English, at any rate."

The man smiled and nodded. Moustafa supposed that was a good enough answer for him. The clerk handed him a form and he filled it out. He guessed at the hotel where Mr. Wall would stay, figuring he'd stay at the nicest and most famous, and made up a name for himself.

"Mr. Augustus Wall, Winter Palace Hotel, Luxor.

This is in regards to our previous discussion of the great pharaoh Taharqa, the study of which I have recently had to discontinue in favor of that of a more recent epoch. I must point out to you that you are erroneous in your matter. The specialist you have gone to speak to is not your man. I am afraid that I do not know with whom your interest really lies. We shall speak in person at the earliest available opportunity. Until then, have a safe journey.

Kindest regards,

Muhammad ibn Baatin."

Moustafa hoped Mr. Wall would be clever enough to read between the lines, especially with the false name. "Baatin" in the Soudanese dialect meant "unseen", a common term for God. That made the connection between the

Islamic faith and the Soudan, which should help Mr. Wall figure out who had wired him.

The clerk took it, his brow furrowing slightly as he read the obscure lines. Moustafa tensed.

"That will be seven piastres, please," he said.

Did Moustafa detect a note of tension in his voice, a certain stiffness of manner? Without a word Moustafa handed over the money. As the clerk counted it, Moustafa bent closer and whispered, "We will have our freedom soon, brother."

The clerk glanced at him, glanced down at the paper, and back again at Moustafa, eyes gleaming.

"I'll be happy to deliver this message, brother."

The fool must think it's a coded message for the independence movement, Moustafa thought. He gave the man a conspiratorial nod and left.

Moustafa was once again at loose ends. He resisted the urge to go home and see Nur and the children. It might put them in danger and even if the Invisible Scorpions weren't following him, it would only be too painful to have to leave once again. Instead, he checked in to a cheap hotel, one well away from the train station. The ones close to it might be watched. Then he decided to check up on the two contacts he had questioned. Perhaps he could get more out of them.

He decided to try the waiter first. Dressed respectably as he was, he would have no trouble entering Shepheard's Hotel. The Europeans, and sadly the Egyptian staff, would simply assume he was a manservant.

Moustafa affected that air as he entered the hotel, stooping slightly, and putting on a self-effacing smile.

Not that he needed to bother. They took one look at him and made their assumptions.

Oh, to be a guest in a place like this! The entrance hall was grandiose, with plush carpet and liveried servants rushing to and fro handling the guests' baggage or delivering food and drink on silver platters to the rooms. Europeans lounged in soft armchairs of red velvet, reading the newspaper or chatting amicably. A long counter of mahogany staffed by managers in fashionable suits took up one end. This is where newcomers checked in, or those already staying at the hotel got their letters or telegrams.

This was the leading hotel in all of Africa. Here the guests could expect the finest service, eat the best dishes, and sleep in the most luxurious rooms.

And yet all those guests, Moustafa saw sadly, were white. Oh, perhaps the occasional Turk might check in, although not as many as before the war, but Egyptians? No. Soudanese? Certainly not! While there was no sign strictly forbidding such people from staying here; there didn't need to be.

With a sigh Moustafa left his daydreaming and returned to his grim task.

He glanced at the terrace and didn't see his man. Peeking into the dining room, he didn't catch sight of him either.

A passing waiter stopped. "May I help you?"

"Um, yes. I'm looking for one of your coworkers, actually my boss was. I don't know the waiter's name, but he was about your height, thin pencil moustache, about thirty, a chip on his front tooth?"

The man's face fell. "You mean Mahmud Idris?"

"I suppose."

"So you haven't heard."

"Heard what?"

"He was killed in an accident last night. A motorcar ran him down in the street. The driver didn't even stop."

The waiter said more, but Moustafa couldn't pay attention. The man he had questioned had predicted he would come to a bad end. Moustafa had urged him to leave town and he hadn't. Now he had paid the ultimate price.

Moustafa gave his condolences to the waiter, left the hotel, and composed himself outside. Then he went to the tobacconist's a few doors down, where he waited in the street until a European entered. Moustafa walked in right behind him.

The tobacconist spotted him immediately and his jaw dropped. The man started trembling from head to toe. The European, oblivious, made his order in English.

"Excuse me? Did you hear me?" the European asked, snapping his fingers in front of the tobacconist's face.

That woke him up.

"Um, yes. Sorry, sir. What is your pleasure?"

"My pleasure is to have a pack of Benson & Hedges like I asked."

"R-right away, sir."

The tobacconist handed over the cigarettes, fumbled the change, eliciting a grumble from his customer, and then stood there pale and awkward as the man left. Moustafa moved in close to keep the man from getting up to any tricks.

"Keep your hands on the counter," Moustafa ordered as the customer left.

Moustafa went around behind the counter, found the gun in its usual place, and took it. Then he moved to the door, switched the sign from "open" to "closed", and locked the door.

"Now let's have a little chat, shall we?"

"I told you everything I know!" the tobacconist wailed, sweat breaking out on his brow.

"No, I don't think you have. Who is your contact?"

"It changes. I never know who might come."

Moustafa moved close to him, towering over the man, who shook like a palm frond in a strong wind. "Then how do you know the man is from the Invisible Scorpions?"

"T-there's a code word."

"Which is?"

The tobacconist shook his head. "No. I cannot tell you that."

Moustafa slapped him upside the head. "You can and you will."

The tobacconist shook his head. Moustafa glanced at the window to make sure no one was looking, and jabbed the man's revolver in his stomach, forcing out a loud "oof!"

"Talk."

"The … password is to ask, 'where is the most select of places?' The countersign is, 'Where Sekhmet rises.'"

"What's that supposed to mean? It sounds like a cipher."

The tobacconist shrugged. "How am I supposed to know? It's just what they told us to use."

"And where do these contacts for the Invisible Scorpions meet you?"

"They come here."

"Nowhere else? They never have you go to a cafe or a bar or anything?"

"No."

Moustafa studied the man. No, he did not look like he was lying. Perhaps the Invisible Scorpions used different techniques with different people. Maybe their more trusted, active tools, like the waiter, were asked to go to that low drinking den. That would explain why the waiter was killed and not the tobacconist. They might have been keeping a closer eye on him.

"All right," Moustafa said, nodding.

His hand lashed out and grabbed the tobacconist by the throat. Slamming him against the wall, he shouted in his face, "Tell me where you meet or I'll tear out your gullet and give it to my daughters to jump rope with!"

The tobacconist choked out something, his face turning red.

"Speak, damn you!"

The tobacconist clutched at Moustafa's hand, which was clamped like a vice around his neck.

"Oh, I suppose I'll have to let you breathe. If what comes out of your stinking gullet turns out to be a lie, it will be the last breath you take."

Moustafa held on a moment longer to prove his point, then eased up his grip.

The tobacconist took a moment to catch his breath, then whined, "They'll kill me if I tell you!"

"I'll kill you if you don't."

"There's a bar we meet at, on Al-Musta'in Street. I'm only supposed to go there if I have urgent news. Usually they come to me."

"And how do you make yourself known?"

"You order a sheesha. They tell you what varieties they have, and then you ask if they have Syrian. They say they have a little bit left and you say you don't mind paying more for your favorite."

"When was the last time you went to the bar?"

"Months ago. I've only been a couple of times. They come to me, like I told you."

"How often does a contact come and speak with you?"

"It's irregular. Once every ten days or so."

"And when was the last time?"

"Last week. The time they wanted me to keep an eye out for the American."

So the representative from the Invisible Scorpions might not show up for a few days or more. Waiting for him would be fruitless.

Which left him only one option, an option that chilled him.

He had go to that bar and try to make contact himself.

CHAPTER TWENTY-FOUR

Faisal had trouble getting to sleep that night. The Englishman had told him to go back to his own cabin, saying it was safe now. Faisal had tried to argue with him. He pointed out that the magician might have a key, or that someone else in the crew might be in on the plot. The Englishman didn't listen.

He acted strange, though. He did not get angry, even when Faisal brought up djinn. Instead he talked in a quiet voice as he stood at the railing looking out over the river in a way that made Faisal know he was not really seeing it. He spoke in a quiet, steady voice and told Faisal to stay in his own cabin.

Faisal did not ask a second time. Something in the way the Englishman acted made him worried. He had never seen him act that way before, and Faisal began to wonder if the magician had put a spell on him.

He bumped into the German on the way back to his cabin. Faisal tried to talk with him, using his few words of English and pointing to the Englishman's cabin. The German made a face, pointed to the cabin, and shook his head.

Did that mean the German agreed about the spell? Faisal wasn't sure. He was sure that the German didn't want him bothering the Englishman again.

Faisal hoped that the German would invite him for more chocolate and chicken, but that didn't happen either. Crestfallen and worried, Faisal reluctantly returned to his cabin.

Before going to bed, Faisal tried to secure his cabin door as much as possible. It only had a simple lock with no bolt or chain, and Alaeddin Bey might have a key. The Englishman had said the magician would never come down to the servants' deck because it would look suspicious. Faisal wasn't so sure. Alaeddin Bey could turn invisible or summon up a hundred cobras to hide under Faisal's blanket and bite his toes. There was nothing that magicians couldn't do.

As Faisal stood inside his little cabin, which he had been so proud of before, he now saw it as a deathtrap.

Then he had an idea. From his travel bag he pulled out a ball of twine he had stolen from a tailor's back in Cairo, knowing it would come in handy sooner or later. Tying it around the doorknob, he looped it around the light fixture next to the door and back to the doorknob, where he tied it off.

Now no one could force open the door unless they yanked the light fixture off the wall. That would make a big crash and wake up everybody.

Faisal got into bed and shut off the light. He sure was clever, so clever that the second break-in of the magician's cabin had gone off without a hitch. He'd gotten in through the window like last time, found the packet of magic powder, poured it into the sink, and washed it down the drain. Then he had poured Cordelia's fake powder into the packet and tied it up exactly as before. After that he had snuck out without anyone seeing him and tossed Cordelia's piece of paper over the side.

Only one thing troubled him—Cordelia being clever. That had been a good idea of hers. When he had seen the two powders side by side he couldn't tell any difference between them at all. Faisal didn't want Cordelia to be clever. If she was clever then she would be useful, and if she was useful she might be brought along the next time someone got murdered.

Faisal didn't want that. He didn't see any way to stop it, though.

He lay in bed, waiting for sleep to come. While his door was secure, magic could still get him. That made him edgy, but the soft bed with its clean sheets and soft pillow and blanket were luxurious. He could get used to this. Lying in this bed was like being in a dream, and soon his muscles relaxed, his mind cleared, and he began to dream for real.

Faisal found himself in a sandstorm. He walked through a harsh desert, sand swirling all around him and scraping his face. Even though he could barely see, the sun shone bright and clear above, hammering him with its heat. He felt thirsty, and hungry too, and he knew he had a long way to walk.

Blinking out the grit in his eyes, he saw a crumbly old building up ahead. It was a big tower, an ancient one with all the stones all jumbled up and looking ready to fall.

Faisal made for it. The wind blew harder, and the sand got in his eyes so much that he almost couldn't see his way. The sun grew stronger too, and he thought his head would burst from the heat.

Finally, he reached the tower. He opened up a huge, creaking door and went inside.

Everything was better in there. There was no heat or blowing sand. Instead there was a big table covered in good food. There was chicken and beef and piles of fruit. There was even a stack of sugarcane and a box of German chocolates the size of a table. He went over to the box and looked at the picture on the top. It was like the one he had seen before, with a village covered in white stuff and trees with no leaves.

But unlike the real box of chocolates, this one was like a moving picture. Children in bright coats of many colors played among the houses, laughing and performing somersaults. Ahmed came along, kicking a football. He grinned at Faisal and kicked the ball to him. Faisal laughed.

Then Faisal saw himself. He wasn't a boy anymore. He was a man, a cowboy. He had the cowboy clothes and the cowboy hat and the guns and the funny rope thing cowboys used to grab cattle and bandits. He admired his new self as if he was looking in a mirror, but there was no mirror.

"Eat," his friend Ahmed said. "They say you've earned it."

Faisal turned to the table, licking his lips. Yes, after that big trip through the desert he certainly had earned it.

"Not the trip," Ahmed said. "You did more for them than that."

Faisal looked at all the food, wondering what he should eat first. Next to the table he saw a stack of blankets and pillows and that made him feel great. He could sleep after he ate.

The tower crumbled in the wind, and he was standing in the sandstorm again.

"This way, Faisal!" a woman called. He did not know who she was.

Nearby was a little house, solidly built.

"Come in here. Get out of the sandstorm."

Faisal entered, and he was a boy again. There was a table with food on it, and a stack of blankets and pillows. He could sleep after he ate.

"What happened to my cowboy clothes?" Faisal asked. "What happened to my beard?"

"You're not a cowboy," the woman's voice said. "And little boys don't have beards."

"I am too a cowboy!"

"Sit, Faisal, and eat as much as you like. Then you can sleep. Don't worry, this house is well made and the sandstorm can't wreck it."

He heard a crumbling sound and looked out across the desert. The tower was building itself up again.

"It's back!" Faisal tried to run for it, but he couldn't get out the door.

"No, Faisal, stay here. It's much safer here."

The confusing pictures in his mind vanished with the sound of a faint click of metal on metal.

Faisal was awake instantly, eyes popping open to the pitch black of the cabin.

Someone was at the door.

Life on the street had honed his senses, and he had learned to wake up to unusual sounds. The splash of the water against the hull, footsteps in the corridor outside, the cook clattering around in the kitchen getting his midnight snack—none of these aroused his notice after the first night on board. They were normal sounds, safe sounds.

This sound hadn't been. This sound had been like the soft step in the alley, or the stealthy movement of one of the other boys trying to slip a thieving hand into his pocket. The sound at the door had been an unusual sound, and unusual sounds were dangerous.

He lay in bed, not moving a muscle, and listened.

The sound came again, a quiet scrape of metal on metal coming from his door, and Faisal knew what he was hearing.

Someone was trying to pick his lock.

The sound didn't repeat. He heard movement on the other side of the door, a faint rustle of clothing and the softest creak of the wooden deck as someone adjusted their weight.

Faisal stared at the door. A dim lamp burned in the hallway all night. The door was well-fit enough that he couldn't see light through the bottom or sides, but normally he could see some through the keyhole.

Not now, though. Either someone had turned off the lamp, or they had put an object in his lock.

That made sense if they were trying to pick it, but then why weren't there any more sounds? With a lockpick you had to turn it this way and that, feeling the mechanism inside to find the right way to move all the parts. Whoever was on the other side of the door had stuck the lockpick in and stopped.

Another slight movement on the other side of the door. Faisal clutched his blankets, paralyzed with fear.

Shhhhh.

The sound cut through the air, coming from the direction of the door. Faisal trembled. It was the magician. He wasn't trying to pick the lock, he was casting spells!

Faisal clutched his talisman, hoping it would protect him from whatever djinn Alaeddin Bey was sending for him.

Then something unexpected happened.

He smelled a strange smell, and it made his nose tickle.

Faisal buried his face in his pillow and tried to hold his breath as he sneezed.

Of course you're not supposed to hold your breath when you sneeze, because it can make your head explode. Everybody knew that. It sure felt like his head was exploding. His ears popped, stars flashed in front of his eyes, and his cheeks puffed out.

He kept from making any sound, though.

That was his street instincts again. If there was danger, you kept silent, even if it might make your head explode.

He removed his face from the pillow and got that tingly feeling again. A strange smell too. Was the magician trying to poison him with some sort of magical dust?

Wait, that wasn't it. He was trying to put him to sleep with the sleep dust he used on Ms. Trasher. Since Alaeddin Bey couldn't slip it into his food, he blew it through his door with a little metal tube so Faisal would breathe it in and fall asleep.

Which meant he was going to come in and kill him. He wanted Faisal to be quiet so he could murder him and nobody would hear.

At least he had switched the sleep powder with something Cordelia had given him, and at least he had tied the door shut with strong twine. That would slow down the magician for a time.

But he'd get in. Oh, he would get in.

Noise! Alaeddin Bey wanted silence, so Faisal needed to make noise and scare him off.

Faisal sat up in his bed and was about to scream at the top of his lungs when he heard another unexpected sound.

The metal being pulled from his lock and footsteps moving away.

The magician had just walked down the corridor.

Light shone through his keyhole again.

Now thoroughly confused, Faisal switched on the lamp in his cabin, sprang out of bed, and started to untie the string securing his door. Twice he had to suppress a sneeze. He could see the fine dust hanging in the air. What had Cordelia given him to replace the sleep dust with? He didn't know, but it was making his nose all tickly.

Faisal kept one ear pressed against the door to listen as the footsteps went up the stairs to the lower deck and faded away.

He got the string untied and poked his head out into the hallway. A little oil lamp burned at the end, as it did all night. Faisal slipped out, locked his cabin door behind him, and moved down the hallway. Now that he was out of the cabin he could hear the magician's footsteps again. It was crazy going after the person who had tried to break into his cabin, but crazier to stay in his cabin and wait for him to return. Faisal would try to spot him, see what he was up to, and then go warn the Englishman. Then he'd have the perfect excuse to stay in his cabin again. It was bigger, more comfortable, and a lot safer.

Faisal followed the sound of the receding footsteps to the lower passenger deck. The hallway was lit here too, and he briefly thought of waking the German.

But no, he couldn't make himself understood. It was up to Faisal to take care of this himself.

So he padded along the lower deck, his bare feet making no sound. He heard the magician move up the stairs to the main deck. A door opened and closed.

Faisal crept up the stairs to the main deck, cautious now. He knew the old trick of opening a door and closing it without passing through. The magician might be waiting for him. Maybe Alaeddin Bey had heard Faisal follow. He didn't think so, but the magician was a tricky one and it paid to be careful.

Faisal got near the top of the stairs and noticed something. Since it was darker outside than the lit deck inside, the window in the door acted like a mirror. He could see right around the corner and tell that the magician wasn't waiting to grab him as he came to the top of the stairs.

That didn't make him feel better, though, because Alaeddin Bey could be standing outside looking right at him and Faisal wouldn't be able to see him at all.

He'd have to risk it. If Alaeddin Bey wanted to put him to sleep but didn't want to murder him, that meant he wanted to get up to some sort of mischief on another part of the boat. He must have figured out how clever Faisal was and didn't want him to spoil whatever evil he was planning.

Faisal eased open the door, wincing as it gave a soft creak.

Peeking either way, he did not see Alaeddin Bey.

Faisal closed the door behind him and listened. Nothing. Had he lost him? Maybe he had gone to the upper deck to attack the Englishman.

Or someone else. He'd check the main deck first to make sure Alaeddin Bey didn't attack Jocelyn or that Australian soldier. They were both on this deck and maybe he wanted to kill them for arresting Abdelkarim.

He hurried as quietly as he could to the prow and peeked around to the other side of the ship.

At the far end, he saw a dark shape next to one of the doors.

But not Jocelyn's or the Australian's door. Those were close to him. Alaeddin Bey was on the other end of the ship. Who was on that end?

Cordelia and Aunt Pearl.

Faisal looped back around and ran along the other side of the ship to get to the stern. Once there, he stopped. He heard a door open, and soft whispers.

Cordelia's scream tore through the night air.

CHAPTER TWENTY-FIVE

Augustus was awoken by a rapid pounding on his cabin door. Struggling out of the sheets and up from the stupor his single drop of tincture of opium had given him, he managed to switch on the light and mumble, "Who's there?"

Faisal's voice replied. "It's me! Come quick!"

Augustus pulled the automatic pistol from beneath his pillow and opened the door.

"What happened?"

"The magician is attacking Cordelia!"

Augustus rushed out of his cabin, not even noticing that he knocked down Faisal in the process. He rounded the ship, then hurried down the stairs, following the sound of shouting.

Several passengers and the night watchman crowded around the front of Cordelia's cabin, looking like ghosts in their nightshirts. The baronet had Alaeddin Bey in a headlock as the Egyptian from the Ministry of Agriculture berated him for sullying the name of Islam. The captain of the *Arabia* was apologizing profusely to Cordelia, who looked shaken but unharmed as she stood in her doorway.

"What happened?" Augustus demanded.

A babble of voices replied.

"Quiet, all of you!" Augustus snapped. Everyone flinched. Some even took a step back. He turned to Cordelia. "What happened?"

"He broke into my cabin. He picked the lock and came right in. Oh, it was terrible! I awoke when he bumped into the nightstand. If I hadn't, Lord knows what might have happened!"

"That's not true," Alaeddin Bey choked out. "She invited me in."

The baronet used his free hand to punch him in the face.

"That's enough out of you!"

Augustus smiled. That was hardly Queensberry rules, but the fellow deserved anything he got.

"How dare you say I invited you in?" Cordelia shouted. "If that were the case, why is that lockpick lying in front of my door?"

Everyone looked to where Cordelia pointed. There was, indeed, a lockpick lying just before her door.

The baronet punched Alaeddin Bey a second time. The Egyptian took off his sandal and smacked him with it.

"Viper!" the Egyptian shouted.

Aunt Pearl pushed her way through the crowd, wielding a chamber pot, which she brought down on Alaeddin Bey's head. Fragments cascaded on the deck. Augustus leapt back to avoid the spray but it turned out the chamber pot was unused. Alaeddin Bey went limp.

"Enough," the captain said. "There's a storage closet on the lower deck. We'll lock him in there."

He turned and gave instructions to some of the crew who, awoken by the hubbub, had emerged from below decks. They hurried away, led by the baronet, still holding the mesmerist in a tight grip, his sleeve powdered with fragments of chamber pot.

"Thump him a few more times on your way down!" one of the English passengers called after him.

A loud thump and a groan came as a reply.

"I better go check on everything," the captain announced. "Now it would be best if everyone returned to their cabins. I promise you there will be a full investigation when we reach Luxor tomorrow afternoon."

The captain hurried after his crew. The crowd remained, still babbling amongst themselves.

"All right, all right," Augustus said. "It's all over. Do as the captain says."

No one listened.

"Move on!" he shouted.

Still they babbled.

Aunt Pearl shook her fists in the air. "Did you not hear the man? MOVE!"

They moved.

Aunt Pearl clutched her chest. "Oh dear. This was too much. I need a constitutional."

"It's best if you return to your cabin too, Aunt Pearl," Cordelia said. "I'm quite all right now."

Aunt Pearl embraced her niece, scowled at Augustus, and returned to her cabin.

Once they were alone, Cordelia turned to him with a smile.

"So what really happened?" Augustus asked.

Cordelia put on a look of injured innocence. "What? You don't believe my story?"

"No."

She shrugged. "Our investigation wasn't getting anywhere. So I decided to hurry it along."

Augustus's jaw dropped. "You set this up. All those glances you cast at him. All those whispered conversations. You were making love to him this entire time!"

"Do keep your voice down. You'll injure my reputation."

"You've injured your own reputation. You—"

"I've injured the reputation of Cordelia Ruskin of Hampstead, not Cordelia Russell of Knightsbridge."

"You could have gotten hurt!"

Cordelia glanced around and then spoke in a low voice. "Nonsense. I had it all planned. I was never in any real danger. In fact, I was protecting myself. I could tell Alaeddin Bey was smitten with me, and I could tell he was the kind of man who would get his way, one way or another. So I made it known to him that I would be staying up late tonight and a visit from him would not be unwelcome. He knocked on the door very lightly so no one would hear. That told me my suspicion was correct and that he was an experienced seducer. So I opened the door and embraced him."

"Embraced him!"

"I had to play the part, didn't I?"

"How could you so shamelessly—"

"Come now, Augustus, are you jealous?"

"Certainly not!"

"There was nothing shameful about it. I was only playing a part, and it was only a hug. I did it to get the lockpick from him."

"Really?"

Cordelia bit her lip. "Only that part didn't work out so well. One should never try to pick the pocket of a pickpocket. They know all the tricks."

"So he caught you?"

"He did. That's when I screamed. I was going to scream soon enough anyway."

"You're lucky you had the chance. Did he …" Augustus's words trailed off. He couldn't quite figure out how to frame the question.

"Did he paw me with his hands? Did he steal my virtue? Not at all. And why is everyone so concerned with that all of a sudden? You know how many times I was asked that, and in so many different ways, before you managed to make it here?"

Cordelia's words stung. He had been one of the last to arrive. But if she had behaved, he wouldn't have had to come in the first place.

Augustus wagged a finger at her. "You put yourself in unnecessary risk, not to mention an indecent situation."

Cordelia laughed. "Indecent? You forgot I was a nurse during the war. I gave sponge baths to entire hospital wards."

"I don't want to hear this."

"I'm not some shrinking violet who must be protected, Augustus, and we're not in the reign of Queen Victoria anymore." She moved closer to him. "But it is nice to know you care."

"I care about not getting hanged by your brother."

Augustus moved past her and retrieved the lockpick. "This will make a nice gift for Faisal."

"I've helped the case along more. You should give me a gift."

"Faisal is less annoying. Now I must go speak with the captain. I will reveal to him my purpose on this ship and ask to question Alaeddin Bey."

"Assuming he doesn't have a concussion from getting hit over the head by a chamber pot."

"Why does Aunt Pearl have a chamber pot, anyway? All the cabins on this deck are en suite."

"She doesn't trust Egyptian plumbing. She thinks it might suck her down."

"I'm sorry I asked."

Augustus moved away, thankful to be rid of her. Just as he rounded the side of the ship, Faisal dropped down from the railing above.

"Is that lockpick for me?"

"How did you know I retrieved Alaeddin Bey's lockpick? Oh, you were watching from the upper deck. How silly of me. I really must remember that wherever I am, you're lurking somewhere in the shadows."

Augustus reached into his pocket to retrieve the lockpick and discovered Faisal was already holding it up to the light.

"This is a good one. The real professionals use ones like these."

"Faisal?"

"Yes."

"Do not pick my pocket."

Faisal cocked his head. "You were going to give it to me anyway. It doesn't count."

Augustus took a step forward. "Faisal. Do not pick my pocket."

Faisal slumped a little. "Sorry."

"Now go back to your cabin and don't cause any more trouble. I have to go speak to the captain."

Faisal raised his hands in the air. "More talking. Just like with Cordelia. That's all you foreigners do. Blah blah blah."

"Go to bed, or no moving picture when we get back to Cairo."

"But you promised!"

"Go to bed."

"I did more to solve the case than Cordelia!"

"Go to bed!" Augustus stormed off. Why did everyone have to be so irritating?

He found the captain below decks, having secured the mesmerist in a storage room, locked it from the outside, and posted a watchman. Augustus asked to have a word and, over a nightcap in the abandoned library, told him everything about the case that decency would allow. That meant leaving out Cordelia's true identity and the content of the stolen papers.

"I would like permission to search Alaeddin Bey's quarters," Augustus finished. "I still must find certain papers stolen from Mr. Beechcroft."

"I'm afraid I cannot allow that," the captain said. "That cabin is now a crime scene. It will remain locked until we reach Luxor. Once there, I will wire Sir Thomas Russell Pasha in Cairo to check on your story. I apologize for this, Sir Augustus, but having had two crimes in as many days on my ship, I must proceed with care. The reputation of the Thomas Cook travel company is at stake."

"I understand. The papers have waited for five years. They can wait another day."

Except they didn't. A couple of hours later, Augustus was woken by a crew member and brought to the captain.

The watchman reported he heard a splash near the ship just before dawn. When he went to investigate, he saw rippling water but no sign of any swimmer. While he would have normally shrugged this off as the act of a large fish, recent events had made him more suspicious. He went to check on Alaeddin Bey's cabin and found that it had been broken into, his steamer trunk and other belongings rifled through.

Together, the captain, the watchman, and Augustus made a cabin by cabin search and discovered that everyone was in place except the Egyptian official from the Ministry of Agriculture.

He was nowhere to be found.

"He could have swum out of range of the ship's lights quickly enough," Sir Augustus told the captain. "If he was a strong enough swimmer he could have swum underwater that distance."

"But if he stole the papers, wouldn't they get ruined in the river?" the captain asked.

"Not if he brought along some sort of waterproof container. He must have known Alaeddin Bey was on board and targeted him specifically to get the papers. He must have been Alaeddin Bey's accomplice, or a rival criminal who knew about the value of the papers and decided to get them for himself."

"But how did he know we would stop at Assiout?"

Augustus lit a cigarette. "I am afraid, captain, that your company has a spy in its Cairo office. Abdelkarim was working with Alaeddin Bey, so Thomas Cook was already dealing with one crooked employee. It isn't such a stretch to think there might be another."

The captain shook his head and took a sip of his whiskey, glancing at Augustus over his glass. Augustus knew what was coming next.

The captain leaned forward and in a low voice said, "I hope I can rely on your discretion in this matter?"

"As much as is possible. A passenger attacking a fellow passenger should not reflect badly on the boat … or its captain."

The captain looked down at his glass. "The press will make a stink of it, of that you can be sure."

"I have no doubt that they will. Thomas Cook has more than a little pull. Can't you wire him and have him do something to keep the police mum?"

"I will, but that's not the issue. The press always interviews leading figures who come to town. They're sure to interview the baronet, and perhaps Herr Schäfer, given his prominence in scientific circles."

"You can rest assured Herr Schäfer won't say a word. As for the baronet, I'll have a gentleman's chat with him."

The captain nodded. "I would be most grateful to you. Unfortunately, it will be difficult to keep all the passengers silent. This will get out sooner rather than later."

Augustus sighed. That would put the thief on his guard. He needed to solve this with as much haste as he could.

But how could he do that when he had no idea who the thief was, or how he operated?

CHAPTER TWENTY-SIX

The bar that acted as the rendezvous for the Invisible Scorpions was quiet in the late afternoon. Moustafa supposed, not knowing much about bars and being quite proud of that fact, that its main business was done after dark. It suited his purposes to be one of the few customers. He would stand out more.

Heart pounding, Moustafa approached the low, open doorway. He noted the sides were scrawled with the same strange graffiti he had spotted in the alley. He had no idea what those odd symbols and crude pictures might mean, and he could not very well stand there puzzling over them. At least now he had an idea who had drawn them. Taking a deep breath, he ducked through the doorway, took the three steps down, and entered the bar.

He came into a long, low room with windows high on the walls that gave little light through their shutters. Moustafa got the impression that those shutters always remained closed. A few heavy wooden pillars broke up the room. They were of old timber, holding up a building that may have been a couple of centuries old. The building had definitely seen better days, or perhaps it had always housed sin and crime. That was nothing new to Cairo.

Several large round tables stood scattered around the room, with chairs crowded around each. Only one was occupied by a group of ten men, drunk and loud even at this early hour. The bar, a cheap counter of warped wood stretching along one side of the room, had a few more customers. At the opposite end of the long room were a few stalls where men hunched close together in the shadows, speaking softly.

Moustafa tried to look like he belonged, resisting the urge to glare at these lapsed Muslims.

He walked up to the bar.

"What do you want?" the sour-faced Egyptian behind the bar asked. He had a razor scar across his face, which made one of his eyelids droop.

"A sheesha and a tea," Moustafa said, "and a beer for afterwards."

He couldn't believe those words had just passed his lips. He didn't dare sit in this place without some alcohol at his table, though.

"What kind of tobacco do you want with the sheesha? We have Egyptian and Lebanese."

"Do you have Syrian?" Moustafa asked, feeling a trickle of sweat go down his back.

The bartender didn't bat an eyelid. "We have a little left."

"I don't mind paying extra for my favorite."

The bartender nodded. Moustafa moved to a table close enough to the bar that he could overhear any conversation.

"Hey, Nubian!" the bartender called after him.

Moustafa turned, trying to look casual. "Yes?"

"Come here and get your damn drinks and sheesha. Did you think I was going to walk over to your table?"

Moustafa resisted the urge to grab the man by his throat and bash his head repeatedly on the bar.

"Why not? It wouldn't kill you," Moustafa growled, coming back. He figured he shouldn't act too meek. At the same time, he worried that he had shown his ignorance of a custom in this place. Perhaps regulars knew there was no table service.

Or the man had already spotted him as an outsider and was trying to get him to leave.

But he knew the password, assuming the tobacconist had told him the truth. Assuming the sneaky fellow hadn't warned the bartender. Assuming a lot of things.

Why do I always get myself into these situations?

The bartender brewed up some weak tea from a kettle kept warm on a filthy stove behind the bar, then poured a beer into a chipped glass. Moustafa took both.

"I'll make your sheehsa. Come back for that."

The man grunted out a price and Moustafa paid, counting out the exact amount because he did not trust the man to give him real coins in change. Forged coins and banknotes had been making the rounds lately, and he would not trust anything that passed through the hands of this degenerate son of a syphilitic donkey.

Moustafa moved over to the table and sat. He sipped the tea, which was even worse than the camel's piss brewed in the cafe across the street, and gave up a silent prayer for forgiveness for ordering a beer.

Of course he had no intention of drinking it, but merely buying it, supporting such a place as this, must surely count as a sin.

He listened in on the desultory conversation at the bar, which mostly consisted of lewd jokes and boasts about the speaker's prowess at gambling. As disgusting as this sort of speech was, he kept his ears perked and learned a few things. Firstly, the upstairs was not a bawdy house as he had initially supposed. Someone mentioned that they wanted to go to one, and someone replied that the nearest was just down the street, meaning there wasn't one on the premises. He also learned of a good place to buy a knife. Not that he needed that particular piece of information, but it told him something about the company that he was keeping.

A verse from the Hadith came to his mind.

"Whoso of you sees wrong, let him undo it with his hand; and if he cannot do that, then let him speak against it with his tongue, and if he cannot do this either, then let him abhor it with his heart, and this is the least of faith."

Well, he certainly abhorred this place with his heart. But if he had the power, he'd rather tear it down with his hands.

A man sauntered in, not from the street but from a back room, passing through a bead curtain in a darkened doorway just to the left of the bar. He was on the younger side of middle age, and moved with a lithe confidence. He dressed as a Westerner in khaki trousers and a loose-fitting workman's shirt. His heavy boots clomped on the cracked tiles of the floor. On his face was pasted a tight smile.

The newcomer went over to the bartender, who poured him a beer without having to be asked. As he did so, he nodded first toward one table, where a solitary man in a tram conductor's uniform sat drinking palm wine, and then toward Moustafa.

The man in the Western clothing, still smiling, went to the tram conductor first.

Wonderful, so they have a spy on the tram as well as Shepheard's Hotel.

Moustafa looked around, suddenly noticing something about the crowd—most were in uniform or livery of some kind or other. There was a man wearing the blue uniform of the Continental Hotel. Another wore the loose dun uniform of a railroad porter. And there was a fellow in the livery of the Gizereh Sporting Club.

Another man wore no uniform at all, just the clean djellaba and turban of a working man but not a poor one. He had the erect bearing, fine physique, and close-cropped hair of a soldier or policeman.

Moustafa felt a chill go through him. The Invisible Scorpions had eyes everywhere.

Then he noticed another detail. Those in uniform, and that military-looking fellow, all sat alone. The gang that boasted about bawdy houses and gambling, and that trio who were talking about knives, were the only ones in a group. He suspected that they weren't connected with the Invisible Scorpions. They were simply low people who had come in here because it looked like their sort of place. The Invisible Scorpions tolerated them in their den because they acted as camouflage.

He raised his glass to his lips and peeked over the rim at the newcomer and the tram operator. They spoke too quietly for Moustafa to hear, but from their body language he could tell the man from the back room was giving orders and the tram operator was meekly saying he would obey. The smile remained on the man's face, and it now looked even more sinister than before.

The two shook hands, and when they unclasped, the tram operator put his hand in his pocket.

He just got paid, Moustafa guessed.

He tensed as the newcomer got up and headed for his table, still smiling that disturbing smile. Once again Moustafa felt sweat trickle down his back.

"Good to see you again," the fellow said.

"And you," Moustafa replied, his voice coming out hoarse. He cleared his throat, trying to remain calm and reminding himself that most people probably showed a bad case of nerves when they came here.

His nerves strained even further as he realized how hasty he had been. He had assumed that the Invisible Scorpions was a large enough organization that its agents here would not know all its informants by sight. He had assumed the series of code words were a way to identify everyone. He had assumed, as well, that the tobacconist had told him the truth.

All of those assumptions were flimsy, and all of those assumptions could get him killed.

The smiling man sat in the chair opposite him, his hands folded on the table.

"You haven't tried your beer."

Moustafa's mind scrambled for an answer. "I drink at better places than this. I prefer real Belgian brew rather than this monkey's piss."

The man chuckled. Moustafa wondered if there was any real mirth in it. "Yes, this stuff is pretty foul. What's your favorite Belgian beer?"

Moustafa could have punched himself in the face for being so stupid. How could he have broached a subject about which he knew nothing? All he knew was that Europeans said Belgians brewed the best beer.

Trying to look casual he waved his hand, "Oh, whatever is available. During the war one couldn't be too picky. Some of the brews coming out of Liège are pretty good."

The smiling man nodded. "Yes, this isn't much of a bar, I'm afraid. I know you prefer more exclusive joints. Do you know where is the most select of places?"

And there it was. The code word. Moustafa felt a chill run through him. He licked his lips, tried to look the man in the eye, and replied in a low voice, "Where Sekhmet rises."

The man nodded slowly. "That's right, my Nubian friend. That's right. And what do you have for us today?"

Moustafa lowered his voice even more and leaned forward a little. The man leaned forward too, still smiling. "Not here. I have information about a leak in the operation. One of the informers has been spilling to some investigators, and I think there might be some more people in on it. I cannot say for sure that one isn't here right now."

The agent of the Invisible Scorpions leaned back in his chair, his hands flat on the table. Moustafa noticed a heavy silver ring with a prominent stone on it. That would hurt if the man punched him with it. "All right. We'll go to the back room. Come."

The man stood, still smiling. Moustafa followed, carrying his beer. The glass was bigger than his tea glass, it was still full, and he had an idea of what he could do with it.

He also had an idea what he could do with the clasp knife that lay open in his pocket.

He'd run the risk of arrest carrying that here, but had felt it was the safer option.

Then another thought struck him.

Just how many burly, well-dressed Nubians in their early thirties did these people deal with? If the assassin had given a good description of him, he could be walking into a trap.

"Mind the beads," the representative of the Invisible Scorpions said.

"All right."

Moustafa hoped the assassin had been in too much of a hurry, that the fight had been too confused, the street too dark, for him to have gotten a good look at Moustafa. He hoped the bordello where he had sat in clear light for half an hour hadn't been in on it. He hoped everything would be all right.

It wasn't.

Past the beaded curtain was a side door and a steep staircase leading up. A dirty gas lamp flickered at the top.

"We'll go upstairs," the smiling man said.

Two things tipped Moustafa off.

The man had said it in a voice that was slightly louder than it necessary, and the side door stood slightly ajar.

As they ascended the steps, a third thing rang an alarm in Moustafa's head. The stairs were well-made, unlike any of the rest of this place, with firm treads and a thick carpet that made the people going up or down completely silent.

They'll come up behind me from that side room, Moustafa said. *They'll wait until we're upstairs so the sound of the struggle won't be heard in the bar. My only advantage lies in the fact that I'm onto them.*

A faint sound came from behind and below, nearly drowned out by Moustafa's heavy breathing. Were they following him already? He lowered his beer and looked at the side of the glass. Was that a reflection of movement he saw inside?

The smiling man walked just in front of him, giving him no room to move. The sweat poured down Moustafa's face and back now, making him blink and itch.

They got to the top of the stairs. At the landing was another door to the left, this one fully open. A small room had a couple of chairs and some cushions on the floor, as well as a sheesha tucked into a corner and a closed door on the opposite wall. A gas lamp on the wall lit the scene. Moustafa got the impression of a waiting room.

The smiling man turned, still smiling, his hand moving to his pocket. Moustafa felt more than heard something rush up behind him, a thump and a creak of hinges as the heavy door was kicked closed.

Now.

Moustafa splashed the beer into the smiling man's face and swung the glass back just as the garrote went around his neck.

The glass smashed into the face of the man behind him, shattering and making the man cry out and stumble back, the garrote falling to the floor and the man thudding against the door, clutching his ravaged face.

Moustafa rushed at the smiling man, who although blinking and trying to wipe beer from his face with one hand, still had enough presence of mind to pull a switchblade from his pocket.

He flicked it open just as Moustafa brought his fist down on the man's wrist. The smiling man's smile finally vanished as he cried out, his hand opening, the switchblade falling to the floor.

Moustafa followed up with a punch to the face, but his opponent ducked, diving to the side to grab one of the chairs. Still half blind, he didn't get it ready to strike in time before Moustafa was on him again, and only managed to get the chair between them to keep from getting punched.

Moustafa grabbed the chair and tried to pull it out of the criminal's grasp. For a moment they played tug-of-war. Just as Moustafa wrenched it from his opponent's hands, the door on the opposite wall opened.

Moustafa tossed the chair into the face of a Nubian coming into the room.

He meant to slug the smiling man and then rush at the newcomer before he could recover, but they had other plans.

The smiling man, his beer-drenched face now a mask of rage, blocked Moustafa's punch and landed a counterpunch in his gut. That made Moustafa wince in pain and switch tactics. He hunched over and rammed into the leader with his shoulder, slamming him into the wall. Enduring a couple of weak blows to the side and head, Moustafa tried to pull the clasp knife from his pocket.

The leader sensed what his intentions and grabbed his wrist. Although Moustafa was stronger, the move got the knife tangled in his pocket for a precious second as the Nubian recovered from getting hit by the chair and surged forward.

Moustafa stepped back, grabbed the leader's shirt with his free hand, and flung him into the Nubian's path.

A quick glance over his shoulder showed the man with the garrote still on the floor, his back against the closed door and his hands clutching a face streaming with blood, and then Moustafa pulled the knife from his pocket and lunged at the two enemies who remained standing.

As he did so, it struck him how quiet all this was. The floor had the same thick carpet as the stairway. The door to those stairs was thick. None of three gang members, not even the man who was so horribly wounded, had made so much as a shout. He wondered how many men had died silently in this room while the people below drank their beers, utterly unaware.

Moustafa, too, kept silent, as if in unspoken agreement with the men trying to kill him. He didn't want a rush of people from downstairs either. None would take his side.

He struck at them just as they were untangling themselves. A quick slash caught the leader on the forearm, eliciting a hiss of pain, nothing louder. Moustafa could not help but admire the man's restraint.

Admiration turned to near panic as the leader ducked to the side and the Nubian came at him, bearing a curved blade two handspans long that Moustafa instantly recognized as a Beja dagger. The man had the dark skin and lean Semitic features of one of the Eastern Desert tribes. They were nomads, once loyal fighters for the Mahdi, and their skill at knife fighting was legendary.

As were their knives. That blade was honed to a keen edge on both sides. The man could slash with the outer curve and hamstring him with the inner curve.

And all Moustafa had was a little clasp knife less than half the length of the Beja man's dagger.

Moustafa backpedaled. The Beja moved in, sizing Moustafa up, taking his time.

Ducking to the side, Moustafa tried to grab one of the cushions to throw in the Beja's face to distract him, but didn't get the chance. The Beja swept down with his blade, forcing Moustafa to dodge back. Another swipe made him step away again.

And now he was out of room. Cornered.

He had only one way to go—forward.

Moustafa waited until the Beja tribesman made another swipe, barely dodged this time, and then leapt at him, stabbing with his clasp knife while bringing up his free arm for protection.

A line of fire ran down his forearm as the Beja brought up his knife to run the sharpened back edge along Moustafa's flesh. An instant later Moustafa slammed his knife into the man's belly, right up to the hilt.

Pulling out, he made four more rapid thrusts into the man's stomach and chest. The tribesman stiffened, eyes going wide before giving Moustafa an admiring look and falling to his knees.

Moustafa wrenched the knife from the tribesman's still-strong fingers before the man was able to swipe at him again, and looked around the room.

The man with the garrote stumbled to his feet, leaning hard against the wall, his face bleeding profusely. The leader, the man who had led Moustafa into the trap, was heading through the opposite door.

Moustafa kicked the tribesman out of the way, took two steps to the man who tried to garrote him, and slashed his throat with a single upward movement. Then he went in pursuit of the smiling man.

Not smiling now, are you?

The door led to an office. A surprisingly sumptuous desk with a leather-backed chair faced two similar chairs, an odd contrast to the decrepit scene below.

Moustafa did not get to see anything more, because the man he pursued was fumbling in one of the desk drawers, hampered by the fact that he, like Moustafa, only had the use of one arm.

It did not take a genius to figure out what he was going for.

Moustafa threw the dagger. Curved and overly weighed on the thick horn handle, it did not make a good throwing weapon. Moustafa only hoped it would slow the man down long enough for Moustafa to close.

It did. As the knife flew at him end over end, the bandit ducked, but not so fast to avoid the end of the hilt from hitting the top of his scalp. His head jerked back and he stumbled, righting himself the next moment.

That was all the time Moustafa needed. In a few quick steps he made it across the room and landed a punch square on the man's jaw, sending him flying back to crash against the wall and slump to the floor unconscious.

Rounding the desk, he reached into the half-open drawer and retrieved the snub-nosed .38 inside. This he tucked in his pocket, along with the box of spare shells that he also found in the drawer.

The pain in Moustafa's arm wasn't so bad yet. It felt more like a burning sensation, with a bit of nausea in the pit of his stomach. But he knew from the free flow of blood spattering the desk that it was a bad cut, and that the pain would become excruciating once the initial shock wore off.

Excruciating, but not crippling. He had been injured enough in service to that madman that he could gauge just how much he would suffer from a wound.

He bent down to pick up the dagger and check the gang leader was still unconscious. He was, but was he actually the gang leader? His informant had said that the leader was a woman who called herself Sekhmet. Perhaps this fellow was only in charge of this building.

As Moustafa stood up, his head swam. The shock was beginning to wear off. He glanced around, taking in the rest of the office. A window was covered with thick curtains. To one side stood a glass-fronted liquor cabinet, well stocked with the finest bottles. Moustafa went over to it, grabbed a bottle of vodka bearing the image of the late czar, and poured it on his wound.

The pain flashed like lightning through his body, making him stagger. He ground his teeth to keep from crying out. Setting the bottle on the desk, he cut a length of the curtain, soaked it in vodka, and wrapped it tightly around his wound.

That was all he could do about that until he found some proper treatment. Moustafa stumbled over to the desk and began a methodical search. On top of the desk was a telephone, a train timetable, an ashtray so weighty that Moustafa suspected the owner had bought it to double was a weapon, and today's newspaper.

Other than the drawer where the gun had been, all the drawers were locked. Moustafa rummaged through the pockets of the man he had punched out and retrieved the key, as well a large roll of bills. Moustafa hesitated, then pocketed the money. He would need it to get down to Luxor, assuming he could find a way. Using dishonest money to stop a murder surely couldn't count as stealing, could it?

With the key he opened every drawer, and found stacks of files too numerous to go through. At a brief glance they appeared to be financial forms for a variety of legitimate businesses. He also found a briefcase with more forms. He took a sampling of the loose papers and stuffed them into the briefcase. While he couldn't take everything, just these samples would help the police investigate the gang.

Moustafa stopped. What police? That man downstairs had looked like a police officer, and hadn't his informants hinted that there were corrupt men on the force?

He took the briefcase anyway. Just as he was about to head out the door, he had second thoughts and retrieved the scabbard from the Beja warrior's belt. He cleaned and sheathed the dagger and stuck it in the briefcase. He might need a knife as well as a gun on this job.

Then he hesitated a second time. Crossing the front room back to the office, he studied the unconscious man, the only member of the Invisible Scorpions upstairs who was still breathing.

I should kill him. He'll wake up and get the whole gang hunting for me. I'll be a dead man before sunrise.

Moustafa reached for the knife hidden inside the briefcase, then stopped. He had never killed a defenseless man before. Even that man with the garrote whose throat he had slit had been standing on his own two feet, gathering strength to get back into the fight. But the man slumped on the floor posed no immediate threat.

He'll be a threat soon enough.

Moustafa's hand inched toward the briefcase. He began to shake all over.

I can't do it. I must do it.

Moustafa leapt in the air as the telephone rang.

It rang a second time. Moustafa shrank away from it.

The Beja was in here. There's probably always someone manning this telephone. If you don't answer they'll know something's wrong.

The phone rang a third time.

He picked it up. The line was crackly, probably one of the older, cheaper lines installed before the war. Good. That made a voice difficult to recognize.

"Hello?" he said, keeping the mouthpiece well away from his lips to muffle his voice further.

"Where is the most select of places?" a crackly voice on the other end asked. Male, speaking in Arabic. Cairene accent. Other than that Moustafa could tell nothing.

"Where Sekhmet rises," Moustafa replied.

"Taha?" the voice asked. A typical Beja name. The man must have caught Moustafa's Soudanese accent.

"Yes."

"Tell the boss the line's fixed. The next train leaves in an hour."

"I will."

"Tell him to give my greetings and praise to Sekhmet."

"I will."

The man hung up.

Moustafa put down the mouthpiece, his mind racing. His arm throbbed with pain. He should see a doctor, but he didn't have the time.

He said they got the line fixed. Only the southern route had been sabotaged. That meant he could get a train to Luxor. Moustafa studied the train schedule. There was, indeed, a train to Luxor scheduled in an hour. It was a local train, making several stops along the way, but it stopped at Luxor before continuing further south to Aswan.

So this man at his feet was supposed to be going south too? Where? And wouldn't they notice when he didn't get on the train?

Moustafa tried to think clearly through the pain. No, they hadn't mentioned meeting him at the station, hadn't mentioned anyone else.

He looked once again at the man who had led him into this trap. If he was going to one of the nearer stations, Beni Suef or Minya, wouldn't the gang suspect something when he didn't get off? And when he woke up, wouldn't he and his comrades put two and two together and realize that it had been Moustafa who answered the telephone, and that he may very well be on that same train? Every station could be filled with gang members ready to storm in and kill him.

He had to take that chance. This was far too big. He had to warn Mr. Wall and Faisal.

Moustafa had just enough time to make it back to his hotel, change into a djellaba that wasn't torn and bloodstained, and get to the station.

But first he had to use the telephone again.

He called the Citadel, told the incredulous officer about a double murder at the address of the bar, and then hung up before the man could ask any questions.

Then he struck the unconscious man with the ashtray, hopefully knocking him out for longer, long enough that the police could arrive.

Blood spurted from the man's scalp. Moustafa prayed he had not killed him.

God forgive me if I have.

He hurried out of the office and headed downstairs for the bar. As he passed through the beaded curtain, every head in the place turned in his direction, eyes going wide. Moustafa was relieved to see the man who he guessed was a police officer had left.

Moustafa gripped the pistol hidden inside his pocket. The bartender glanced at it, then backed away, hands raised.

Moustafa didn't bother saying anything as he ran out into the street.

He had a train to catch.

CHAPTER TWENTY-SEVEN

There was a big stink at the dock in Luxor, with many police coming to take away the magician and a long meeting between them and the Englishman, the captain, Cordelia, Jocelyn, and that Australian soldier. It went on forever, and Faisal had to sit on the ship being bored as all the other passengers left to go to some hotel. The Germans motioned for Faisal to come with him but Faisal shook his head. He would wait for the Englishman.

The crew busied themselves cleaning the cabins and common areas, and he was left alone with nothing to do.

At least he didn't have to go to the police station too. If he ever set foot inside a police station, something bad would happen, that was for sure. This was one time he didn't mind not getting credit for solving a case.

From the docks he could look out on the town. Luxor wasn't very big compared to Cairo, but there were some big hotels along the riverbank. He hoped they were going to stay in a nice one, preferably one that was far, far away from the palace of the giant pharaoh. He recognized it from the book the German had shown him. It was close to the river too, and had giant columns covered in old picture writing plus those big gates the ancients liked that had carvings on them of animal-headed jinn and huge battles. Most of the figures looked fifty feet tall. He could see them clearly even from a distance.

He wouldn't want to go into that place at night. It looked like it was crawling with djinn.

Rashid passed by, carrying a basket of dirty laundry. He stopped.

"You still here?"

"Waiting for my Englishman. He's with the police."

Rashid made a face. "I've lost some nice tips, but I'm not sorry to see them go. Abdelkarim was a bully."

"Maybe you can rob the passengers now," Faisal said.

The tea boy grinned. "I've already been thinking about it. Hey, why don't you get a job on the boat too? You know how to break into cabins. We could be a team."

Faisal shook his head. "My place is in Cairo."

"Suit yourself. But if you ever change your mind, you know where to find me."

Rashid left.

Finally, the Englishman came back to fetch him.

"So what did the police say?" Faisal asked, picking up his bag. He was glad to be getting off this ship. The boat ride had been fun in some ways, but too dangerous. Plus, that European boy was annoying. Imagine getting thumped and crying for your mother!

"Alaeddin Bey is keeping his mouth tightly shut. While they can charge him for attacking Cordelia, they can't pin any robberies on him."

"Why not?"

"Because the only stolen item in his possession, the papers of Mr. Beechcroft, were in turn stolen from him. So there's no evidence he ever had them."

"What did they say about that Egyptian who swam away?"

"We wired Assiout. The local office of the Ministry of Agriculture had never heard of him. His papers had obviously been forged."

They walked down the gangplank and onto the pier. A porter from Thomas Cook walked ahead of them, carrying the Englishman's luggage and shooing away all the hucksters crowding the pier. Several of them waved cheap carpets and old things from the pagan times, calling on the Englishman to buy them.

"They have some old things," Faisal said. "Are you going to buy some for your shop?"

"No."

"Why not?"

"Because they're all fake."

"You sell fake things."

"I sell fake things that aren't obviously fake. I have my reputation to think of. Most of these are terrible fakes, and those that aren't are probably good fakes."

"How can you tell?"

The Englishman stopped and plucked a little statue out of a vendor's hand. That got the vendor all excited.

"Good quality, sir. Very old," he said in Arabic, then turned to Faisal. "Can you translate for me?"

The Englishman ignored him and all the other vendors that crowded around. Showing the least bit of interest always created a lot of noise. Faisal had seen that before.

"Look here," the Englishman said. "Now this statue is of bronze. But it's not the kind of bronze used by the ancients. See how it's all shiny? An ancient one would have more of a green patina, that's staining. Also, notice how the features are all dull and rounded? That wouldn't happen in an original."

"It is original!" the vendor said. "Very old! Dug up not two miles from here."

The Englishman kept ignoring him. "This is probably a cast of an original. If you do that, you lose some of its sharpness. Now take a look at this shabti." He plucked a little statue from the hands of another vendor. "First off, the hieroglyphs are wrong."

"Most tourists won't know that," Faisal said, barely able to hear himself over the angry protests of the vendors.

"True. But look." He scratched at the little blue figure with his fingernail. Some of the paint came off, showing plaster underneath. "This is only blue paint, not faience. This is a terrible fake. You could make something better."

He tossed the two fake objects back to their owners, who started cursing at the Englishmen. The one with the fake shabti shouted the most.

"You damaged it! You have to buy it now!"

"Get out of the way!" the porter from Thomas Cook shouted back at him.

They moved on, pushing through the crowd. The crowd pushed back and the porter spun around, using the Englishman's steamer trunk, which was balanced on his back, to clear a big swath through the antiquities vendors.

"So you think I could make fake things?" Faisal asked, cringing as one of them screamed vile things in his ear.

"Certainly, and make good money too," the Englishman replied, smacking away a hand clutching at his sleeve.

Faisal stumbled as the vendors surged at them. "I wouldn't want to be stuck in this crowd selling them all day."

"You won't. Help is on the way."

Several policemen shoved through the crowd, thwacking out a path with their sticks.

"This is the first time I've been glad to see a policeman," Faisal said.

The crowd retreated. Faisal could breathe once more. The Englishman didn't seem phased at all.

"There are many other ways you can tell if an antiquity is a fake," he said.

"I think that's enough of a lesson for today," Faisal replied. "I don't want you to start another riot."

The Englishman looked down at him and smiled. "Are you finally tiring of my company?"

Faisal didn't reply. They climbed aboard a waiting horse-drawn carriage that took them along the broad street running alongside the river. Although the afternoon was still hot, he saw Europeans out for strolls in big hats, the ladies carrying parasols. Each European had one or two Egyptians following trying to sell something. Feluccas sailed on the river, some carrying tourists, others fishing. On the landward side of the street were big hotels made of stone, each flying a bunch of European flags. They all seemed to compete with each other to have the freshest paint, the longest staircases, and the most windows. After a few minutes, the carriage turned into one of the front drives.

"Can we get another hotel?"

"This is the Winter Palace. It's the best hotel in Luxor."

"It's too close to the ancient palace of the giant pharaoh."

"It's called Karnak, and it wasn't an ancient palace, it was a temple."

"That's worse!"

"Karnak is a mile away."

"A fifty-foot-tall djinn could make it here in three steps."

"Nevertheless, we're staying here."

The carriage clopped up a long, curving drive to the hotel. Faisal stared. It was even nicer than the one the Englishman had breakfast at. Painted a pale yellow, it was four floors tall. The lowest floor was all shops, their display windows tucked under archways. He saw a photography shop, a barber, and several offices. Hanging over one of the arches he recognized the flag of the Thomas Cook company. A grand staircase led up to the second floor and a huge doorway to enter the hotel.

As they got out of the carriage, a trio of servants in red uniforms with bright brass buttons hurried down the steps. Two took the Englishman's luggage, except for the gun case that he always carried himself, while the third bowed deeply and greeted him in English. No one paid any attention to Faisal.

As they entered the front hall, Faisal gasped. It was a huge open space, with a ceiling way high up and a big crystal chandelier hanging from it. A sweeping staircase led upstairs. A rich red carpet covered the floor, and everywhere he looked he saw burnished brass, marble, and fine furnishings.

Fine people too, and not just the Europeans. Even the hotel staff in their uniforms looked wealthy. Suddenly Faisal felt a bit embarrassed in his clean but common djellaba and his unkempt hair. He felt people were staring at him. At least he had washed before leaving the *Arabia*. He'd stolen some soap too, in case the hotel didn't have any.

Faisal stuck close to the Englishman, who went up to a big desk of dark wood and spoke someone in English. Faisal was surprised to see the man was European. Wow, this hotel was so rich it even employed Europeans! The man glanced down at Faisal, frowned a little, then looked back at the Englishman and spoke with him.

"Am I allowed in here?" Faisal whispered.

"You're fine. I told them you were my servant."

Good. They couldn't kick him out. He hoped.

The Englishman signed something and talked some more with the European behind the counter. Faisal looked around again.

"Hey! Our bags are gone! They stole them!"

"Relax, they took them to my room."

"Oh."

The European hotel man looked at him and asked the Englishman something in English. When the Englishman replied, the hotel man laughed.

Great. They're laughing at me already.

Another hotel employee led them upstairs. Faisal ran his finger along the marble railing, admiring how smooth and clean it was. Everything was clean. Impossibly clean. Faisal suddenly felt like he needed a bath. He'd washed his face and hands, but even so he felt dirty compared to this shiny place.

The member of staff led them down a broad hallway, his shoes making no sound on the plush carpet. Good. This place would be easy to sneak around in. The servant stopped at a door, took out a big brass key, and opened it.

Faisal gasped. The room was enormous, with a huge bed, a writing desk with a telephone, a dressing area with a washbasin and full-length mirror, paintings on the walls, and an attached bathroom.

"Wow."

Faisal followed the Englishman into the room and looked around. He went over to the windows, which turned out to actually be glass doors, and opened the curtains. The room looked out over the river. He could see the crowd of Europeans and Egyptians moving along the esplanade, and the carriages moving along the road between the esplanade and the hotel. There was a honk and a motorcar sped through the traffic.

"Are we going to hire a motorcar?"

"It depends on if we need one."

"We need one," Faisal said with a nod. He turned back to the room. The Englishman was giving the servant some money. The suitcases and steamer trunks were set to one side. Good. The servants hadn't really stolen them. He should warn the Englishman to check all his things were still inside, though.

Faisal went over to the bed and bounced on it. It was soft and very springy. Perfect for bouncing.

"Get off there, you little scamp!" the servant shouted.

"Get off there, Faisal," Augustus said.

"What?" Faisal asked, still bouncing. "I'm only trying out the bed. Where are you going to sleep?"

"Here," the Englishman snapped. "You sleep in the servants' quarters."

"Servants' quarters again? The last ones were dangerous."

"This is a respectable hotel. You'll be perfectly safe here."

"Not if you're staying here," Faisal grumbled, tromping out of the room.

The servant, after smacking him upside the head, led him back downstairs and through an amazing garden that stretched behind the hotel. Gravel paths wound between big stretches of grass shaded by palm trees. Here and there were big bushes cut into funny shapes. Off to one side, near a gushing fountain, Europeans sat on canvas chairs sipping drinks. Birds twittered and the air felt cool and moist.

"This is nice," Faisal said.

"We are the finest hotel in all of Egypt," the servant said with obvious pride.

"Gah! What's that?" Faisal leapt behind the servant to avoid a monster walking across the lawn. It wasn't very big, and kind of looked like a bird with a fat body, skinny legs, and a beak, but it had a huge fan sticking out of its rear end with a bunch of eyes on it.

"You little idiot. Don't you know a peacock when you see one?"

"A what?"

"A peacock. Haven't you ever seen peacock feathers in the market?"

"Sure. Rich people buy them. Not sure why."

"Don't try to understand rich people. I've worked in this hotel for fifteen years and I don't understand rich people. Just do as they tell you."

"So peacock feathers come from peacocks?"

"Where else would they come from? Camels? Don't be afraid of it. It's just a bird."

"Looks more like a monster."

Faisal watched it, still concerned, as it slowly stalked away. The peacock folded up its feathers and reopened them, shaking them so all those eyes on the end vibrated back and forth. Faisal shuddered.

"What you really have to watch out for are crocodiles," the servant said, leading him further through garden. "We haven't had any this far north in years, but if your master takes you south of the First Cataract, don't swim in the Nile."

"I've seen crocodiles," Faisal said, proud of his knowledge. "A marabout came to our neighborhood once. He had one on a golden chain and made it do tricks."

The servant chuckled. "How many fingers was he missing?"

"I can't remember. I don't think he was missing any."

"Then he must have truly been blessed by God. Here we are."

They came to another building, smaller than the hotel but grand enough that Faisal would have thought it was another hotel if the servant hadn't told him it was the servants' quarters. The room the servant led him to was almost good enough for the Englishman. Once again he got a nice bed and a washbasin, one of those full-length mirrors that stand on little wooden feet, and a little closet to put his things in. He even got a window this time, looking out over the garden.

There was also a telephone on the wall. Faisal stared at it.

"Why is there a telephone here?"

"So your master can call you. When you master checked in and said that you'd need a room in the servants' quarters, the switchboard linked your room to his. No need to go through the operator. All you have to do is pick up the receiver and it will ring in your master's room. He can do the same to ring you."

Faisal looked at the funny box on the wall. It had a little horn on the front, and on a hook on the side hung another little horn attached by a string to the box.

"So how does it work?"

"Some electricity thing. How am I supposed to know?"

"No, I mean how do you use it?" Faisal thought you only used electricity for lights.

"If you master wants to call you, that bell on the top will start to ring. Pick up the earpiece on the cord and put it to your ear. Talk into the speaking horn on the front there. If you want to ring him, just pick up the earpiece and do the same thing as before."

Faisal glanced at him doubtfully. "Should I try it?"

"Does your master want you to call him?"

"Um, sure."

"Then try it."

Faisal picked up the little horn and put it to his ear. He heard a ringing sound inside. Then a click.

"Hello?"

Faisal almost dropped the horn in surprise. That was the Englishman's voice!

"Hey Englishman! I'm talking to you on the telephone!"

The servant smacked him upside the head. "Address you master in the proper manner, and lean closer to the mouthpiece. He can't hear you."

"Hello, um, Sir Augustus. Can you hear me now?"

"Oh, it's you Faisal. Come on over. I have some things for you to do."

"All right."

Faisal dropped the earpiece so that it swung on its cord. He jumped up and spun in the air.

"I just talked on the telephone!"

"Put the earpiece back on the hook after you use it," the servant said.

Faisal did as he was told. "It's not a toy. Only use it if you wish to speak to your master."

He's not my master, Faisal thought, *and I'm not his servant.*

Faisal hated having to pretend.

The servant handed him a room key. "Now behave. Your master has obviously not trained you right. I don't want to hear about any trouble from you."

The servant left, closing the door behind him. Faisal locked the door and looked at the telephone again. He went over to it and tried to look at himself in the mirror, but the angle was wrong. He moved it to the side, had to grab it to keep it from toppling it over, then adjusted it.

He went back to the telephone. Perfect!

Faisal stood straight admired himself in the mirror—nice blue djellaba, new sandals, and standing in a luxurious servants' quarters.

No, it's a hotel room.

His hair was a bit messed up, though. It had a mind of its own and flew every which way no matter what he did with it. He licked his palm and tried to plaster it down. No luck.

Oh well, he still looked pretty special. Faisal stuck his nose in the air like a European.

"I'm staying at a fine hotel. The Winter Palace. I sailed here on the *Arabia* and now I'm going to hire a motorcar and go to the moving pictures."

Faisal pranced around the room. "Yes, perhaps I'll go to the garden first and have a sugarcane juice." Faisal paused. Did Europeans drink sugarcane juice? He didn't know. Mostly they drank alcohol, didn't they?

He bounced on the bed. Nice and bouncy. Not as good as the Englishman's bed, but there was no one here to tell him he couldn't bounce on it.

Going back to the phone, he admired his reflection in the mirror.

"I think I'll order my motorcar now." He picked up the earpiece. "Waiter, please order my motorcar. I wish to go to the moving pictures. But first I'll have a sugarcane juice in the garden."

"Faisal, stop messing about and come over to my room like I told you!"

Faisal leapt into the air, dropping the ear piece. He scrambled to get it. "Sorry!" he shouted into it. Whoops, wrong horn. "Sorry," he repeated into the mouthpiece, then hung up.

He made it to the Englishman's hotel room in just a couple of minutes, although he nearly knocked over a waiter with a platter of food as he ran across the garden.

"I'm hungry," he said and the Englishman opened the door.

"What else is new?"

"They're serving lunch in the garden."

"Good. I'll go eat while you check out the hotel. Look for all the ways to get in and out, and check how easily you can climb to various windows."

"I'm hungry too," Faisal said. He clutched his stomach to prove it. Sometimes the Englishman needed things explained to him.

The Englishman sighed. "Fine, here's a piastre. Go get something on the street. It wouldn't hurt to check out the neighborhood too."

"All right! Where's Jocelyn and the German?"

"They're staying here. All the passengers from the *Arabia* are staying here. Now run along."

Faisal ran along.

Exploring the inside of the hotel was going to be tricky. The staff here didn't know him and might think he had snuck in. So he went over to a trolley full of bottles sitting outside a big room where a bunch of European men were drinking and swiped a big glass bottle with a funny steel nozzle on top. There were a bunch of bottles on the trolley with liquids of all different colors. He picked the clear one because that looked like water. Alcohol always had a color and he didn't want to carry alcohol.

So he carried it around with him like he was delivering it to someone. He made sure to keep his back straight and put on a serious face like the hotel staff did.

That worked. Almost.

A waiter passed by with a tray of sandwiches and frowned at him. "Where are you taking that seltzer?"

So this was seltzer? He thought it was water. He hoped it didn't have alcohol in it.

"To my master. He asked for it. I went to the front desk to get it." Faisal stared at the sandwiches. His stomach growled, but he knew better than to ask for some.

"You go to the head waiter or head bartender for that. Don't bother the concierge."

"OK. Sorry."

The waiter hurried off, leaving Faisal wondering what a concierge was.

The hotel had a pretty simple layout. It was basically a big rectangle with long hallways to either side of the stairs. The tricky bit was to know which rooms he could go in and which he couldn't. He figured the ones with numbers on the doors were rooms for guests, just like the cabins on the *Arabia* with their numbered doors. Other rooms were harder to figure out. One turned out to be a big bathroom. The place even had its own servant, a Nubian who passed soap and some sort of stinky perfumey watery stuff to the Europeans who came in to pee. He had to pee too, but the Nubian chased him off.

Faisal continued to explore. A lot of the rooms, even the common rooms, were empty. He remembered the Englishman saying that the big war had kept a lot of tourists away and business hadn't picked up yet. That surprised him. There seemed to be a lot of Europeans in Egypt already. Were there going to be even more soon? He couldn't really remember much about Cairo before the war. That was almost half a lifetime ago.

Faisal tried to imagine this hotel full. That was a lot of Europeans!

He came to one room that looked like a lounge. Big leather chairs were placed along the wall or around little tables. The air smelled of cigar smoke. On the walls hung a bunch of paintings. Most were of old Europeans. Others showed Egyptians fighting crocodiles or hunting lions. Those were more interesting than the old Europeans.

One painting was better than all the others. It showed some European soldiers in bright red uniforms fighting Egyptians in white uniforms. Everyone was shooting or slashing with swords or stabbing with bayonets. He wondered if this was a real battle and who won. The Europeans, probably.

They always won battles. Except if they fought each other, that is. That was why the war in Europe was so bad. Europeans fighting Europeans.

He imagined being in that battle. He'd be on the Egyptian side, of course. Maybe those red-coated soldiers were German. That's it! The Egyptians defeated the Germans and that's why the British ruled over Egypt and not the Germans.

Faisal would be right in the front line, firing his gun like a cowboy and knocking down a German with each shot. He held the seltzer bottle like a pistol.

"Pow! Pow! Pow!" *Pssssht!*

A spray of water shot out of the bottle and hit the painting. Faisal yelped, dropping the bottle. It landed on the nozzle and shot another spray, soaking a chair and the nearby carpet. Faisal grabbed it before it could cause any more trouble.

He looked at the painting. It now looked like a melting rainbow. Whoops. Tucking the seltzer bottle behind one of the chairs, he hurried out.

That spray of water reminded him he needed to pee. Time to search the grounds.

First he went into the garden. It was huge and it was easy enough to find a bush out of view, crawl inside, and relieve himself.

As he came out, that peacock was standing there watching him.

"Gah! Stop looking at me with all those eyes. Go look at the Europeans or something."

Faisal moved away as the peacock's eye feathers stared at him.

He looked around, realizing this garden might come in handy as more than just a bathroom. There were lots of places to hide and spy on people. He saw the German from a distance, talking to some other Europeans. Too bad. If he had been alone Faisal could have asked for some chocolate.

The back garden was enclosed by a high iron fence with big spikes on top. That would be tough to climb. He bet at night the hotel posted watchmen. It didn't look like anyone was going to break in or out of this garden.

He noticed something else too. Walking around this garden, the

Europeans took no notice of him, and only once did a servant ask where he was going. The servant, like the waiter inside, was too busy to bother thinking about the excuse Faisal gave and walked off.

Faisal was being treated like he belonged here. That gave him a funny feeling.

Time to check the outside. He passed through the front lobby and made a study of the hotel along the street. The walls were smooth and looked difficult to climb. In fact, they looked like they had been designed that way. How annoying! The silly foreigners hadn't been as clever as they thought, though, because each room had a little balcony enclosed by a low stone railing. They were close enough together that you could leap from one to another. That would make noise, and of course you'd be visible to anyone below, but once you got to the right balcony, the glass doors that led to the room were easy enough to pick. He'd already checked that when he had first entered the Englishman's room.

They had been clever in other ways, though. The ground floor windows on the front of the hotel didn't have balconies, so there was no way to climb up. The same was true at the back of the hotel. Plus, in front anyone trying to sneak from window to window would be visible from the street and esplanade. Faisal saw big lights tucked behind the bushes in the front of the hotel that he supposed lit up the front at night. He'd seen other European buildings with that.

So the hotel was pretty safe from people trying to break in, but not so safe from people staying or working there. The Englishman said one of the waiters at Shepheard's hotel must have been a spy, and Abdelkarim had been a spy. Who knew how many there might be in this big place?

A growling stomach reminded him of a more important problem. It was time to buy some food with that piastre the Englishman had given him. He remembered seeing a lot of vendors on the esplanade, so he scurried through traffic to get to the broad riverside walkway.

Then he stopped dead in his tracks.

The magician was walking through the crowd!

CHAPTER TWENTY-EIGHT

Augustus couldn't believe what he was hearing.

"Are you quite sure?"

"Of course I'm sure!" Faisal said. "I saw him walking along the esplanade. Except he wasn't wearing his turban and robes. He wore that suit I saw in his closet. And he had a big bandage on his head from where Aunt Pearl smacked him."

"He was charged with attempted assault on a woman! How the blazes did he get out of jail?"

"Well, he didn't escape. He wouldn't be walking on the esplanade if he had. They must have let him out."

"Where did he go?"

"I had to hide behind a newspaper seller until he passed. I don't think he saw me but you don't know because he's tricky and knows magic and his djinn—"

"Get to the point, Faisal."

"I followed him for a while and then he got on a carriage so I lost him."

Augustus sighed and rubbed his temples. "All right, keep an eye out around the hotel in case he comes here."

Faisal's face fell. "You don't think he's still going to stay here, do you? Not after the passengers all beat him up?"

"Who knows what that snake will try to do."

"I'll keep an eye out, Englishman. Don't worry, he won't get by me."

After Faisal left, Augustus went to Jocelyn's room to warn her, searched for Heinrich and couldn't find him, and then reluctantly knocked on Cordelia's door. She wasn't there and neither was Aunt Pearl.

Nervous now, he searched the hotel and found them having tea on the back veranda.

"Augustus, how nice of you to join us!" Cordelia said.

"What did you do?" Augustus demanded.

She put down her teacup. "Whatever do you mean?"

"Alaeddin Bey is free! Faisal saw him on the esplanade," he said, sitting down without an invitation.

The shocked looks Cordelia and Aunt Pearl traded proved his suspicions wrong.

"Free? How can that be? I gave a written statement. So did several witnesses!"

"Well, he's free."

"And why did you ask me 'what did you do'?"

Augustus flushed. "I, um, apologize. For a moment I thought you let him go so that we could track him. Silly of me to think that."

Aunt Pearl harrumphed. "My niece may be a foolish, impulsive girl, but she is not that foolish and impulsive."

Augustus glanced at the older woman. Did she know that Cordelia had entrapped Alaeddin Bey? Best not to mention it.

A waiter appeared. Augustus waved him away. After this case, he would never trust a waiter again.

"Take care with what you say and do," he said in a lower voice. "There may be people listening. Take special care among the servants."

"After this trip I'll be taking her straight back to England," Aunt Pearl said.

That was music to Augustus's ears. The look on Cordelia's face ruined the melody. The only way Aunt Pearl could assert her authority over that girl was to smash a chamber pot on her head.

Cordelia stood. "We should go to the police station and get to the bottom of this."

To that, Aunt Pearl could not object, so the three of them got a carriage.

The Egyptian desk sergeant who greeted him was apologetic but unhelpful. He explained it was out of his hands. A stern lecture and a mention of his knighthood got Augustus in front of the captain, an Englishman who would obviously have rather had this discussion man to man but could not stop Aunt Pearl from barging into his office, Cordelia in her wake, impressively playing the role of the dishonored innocent.

The captain's opening gambit did not prove a success.

"Miss Ruskin, I can understand your disappointment, but—"

His words were cut off by Aunt Pearl's parasol smashing down on his desk. Papers and pens flew everywhere.

"Disappointed? Disappointed doesn't cover the half of it! This is outrageous!"

"He tried to enter my cabin!" Cordelia wailed. "That beastly man tried to have his way with me!"

The captain rallied. He looked at Cordelia with a steady gaze, ignoring further choice remarks from Aunt Pearl, and said in a level voice, "That is not quite the whole story."

Cordelia's jaw dropped and her hand went to her chest. "I beg your pardon?"

"You were seen with him alone on deck on numerous occasions. He says you invited him to your cabin."

"Now look here," Augustus said, jabbing a finger at the captain as the ladies sputtered with rage. "Are you going to believe the words of a man who was found with a lockpick in his possession?"

"I screamed!" Cordelia screamed. "Isn't that evidence enough?"

The captain was unflustered. "Alaeddin Bey stated that you invited him to your cabin, and that you screamed when you changed your mind at the last minute." He turned to Augustus. "As for the lockpick, where is it?"

Augustus stiffened. He had been hasty giving it to Faisal.

"I'm not sure. Several people saw it."

The captain nodded. "That was indeed in their statements. But I ask you, do any of you know what a lockpick looks like? Does the baronet?"

Augustus couldn't answer that without being put in a position to answer a series of awkward questions.

I've constructed my life in such a way that it is impossible to speak frankly with ordinary people.

The captain went on. "You all saw a strange piece of metal by the door to Miss Ruskin's cabin. You assumed it was a lockpick, because you assumed, in your gentlemanly or matronly manner, that Alaeddin Bey had broken in. What in fact you saw was mostly likely some piece of marine machinery unfamiliar to you. And I cannot check because it has gone missing."

"But why did you release him?" Cordelia asked. "Surely he should be kept until there's been a hearing. You yourself told me you would get in touch tomorrow and tell me the court date."

The police captain stiffened. "I am sorry, madam, but we have decided not to press charges. The evidence is only circumstantial. We have numerous witnesses who said you made unseemly advances on Alaeddin Bey throughout your trip from Cairo. Whatever happened when you opened your door to him, the fact of the matter is that you have no real case. No one saw what happened, and no one has any real evidence against him."

"This is ridiculous!" Aunt Pearl bellowed. "The Turk laid hands on my niece and all you do is talk about evidence?"

"Let's go," Augustus said.

"But—" Aunt Pearl protested.

"Let's go," Augustus insisted.

Cordelia sighed. "Yes, Aunt Pearl. We should go."

Outside, the afternoon sun searing into them, they huddled under the shade of a dusty palm tree by the sidewalk and conferred.

"This is a cover up," Augustus said. "Alaeddin Bey has connections among the local constabulary. There's no other explanation."

"You think the captain is a party to Alaeddin Bey's crimes?" Cordelia asked.

"To some extent, I think he is," Augustus said. "He would have surely held him for a hearing. While he's technically correct about the circumstantial nature of the evidence, any honest English policeman would take the side of two women, a knight, and a baronet over a Turk."

"So now what?" Cordelia asked.

Augustus rubbed his chin. "Good question. Thank you, both of you, for not revealing your true identities."

Aunt Pearl thumped the tip of her parasol on the pavement. "At this point it would bring shame on the Russell name."

Cordelia gave her aunt a smile. "Be that as it may, I'm more concerned with the case. If we let the cat out of the bag now, we'd never solve it. Thomas would just come down and muddle the whole affair even further."

Augustus cocked his head and studied the girl for a moment. Was she actually trying to one-up her brother, just as he so enjoyed doing?

They hailed a carriage and made their way back to the hotel. The heat was oppressive. It had been a year since Augustus had last been to the south and he had forgotten just how bad it could be, even in the winter.

Once the ladies had bidden him goodbye in the lobby, he got another surprise.

"There are two messages for you, sir," the concierge said. "A telegram and a note."

The telegram was a cryptic message that must have come from Moustafa, judging by the Nubian name of the sender, a name that belonged to none of his associates. While he couldn't quite puzzle it out, it seemed to warn of some greater danger than the mesmerist and that Moustafa was on his way.

Augustus smiled, his mood lightening. Good old Moustafa. He knew that man couldn't keep himself away from a mystery!

But when would he get here? The papers said the railway had been cut.

Next he looked at the note—a plain white envelope containing a single sheet of paper with elegant handwriting in French.

He could not have been more surprised at what it contained.

"Dear Sir Augustus,

"My deepest apologies to Miss Ruskin for falling for the trap that she set. I should have known that she was too virtuous of a woman to ever make the suggestions she did. Do let her know that my apology is mixed with admiration for a game well played.

"Now on to other matters. For the sake of both our sides I suggest a truce. We have a common enemy, one known only partially to me and not at all to you. I cannot risk putting this information down on paper, so I suggest that we meet on the riverside at 5 PM tonight, one mile south of the Winter Palace. It is an open area, well in view of the esplanade and some of the lesser hotels. The landmark you should look for is a statue on the esplanade of General Stewart. You will be in no danger and you may bring whatever reinforcements you see fit. I will come alone. I wish to discuss our mutual problem and come to an understanding and, if I dare hope such a thing, a resolution."

Kindest Regards,
Alaeddin Bey"

Augustus read the missive a second time to assure himself his eyes weren't deceiving him, and then folded it and put it in his pocket. A strange feeling came over him. What had the mesmerist said in their last session, something about allowing foes to become friends?

He returned to the concierge, intending on asking about how the note was delivered.

Instead he got cut off by Faisal.

"He was here!" the boy said.

"I know. He left me a note."

Faisal's eyes widened as Augustus told him its contents.

"What could it mean?" Faisal asked.

Augustus made a helpless gesture with his hand. "For once I am at a loss. What did the mesmerist do?"

"I saw him come in. I was outside. There was … a disturbance here in the hotel. Some people complaining about a painting or something. Silly foreigner stuff. Anyway, I saw him get out of a carriage and walk right up the steps like he wasn't afraid of anything. I hid behind a potted plant but he saw me."

"What did he do?"

"Nothing. That was the strange part. I thought he was going to cast a spell on me or something, but he just said, 'Good day, Faisal' and passed on through to the lobby. I peeked in and saw him writing a note at that big desk in front."

"That was the note for me."

"Maybe. He wrote two notes."

"Two notes?"

Faisal nodded. "Then the magician came out, said goodbye to me even though I had hidden behind a different potted plant, and got into a carriage."

"We must find out who the other note was for."

"You could ask the man at the desk," Faisal suggested.

"No, they'll honor the guest's privacy, whoever he or she is. Oh, the cheeky cad might have written a note to Cordelia!"

"Is she all right?"

Augustus looked at him. "I'm surprised you care."

Faisal shrugged. "She's not bad, just annoying."

Augustus laughed. "Right you are. I have an idea. Come."

He entered the lobby, the boy staying close behind and looking nervously around him. Faisal probably thought Alaeddin Bey might appear in a puff of smoke. Considering the twists and turns this case was taking, Augustus wouldn't be surprised.

He went up to the concierge. "May I trouble you for a pen and a piece of paper?"

The man got them, and Augustus wrote a note. It was to no one, and contained nothing. He merely wanted the chance to study the letter boxes, having memorized the room numbers of each of his companions.

The only one with a note was Heinrich's.

After some searching, they found Heinrich tucked comfortably in an armchair in one of the hotel's several lounges, a whiskey by his side and his nose in a book.

"Holiday over, my friend. You have a note from Alaeddin Bey."

The German scholar stared at him in shock. "How truly remarkable. Spending time with you is full of surprises."

He retrieved the note and read it to Augustus.

"*Dear Herr Schäfer,*

"*I must thank you for a most intellectually stimulating time aboard the* Arabia. *Our discussions on hypnotism, psychology, and Egyptology will be treasured memories for many years to come.*

"*I must regretfully, however, add a slight criticism to my praise. You are a clever man, very clever. But you made one slip. I recognized your name. I have an excellent memory for names, and just a few months ago you wrote a letter to the* Egyptian Gazette *in response to an article they printed on hypnotism in which the reporter called it chicanery. You defended the new science, but added, and I will never forget these words, 'any so-called hypnotist who stands on stage rather than sits in front of the psychologist's couch is nothing but a cheap vaudeville clown.' And then you make friends with the likes of me! So I began to watch you, and saw how you would confer and sneak around the ship. Soon the connection between you and Sir Augustus became apparent. I saw that his servant boy was far more than that, and that strange woman with the daring mode of apparel was in on it too.*

"*What I did not see was that Cordelia was also part of the plan. Bravo. You took the intellectual front, trying to discover my intent and get me to let down my guard. Sir Augustus and Faisal took the investigative duties. Jocelyn was surprisingly effective at a certain juncture. But it was Cordelia who truly fooled me. While I could tell that she was familiar to all of you, I underestimated her intelligence (might I say craftiness?) and became besotted with her beauty. That made me fall into her trap.*

"*But there are bigger traps set for all of us, my German friend. I have offered an olive branch to Sir Augustus. I am hoping that you can reason with his overly impulsive nature to accept. For all our sakes.*

Kindest Regards,

Alaeddin Bey"

"Overly impulsive nature!" Augustus repeated. "What cheek!"

"What does it say? What does it say?" Faisal asked, tugging on his sleeve. The note had been in French.

"One moment," he said, dismissing the boy with a gesture. He turned back to Heinrich. "This man is daring, I'll give him that. Why do you think he's doing this? He got released from jail. Why on earth would he come straight back to the people who tried to imprison him?"

"This 'bigger trap' he mentions sounds serious," Heinrich said, and glanced at Faisal who was bouncing from one foot to the other. "Do translate for the boy before his head explodes."

Augustus did so. Heinrich was right. Neither of them would be able to think straight until the boy stopped bothering them.

Faisal listened with rapt attention.

"He knows us well, Englishman."

"Nonsense. I'm not impulsive."

Faisal rolled his eyes. "Of course not, Englishman. But he's fooled us all. Well, almost all of us. I think he's not up to any tricks with the truce. I think he really wants to talk."

"Why do you say that?"

"Because he's afraid. Not of us, though. If he was afraid of us he'd get out of Luxor on the first boat or train. He's afraid of someone else, so afraid he thinks that running won't save him. He wants our help."

"And the police captain was told to back off," Augustus said, rubbing his chin. "Very well, we'll meet him at this rendezvous, but we will not do it under his conditions."

"What do you mean?"

"We'll get there early, and we'll come armed. If this turns out to be a trap, we'll be ready for him."

So an hour before the arranged meeting, Augustus and Faisal found themselves on the baking bank of the Nile. It had taken some time to shoo away the hucksters trying to sell them antiquities, or a ride on a donkey or felucca, but they had finally managed when Augustus foolishly agreed to buy Faisal a melon, at which point all the hucksters returned and the entire process had to start again.

At last they had the strand to themselves.

Or at least it appeared so.

Jocelyn was positioned on the shaded terrace of a second-story cafe that, while being a cafe of the lower sort for middle-class travelers mixed with some of the more well-to-do locals, offered a fine view of the riverside. Given the glare of the sun and the shade of her position, she could not be seen from the riverside while she could see all. If she spotted danger she was instructed to fire a shot from the revolver she kept in her handbag, whether in the air as a warning, or into the body of some suspicious individual, was left to her own discretion.

Now all they had to do was wait.

Faisal grew restless, and annoying. The melon had disappeared all too quickly and now he pestered Augustus with questions and doubts.

"Why are we falling into his trap? You know he's going to cast a spell on us."

"There's no such thing as spells. And if you say he's going to summon a river djinn to drown us, I'll drown you myself."

"Fine. He's going to shoot us."

"Unlikely. He doesn't appear to be the violent sort. And I believe he wants to make peace."

"How can you trust someone like him?"

Augustus didn't have an answer to that. He just felt, in a strange, inexplicable way, that it was true.

Spotting the skeletal remains of a calf at the edge of a field by the river, he hit upon an idea to keep the boy quiet.

The Englishman walked over and picked up two of the calf's knuckle joints.

"What are you going to do with those, you silly Englishman? They're too old to make soup."

"I'm not going to make soup, you silly Egyptian, I'm going to make a pair of clubs."

"Hey! Who are you calling silly? You'd never solve these crimes without me."

"That is entirely possible."

"I wish Moustafa was here," Faisal said more quietly. "Things are a lot easier with him around."

"But he always smacks you."

"Yes," Faisal said, nodding. "But things are easier too."

"Look, there's a stroke of luck. A leather worker is passing with his cart. We can do this right now."

"Do what?"

"You'll see."

Augustus went over to the leather dealer and bought a cured hide from him. By now the afternoon had advanced enough that hardly anyone remained in sight, and they didn't get mobbed as was typically the case any time a foreigner spent money.

Returning to the riverside, Augustus cut the hide into long strips, hunted up a pair of stout sticks that he cut to the correct length, and started wrapping one of the bones on the end of each stick.

"That sure would hurt," Faisal said, squatting next to him and watching.

"That's the intention."

"But why make two? Am I getting one?"

"Certainly not. It's for someone back in Cairo. He had one and it got taken."

"Who?"

"Sir Thomas Russell Pasha."

Faisal recoiled. "The policeman!"

"The same."

"But he's bad! He's killed thousands of Egyptians."

"Only a few dozen during the riots, and the rioters killed at least that many Europeans and fellow Egyptians."

Faisal stared at the Englishman.

"How could you be so foolish? Everyone knows Russell Pasha had gunned down the independence crowds and packed the Citadel full of heroes."

"I didn't know you've become an independence activist."

Faisal shrugged. "I'm not. Why should I be? If the Egyptians were in charge they wouldn't care about the street boys any more than the English do. But I hear things. Lots of things. You hide inside your house so much it's like you're deaf."

"Just because I gave you a boat ride and a hotel room doesn't mean you get to be familiar. Here, hold this."

Faisal held the handle up to the knuckle bone as Augustus worked on it. After a moment, Faisal said, "I thought you didn't like him. You always say so."

"He's an ass."

"Then why do you want to make him a club?"

"I've been told that I should value the people around me more than I do at present. Jocelyn said so. Oddly enough, so did our mesmerist friend. If I can value a fool such as Sir Thomas, then I suppose I can value anyone. Here are some strips of leather. You make one and I shall finish the other, all right?"

"All right. But I'm making yours, not Russell Pasha's."

"Fair's fair."

They set the bones against the end of the sticks and wound the leather straps around them, leaving the round part of the knuckle bone exposed before tying off the leather. Then they soaked them in the Nile and set them out to dry.

"Don't leave yours in the sun, you silly Englishman. It will dry too quickly and the leather will crack. Put it in the shade of this palm tree like I did."

"Hmm. Good point. How do you know so much about it?"

"I know lots of things."

"The sun is weaker in England. If you want to dry something there, you have to leave it exposed."

"Is that why English people are so pale?"

"I suppose so."

"They are only pale when they first get here, or if they are women and hide from the sun. Englishmen who have been here a short time are all red.

They look very funny. Only after you've lived here for a while do you look brown like normal people."

"It's been a long time since I've been accused of looking normal."

Faisal gave him an angry glance. "I wish you'd stop that."

"Stop what?"

"Thinking about your face all the time."

As soon as Faisal said it, he got a frightened look.

Augustus turned away and looked out over the river.

It always comes back to that, doesn't it?

He lit a cigarette to give his hands something to do.

Faisal stood still for a moment, then started moving around, gathering up all the spare bits of stick and leather left behind from the job. After a minute he stopped.

"Sorry, Englishman."

Augustus half turned his head. "Sorry for what?"

"Saying that."

"Oh, I'm not angry, just curious."

Faisal scratched his head. "Curious about what?"

"Just what the hell am I supposed to think about."

"Your friends, Englishman."

"And who would those be?"

"What do you mean? You have breakfast with Russell Pasha at Shepheard's Hotel all the time. And Moustafa felt really bad about having to leave,"—Augustus made a derisive snort and Faisal hurried to continue—"and then there's Mr. Jocelyn and the German with the chocolate and um, lots of people."

"You're leaving out Aunt Pearl and Cordelia."

"The first time I met Aunt Pearl, she hit me with her parasol."

"Yes, she did," Augustus said, amusement breaking through the darkness. "Cordelia never hit you."

"No, but you don't want to marry her."

Augustus turned. Faisal clamped a hand over his mouth.

"You seem to know quite a lot about me. How do you know I breakfast with Sir Thomas at Shepheard's? And how did you know that silly girl was still pestering me? Haven't I told you not to follow me?"

"But I'm useful!"

"That doesn't mean you can dog my footsteps everywhere I go."

"I don't … all the time."

"Well, don't do it any of the time."

"Then I won't be around when you need me."

"Well, maybe I don't need you all the time!" Augustus snapped.

Alaeddin Bey's voice called over the riverside. "Perhaps you need to see further than your own mask, my English friend."

The two of them whirled. The mesmerist, dressed in a western-style suit and with a fedora perched atop a large bandage wound around his head, came off the esplanade and across the sandy riverside toward them.

"How the devil did he get past Jocelyn?" Augustus muttered, his anger at Faisal forgotten.

"Magic," Faisal whispered. "He's too clever for us, Englishman."

CHAPTER TWENTY-NINE

Moustafa stumbled through the hot Luxor sun, exhausted and dehydrated. He had spent the last of his money getting here, and had none for a carriage ride from the train station to the Winter Palace Hotel.

The train ride down had been a nightmare, eighteen hours of constant vigil and pain, his head and body weak from loss of blood and his nerves torn to shreds by the fear that at every stop, a gang of killers would gun him down through the windows or rush onto the train to stab him to death. He had taken to feigning stomach upset and hiding in the privy at every stop, but that only made the fear worse, because each time he returned to his seat there would be new people in the carriage, new people who could easily be assassins.

By the grace of God he had made it, and now he stumbled along the esplanade—weak, hot, tired, thirsty, the paving stones wavering under his uncertain steps. He thought he caught disparaging comments called after him, the occasional taunt, but he paid no attention. He had to get to the hotel, had to warn the others.

At last it appeared up ahead. Staggering up the sweeping staircase, he found the front entrance blocked by a glowering doorman.

"The hotel bar is for guests only," he said. "Find some place in town."

"I'm not here to drink," Moustafa gasped, leaning against the doorframe. "And I'm not drunk. I'm sick, and I need to see my boss. He's staying here."

"If your boss is really staying here, he won't want to see you in the state you're in. Go to a hammam and make yourself decent."

"Out of my way you louse-ridden son of a dog!" Moustafa bellowed.

The man leapt backwards as if his shoes were fitted with springs. Moustafa stormed through the door. Everyone in the lobby stared at him.

By sheer good fortune, Herr Schäfer walked by just as several members of staff converged on him.

"Leave him alone!" the professor said, raising a hand. "He's with me."

"Thank God I've found you," Moustafa said, practically falling into his arms. Now that he saw a friendly face, he knew everything would be all right.

At least he hoped so.

"Are the others all right?" he asked as Herr Schäfer led him to a chair.

"Yes, at the moment. Alaeddin Bey asked to meet Sir Augustus. Faisal went with them. I'm afraid it might be a trap, so Jocelyn is on lookout. At least it's in a public place. There's so much to explain I don't know where to start."

Moustafa shook his head. "He's not the real danger."

Herr Schäfer ordered a waiter to bring some lemonade and sandwiches. Then they traded all the information they had, only stopping when the waiter brought the meal and Moustafa gratefully wolfed it down.

Once he finished, he said, "That false official from the Ministry of Agriculture, he must be one of the Invisible Scorpions."

Herr Schäfer nodded gravely. "It sounds like the local chief of police is one too, or at least in their pocket."

"We're all on our own, as usual," Moustafa said with a sigh. "At least I was able to sneak a gun and a knife down here. Every time a conductor asked to see my ticket I thought I was going to have a heart attack. Now show me where Mr. Wall and Faisal are. I must join them and make sure they're safe."

Herr Schäfer looked past him. "They're safe. In fact, here they are."

Mr. Wall, Faisal, Jocelyn, and a man of indeterminate race with a bandage on his head entered the front door. Moustafa stood, already feeling better from the refreshment, and waved. Faisal spotted them from across the lobby.

"Moustafa!"

The boy ran over and hugged him around the middle.

"You came! I knew you wouldn't give up on us!"

Moustafa hugged him back and smiled. "I'm glad to see you're all right, Little Infidel, and the cleanest I've ever seen you. Now keep your voice down. We're in danger."

Mr. Wall came up and shook his hand. "Glad you could make it."

"I have some information about what we're facing," Moustafa said. "I've been busy back in Cairo."

"Let's go up to my room and discuss it. But first may I introduce you to Alaeddin Bey."

Moustafa blinked. "You have always been full of surprises, Mr. Wall, but I didn't expect this."

Herr Schäfer looked equally surprised. "I was half expecting your meeting to be a trap."

"So did I, but it turns out Alaeddin Bey is in as much danger as we are, and is willing to make a deal to save his own skin and no doubt ours. We're after bigger prey than a pickpocketing, philandering mesmerist."

"Yes," Moustafa said, lowering his voice. "We're after the Invisible Scorpions."

Alaeddin Bey trembled a little. "So you know of them."

"They nearly killed me. I need a hotel doctor. Perhaps we can go to one of the rooms to discuss all this and you can call one?"

"We can't risk that," Mr. Wall said. "I'm sure Heinrich has mentioned that Cordelia came along. She's a nurse."

"You can't seem to shake her, Mr. Wall," Moustafa said and laughed. They moved to the stairs.

"Mr. Jocelyn is here too," Faisal said, skipping along beside him. "I'll go get him. He's been very helpful."

Within a few minutes, they had gathered in Mr. Wall's room. Propriety was forgotten as Cordelia and Jocelyn came too. Aunt Pearl was taking a nap and would know nothing.

As Cordelia came into the room, she strode up to Alaeddin Bey and gave him a hard slap across the face. The mesmerist appeared unphased.

"I most certainly deserve that, madam, for thinking so ill of you as to fall for your ruse, but I feel compelled to point out that it was you who initiated it."

That earned him a slap on the other cheek. Moustafa looked on in confusion.

Alaeddin Bey bowed and turned to Mr. Wall. "Now that that's done with, may I say what you brought me here to say?"

"You may," Mr. Wall said.

"Everything you suspected of me is true. I will tell all, but first I ask that Faisal leave the room so as not to sully his innocent ears."

Moustafa snorted.

"I want to stay and hear this!" Faisal whined.

"Out you go," Mr. Wall said, ushering him out of the room. "And no listening at the door. I'll be checking."

"I will speak English as an extra precaution," Alaeddin Bey said. "Although he probably knows more of that language than he lets on. No matter how much you check on him, Sir Augustus, he will outwit you."

"You're a perceptive man," Moustafa grumbled. "I'll give you that."

Alaeddin Bey smiled and addressed the gathering. "To the ladies I must apologize in advance for what I am about to say, but you are both women of some worldly experience and have no doubt guessed much of the truth. I have made my living fleecing tourists in the most efficient way possible. I have played on their own weaknesses. So many foreigners come here to sample the supposed sins of the East, both men and woman, that I was easily able fool the men and seduce the women. I apologize once again, Miss Ruskin, for assuming you were one of that sort, but I must tell you that not all of the fair sex share your sense of virtue. Mr. Beechcroft's daughter Harriet was one of them. Through her I got the combination to their safe and took the money and papers you mentioned."

"Now wait a moment," Herr Schäfer said, "It is well known that one cannot make the hypnotic subject do anything they do not truly want to do."

The mesmerist nodded, smiling slightly. "Your natural decency outweighs your scientific vigor, my friend. Everything my subjects did they did entirely of their own free will. Harriet Beechcroft visited me in my cabin out of desire for me and a rebellious streak against her father, who portrayed himself to the world as a social conservative, as most secret sinners do. But she was not a stupid girl. She saw quite clearly that her father was a hypocrite, and while she did not know the true nature of the acts he committed on his 'evening walks' in Cairo, she had her suspicions. To punish his hypocrisy, and out of love for me, she gave me the combination to the safe."

"But what about your other victims?" Moustafa asked as Cordelia set a washbasin beside him and opened up her medical bag. Moustafa rolled up his sleeve to reveal his homemade bandage, caked with dried blood.

"Oh my, you have had a run-in with our common enemy," the mesmerist said. "I'll get to them in a moment. To answer your question, all my victims have been willing to some extent. Well, not the ones I pickpocketed, although many of those were men I brought to houses of ill-repute. For the weaker-minded among them, I gave hypnotic suggestions to act with more generosity in their lives. That sparked their guilt complexes and more often than not turned into a good tip for me."

"Ah, I see!" Herr Schäfer. "And the regression to childhood was to bring them back to a purer time, so they would feel guilty about what they had become and thus not press charges against you, blaming themselves for being victims."

"Quite correct, Herr Schäfer."

"You tried that on Cordelia and I," Mr. Wall said. "What was the motive there?"

"Well, in Cordelia's case it was to gain her trust. She played her part well and fooled me into thinking she was another Harriet Beechcroft. In your case, Sir Augustus, it was to gain your belief. After the first session you took the science of mesmerism more seriously, did you not?"

"I did," Mr. Wall conceded. It was a rare sight to see him admit he was wrong. Moustafa would have given much to have been present at the hypnotism session.

"And after that you were much more open to my suggestion at the second session. Do you remember what that was?"

Mr. Wall looked away. "To forgive those I saw as enemies."

"Indeed. I saw you as a man with no shortage of anger at the past, if you forgive my saying so. And because of the psychological preparation I gave you in that second session, you were open to meeting with you when I suggested it."

"Nonsense! I did that because you yourself were robbed, and I saw we were dealing with a larger conspiracy."

Alaeddin Bey bowed. "Whatever you say, Sir Augustus."

Moustafa hissed as he felt a pain in his arm.

"This is a nasty cut," Cordelia said, working on his wound as he held it over the washbasin. It took some time to remove his crude bandage, and that got the cut bleeding again. "Fortunately it isn't too deep. You won't require stitches if I bind it tightly enough. You'll have a nasty scar, I'm afraid."

"The latest of many," Moustafa couldn't help but grumble. He turned to Alaeddin Bey. "So you got robbed of Mr. Beechcroft's papers, eh? Tell us about that."

"I was just about to, good sir. Yes, I did get robbed by that man pretending to be from the Ministry of Agriculture. He was an agent of the Invisible Scorpions. Let me assure you that I have never worked for them, although I have known about them for several months now. I heard rumors of a large, secret criminal gang of that name, but had paid little attention. The gangs tend to be based in the cities, especially Cairo and Alexandria and Port Suez. And then of course the Bedouin have their own criminal activity. I thought myself safe, working mainly from tourist boats and the finer hotels. The Bedouin have no power on the river, and the gangs, when they use the river, use it for smuggling or for escaping justice, and steer clear of the tourist boats."

"So what changed?" Moustafa asked.

Alaeddin Bey sighed, and rubbed his temples. "The Invisible Scorpions are ambitious. They've spread to most cities. I now hear they're trying to get the Bedouin tribes to submit to them. They want to run all crime in Egypt, and they see the tour boats as an opportunity. During the war, tourism all but died out, and so they didn't bother with it. But now that the tourists are beginning to return, they want to get their fingers in the tourist trade."

"And so they contacted you," Mr. Wall said.

"They did indeed, and when they did I realized I was up against a formidable foe. I take it you know what is in the Beechcroft papers?"

"I know enough," Mr. Wall said.

"Then we will not discuss the matter in front of the ladies. I will just say that my command of English in 1913 was not what it is today. The Beechcrofts and I conversed mostly in French. When I stole the papers, I had a bit of trouble understanding certain … technical terms. I knew a backstreet surgeon who had been educated at one of the English-run medical schools, a surgeon who specialized in removing bullets no questions asked. I assumed he would be discreet. For a fee he explained the papers to me. I had struck gold, but then the war intervened and I had no chance to act. Even after the war I had difficulty tracking down Mr. Beechcroft's address, since he had moved within the United States by then. I was just planning to act when the Invisible Scorpions contacted me."

Alaeddin Bey rubbed his temple again, and this time his hand trembled.

"It turns out that surgeon wasn't so discreet after all. The Invisible Scorpions had him in their pocket, using him to patch up their men after their frequent battles with other gangs. He got into some trouble with them, I have not been able to ascertain what. He lost their trust, and with the Invisible Scorpions that is a death sentence. To save himself he told them about me and the papers I had in my possession. So they made me an offer—work for them, splitting the take fifty-fifty, or leave Egypt."

The mesmerist raised his hands in the air.

"But I cannot leave Egypt. For reasons I do not wish to explain, there is nowhere else for me to go. And I will not be bullied by some gang of street thugs. I am no man's slave. So I temporized. I said I would do as they wished. That was two voyages ago. On the first voyage I managed to trick them into thinking I got very little. Their share was so low, I hoped they would lose interest. They searched my cabin and hotel room and found almost nothing. I had tricked my prey into giving me gifts, you see. A month's stay at one of the nicer residential hotels, for example. There was precious little for the Invisible Scorpions to take."

"I'm surprised they fell for that," Jocelyn said.

"They did the first time. Not the second. After receiving another disappointing share, they said that a third time would mean death. I was left with a stark choice. Then I heard of Ms. Trasher's collection for the orphanage. This could be my salvation. I would rob her, and then continue up the Nile to Khartoum. Although the Invisible Scorpions have agents in the Soudan, they are not as strong there as they are here. With a change of costume and modus operandi, I could disappear there and resume operations on a quieter level."

"But they suspected you'd flee?" Moustafa asked.

"I do not think so. But they worried I would disappear with the Beechcroft papers. Those were more valuable to them than myself, so they sent an agent to steal them."

"Do you have any idea where they took them?" Mr. Wall asked.

"None."

Moustafa hissed as Cordelia started binding his wound. "So you had nothing to do with the murder of Detective Lowell?"

Alaeddin Bey gave him a hurt look. "I have many sins marked against me in the Book of Life. Murder will never be one of them."

"So it was the Invisible Scorpions all along," Moustafa said. The killer must have left the bloody cloth behind the brothel to implicate Alaeddin Bey, since he was known to bring tourists there. Perhaps the gang wanted extra leverage against him.

"Right. We need to plan what to do," Mr. Wall said. "Alaeddin Bey, you will have to leave us for this part."

"I understand. I will wait in the library downstairs."

"Not on your life." Mr. Wall opened the hotel room door. To Moustafa's surprise, the Little Infidel wasn't on the other side. "Faisal! Where are you?"

Faisal appeared a moment later. "What?"

"Come in. We need to plan. Alaeddin Bey, go into the bathroom and close the door. Everyone, we'll speak in a whisper so he can't hear."

Alaeddin Bey did as he was told. After the door shut, Faisal hurried out onto the balcony.

"What are you doing?" Moustafa asked.

"Keeping an eye on him."

"The window is too small for him to get out," Mr. Wall said, "and besides, it's a sheer drop down two floors."

"He could turn into a bird."

"You have the brain of a bird, you idiot street runt!" Moustafa shouted.

Faisal grinned. "It's good to have you back."

"Keep still," Cordelia said, "I need to finish with this bandage."

Moustafa did as he was asked.

"Thank you," he said, examining her handiwork. She had done an excellent job.

"Now recount everything you learned in Cairo," Mr. Wall said.

Ignoring the pain that still lingered in his arm, Moustafa retold his story from the start, not leaving anything out. He had long since learned that even the smallest detail could be important.

When he got to the part about the code words, Herr Schäfer leapt to his feet.

"I have it!" he cried.

"What?" Moustafa asked.

"'The most select of places.' That's what the ancients called Karnak temple," the German scholar said.

Mr. Wall smacked a fist into his palm. "Good job! That must be their meeting place. It sounds like this Sekhmet woman has a taste for ancient history, and wishes to evoke the same sort of feeling in her followers."

"And the same sort of dread," Moustafa said. "Sekhmet was hardly a kind goddess. But listen to this. I think they might be meeting here very soon."

He went on with his story, finishing by emphasizing the conversation with the man on the telephone.

After he finished, everyone in the room fell silent for a moment.

"We've stumbled into something big," Jocelyn said. "Their meeting at Karnak and their theft of the Beechcroft papers could not be coincidental."

"Mr. Beechcroft is a very wealthy man," Moustafa said. "Perhaps they hope to use the blackmail money to expand their operations."

Mr. Wall nodded. "Indeed. What we need to do now is—"

A knock on the door made everyone whirl in that direction. Moustafa, Mr. Wall, and Jocelyn all reached for their guns.

"Who is it?" Mr. Wall demanded without approaching the door.

"Room service."

"I didn't order room service," Mr. Wall said in a whisper.

Moustafa crouched behind the chair, which was heavy and might stop a bullet. He leveled the revolver he had taken from the Invisible Scorpions. Mr. Wall and Jocelyn moved to opposite sides of the door, Jocelyn crouching so she wouldn't be in Mr. Wall's line of fire.

"*Eroom servisss?*" Faisal said in a poor imitation of English before switching back into Arabic. "Don't worry, I ordered that."

"Who said you could order room service?" Moustafa demanded, not leaving his post behind the chair.

"The Englishman."

"I most certainly did not."

"You wanted me to pretend to be your servant. That means I get to tell the hotel staff what you want." He turned to Moustafa, his eyes going wide. "Have you ever heard of room service? They bring food right to your room. Whatever you want!"

Faisal opened the door as the adults quickly held their guns. Moustafa and Jocelyn stood so as not to look strange. Just as the boy promised, one of the hotel staff pushed in a large cart, its wheels groaning under the weight of an enormous feast.

"This must cost a fortune!" Moustafa said once they had gotten rid of the servant.

"You gave us some good clues," Faisal said as he sat down and started uncovering the dishes one by one. "So you deserve your share. So do I."

With that, Faisal tucked in.

"You might as well eat, Moustafa," Mr. Wall said. "I think we all have a long night ahead of us."

CHAPTER THIRTY

Faisal felt so much better now that Moustafa was back. He was the best fighter ever, and even wounded he'd make everyone a whole lot safer.

And they'd need to be safe, because now the Englishman was leading them into the giant temple Faisal had seen in the German's book.

As if magicians and murderers and thieves and secret societies weren't enough, now the Englishman wanted to go into a temple full of giant pharaohs and djinn!

There had better be a moving picture theater in Luxor. The Englishman was going to owe him a lot.

He walked with the Englishman and Jocelyn. They pretended to be tourists while Faisal pretended to be a servant and walked with a picnic basket. Jocelyn had explained what a picnic basket was. It was a covered wicker basket where you put a bunch of food to eat outside. That sounded like a good idea, because you never knew when you'd get hungry.

But being Englishmen, they hadn't put anything in the basket except some spare ammunition and a couple of knives. No food at all! Faisal had told them it would be better for their disguise to put in some bread and some olives and some falafel and maybe a few sweets. Not too many, just enough to make it look realistic. But they said they "didn't have time to go food shopping."

No time? The temple or giant's palace or djinn city or whatever it was had been around for a million years and they had to get to it right away? Silly Englishmen!

Faisal soon forgot about his stomach as they walked down a wide road with rows of sphinxes on either side. They weren't as big as the sphinx at Giza, but there were hundreds of them, a whole army of djinn turned into stone. Good thing they were visiting in the daytime. The sun wouldn't set for another couple of hours.

"What did you do with the magician?" Faisal asked.

"Alaeddin Bey is handcuffed to the pipe in my bathroom. Aunt Pearl is guarding him," the Englishman said.

"Is that why you had me steal a chamber pot from the servants' quarters?"

The Englishman smiled. "Yes."

Moustafa and Heinrich walked well behind them, almost out of sight. The Englishman wanted to split up to look around better. He said this was the biggest djinn place in all of Egypt.

Great.

Far behind them, almost out of sight, the Avenue of Sphinxes, as the Englishman called it, led to another temple, big but not as big as the one they were heading to. Of course they had to go to the biggest one.

"Is there a moving picture theater in Luxor?" Faisal asked to take his mind off the crazy amount of danger they were walking into.

"I haven't checked," the Englishman replied.

"I noticed in the local newspaper that there is," Jocelyn said.

"Oh, that's good!" Faisal said. "Let's go see something."

"We have more important things to do, Faisal," the Englishman said.

"I was afraid you were going to say that. So what are we looking for? These Invisible Scorpions aren't going to meet in the temple in the daytime, are they?"

"Probably not. This is a scouting mission. You see, while Karnak is dedicated to Amun-Re, the Sun god, there are several temples to other gods and goddesses within the precinct. One of them is dedicated to Sekhmet. I have a hunch we might find something interesting there. Heinrich knows where it is."

They approached one of those big gates the ancients liked. An Egyptian stood at the gate selling tickets.

"Oh, look, you have to buy a ticket," Faisal said. "I bet they don't let Egyptians in."

"I'll get you in," the Englishman said. "Don't worry."

The Englishman paid while Faisal looked around uncertainly. Those rows of stone djinn seemed to stare at him. He gave a little shiver as he and the Englishmen passed through the gate into a great big courtyard filled with statues. On the back side of the gate were carvings of a pharaoh smashing Libyans.

"Hey, that's the picture I saw in the German's book!"

"What a good memory," Jocelyn said. "Isn't he a clever boy, Augustus?"

"He has his moments."

I'd rather not be clever and not be here.

They continued deeper into the temple. The German got all excited and pointed this way and that, talking very fast to Moustafa, who looked all around him eagerly. The Englishman and Jocelyn were talking too, in English this time. From some of the words he could tell they were talking about ancient stuff. Faisal didn't mind being left out.

A few other foreigners walked around, the men in great big sun hats and the women with white dresses and parasols. Some were led by Egyptian guides who pointed out the statues and carvings to them like they couldn't see anything themselves.

They passed through another gate and Faisal stopped short with a gasp.

Before him stood a forest of massive stone columns stretching as far as the eye could see. Each of them was covered in the old picture writing. High above, he could see parts of the roof still in place, big rectangular blocks resting on the tops of the columns. On the lower sides were carvings of big vultures. At night, he bet they came to life, detached from their perches, and went searching for people to swallow.

He'd seen this in the book too.

For a moment he was too awestruck to be afraid.

A heavy hand rested on his shoulder. Faisal didn't look to see who it was. He was too busy staring at the columns.

"Before you say that djinn made this," Moustafa said, "let me tell you that you made it."

"I never made anything like this."

"No, but people like you did. Egyptians. When the Nubians ruled over this place, we added to it. This is what we can do when we set our minds to it. Do you remember what I told you?"

"That I'm a good-for-nothing lazy guttersnipe?"

"Besides that."

"That's I'm a filthy, flea-bitten sewer rat?"

"That too. Can you think of anything else? Something that I told you to not to forget?"

"You told me not to forget that I'm Egyptian."

"That's right."

They began to walk between the columns. Everyone had stopped talking. A few other tourists were around, but they weren't talking either. Everyone stared at the columns that seem to rise up to the very sky. Each column had different picture writing on them, and Faisal realized there must be a whole book written here, a whole library of books.

Faisal stopped and leaned against one of the columns, looking around. It was hard to see far. The columns blocked your view.

"It would be easy to get lost in here," he said.

"Don't worry, Little Infidel. All you have to do is follow the columns in a straight line and you'll get to one of the walls surrounding this place. From there you can just follow the wall around until you find one of the gates."

Faisal nodded. He'd be sure to remember that.

"What does all this picture writing say?"

"They're called hieroglyphs," Moustafa said. "I taught you that word before. You should try to remember it. They're prayers to the gods, mostly, or boasts by the pharaohs of things they did during their lifetime."

"So spells, mostly?"

"Don't worry. They can't hurt you."

Faisal tore his eyes away from the sight of all those columns and looked at Moustafa.

"Thanks for coming to help us."

Moustafa nodded, his face grave. "Once I discovered you were in more danger than you realized, I knew I had to come."

"Good thing that man only wanted to steal those papers instead of killing us."

"They're being careful. That's a good sign. They don't want to attract too much attention from the authorities before getting a grip on every crime racket in all of Egypt. We can use that against them."

"How?"

"I'm not sure yet."

The German was leading the others in one direction. Faisal and Moustafa followed.

"He's taking us to the temple of the god Ptah," Moustafa said.

"I thought we were supposed to go to the temple of Sekhmet."

"Sekhmet was Ptah's consort."

"What's a consort?"

"His, um, friend. Look around you. You'll need to know every inch of this place."

They passed through a little side gate into large open space filled with broken statues and ruins. A high wall enclosed it. In fact, Faisal noticed it enclosed everything. He felt relieved to see it was broken in places. He wouldn't want to be trapped inside this huge collection of temples.

"Don't worry," Faisal said, his voice trembling a little. "I'm paying attention."

Up ahead, a small temple stood amid the rubble. Well, it wasn't really a *small* temple, but it looked pretty small compared to the giant one they had just left.

It also looked pretty battered, with big gaps in some of the walls and heaps of rubble all around. There were even some palm trees growing inside and around it.

There were still plenty of places for djinn and murderers to hide, though.

They approached from the front, where a few columns stood among the remains of what had been a front hall. It was like a miniature version of the place they had just left. Beyond stood a gate, and through that must be the temple. It looked dark in there, and Faisal realized that more of the roof had survived in this place than in the bigger temple.

Great.

Moustafa and Jocelyn put their hands in their pockets to hold their guns. The Englishman gripped that cane that could turn into a sword. The German didn't have any weapons. Why was he along?

"This temple was built by Thutmose III," Moustafa told Faisal. "He ruled 3,400 years ago."

"Wow."

"The Nubian pharaoh Shabaka restored it about 2,700 years ago, and the Romans did the same."

"Oh." Faisal wasn't really interested in a history lecture right now. He was too worried about what might lurk inside that temple. It was quiet here, away from the main site. He didn't see or even hear any tourists, and because there were no tourists, there were no Egyptians either.

"So what was this Ptah thing? A djinn? A monster?"

"No, Little Infidel, he was the god of creation, who lived before anything was made and created the world. Sekhmet was the goddess of war and has a shrine here too."

"How could they be smart enough to build all this and believe in more than one god? Even the tourists believe in only one god."

Moustafa didn't reply. They had come to the temple. He drew his revolver as they walked through the small hallway of columns, passed through the gate, and entered the shady interior.

They came to a small chamber with two thick columns holding up the roof. Only a few gaps in the roof allowed in light, and the corners of the room lay in shadow.

All the adults had drawn their guns now, except for the German, who looked around curiously as if he was in a museum. As Faisal's eyes adjusted to the dimmer light, he saw the columns and the walls were all decorated with the old picture writing and lots of carvings. Some showed rows of people wearing funny hats and carrying strange things in their hands. Others showed the animal-headed djinn the ancients liked so much. Faisal shuddered and looked away.

A staircase against the inside of the gate led up to an opening in the ceiling. Moustafa went up to check.

"No one," he said when he came back down. "It would make a good sentry post. You get a good view all around."

The German said something and pointed forward. Moustafa and the Englishman led the way.

They came to a strange room, darker than the last one, its walls and ceiling nearly complete. Partial walls separated it into three little niches big enough for them to stand inside.

Two had the remains of statues. At the back of one of the niches was a broken portion of wall Faisal could climb through. A palm tree growing right outside of it kept the opening from letting in much light. Everything in this back room was gloomy and cold.

The third niche held a complete statue.

Faisal's breath caught. It was a female djinn with the head of a lion. She stood taller than a man with a staff in her hand and looked like she had a smile on her animal face.

Smiling because she can't wait to come to life and eat us all.

"Sekhmet," the German said with obvious excitement.

What are you so happy about?

Then Faisal noticed something else—a dark stain on the floor in front of the statue.

"A bloodstain!" Faisal cried, then stopped himself in case the noise woke the djinn. He continued in a lower voice. "She must come alive at night and bring people back here to eat."

"Don't be stupid," Moustafa said.

"He's partially correct," Jocelyn said, kneeling down to examine the stain. Faisal tensed, thinking the djinn would take the chance to bite Jocelyn's head off. "This is a bloodstain. You don't think …"

"A human sacrifice?" Moustafa asked. "I've met these people. I wouldn't put it past them."

The Englishman looked around. "Well, they're not here at the moment. Let's take a look around. Jocelyn and I will study this back area. Moustafa, take Heinrich and study the front chamber and the columned entrance. Faisal, go through that crack in the other niche. That might be a handy back entrance to this place. Check around the temple and the surrounding area. Keep a lookout for anyone coming, and see if you can find anything of interest."

"Do I have to go alone?"

"You're quite safe here in the daytime."

Faisal groaned.

He moved to the far niche. Jocelyn walked with him, which made him feel a bit better, but not much. The djinn could kill the two of them just as easily as Faisal alone.

He took off his sandals, tied them together around his neck, and climbed up the wall. It was easy enough. The cracks between the old stones gave plenty of holds for his fingers and toes. Hauling himself up onto the triangular gap in the wall, he peeked out, blinking at the bright sunlight.

No one was in sight. Heaps of rubble lay on the opposite side of the wall, plus several palm trees. If he had to come into the temple from the back way, he could approach it with a bit of cover and climb in easily. The outside wall was even rougher than the inside.

He let himself down the other side. A few small stones skittered under his feet, rolling down the heap of debris. That was too noisy. He took some time to remove all the small stones around the area so that if he had to sneak in, he could do it quietly. In the distance, he saw a trio of tourists being led by a guide through the main temple. There was a break in the wall at just that spot. Faisal ducked behind the broken head of some pharaoh and waited until they passed out of sight. They didn't even look in his direction.

It sure was quiet and lonely out here. He bet it wasn't at night, though. This place would be crawling with djinn and murderers. He wondered if the Invisible Scorpions were magicians. Maybe they could really turn themselves invisible. Maybe they were watching him right now!

Faisal started studying the outside of the temple. The sooner he got through this and got back to the others, the better.

He didn't have to look for long. On the back corner of the temple he found some strange carvings. They looked sort of like the old picture writing (*hieroglyphs*, Faisal reminded himself) but they weren't old. He could see they had been carved very recently. There was a stonemason in his neighborhood back in Cairo who carved words on the plaques that they put on buildings. These carvings looked like those—all sharp and new, not old and worn like the ancient stuff.

He hurried to the crack in the back wall and climbed back in.

"Hey, I found something!" he cried as he rounded the corner to go back to that djinn statue.

Faisal stopped short. The Englishman and Jocelyn were kissing! On the lips!

Kissing was normal between Egyptian men, but not on the lips. You gave a kiss on each cheek, and the Europeans didn't even do that. And men never, not ever, gave each other kisses on the lips.

"Why are you kissing a man, you silly Englishman!"

Jocelyn turned to him with a smile. "Because I'm a woman, you silly Egyptian."

Faisal blinked. A woman? Was Jocelyn teasing him? But if Jocelyn was teasing him, why would Jocelyn and the Englishman be kissing on the lips?

Faisal looked at Jocelyn's trousers, then at her shirt, which was always puffier than most Englishmen's shirts. He had always thought Jocelyn just liked loose shirts. Then he looked at Jocelyn's beardless face, then back at the trousers.

He remembered the Englishman saying that it wouldn't be appropriate to go to Jocelyn's cabin, and back in Bahariya Oasis they had bathed in the pool separately.

But those trousers …

Wait. She had ridden through Libya alone! How could a woman do that?

"Are you sure you're a woman?" Faisal asked.

"Quite sure."

"So you disguised yourself as a man to sneak through Libya?"

"Well, I suppose you could put it that way."

"Then why are you still in disguise?"

"She's not," his Englishman said. "Everyone here knows she's a woman. Everyone except you, that is."

Faisal ignored him. He was too silly to figure these things out himself.

"But why are you wearing trousers?" he asked Jocelyn.

"Because they're more comfortable than a dress. More practical too."

"But they're for men!"

"Why?"

"Because they are."

"Not for me they aren't."

Faisal cocked his head and studied her. Or him. Or whatever Jocelyn was.

"Are you sure you're a woman?"

"Do I need to prove it to you?"

"Gah! No!"

That got both the Englishmen laughing. Faisal didn't like being laughed at.

Then he had a horrible thought. If Jocelyn was a woman, and they were kissing, it could only mean one thing.

"Are you two getting married?"

"No," Jocelyn said.

The Englishman gave her a look like he wasn't really happy with that answer.

"You sure?"

"My husband was killed in the war. I have no desire to be married again."

Whew! That meant his house on the Englishman's roof was safe.

"You completely, absolutely, positively sure?" Faisal asked.

Jocelyn's face stopped being amused and got that look that mothers get when comforting their children. He'd seen that look lots of times. Of course it had never been directed at him, and it made him feel funny. Happy and sad at the same time.

She bent down and put a hand on top of his head.

"You're worried I'll take him away, aren't you?"

"No."

I cast a spell against that. And it even works for women in trousers.

"I think you are, but you shouldn't be. He pretends he doesn't want you around but he always spends a lot of time with you, doesn't he?"

He does when there's work to be done. Otherwise, not so much.

The Englishman wasn't even looking at them. Instead he was pretending to study the sculpture.

"He does," Jocelyn said, answering her own question. "Now what was this about finding something?"

"Um, right. I found some carvings. But not old carvings. New ones!"

The Englishman turned to him. "Really? Show us."

"This way." Faisal was glad to get out of this conversation and talk about something that made him look useful.

He led them to the carvings.

"Interesting," the Englishman said, nodding appreciatively. "You're quite right that these are new. Look at how fresh the lines are, and how white the stone where it's been chiseled. No weathering at all."

Jocelyn smiled down at him. "I remember Ahmed teaching you some things about Egypt's past when you were in Bahariya. Perhaps you'll be an antiquities dealer like Augustus when you grow up."

Faisal didn't reply. He could tell that Jocelyn was trying to be nice, but he was still confused by what he had just learned.

"These are interesting, very interesting," the Englishman murmured. "Faisal, go find the others. They need to see this."

Faisal ran off, relieved to be out of the situation. He found Moustafa and the German quickly enough and brought them back to study the strange carvings. The German said something in English and shook his head.

"What did he say?" Faisal asked.

"He said that these aren't real hieroglyphs, but rather modern imitations that don't mean anything."

Moustafa talked excitedly to the others, then switched to Arabic.

"But they do mean something, Little Infidel. You've done very well to find these."

Faisal blinked, surprised to be getting a compliment from the Nubian. "So what do they mean?"

"They're similar to the signs I saw in the alley, and near that drinking den the Invisible Scorpions use. I wish I had copied those down, but there wasn't much of a chance either time."

The German must have thought the same thing, because he had pulled out a pencil and a notebook and was drawing a picture of the whole section of wall, including the real picture writing next to the modern stuff.

"But what do they mean?" Faisal said.

"It's some sort of code," the Englishman said., "and it means our hunch was correct. The Invisible Scorpions do use this place for meetings. I suspect they don't come here in the daytime, however."

Faisal's heart sank. He'd been around the Englishman too long not to figure out what he was getting at.

"You don't mean …"

"Yes. We need to come here tonight."

Faisal groaned. Sometimes he hated being useful.

CHAPTER THIRTY-ONE

Back at the hotel, Augustus found Aunt Pearl still on guard in his bathroom, and Alaeddin Bey still handcuffed to the pipe that led to his bathtub.

"Thank you very much for your help," Augustus said to the woman. "Where's Cordelia?"

"In her room or the library. You think I'd let her anywhere near this cad?" Aunt Pearl shot the prisoner an evil look.

"Well said. You are relieved of duty."

"Thank you. I think I'll have my afternoon constitutional and take a nap."

"Place it on my tab."

After she left, Augustus turned to Alaeddin Bey.

"Did she give you a beating? I see the chamber pot is still in one piece."

"I few slaps. I really must protest at this treatment. Can I go now?"

"Protest all you like, and no, you cannot go. Have you ever seen these?" Augustus showed him the glyphs Heinrich had drawn.

"These are astrological symbols."

"Indeed? What do they signify?"

The mesmerist shrugged. "How should I know? Astrology is mere fiddle faddle."

"I won't argue that point, but I thought you studied the mystical arts."

"I study hypnotism and eastern philosophies, not cheap magic and superstition."

"Oh, right. You're a scientist. I forgot."

Alaeddin Bey frowned. "Sarcasm is unbecoming in one of your station. My methods have proven very effective."

"So effective you're handcuffed in my bathroom."

Cordelia's voice came from behind him. "And yet you're listening to him."

Augustus whirled around.

"What the devil are you doing here?"

"Aunt Pearl said you were back so I wanted to see how you were getting on."

"So you just walked into my room? Have you no shame?"

Cordelia smiled and gestured to the mesmerist. "It isn't like you were about to take a bath, not with him shackled there."

"What if people saw? Think of the scandal!"

"No one saw. What's this about astrological symbols?"

Augustus remembered something her brother had said in the garden at Shepheard's Hotel. *Cordelia is enchanted with all the pseudosciences.*

Augustus handed her the notebook. "Do you know what these signify?"

Her eyes lit up. "Oh, how very interesting!"

"I'm glad they're interesting, but what do they mean?"

"It's a set of horoscopes."

"Horoscopes?"

"Yes. But it's a different system than what we use in the West. You probably recognize our astrological symbols even though you are not a student of the science."

"I've seen the symbols in the cheaper papers."

Cordelia did not take up the bait. Instead, she went on as eagerly as before. "These are an old system of symbols used here in Egypt. Not ancient Egypt, but the medieval Egypt of the Mamluks. See, here is the symbol for Saturn in conjunction with Venus. Oh, how appropriate! And the Moon in

Libra. Oh yes, and here's another set with—"

"Yes, but what does it mean? Who are the horoscopes for?"

"It's impossible to say. Perhaps we shouldn't be asking *who*, but *when*."

"I don't follow."

Alaeddin Bey chimed in. "She means they give certain dates."

"Quiet," Augustus snapped.

"He's quite correct," Cordelia said. "It's a list of dates. Despite his many faults, Alaeddin Bey is quite a perceptive man. You should listen to him, especially the advice he gave you during your second hypnotic session. Actually I think you have. You're far less grumpy than you used to be. Yes, much more agreeable."

"That will end quite quickly if you don't tell me the blasted dates!"

Cordelia took a step back and blinked. "Are you getting angry just to prove me wrong?" When Augustus replied only with a grumble, she went on. "These horoscopes are quite complex. I'll have to look them up. Luckily, I packed a reference book on astrology in my luggage."

Of course you did.

Cordelia left.

"It appears you are less susceptible to hypnotic suggestion than some of my subjects," Alaeddin Bey said.

"I beg your pardon?"

"I noted you keep a certain distance from those around you. I was trying to help you with that."

"You should be more concerned with yourself," Augustus growled.

"Did Cordelia make love to me in order to make you jealous?"

"She did it to entrap you, and she succeeded."

"Ah yes," the mesmerist said, nodding, "you like that strange woman in trousers. Tell me, do you think she will stay with you? The call to adventure is just as strong with her as it is with you."

"Do you want to get hit by another chamber pot?"

Alaeddin Bey smiled. "Threats of violence only prove that I am correct."

"No, they only prove you're in mortal danger."

The mesmerist's smile faded. "Look, Sir Augustus. You are not such a cipher. The war traumatized us all. That is no reason to shrug off one's friends."

"Says the man who lives alone, works alone, and spends his time tricking people out of their money and virtue."

The look on Alaeddin Bey when he said this immediately made him sorry.

"Yes, I am alone," Alaeddin Bey said, his voice sounding distant. "You said you did not think I am Turkish. You are correct, although I am from the Ottoman Empire. I am Armenian. When the war came I was living in a small town in Anatolia. I was a scholar, a teacher at a local school. I had a house with a little garden and a big library. I had my aged parents and my brothers and sisters. I had a woman who wanted to become my wife. Life was simple and promising. When the war came I did not think it would affect me. Life, you see, was too pleasant, too easy, as if nothing could break the rhythm of lectures and dinners and walks in the park."

Augustus leaned against the sink and took out a packet of Woodbines. He lit one, then found himself offering one to Alaeddin Bey. The mesmerist didn't even notice the gesture. He was elsewhere.

"We were patriots, Sir Augustus. While we thought joining the European war was a mistake, we were proud of the Ottoman Empire. My youngest brother even enlisted. But there were Armenians who saw the war as a chance to free our people from what they called the 'Ottoman yoke.' Some on the borderlands took up arms and helped the Russian invaders. When the news hit the papers, many of my Muslim neighbors, people with whom I had shared conversations with over coffee or said hello to in the street, people whose shops I patronized or whose children I educated, they changed. They changed as quickly as day changes into night. I suffered insults. Got spat on in the street. My school, which was run by a Muslim who I thought was my friend, sacked me. And then it got so much worse. People began to get attacked in the streets. People threw rocks through our windows. A group of Muslim men caught my sister alone in the marketplace and … well, we knew we had to leave.

"We never even made it out of town. We were stopped by soldiers just two blocks from our house. They tried to grab my sister and when my brother and I intervened, they shot us both. Here is the wound."

Alaeddin Bey opened his shirt to reveal a puckered scar on his chest.

"I awoke that night in the ditch where they had thrown me. My brother lay beside me, dead. My father too. They had stabbed him to death with bayonets. My mother and sister I did not see. I never saw them again, but I know what happened to them. I know what happened to hundreds of thousands of my people."

The mesmerist passed a trembling hand over his face.

"They had left me for dead, but I had been fortunate. The bullet struck bone, and while it had bled freely and the shock had knocked me out, the wound wasn't too dangerous. I had been robbed, of course, and had nothing on me. I fled into the countryside. From a distance I saw a long column of Armenians being led along the road by soldiers. The roadside behind was littered with corpses to mark their passing. I fled further into the wilderness, robbing isolated farms to get food. I had never stolen before, but now I had to do it to survive.

"I headed for the coast, hoping to find a boat to get out of the country. For days and days I walked, avoiding all human habitation except when I needed to steal food. My shoes wore out and the winter grew cold. Ah! I'm telling a tale. Why make it sound poetic? I was miserable and filthy and the loss of my family made me feel like someone had punched me in the stomach over and over again. You've lost. You know. I don't need to explain it."

Augustus shook his head but did not speak.

"Have you ever been to the Anatolian plain in winter? No, of course not. Only a madman would volunteer to go there. That's where they led my people, out into the plain to freeze and starve. I froze and starved too. But at least I was free. I had a chance. Not like the others. One day my luck changed. Fate handed me a new page in life. I was stumbling along over barren hills and came to a road. There I saw a lone man riding a horse. He had stopped by the side of the road, his back to me, and the horse was nibbling on a little patch of grass that had somehow survived the cold. He did not see me.

"You may think you know what I did next, but you are half wrong. I snuck up on him, yes. I picked up a heavy stone, yes. He did not see me until I was almost upon him. Then he heard me. He twisted in his saddle and was so startled by my appearance he fell off his horse. I must have been quite a sight. My clothes were in rags, my feet bloody, my hair matted. And there was murder in my eyes, I assure you.

"He was a Turk, a rich one. I do not know why he was riding alone in such a lonely place. It was as if God himself had delivered him to me for vengeance. I raised the stone over my head, ready to dash his brains on the road.

"But I did not. Perhaps I should have, but at that moment I saw God had given me another path. I threatened him, swore at him, screamed like a lunatic until he had given me his money and his horse and revealed he had spare clothes in his saddlebag. I took them, and left him by the side of the road. He had clothes and a water skin I left him. I did not want his death on my hands. He had not killed my parents or brothers. He had not insulted my sister. He had not done me wrong.

"So I became a thief, and not a murderer. And I have been a thief ever since. I have lied and stole and seduced, but I have never taken a woman by force and I have never killed. There are those I wish to kill, Sir Augustus, those who deserve it. But they are not the people I meet now. I save my anger for those who created it."

Augustus found his voice. "Why do you imitate a Turk?"

Alaeddin Bey gave a little shrug, attempting a smile. "My Turkish is fluent, and Turks have the mystical aura of the East clinging about them, at least the Westerners think so. To be an Armenian in 1919 is to have everyone look at you with one thought in their head. I do not wish for my loss to be my identity."

Augustus shuddered.

"I got it!" Cordelia said, coming back in. She stopped at the door. "Whatever is the matter?"

"Nothing," Augustus said, clearing his throat. "You have the book?"

"Yes. Are you sure you're—"

"Good. Get to work. I'm going for some air."

Augustus went onto the balcony and looked out over the garden for several minutes, smoking one cigarette after another. At last he knew he must go back inside, so back inside he went.

Cordelia sat at the desk, the open book and several pieces of paper in front of her, filled with strange symbols and notes.

"What did you find?" he asked.

"It's just as I thought," Cordelia announced. "It's a list of several dates, twelve in fact, one for each sign of the zodiac."

"Meeting dates?" Augustus asked.

"Perhaps. But I found out something even more significant. One of those dates is tonight."

So that night, two hours after sunset, they set out. Cordelia, Aunt Pearl, and Herr Schäfer stayed in the hotel guarding Alaeddin Bey.

Augustus felt more than a little obtrusive walking out of the Winter Palace Hotel with a large, heavy bag accompanied by a woman in trousers, a hulking Nubian with a bandaged arm, and a young Egyptian boy. He hoped people would simply stare at his mask and miss all the other details.

It was a simple enough task to walk along the esplanade for a while, shooing away the hucksters who even at this hour dogged their footsteps, and then cut over to the Avenue of the Sphinxes that connected Luxor and Karnak temples. Both temples were off-limits after dark and had watchmen, but Karnak was too vast to patrol properly and they soon managed to sneak in through one of the many gaps in the surrounding ancient wall that enclosed the sacred precinct.

A thin crescent moon gave scant light as they moved through the outer ruins of the giant collection of temples. Augustus opened the bag and produced a German submachine gun from the last war. To Moustafa he gave a Lee-Enfield rifle. Jocelyn had her own rifle. All three of them had handguns as well. They moved as silently as they could, taking a meandering path between the broken walls, column bases, and heaps of rubble. The main part of the temple stood before them, shining with the palest light from the moon.

"They're watching us," Faisal whispered.

Augustus stopped. "Sentinels? Where are they?"

"No, the djinn."

There was a soft smack as Moustafa cuffed him. Faisal was too frightened to even object.

"The boy does have a point," Jocelyn whispered as they moved on. "If they really are meeting at the temple of Ptah and Sekhmet tonight, there will be at least one lookout."

"We'll deal with that when we come to it," Augustus said. "Let's cut through the main temple. It will give us more cover."

Faisal made a strangled sound in his throat, but didn't say anything.

As they drew closer to the temple, even Augustus felt a prickle of superstitious dread. The crescent moon made the pharaohs flanking the gate glow with an eerie light. They moved into the shadows and peeked around the gate before entering the more open area beyond. All was silence. Augustus tried to reassure himself that the temple precinct was far too large to guard, and that any sentry would be closer to the meeting place.

Nevertheless, he took care as he moved past the gate a little ahead of the others and came to the Grand Hypostele Hall.

A forest of columns confronted him. The moon was still too low for more than the top halves to be lit, the moonlight slashing down at an angle. The lower halves of the columns and the temple floor remained swathed in shadow.

He crouched, listening, for several minutes. When he heard nothing, he signaled for the others to follow and skirted the edge of the columns, keeping to the wall as he moved left to where the wall turned. Then he moved forward to the gate that led to the open area in which stood the temple they sought.

Keeping to the shadows, Augustus peered out the gate.

The Temple of Ptah and Sekhmet stood ahead, past an open area that looked all too broad and exposed. Augustus studied the temple for a minute, averting his gaze slightly in order to improve his night vision. The others waited several paces behind.

For a while he saw nothing out of place. He kept looking.

Always give it a good look before going out.

Sergeant Guthrie had told him that before his first night patrol, back when Augustus had gone under a different name and was a fresh junior officer straight out of military academy and new to the front.

Things that look like nothing can suddenly rise up and kill you. Take your time before you make a move.

The view of the dimly moonlit temple precinct wavered, a view of No Man's Land superimposing upon it.

Not now, Augustus told himself. Or was it Sergeant Guthrie speaking? *See things clearly. See things for what they are.*

His vision steadied. The temple stood out plainly again.

And then something moved.

It was a lump on top of the wall that Augustus had mistaken for a weathered, irregular stone. But stones do not move a couple of feet to the right.

Augustus gestured for his companions to come up. He pointed out the sentry.

"He must have gone up those stairs to keep watch," Jocelyn whispered. "And if he's there, then the rest will be too."

"What do we do?" Faisal asked. "Even I couldn't make it across there without being seen."

Augustus bit his lip, lost in thought. The boy was right.

"You told me the police we're in their pocket," Moustafa said. "So they'll be of no use. And I don't like the idea of a frontal assault on that place. Considering how good fighters the other Invisible Scorpions have been, I suspect that sentry is a crack shot."

"And those inside the temple will be heavily armed as well," Augustus agreed. "We'll have to distract them. Moustafa, give me your rifle and take the submachine gun."

"I've only practiced with it once," Moustafa objected as he made the trade.

"You're a good shot in any case. I only hope your wounded arm can withstand the recoil. Here's what we'll do. Jocelyn and I will go far to the right, over there by the outer wall. Out of easy range but well within sight. We'll turn on the flashlight and talk in a normal voice as if we're sneaking into the temple at night. That will get the sentry's attention as you and Faisal sneak up from the other direction."

"Won't they run over and shoot you?" Faisal said.

"They won't want to risk the noise. I'm sure they have the watchmen in their pay, but gunshots would bring too much attention. What they'll most likely do is send one or two watchmen after us. We'll be trespassing, after all, so they can kick us out. I'm sure it happens often enough. We'll pretend to follow the watchman, and once we're out of sight of the temple, we'll overcome him and return. By then you'll have taken out the sentry and, with a bit of luck, stuck up the entire gang."

"That sounds like a lot more luck than we usually have, Mr. Wall," Moustafa said.

Augustus grinned and clapped Moustafa on the shoulder. "Where's your pluck? Taking that museum job has robbed you of your sense of adventure. Now judging from the distance we should both be able to get into position at about the same time. Don't make a move until you see our flashlight."

"This is a bad idea," Moustafa grumbled as he and Faisal moved off and were swallowed by the shadows.

Augustus tensed. Moustafa was right. It was a bad idea. But it was the only idea he could think of.

CHAPTER THIRTY-TWO

Moustafa and Faisal barely made it a hundred yards through the Grand Hypostele Hall before trouble started.

Faisal grabbed his arm and stopped him. Fear made his grip surprisingly strong. Moustafa could barely see the boy's face in the dim light, but he did see him put a finger to his lips. Moustafa cocked and ear and listened.

And then he heard it.

Footsteps. Approaching from behind.

Moustafa got behind the cover of one of the broad columns, slung his submachine gun, and drew the curved Beja dagger he had won in the fight back in Cairo. He'd need to kill this sentry or watchman quietly, or this whole plan would unravel before it truly got started.

The footsteps drew closer. Faisal disappeared into the shadows. The boy had a talent, Moustafa had to admit. Even though Moustafa looked directly at the spot where he knew Faisal to be, he could not see him.

Moustafa envied him. He wouldn't mind disappearing right now too.

The footsteps drew closer.

A shadow passed into view—a slight figure, in what looked like a dark djellaba. Moustafa did not have the time to take a close look. He drew up behind the intruder and raised his knife arm.

Only at the last instant did he stop from slitting the newcomer's throat. As he clamped his free hand around the person's mouth and moved in for the kill, he felt the smoothness of the cheeks, and the long hair brushing against his arm, and smelled the faint perfume of a woman.

The woman tried to scream, her cry muffled by Moustafa's strong grip.

"Who are you?" Moustafa whispered.

"It's Cordelia," Faisal said, appearing from the shadows.

Moustafa let go. "What are you doing here?"

"I came to help," Cordelia whispered, her voice wavering from the shock she had been given. "Would you mind ever so much taking that knife away from my throat?"

"Oh right, sorry." Then anger rose up in him. "What do you think you're doing? I could have killed you."

"I came to help," Cordelia repeated, this time lifting up her medical bag. "If this turns out anything like your last adventure, someone is going to need a nurse. Where are the others?"

"We split up. They're going to distract the guard while I sneak up on them. You need to leave. The shooting will start soon."

"I will not. You'll need me."

Moustafa hesitated, looking back the way they had come. Mr. Wall and that crazy woman were long gone. He would have trouble catching up to them now, assuming he could find them. And even if he did, that would set the timing of the attack off. The meeting might be finished by the time they sorted this out.

Of course he could leave Cordelia here with the instructions to either hide or return to the hotel, but he felt sure she would only start following them again.

"All right," he said with a sigh. "But keep well behind us and try not to make any noise."

They started moving again. Faisal, who had understood none of the conversation, whispered to him, "Why are you letting her come along?"

"No other option," Moustafa grumbled. "Just like I had no other option but to chase you and that madman all the way up the Nile to solve another case."

For once, Faisal didn't object to Moustafa calling Mr. Wall mad. Perhaps he had finally opened his ignorant eyes. More likely he was too scared of attracting djinn to speak more than absolutely necessary. As they passed through a patch of moonlight shining slantways between the columns, he could see the Little Infidel clutching the charm around his neck.

Moustafa felt grateful for all the hours he had spent in this place as a younger man. He knew it like the back of his hand. Otherwise he could have never found the side gate in the near-darkness.

But find it he did. He peeked around the corner and found they were to the southwest of the Temple of Ptah and Sekhmet, facing the entrance at an angle. He paused there, waiting, unable to see the sentry he knew was on duty.

That made him nervous.

A sudden light made him jerk back.

A few hundred yards away, past the temple, he could see the light of a flashlight bobbing through the ruins.

Female laughter carried through the night. Jocelyn, playing the silly woman sneaking into the temple after dark. In response he could hear Mr. Wall's voice, unusually mirthful. They were too far for him to pick out the words.

It didn't matter. He saw movement on top of the temple and knew the sentry had seen. The shadow shifted to the far end of the temple roof and out of sight.

"Now's our chance," Moustafa said. "Miss Russell, you stay here. It's too dangerous out in the open. Faisal, let's go."

"You're letting a child go into danger but not me?"

"He's useful as a scout, and he can take care of himself."

To avoid hearing Cordelia's response, he started to run, staying low and trying to keep to as much cover as possible.

That was difficult. The area was fairly open and the moon, although only a crescent, cast sufficient light to expose him.

Faisal did better. He zigzagged between statue fragments and heaps of broken building blocks, his smaller form being able to slip into shadows that Moustafa could not. He also kept well away from Moustafa.

Smart boy. Moustafa felt like he had a big target painted on his chest. *Dear God, please don't let Nur's dream come true. I need to get back to them.*

As they approached, Moustafa and Faisal slowed, silence being more important than speed at this point. Moustafa kept his gaze between the roof, where he saw no one, and the temple gate, where he expected to see the muzzle flare of a gun at any moment.

Moustafa crouched behind the low remains of the wall enclosing the columned front hall, the submachine gun trained on the black rectangle of the gate beyond. He could see nothing. Couldn't see the Little Infidel either, which was for the best. He'd be out scouting and would no doubt come back with some useful information. As annoying as that guttersnipe was, he had his uses.

He heard a distant call in heavily accented English.

"Sir! Madam! The temple is closed!"

That would be the watchman. Mr. Wall and his unseemly friend would act abashed, talk with him for a moment, and allow themselves to be led out. Once they got out of sight of the Temple of Ptah and Sekhmet, that watchman would get a quick hit on the head and be put out of order. Then those two would sneak over here to help.

But Moustafa couldn't wait that long. Sooner or later, the sentry on the roof would stop watching the distraction and get back to looking all around.

Time to move.

Studying his path with care so as not to dislodge a pebble and make some noise, he moved into the columned hall. He angled left, out of sight of the black gate, and moved to the wall. Pressed against it, he was invisible to the sentry above unless the man leaned over the edge and looked down.

Moustafa edged along the wall to the edge of the portal. Across the opening, he saw a small hand emerge from shadow into the moonlight. Faisal.

The hand put up all five fingers, then two, and pointed inside the temple. Then the hand slipped back into the shadow and disappeared.

So there were seven people inside. How had the Little Infidel managed to determine that without revealing himself?

The tyke did have one advantage. His side of the gate was in a shadow cast by one of the columns. The moon shone on Moustafa's side. He couldn't take a peek into the temple interior without revealing himself.

He should have thought of that before choosing to go left instead of right.

A low whistle from above made him tense. From within the temple and above he heard a whisper.

"They're gone," a man said in Arabic. "Just some stupid tourists."

A soft light appeared within the temple, visible only by the pale glow it cast out the gate.

"Brethren," a woman's voice intoned. "We are gathered here at a key time. Most of the gangs have sworn fealty, and the others will soon be defeated. The operation on the river went well and we have the papers that will put that foreigner in our pocket. We will soon have even more cash coming in."

"All thanks to you, oh great Sekhmet!" a man called.

Moustafa's lip curled in disgust. How could an Egyptian woman of the modern age sully herself so much as to be called by the name of a pagan goddess? Not even belly dancers did that!

The woman kept talking.

"Ahmed, you will take the case to Cairo. Mohammad, Tarek, you're to guard him. The rest of you, continue with your work in the south. That is all we need to discuss tonight. Now let us show obeisance to the great goddess."

Rage rose up within him. They were going to perform a pagan rite?

Moustafa had enough sense to only expose part of himself as he looked around the edge of the gate, leading with his gun.

He took it all in within an instant—the lamp on the floor of the main room, the small group of Egyptians moving toward the rear sanctuary, and the sentry atop the wall, turning to face him and bringing up his rifle.

A short burst from the submachine gun toppled the man off his perch. Ignoring the jab of pain the recoil sent through his injured arm, Moustafa leveled the gun at the small crowd of bandits.

"Stop where you are! You're—"

Moustafa ducked back as half a dozen men drew guns with remarkable speed and poured fire out the gate. Bullets cracked off the ancient masonry.

"Why didn't you wait for the Englishman, you silly Nubian!"

"Keep out of the way!"

Moustafa reached around the doorway and fired a blind burst before poking his head around. Just by luck he had gotten one gangster and scattered the rest.

He kept firing, the gun stitching a line across the wall and hieroglyphs but not hitting anyone as they ducked behind cover. He struggled to aim, but the submachine gun pulled up and to the left.

Then it ran out of bullets.

Cursing, Moustafa got back behind cover and fumbled for another magazine, his arm singing with pain. He hoped the Invisible Scorpions were cowed enough to give him time to reload.

How had Mr. Wall fired this thing? Oh right, short bursts. He had told him long bursts only wasted ammunition.

Moustafa snapped a new magazine into the gun just as one of the Invisible Scorpions rounded the corner, pistol leveled.

Moustafa gave him a burst in the stomach that threw him back, doubling over and gouting blood.

Continuing to turn around the corner while going down on one knee to make less of a target, Moustafa gave a short burst at the next figure he saw, a man with a pair of pistols half behind the inside of the gate.

The man ducked back into cover. Although he was only a few feet away, he moved like lightning and Moustafa had no idea if his bullets had struck flesh.

"They're going to get away out back!" Faisal shouted. "And they're going to get on the roof and fire down on us!"

Time to move. Moustafa retreated into the columned hallway and made for a gap in the masonry. The Little Infidel disappeared into the shadows, no doubt doing the same.

Moustafa clambered through the wrecked wall, trying to keep an eye on the roof and the temple's back corner that had now become visible as he got out of the columned hall.

Just as Faisal had predicted, he caught sight of a dark shape on the roof.

He and the gang member fired at the same time.

A bullet cracked off a piece of rubble at Moustafa's feet. In the flare of his submachine gun, the figure flailed and dropped.

Moustafa rushed for the rear corner of the temple, staying close to the wall to make it harder for anyone remaining on the roof to fire down on him and keeping his sights trained on the corner in case those retreating out the back came around it to fire.

He almost got there before they tried. One peeked around the corner and Moustafa gave him a short burst, but the man had already ducked back.

Moustafa pressed himself against the wall just a couple of feet short of the corner. Through the ringing in his ears he heard a woman shout, and what he thought was the sound of running feet. Were they already making their escape?

If they had left a rearguard at the temple, Moustafa would get a bullet if he tried rounding that corner.

But if he didn't, they'd get away.

He had to chance it. Leading with a burst of bullets, he rounded the corner.

Only to find he was firing at nothing.

It took a moment to spot them—five dark figures scattered over the field of rubble between the Temple of Ptah and Sekhmet and the Grand Hypostele Hall.

If they get in there, we'll never find them!

Moustafa gave two short bursts at the receding figures, but they were already a hundred yards away and flickering in and out of the shadows. None of his bullets hit.

A quick movement to the right caught his eye. Faisal darted from shadow to shadow, following alongside the fleeing gang but staying well out of range. They probably didn't even see him.

Shots came from the left. A couple of hundred yards away, one of the temple watchmen stood atop a column base and fired with a rifle at something he couldn't see.

Temple guards were not issued firearms. Mr. Wall's suspicions had proven correct. The guards were in the pay of the Invisible Scorpions.

Jocelyn popped into view about a hundred yards in front of him. A single shot cracked the night air and the watchman flew backwards into the shadows.

"Not a bad shot," Moustafa admitted as he snapped his third and final magazine into the submachine gun. His arm shook with pain. But he had no time to nurse it.

He raced after the Invisible Scorpions, who were halfway to the Grand Hypostele Hall now, headed straight for the side gate. A shot from the left, no doubt by Mr. Wall, made one pirouette and fall.

Three left, Moustafa thought as he huffed over the broken ground. *Three fighters and that wicked woman. Although she's probably a good shot too.*

Two of the Invisible Scorpions stopped a moment and fired a flurry of shots at Moustafa and Mr. Wall, forcing them to seek cover. When Moustafa next looked, he saw them almost at the gate. Both he and Mr. Wall fired more shots, all of which missed as the small group ducked into the gate and disappeared. Off to the right, Moustafa saw Faisal hop out of a shadow and through a small hole in the masonry.

Moustafa smiled. The boy had been terrified of the place in the broad daylight, and now he was chasing criminals into it in the middle of the night.

They approached the gate more cautiously now, afraid one of the gang might be waiting in the darkness as a sniper. Mosutafa was less than fifty yards away and even in the dim light would make a good target. Mr. Wall angled in from the left, pressed against the wall, and edged toward the opening.

As his former boss pulled something out of his pocket, Moustafa ducked and closed his eyes. A low thud and a flash beyond his eyelids told him Mr. Wall had detonated one of his homemade flash grenades.

Moustafa was up and sprinting toward the gate as the detonation still rang in his ears. Mr. Wall moved in, firing his pistol at some unseen targets.

When he caught up, Moustafa came upon a dead gang member and an eerie scene.

The Grand Hypostele Hallway shone in the moonlight. The dim light of the crescent moon angled in through the open roof, casting across the columns to put one side of them in faint light and the other side in deep shadow. The floor was a pattern of light and dark strips. The hieroglyphs on the columns stood out sharply, mutely speaking across the ages.

Mr. Wall moved left and Moustafa veered right into the silent stone forest.

The remaining gang members had gone to ground, hidden somewhere amid these columns.

Moustafa got into a shadow and stayed there a moment, ears straining to hear even the slightest sound.

Nothing.

He feared moving. The entire columned hallway was striped with alternating bands of moonlight and shadow. If he tried to penetrate deeper into this vast hall, he'd have to cross one of the illuminated parts, and would invite a shot.

Yet if he did not move, he would not find the Invisible Scorpions. They were hidden somewhere around here, equally immobilized.

Unless they were far enough inside already that the forest of columns obscured them from view.

The faint sound of a sandal scraping on stone up ahead. Friend or foe? He peered in that direction and saw nothing.

The sound came again, moving to the right. A moment later he heard the snick of a magazine being snapped into place somewhere up ahead.

Had that been Mr. Wall? He had an automatic pistol. But then again so could the Invisible Scorpions.

The sound to his right had been closer, and couldn't have been made by Mr. Wall. His former boss would have had to pass across his view. Faisal was somewhere to the right, but the Little Infidel never made a sound in this kind of situation. It was the only time he stayed quiet.

He rushed from the cover of one column to another. A quick sound of movement came from ahead and a bit to the left, but no bullet came.

As soon as he got to the next column he realized how lucky he had been. While he had run along the shadow of one of the great carved columns, he hadn't realized until too late that from either side his figure would have been silhouetted against the moonlit bands to his left and right.

This strange terrain is going to get me killed.

Another slight movement. Moustafa froze. It had come from the other side of the column.

Did he dare try to draw his knife and kill the man silently? If started to change weapons and the man came around and saw him, Moustafa wouldn't have time to respond. But firing would give away his position. Someone might even spot the muzzle flare before he had time to move to another location.

A thud and a cry from the far left made him pause. Had that been a woman's voice?

A moment later there was a burst of gunfire from that location. He could not see the muzzle flares directly, but they lit up the interior for a moment before going out.

The sound of running feet, one lighter and one heavier. Moustafa couldn't see them and didn't dare move position to look, not with an opponent so close.

"He's after me!" Faisal called.

Moustafa edged around the column. He had to help him.

"Duck!" Mr. Wall shouted.

A single shot from what sounded like Mr. Wall's pistol, followed by a heavy thud.

"You got him!" Faisal cried. "He was the last!"

Moustafa was just opening up his mouth to warn that there was another when Faisal burst into the moonlight twenty yards away, holding a briefcase aloft.

"I got it! Englishman, I—"

A gunshot barked from a nearby shadow. Faisal flew back, his body hitting hard on the stone flagstones.

Moustafa spun, spotted the gunman and poured every bullet from his magazine into him as Mr. Wall appeared from behind a column and did the same. The Invisible Scorpion jerked, erupting blood from a dozen wounds, and fell dead.

With a cold feeling in his gut, Moustafa turned back to Faisal.

The boy lay unmoving on the ground, a pool of blood spreading around him.

Nur's dream, Moustafa thought, his entire body trembling. *It wasn't about me. It was about him.*

CHAPTER THIRTY-THREE

Faisal felt cold. He thought his chest should hurt, but it was more like a cold tightness, as if a big block of ice was stepping on him.

His hands felt warm, though, because he was holding his chest. They felt wet too.

The gunfight raged all around him. Even over all the noise he could hear the Englishman shouting in English. He sounded really afraid.

Oh no, don't get the Englishman too.

Faisal tried to sit up, thinking he should get out of the line of fire, but he found he could barely move.

Trying made the first of the pain come.

He hissed through his teeth, then groaned as another wave of pain passed through him. His eyes filled and he blinked the tears away. He had to keep quiet, or the Invisible Scorpions would find him and they'd get the case. Faisal couldn't let the others down.

He turned his head, the world rocking side to side as he did so, and saw that the case lay near him, tucked away in the shadow of one of the big columns. Good. The gangsters might miss it.

They wouldn't miss him, though. He lay right in the moonlight.

He really should get out of sight, but he was afraid it would hurt more. Besides, he was too tired.

The gunfire stopped. He could still hear the ringing in his ears like he had heard after the other gun battles he'd been in. Now he heard something else too. It was a *whoosh whoosh whoosh* in his ears that he could feel as well as hear. What was that?

He lay there looking at the columns in the moonlight with their funny picture writing. It would have been nice to have learned more about that stuff. He should have asked the Englishman. Or even Moustafa.

Funny. The columns looked taller than before. And the stars above them looked really, really far away.

Suddenly the Englishman came into view, followed quickly by Cordelia. She said something in English that came out sounding all slow and funny and pushed the Englishman away. Then she opened up a bag and took some things out of it.

Where had the Englishman gone? He turned his head and felt the world go all topsy-turvy again.

There he was, standing by the nearest pillar. He sure looked awful. More upset than he had ever seen him, even when the djinn possessed him in the desert. He kept trying to rush forward but Moustafa held him back. Briefly he saw Jocelyn with a rifle in her hand looking around the temple, but then she disappeared.

The Englishman and Moustafa started to disappear too. They didn't walk out of his line of sight like Jocelyn, they just sort of started fading. The columns started fading too.

As they started to fade, Faisal noticed there was someone standing behind the Englishman. Faisal wanted to call out a warning, but then realized that he didn't need to. This wasn't an enemy. He didn't know how he knew that, he just did.

The figure grew clearer, and he saw it was a woman. At first he thought it was Jocelyn, but then he noticed the figure wore a headscarf. The woman put a hand on the Englishman's shoulder but the Englishman didn't seem to notice.

Cordelia blocked his view for a second as she started pressing something against his chest. The pressure made him gasp with pain. When she moved again, the woman was gone.

And then everything was gone.

***

The next thing he knew he was in a room and it was daytime. He only got a bit of a look. It was painted all white and clean and he lay in a bed. Faisal felt very tired and his head felt all fuzzy. He couldn't move. He wasn't sure if that was because he wasn't trying or he really couldn't move. He slept.

***

The next time he woke up, it was evening or early morning judging by the light coming through the window close to his bed. The sun was low in the sky anyway, and had that golden color it gets when it's like that. The Englishman sat in a chair by his bed asleep. He looked pretty bad, his hair and clothing all messed up and even though he was asleep he looked exhausted. Faisal wanted to wake him up so he could have someone to talk to, but decided against it. The Englishman obviously needed to rest. Maybe he had gotten hurt in the gunfight too.

Strangely, Faisal didn't feel much pain, only a heavy tightness in his chest. His head was still all fuzzy and his body had a light, tingly feeling to it.

Cordelia came into the room. She smiled at Faisal but looked concerned too and put a hand on his forehead. Then she took a funny glass stick off a tray by the bed and stuck it under his tongue.

"What's this?" Faisal asked.

Cordelia put a finger to her lips and glanced at the Englishman. Right. Let him sleep.

After a little while she took the glass stick out from his mouth and looked at it, turning pale. She hurried off.

Faisal dozed for a bit, waking up when Cordelia returned with an Egyptian man wearing one of those white jackets the doctors wear.

"Hello, young man," the doctor said. "You're very lucky to be alive."

"Is the Englishman all right?"

The doctor looked confused for a moment. "You mean Sir Augustus? Yes, he's fine."

"Then why does he look all rumpled?"

The doctor smiled. "That's because he hasn't left your side for three days."

"I've been here for three days?"

"And you'll be here for longer than that." The doctor looked through some papers he carried. "Yes, your wound was very serious. It missed all the major internal organs, though. With sufficient rest you should have a full recovery. As I said, you were lucky."

A sharp intake of breath beside him made Faisal turn. The Englishman had woken up and sprung to his feet, his hand going to the pocket where he kept his pistol. He had enough sense not to draw it. There was no danger here and the doctor probably wouldn't like it.

"You're awake," the Englishman said, looking down at Faisal.

"So are you," Faisal replied. "Maybe you should go back to sleep. You look as sleepy as I am."

The doctor got a glass of water and a couple of pills. The Englishman took them from him and held up Faisal's head so he could take the pills and swallow them down with water.

"That will help your fever," the doctor said. "I'm going to do the rest of my rounds and come back in a little bit. I think you're in good hands here."

With a smile at Cordelia and the Englishman, he left.

"Did you get the briefcase?" Faisal asked.

"Yes we did, Faisal," the Englishman said, sitting down beside him.

"Did it have the papers in it you wanted?"

"Yes it did. You did very well."

"What about that woman? Sekhmet?"

"She got away."

"Oh."

Faisal felt disappointed. All this trouble and they didn't even break up the whole gang.

Cordelia said something. The Englishman translated.

"She says not to worry about all that. We solved the case for Mr. Beechcroft."

"What are you going to do about the magician?"

"Alaeddin Bey managed to give us the slip. He filched one of Cordelia's hairpins through sleight of hand and picked the handcuffs. He kept them around his wrists like they were still locked and then when he saw his chance he took off running."

"I bet he's halfway to Jerusalem and still running he's so scared of you," Faisal said and giggled. He stopped because it hurt.

The Englishman smiled. "Oh, I didn't look for him too hard."

That was strange. But the Englishman was always saying strange things.

Cordelia was fussing around the bed, arranging the pillows and tucking in the covers.

"She saved me, didn't she?"

"Yes."

"I was going to die, wasn't I?"

The Englishman looked down at the floor. "Best not to think about it too much."

"Who was that Egyptian woman at the temple?"

"You mean Sekhmet?"

"No, the other one."

"I don't know who you mean."

"Never mind," Faisal mumbled. He thought he knew.

***

Everyone was really nice to him at the hospital, even Moustafa. Faisal slept most of the time because of those pills they gave him, two pills three times a day. One morning, however, they gave him four pills.

He slept really long then, and when he woke up he found himself in a different room. From the small size and the hum of the engine, he knew he was on a steamboat. The Englishman and Moustafa sat in the cabin with him.

"Where are we going?"

"Downriver," the Englishman said.

"You just rest, Little Infidel."

Faisal rested. He was glad to get away from Luxor. He'd never seen a place with so many ancient ruins. No wonder he'd gotten hurt.

He slept through much of the boat ride, eating a little of what Cordelia brought him and talking a bit with the others when they came to visit. Otherwise he slept, and dreamed of getting back to Cairo.

Faisal wondered where he'd stay once he got there. He wouldn't be able to climb up the back wall of the Englishman's house to get to his little shack. No, not for a long, long time. He guessed they'd put him in a hospital like they had in Luxor. That would be nice. The beds were comfy and they brought you food three times a day without you needing to do anything. Mina could visit. Or maybe it wouldn't be good for her to see him all hurt. She might get scared.

Faisal was surprised when they docked after only two days and they put him on a stretcher and carried him onto land.

"Where are we?"

"Assiout," the Englishman said. "We're taking you to a hospital here."

They put him in the back of a motorcar that drove very slowly so as not to give him a bumpy ride. Even so, every little rut or stone in the road jarred his wound and made him hiss in pain.

"Don't worry," the Englishman said. "We're almost there."

Faisal lay on the seat and watched the tops of the buildings pass by. He wished he could sit up and see everything. He hadn't seen anything on the river trip except the ceiling of the cabin. He started to drift off to sleep but then a bump in the road hurt him and he woke up again. When he looked out the window, he didn't see buildings any more, but the tops of palm trees.

"Is this hospital in the countryside?" Faisal asked.

"Yes."

The motorcar slowed to a stop. He could hear children playing somewhere in the distance. The Englishman got out and started speaking with a woman in English. Then the Englishman and Moustafa got the stretcher and took Faisal out.

He found himself in front of a big whitewashed building. Off to the side was a church like the Christians use. He could tell because it had one of those peaked roofs and a cross on top. In the distance, past the church, he saw a bunch of boys and girls running around and laughing in the field.

And that's the last he saw before he dropped out of consciousness.

He didn't know how long it was before he woke again. All he knew was that it was night. The window next to his bed was a big black rectangle and there was an oil lamp burning on the bedside table. Whether it was that night or the next night he didn't know. Maybe it was even the night after that.

He was in a little room that looked like a hospital. There were four beds, but no one else was there. Everything was clean and white and there was a metal tray on a nearby table with bandages, a bottle of the stuff they called iodine, another bottle with some pills that were called pain killers, and a pair of scissors for cutting off bandages before replacing them with new ones. He had learned these things over the past few days.

Faisal rested for a time.

His doze got disturbed by the door opening. A European woman looked in for a moment, then closed the door. He thought he recognized her, but his head was so muzzy from sleep and probably some of those pain killers that he couldn't remember where he had seen here before.

A minute later, the Englishman walked in.

"They told me you were awake." He sat on a chair by the bed. "How are you feeling?"

"Better than before. I'm glad that trip is over. You were right to stop before we got home. It's better to rest in the country, I think."

The Englishman put a hand on his forehead. "No trace of fever. You had a fever the first couple of days."

"I had weird dreams. When do we go back to Cairo?"

The Englishman got an uncomfortable look on the side of his face not hidden by his mask. To his surprise, he took Faisal's hand.

"Faisal, do you know where you are?"

"Assiout. You said so."

"That's correct. Do you remember Ms. Trasher?"

"The American Alaeddin Bey tried to rob? Sure."

The Englishman looked away for a moment and then looked back at him. "Yes, we are at her place."

"Oh, that's why I saw children. I didn't know she had a hospital too."

"Well, many of the children who come here are very sick, so she has a nurse on staff, and a physician who visits regularly. That was the gentleman who examined you when you first got here."

"Oh." Faisal didn't remember that. He had been having trouble concentrating the past few days.

"While you were in the hospital in Luxor I thought of Ms. Trasher and wired her. She said she'd be happy to have you here. Do you understand what I'm saying, Faisal?"

Faisal felt the Englishman's hand tense, like he wanted to pull away but wouldn't.

"Sure. I don't remember much about the Luxor place but it was a big building with lots of other people. Ms. Trasher's hospital is much nicer."

The Englishman shifted in his seat.

"That's not quite what I mean. I feel terrible about what happened to you. I was selfish bringing you into danger like this. I'm afraid it might happen again and I wouldn't want that."

"But I'm useful."

"You are useful, Faisal. Very useful. But you're too young to be coming along on adventures like this. What if you had been killed?"

"But I wasn't. Cordelia saved me."

"She might not be there the next time. I can't risk that. While you've been recovering I've taken a look at Ms. Trasher's institution. It's a wonderful place. There's a nice dormitory for the boys, and plenty of room to play, and brand new classrooms with qualified teachers who teach the children how to read and write and give them marketable skills for when they grow up."

"Sounds like Ms. Trasher is pretty nice."

The Englishman squeezed his hand. Faisal felt confused. What was going on?

"Yes, Faisal. She's very nice. The boys and girls here have been given a wonderful opportunity. The regime is a bit more orderly than what you've been accustomed to, and you'll be required to bathe regularly, but you'll get used to that. And church services are not required. She allows the children to keep their native religion if they so choose."

"What are you talking about?"

The Englishman took a deep breath. "The American who hired me to track down Alaeddin Bey gave me a reward, a rather sizeable one. You deserve a share of that, but since you're a minor I can't in good conscience give it to you right away."

Money? That was great!

"How much? When do I get it?"

"Quite a lot. Enough for a sizeable donation to Ms. Trasher's orphanage, some for a regular supply of clothing and educational materials for you, and once you're old enough to leave, some money to help get you started in whatever trade you choose."

The excitement of a moment before dissipated, replaced with a cold sense of foreboding.

"Why are you giving my money to the American? And what are you talking about, 'old enough to leave'?"

"I've enrolled you as one of Ms. Trasher's wards. I've already signed the legal papers. You can stay here until you're sixteen or eighteen and then—"

"What? You're leaving me here?"

"It's the best thing for you. If I bring you back to Cairo, you'll only keep tagging along and there'll be more trouble."

"I thought you were my friend!"

The Englishman squeezed his hand again. He looked upset. Faisal had never seen him look this upset.

But he looked determined too.

"I am your friend, Faisal. That's why I'm doing this. If we keep going on this way you'll get hurt again, maybe even killed. And it's not fair for you to remain a street boy. This way you'll have a home. Regular food. Friends and a future."

Faisal tried to object, but his throat had clenched. He was frozen with fear and couldn't move a muscle, could only listen to the Englishman's relentless words.

"It's the best thing for you, Faisal. Moustafa agrees. So does Cordelia. You'll be safe and you'll have a future. You know better than I do that street boys rarely make it to adulthood. Now you have that chance. Now you have a future."

But I already had a future.

The Englishman let go of his hand and stood.

"I'm afraid this is goodbye. Trust me. It's better this way. I'll be keeping in contact with Ms. Trasher and I'll make sure you want for nothing. As you grow up you'll see that I'm right, and when you come of age I hope you'll visit me in Cairo. I'll be interested to see what kind of young man you'll have grown into. Goodbye Faisal, and thank you for everything. I mean that."

The Englishman left, and Faisal was alone.

The tears didn't come for a long time. When they did, they didn't stop.

CHAPTER THIRTY-FOUR

Four months later ...

"I got a letter from Ms. Trasher a few days ago."

Augustus sat with Moustafa in his library. The Nubian had come to borrow some books from his library as he did every Thursday and, according to the custom they had settled into, they were enjoying some tea and a chat.

"Was she begging you to take the Little Infidel back? Has the dormitory become infested with lice and fleas?"

Augustus chuckled. "No, all that was in the first letter, the one that came about a month after I left him there. As you know, he recovered fairly quickly, and then raised holy hell. I believe her words were, 'If I crossed a jackal with a lion and fed it on a diet of pure sugar, I don't think I could have come up with a bigger discipline problem.'"

Moustafa laughed. "It sounds like he is on the mend."

"Indeed. Then the letter became more troubling. It said Faisal grew withdrawn. He seemed resigned to his fate and stopped talking entirely. He even refused to eat."

The look on Moustafa's face reflected what Augustus felt. He hurried to go on.

"Thank goodness for the second letter. It was dated a few weeks after the first. Yes, it took nearly two months to get here. Must have gotten lost in the system. The postal workers in Upper Egypt keep going on strike and stashing bags of mail in storerooms as a protest. Even most of the civil servants are supporting the independence movement these days. In any case, Faisal seems to have shaken himself out of it, at least partially. It's impossible to get him to sit still at lessons, and he's had one or two fights with other boys, fights I am happy to say he won, but in other ways he's adjusting to orphanage life quite well."

"Really?"

Augustus nodded. "I was just as surprised as you are. He's been teaching the other children what Ms. Trasher calls, 'A barbaric form of pidgin English' and he's also taught them football."

"He knows how to play football?"

"He learned from that boy in Bahariya oasis. Apparently Faisal scrounged some leather, made a crude ball, packed it with straw, and got one of the girls to stitch it up for him. Ms. Trasher looked at the whole affair with a rather jaundiced eye at first, but softened when she saw the good effect it had on the boys. Released their pent-up energies and made them better able to sit at lessons."

"Even the Little Infidel?"

"Well, no."

Moustafa sipped his tea, lost in thought for a moment. "You know, it's strange. I'm glad the orphanage is changing him, but I'm also glad it's not changing him too much."

"I think he'll be all right in the end. I gave them enough to ensure his place in an apprenticeship once he's old enough to leave, as well as a stipend for his first couple of years so he can find his feet."

"That's very kind of you, Mr. Wall."

"It was the least I could do."

There was an awkward pause.

Yes, the very least.

Clearing his throat, he said, "I should send a wire to see how he's getting on. With the mail being so unreliable, Ms. Trasher has probably sent more than one progress report that I haven't received."

"If you do hear, I'd like to know how he's doing. Have you heard from Ms. Montjoy?"

Augustus shifted in his seat.

"Yes," he said with a sigh. "She's enjoying herself in Palestine and sending me a regular supply of picture postcards."

But no real letters. Jocelyn had been the only one of his friends who thought it a bad idea to send Faisal to the orphanage. "Foisting him off on an institution is irresponsible," she had said. Their relationship has cooled after that, with Jocelyn doing all the cooling.

At least she had promised to return to Cairo after her trip through Palestine. He would patch things up with her then.

In the meantime, he still had to deal with Cordelia, who had seen her chance with Jocelyn's absence and had started petering him tenfold. Annoyingly, she had more freedom to do so now that she no longer lived at her brother's house. When the chief of police learned about her role in the Karnak affair, he insisted on her leaving Egypt. She had replied by getting a nursing job and her own flat downtown. Now she enjoyed more freedom than she ever had in her life.

Freedom to visit him without prior announcement.

Yes, he most definitely needed to patch things up with Jocelyn.

Augustus shook those thoughts away. "So what are you going to do, Moustafa? I feel terribly sorry that you lost your job with Mr. Simaika so soon after getting it."

"It was not written, Mr. Wall. My wife always says that I do not have the temperament to work for someone else."

"Nur sounds like a wise woman."

Moustafa blinked, obviously surprised that Augustus knew his wife's name. It was something Augustus had made a point of remembering after he realized how often he had forgotten it.

Augustus lit a cigarette, "So now what will you do?"

"I will use my share of the reward money to open a bookshop. Besides writing that article you were so kind to read, I've been using the past few months to gather stock. I just need to find a suitable place on a street frequented both by Egyptians and foreigners. The bookshop will have books in all major languages, especially Arabic, and on all subjects."

"With a large section on Egyptology, no doubt."

"Of course. If only I could find some good books on Nubia."

"Perhaps you should write one." After a pause, Augustus murmured, "You said all subjects. Would this include politics?"

Moustafa nodded, his face serious. "Yes, Mr. Wall. We will carry all opinions without censure."

"Not all opinions are treated equally under the law. Take care, my friend, and I will be honored to show up on the first day and be a customer."

"Oh, your money will never be any good in my shop, Mr. Wall."

"Then I'll trade you for one of Suleiman's fake statuettes!"

Moustafa boomed out a laugh and shook his finger. "I will miss selling those to foolish tourists. It is something I know you get great pleasure from too."

Augustus smiled. "I do indeed."

There was a loud clatter as the heavy brass knocker at the front door rapped several times.

Both Moustafa and Augustus rose.

"Sit, Mr. Wall. I don't mind getting it one last time."

Moustafa headed for the door just as the knocker clattered again, more urgently this time.

"I'm coming. I'm coming," Moustafa grumbled.

Curious, Augustus moved from the study to the end of the hallway. At the other end, Moustafa came to the large, old gate and slid the bolt to open the regular-sized door set within it.

Moustafa froze.

Only his head moved to watch as a frowning Faisal, a bag slung over his shoulder and wearing the uniform of a tea boy from one of Thomas Cook's steamboats, stomped through the door and into the front gallery.

Augustus watched in shock.

Faisal stomped right past him and up the stairs. Moustafa was so stunned he even forgot to shout at him. The boy had never been allowed up there.

Augustus was entirely at a loss. He looked to Moustafa for help, but the man merely nodded, said, "I will call you later," and hurried out the front door.

Moustafa ducking out in this situation put Augustus in more of a panic than when he had resigned his job and refused to come south.

Glancing up the stairs, he saw Faisal reach the top and go around the corner. Augustus hesitated a moment, then walked up after him.

As he got to the landing, he saw Faisal stomp up to the third floor.

Where the Devil is the little tyke going?

Utterly baffled, Augustus followed him up to the next floor, which he hardly ever used except for a small reading room that had a small, high window opening on the roof to provide a breeze into the interior. He got there just in time to see Faisal take off his sandals, tie the laces together, and hang them around his neck. Then the boy grabbed a hold of the joints in the room's arched stone doorway and began to climb up. He did it with his usual agility and in a trice he had reached the window and wormed his way through it and onto the roof.

For a moment Augustus simply stared. Then came a series of great crashes, as if Faisal was throwing around large objects up there.

Augustus hurried out of the room and to the narrow staircase leading to the roof, unbolting the little-used door and coming out into the sunlight.

The roof was strewn with dusty old furniture and assorted junk, all the things that had taken up the little shack that still housed the previous owner's discarded bric-a-brac. Cautiously Augustus peered inside …

… and his jaw dropped.

The interior had been made up into a little living space. To one side was a plump cushion next to a box covered in a cloth. A set of silverware was placed on the box beside a rather dusty plate. On the walls hung various boyish mementoes such as ram's horns and shells and bits of pottery. On a little shelf was the Late Period lamp Moustafa had given him in Bahariya.

Beside it were several ticket stubs to moving picture shows. Taking up much of the room was a series of cushions covered with blankets to make a crude bed. Sitting on the bed, arms crossed over his chest, was a very angry Faisal.

Augustus stared at Faisal. Faisal glowered back at Augustus.

"What happened?" Augustus asked. He wasn't sure if he was asking about the orphanage, the hidden room, Faisal's recovery, or all three.

"I ran away from that place and worked on a Thomas Cook steamer to get back here. What do you think?"

"Well, um, yes. I deduced that. But why leave the orphanage? You could have gotten an education there. And three meals a day. And friends. It could have been a home."

Faisal's frown deepened. "I already have one."

"Oh." Then realization dawned. "So that's how you knew my movements. And that's why I so often found food missing from the pantry. I almost sacked the cleaning lady, thinking it was her. Wait a minute, have you been stealing my wine?"

"I pour it out," Faisal said. "Drinking is a sin."

"Not for me it isn't. So while I've been sleeping you've been running around my house?"

Suddenly Faisal looked a bit unsure of himself.

"How do you get up here? You can't get in through the lower floors."

Faisal jabbed his chin toward the rear wall of the building. "I climb up from that alley. No one ever goes in there."

Augustus walked over and looked down. At first glance the wall appeared sheer. A moment's study, however, revealed chinks in the masonry, some of which showed signs of purposeful enlargement.

He walked back to the shed, shaking his head.

"That looks like a dangerous climb."

"Not for me it isn't."

"So how long have you been hiding up here?" Augustus asked with wonder.

"Since the first time I helped you solve a murder. Remember I asked if I could live with you?"

"Did you? Um, no. I don't remember that."

Faisal clucked his tongue and looked away. "Of course you don't."

Augustus tried to think. No, he couldn't remember that conversation at all. He should have felt bad about that, but the anger of having been spied on this whole time, and having been duped, canceled that out.

But the two emotions—guilt and anger—were precisely equal. They balanced each other and left nothing.

Suddenly Augustus felt an overwhelming urge to walk back downstairs, light a cigarette, open up his newspaper, and pretend this wasn't happening.

He did not fight it, and Faisal said nothing as he left.

***

Faisal came back. Moustafa would never have believed it if he hadn't seen it with his own eyes. The Little Infidel had given up a secure place in the orphanage, a place where he could enjoy everything he had lacked on the streets, to travel the length of Egypt and return to that madman.

It was written. Their lives were linked. As a religious man, Moustafa did not believe in coincidence. Of all the places Mr. Wall could have chosen to live, he had picked the street infested by Faisal and his thieving friends. And when that murderer fled Mr. Wall's shop after killing that French archaeologist, who did he bump into but Faisal? And who found the notebook he dropped? Faisal.

That had brought the Little Infidel in on the case. And he had clung to Mr. Wall and Moustafa like a louse ever since.

Even after getting shot.

For all his ignorance, Faisal had seen what Moustafa had not seen—that God had written their fates to be on the same path.

God help them both.

Moustafa walked down Ibn al-Nafis Street and turned a corner to a larger street lined with shops. From there he proceeded until he came to a major street, this one with a tram line. He went to his usual stop to wait for the next tram that would take him to a connecting tram that would make the long journey to the end of the line where he would have to walk the remaining way home.

As he waited, he realized he was smiling. It was good to see the Little Infidel had fully recovered. While he had gotten the best medical care, Moustafa had worried that the gunshot might have done some permanent damage. But Faisal looked just as spirited and willful as ever.

He had found himself missing Faisal.

"Ridiculous," he scoffed.

Moustafa's eyes strayed over the many shops, a mixture of Egyptian, Greek, Jewish, and European, until his gaze settled on one small storefront that had a small sign on it saying, "For Rent."

Curious, he walked over. The steel shutter was down and he could see nothing. The adjoining shop had a sign in Arabic, English, French, and Greek saying, "Andreas Stavropoulos, Fine Watches and Clocks."

He entered. The watches on display actually were not all that fine, just simple pocket watches and mantelpiece clocks for the middle classes. A hunched, older Greek with a fringe of gray hair around a bald pate sat behind the counter, a magnifying eyepiece in one eye as he used a tiny pair of tweezers to remove a spring from the back of a silver pocket watch.

The man looked up.

"Good afternoon. How may I help you?" the Greek asked.

Moustafa smiled. The man had spoken in Arabic. The Greeks, unlike most Europeans, took care to learn the local language. Many had been born here to families that had lived in Egypt for generations.

"I was wondering if you knew who owned the shop for rent next door."

"Oh, that's me." The Greek took out his eyepiece and rose. "The draper who lived there died, sadly. Good man. I rented to him for years. Are you interested in renting a property?"

"I want to open a bookshop."

"Oh! That would be excellent. What kind of books?"

Moustafa paused, then decided it would be best to be open up front.

"All types, especially on Egyptology. There will be political books as well. Of all kinds."

"All kinds, eh? Well, I hope you'll have books telling the fools who burn Greek businesses that most of us want independence as much as other Egyptians."

Moustafa smiled as his tension vanished. "I will make that a priority."

"Let me show you the shop."

Mr. Stavropoulos fetched some keys, led Moustafa next door, and unlocked the shutter. He raised it up with some effort.

"It needs oiling," he said, finally getting it up with a grunt and a loud clatter.

Beyond the shutter was a storefront with large display windows. The watchmaker opened the door and flicked on an electric light.

The empty interior was about thirty feet by fifteen, with a small back room. Moustafa walked slowly around. Everything was clean, with no water stains or cracks in the plaster, and no signs of rats or other vermin. He imagined the place filled with bookshelves, and himself at a little desk by the door, ready to greet customers as they came in. When there were no customers he would read at that desk, and write. Perhaps he could leave an open space near the back where he could run salons or invite speakers to talk on learned subjects to a select audience.

"Do you like it?" the Greek watchmaker asked.

"I do. How much are you asking?"

"Three hundred piastres a month, plus two month's deposit."

Moustafa nodded. "That's fair." It was actually better than he expected.

"It's a very good neighborhood," the Greek said. "Quiet, with no trouble from criminals. As you can see it's right on a tram line, and even though we're on the edge of the Old City we get a nice mix of Europeans and respectable Egyptians."

"I'm familiar with the neighborhood. My former boss lives not far from here. If I take this place, I expect he will still be a part of my affairs."

"Oh? I hope that won't be a problem."

Moustafa laughed and shook his head. "Yes, it will be a problem. It will lead to no end of problems. But it appears God has written that for me, and I will accept it."

***

When the Englishman turned and walked back downstairs without another word, Faisal felt like he was being left at the orphanage all over again.

All the way up from Luxor he had wondered how the Englishman would react to his return. Of course he wanted the Englishman to be happy, but Faisal knew him too well to expect that. Perhaps, he had thought, he would be angry. The Englishman had given the orphanage a lot of money. So Faisal would have understood anger. But walking away without saying anything?

Faisal had turned invisible again. After all he had done, after all the adventures they had been through together, Faisal was still invisible.

And now he knew he would always be invisible.

So he gathered up his things—his spare djellaba, the silverware he had decided not to sell, the ancient lamp that Moustafa had given him, and tied them in a big bundle in his bedroll. Then, with a last look at the little shack that had for a time been his home, and climbed down the rear wall of the Englishman's house and back to his real home.

The streets.

He headed for the shack at the end of the alley where he used to live.

It stank just as much as always. He hated bad smells now. In the orphanage, the boys and girls had to wash every day, and they scrubbed the floors and cleaned the kitchen too. While Faisal hated the work, he liked having a clean place to live.

That was never meant to last, he thought. *Your place is here. You were stupid to think your place was with the Englishman.*

As he climbed over the rubble and heaps of trash, making his way for the shack, he felt a tug of regret for leaving the orphanage. If he had known the kind of greeting he'd get when he came back here, he would have stayed.

Too many rules. Make your bed! Sit up straight! Go to sleep when the bell rings at night!

Ms. Trasher hadn't been bad, though. And the other boys had been nice enough. Faisal had taught them to play football.

He couldn't go back, though, not after stealing a bunch of food from the pantry and fleeing to the port.

A small boy came out of the alley. Faisal recognized Mehmed, the Turkish boy who had been beaten by the sugarcane vendor.

"Hey, Faisal! I didn't think we'd ever see you again."

"Yes, I'm back," he said with a sigh. "You look better."

"Sure. Amira umm Dodi came every day like she said she would and fixed my back up. Thanks for the food."

"Did the other boys swipe any of it?"

"No. They even gave me some more. Where have you been?"

"Nowhere." Mehmed wouldn't believe him if he told the truth. None of the boys believed him. Mina would, though. He'd have to go see her. She must be wondering where he was. Had the Englishman even bothered to tell her what happened? Probably not.

Mehmed followed him back to the shack, chattering away with all the latest news about who had stolen what and who had gotten in a fight with who and who nearly had gotten caught by the watchman. Faisal, who usually loved street gossip, couldn't bring himself to care.

They got to the shack. It looked filthier than ever. Faisal would have to organize the other boys to clean this place up. He changed out of his Thomas Cook uniform and into his blue djellaba, the one that gangster had given him. Ms. Trasher had thrown away his old djellaba. Maybe he should have run away with that gangster when he had the chance.

"You can't beg in that," Mehmed said.

Faisal looked down at himself. "No, I can't."

"Mess it up."

Faisal shook his head. He wouldn't do that.

"Hey, I have an idea," Faisal said.

Twenty minutes later, Mehmed was begging in a crowded street as Faisal stayed close by. Faisal looked clean and respectable, like a boy who had a house and a family and everything. Mehmed looked like a street boy. As he begged the passersby, they ignored him or shoved him out of the way. They paid no attention to Faisal, who walked alongside them and picked their pockets while Mehmed distracted them.

By the end of the day they had twelve piastres.

"This is great!" Mehmed said. "I'm going to eat until I burst."

Faisal's smile did not reach his heart. Although he was glad to help out Mehmed, who wasn't very good at taking care of himself, he felt bad about picking those pockets.

"Stealing is a sin in both our religions," Ms. Trasher had told him. "I don't blame you for doing it when you lived on the streets. Now that you have a home, you don't need to anymore."

Easy for her to say. She was a foreigner with a lot of money. He had to live somehow!

Faisal said goodbye to Mehmed and trudged through the streets. He found himself back in his old neighborhood around Ibn al-Nafis street, or at least what used to be his neighborhood. He had no place here now, even though he knew every shop, every cobblestone.

Hamza, one of the other street boys, called to him.

"Hey, Faisal! I heard you were back. That Englishman you beg from has been busy today. What's going on?"

"What do you mean?"

"He's been going in and out of his house all day. First he brought in some wood. Then he brought in some paint. Then he brought in a big bag full of all sorts of things. I couldn't see what. And for most of the afternoon there's been lots of noise coming from upstairs."

Faisal tried to forget about it. What the Englishman did was no longer his business. He bought some falafel with the money he had stolen and ate it, watching the people walk by, all those lucky people who got to live somewhere better than a shack in an alley that smelled of cat piss. He tried not to think about what the Englishman was up to.

But, as usual, his curiosity gnawed at him. What could be going on in there?

Eventually Faisal decided to find out.

Sneaking into the alley behind the Englishman's house, he peered up at the roof far above. He didn't see anything different, and he didn't hear anything. He hoped Hamza hadn't been teasing him.

He turned to leave, but once again curiosity got the better of him. He put his fingers in the familiar cracks between the big old stone blocks, took a deep breath, and began to climb.

Faisal's life had trained him to be cautious, so once he got to the top, he did not immediately clamber over the lip of the wall. Instead he hung there for a moment, listening.

He heard nothing, but he did smell something.

Fresh paint.

What would the Englishman be painting up on the roof? He never came up to the roof, which is why Faisal had gotten away with living up there for so long.

It sure had been good while it lasted.

Faisal peeked over the lip of the wall. Although the light was beginning to fade into evening, he could see that no one was up there.

He hopped over the lip of the wall and looked around. The roof had been cleaned. A lot of the old trash from the previous owners such as broken pots and splintered old chairs had been removed, and everything had been swept. The shed looked different too.

Faisal stopped and stared.

The entire shed had been painted a sky blue. He walked over. Yes, it was all freshly painted. Hardly believing his eyes, he touched the paint. It was still sticky, and left a little bit of blue paint on his fingertip.

Peering inside, he was in for another surprise. All the old furniture that he used to hide behind was gone. Everything had been scrubbed and swept and there was fresh paint on the inside walls just like on the outside. Where he had put his blankets and old sacking, there was now a narrow bed with blankets and a mattress and a pillow and everything. On the shelf where he had kept his old lamp was a small bottle of lamp oil and a box of matches. A new shelf had been put on the wall next to it, and on that was a small bag. He opened it and found some bread and fruit and vegetables. He also found five piastres.

The smell of roasting chicken made Faisal step out of the shed. The window leading to the upstairs reading room was open and the smell came up from that. This was the time that the Englishman usually cooked his dinner if he didn't go out. Faisal remembered how when he used to live here those smells would make his stomach grumble so loudly he thought the Englishman would hear him. Maybe he should steal some of the food in that bag.

Then he noticed something else.

There was a key in the door leading to the stairs.

Faisal went over and turned it.

The door was not bolted on the inside like it usually was. He opened it and stepped through. Now that he was inside, the smell of that roast chicken was even stronger. It led Faisal downstairs. He knew he shouldn't be inside when the Englishman was awake, but something told him it might be all right this time. Even if it wasn't, he'd already been kicked out of the house. He didn't have anything to lose.

Faisal came to the upper floor and peeked down the stairs. He didn't see or hear anything on the middle floor, meaning the Englishman was probably down in the kitchen or dining room.

The sound of a bell tinkling nearly made him jump out of his djellaba. That had definitely come from the dining room. His sharp ears, honed from years of having to detect dangerous sounds on the streets, could tell almost exactly where and from how far any sound came.

Faisal tiptoed downstairs to the lower landing. Just as he reached the second-to-last step, he felt something brush against his front shin. The bell tinkled again, the sound louder as it came from just down the hall around the corner.

"It's about time you made it down here," he heard the Englishman's voice say. "Get in here before dinner gets cold."

Faisal gaped. A thin wire was stretched across the steps, almost invisible in the dim light of the staircase. He stepped over it and followed a wire set in hooks on the wall that led to the dining room doorway, where a little bell hung on a hook.

And inside the dining room sat the Englishman.

He sat at one end of the table. In the center of the table was a beautiful roast chicken, complete with carrots and potatoes. A plate of fruit sat next to it.

At the other end of the table was a chair, a plate, and a knife and fork.

"Do you like my little alarm? You're not the only clever one in this house."

Faisal hesitated at the doorway. "It's ... very clever, Englishman."

"How are your new quarters?"

"Quarters?"

"The shed. I'm sure you found the money. That's for when I'm not around to feed you. It's also so you can go to the hammam. I cannot abide filth in my home and you are most certainly not sharing my bathroom. I'll renew the money when it gets low. I'll also give you a key to the front door. I don't want you breaking your neck on the back wall. Now there are going to be some rules. First off, you must not touch any of my things. Secondly, you have the run of the house when I'm awake but no sneaking around when I'm asleep. Thirdly, we'll have to see about getting rid of those lice. Oh, and we'll get you a new djellaba to replace the one that criminal gave you. Do you understand everything?"

Faisal stared. No, he didn't understand anything at all.

"Well, don't stand there gawping all day, go wash your hands before dinner. I'm sure you know where the downstairs bathroom is. You'll find soap in there. Ahmed showed you how to use it, so use it!"

Faisal jumped in the air and spun around.

"All right, Englishman!"

Faisal ran to do as he was told, grinning from ear to ear.

HISTORICAL NOTE

While the main characters and story in this novel are fictional, the historical background is as accurate as I could make it. Also, some of the minor characters are real.

The anecdotes and attitudes of Sir Thomas Russell Pasha come from his autobiography, *Egyptian Service 1902-1946*, an excellent glimpse into the mind and times of this important historical figure.

Another real figure is that of Heinrich Schäfer. I am glad to say he finally did finish his *Principles of Egyptian Art* which, while a weighty academic tome, is still one of the most thorough introductions to understanding the art of ancient Egypt almost a hundred years after it was written.

Marcus Simaika was an important leader in the Cairo's Coptic community at this time. He founded the Coptic Museum, which still exists today. With the blessings of the Coptic Pope Cyril V, he scoured the monasteries and churches of Egypt for old artifacts and manuscripts to add to the museum's collection. Now, a hundred years later, the Coptic Museum is one of the most interesting sights in Cairo, with an impressive collection tracing the history of one of the world's oldest Christian communities.

Lillian Trasher was a Christian missionary who lived most of her life in Assiout (nowadays generally spelled Asyut) and ran a missionary that cared for orphans, widows, and the blind. Her story of being inspired to help orphans after learning about the old woman planning to throw her granddaughter in the Nile is true. Trasher saved that orphan from death, and did the same with countless others. The orphanage bears her name and still helps the needy more than a century after she founded it. You can learn more about its work at http://ltokids.tripod.com/.

The information about Shepheard's Hotel comes from a rare pamphlet titled *The Story of a Historic Hostelry: Shepheard's Cairo.* Printed around 1930, this curious little booklet appears to have been a souvenir sold or given to guests.

More details of Shepheard's come from Andrew Humphreys's detailed and beautifully illustrated book, *Grand Hotels of Egypt in the Golden Age of Travel*. Another of his works, *On the Nile in the Golden Age of Travel*, gave me a great deal of information on the boats of the Thomas Cook company. The steamboat *Arabia*, which Faisal enjoyed so much, was a real ship and the pride of Thomas Cook's Nile fleet.

These and many other books on Egypt in the old days I read during various research trips to the Bodleian Library, Oxford, one of the world's great repositories of knowledge, and on frequent visits to that sanctuary for Cairene bibliophiles, the American University in Cairo bookshop.

I also relied on William Edward Lane's classic study, *Manners and Customs of the Modern Egyptians* and the 1929 edition of the *Baedeker's Guide to Egypt and the Sudan*. A more modern guide to the country is the *Blue Guide to Egypt*, now sadly out of print. The 1993 edition has an extensive section on Cairo and proved an invaluable companion on my many rambles through the medieval districts where much of the Cairo action takes place.

The temple of Amun-Re in Luxor is, of course, a real place. I have spent many wonderful hours in its Grand Hypostele Hallway, and have explored all the lesser temples within the precincts of Karnak, including the Temple of Ptah and Sekhmet. I am happy to report there is no visible damage from the gunfight between Moustafa and the Invisible Scorpions. The restoration work must have taken care of that.

Camel cigarettes, which first came out in 1913, used their famous logo of a camel and a pyramid as a way of hinting that its tobacco was really Egyptian. At the time, Egyptian tobacco was widely considered the best in the world. While Egypt is no longer a producer of the crop, Camel has retained its logo.

And of course I would be remiss not to thank my many Egyptian, Sudanese, and expatriate European friends who helped me with their local knowledge and encouragement. You all helped a bunch, and I'll see you the next time I'm in Cairo!

About the Author

Sean McLachlan worked for ten years as an archaeologist in Israel, Cyprus, Bulgaria, and the United States before becoming a full-time writer. He is the author of numerous fiction and nonfiction books, which are listed on the following pages. When he's not writing, he enjoys hiking, reading, traveling, and, most of all, teaching his son about the world. He divides his time between Madrid, Oxford, and Cairo.

To find out more about Sean's work and travels, visit him at his Amazon page or his blog, and feel free to friend him on Goodreads, Twitter, and Facebook.

You might also enjoy his newsletter, *Sean's Travels and Tales*, which comes out every one or two months. Each issue features a short story, a travel article, a coupon for a free or discounted book, and updates on future projects. You can subscribe using the link below. Your email will not be shared with anyone else.

Amazon: http://www.amazon.com/Sean-McLachlan/e/B001H6MUQI
Goodreads: http://www.goodreads.com/author/show/623273.Sean_McLachlan
Blog: http://midlistwriter.blogspot.com
Twitter: https://twitter.com/@writersean
Facebook: https://www.facebook.com/writersean
Newsletter: http://eepurl.com/bJfiDn

Fiction by Sean McLachlan

Tangier Bank Heist: An Interzone Mystery

Right after the war, Tangier was the craziest town in North Africa. Everything was for sale and the price was cheap. The perverts came for the flesh. The addicts came for the drugs. A whole army of hustlers and grifters came for the loose laws and free flow of cash and contraband.

So why was I here? Because it was the only place that would have me. Besides, it was a great place to be a detective. You got cases like in no other place I'd ever been, and I'd been all over. Cases you couldn't believe ever happened. Like when I had to track down the guy who stole the bank.

No, he didn't rob the bank, he stole it.

Here's how it happened . . .

Available in electronic edition. Print edition coming soon!

Three Passports to Trouble (Interzone Mystery Book 2)

Back in the days when Tangier was an International Zone, the city was full of refugees. People fleeing Stalin. People fleeing Franco. People fleeing the Nuremburg Trials. Tangier offered a safe haven from the chaos of Europe.

The International Council had to keep a delicate balance, tolerating everything from anti-capitalist agitators to Germans with murky pasts. It was the only way to keep the peace, and it worked.

Until an anarchist was found dead with a fascist dagger in his chest.

And I got stuck with the case just when I had to smuggle a couple of Party operatives out of town.

Available in electronic edition. Print edition coming soon!

Trench Raiders (Trench Raiders Book One)

September 1914: The British Expeditionary Force has the Germans on the run, or so they think.

After a month of bitter fighting, the British are battered, exhausted, and down to half their strength, yet they've helped save Paris and are pushing towards Berlin. Then the retreating Germans decide to make a stand. Holding a steep slope beside the River Aisne, the entrenched Germans mow down the advancing British with machine gun fire. Soon the British dig in too, and it looks like the war might grind down into deadly stalemate.

Searching through No-Man's Land in the darkness, Private Timothy Crawford of the Oxfordshire and Buckinghamshire Light Infantry finds a chink in the German armor. But can this lowly private, who spends as much time in the battalion guardhouse as he does on the parade ground, convince his commanding officer to risk everything for a chance to break through?

Available in electronic edition.

Digging In (Trench Raiders Book Two)

October 1914: The British line is about to break.

After two months of hard fighting, the British Expeditionary Force is short of men, ammunition, and ideas. With their line stretched to the breaking point, aerial reconnaissance spots German reinforcements massing for the big push. As their trenches are hammered by a German artillery battery, the men of the Oxfordshire and Buckinghamshire Light Infantry come up with a desperate plan—a daring raid behind enemy lines to destroy the enemy guns and give the British a chance to stop the German army from breaking through.

Available in electronic edition.

No Man's Land (Trench Raiders Book Three)

No Man's Land—a hellscape of shell craters and dead bodies. Soldiers have fought over it, charged across it, and bled on it for a year of grueling war, but neither side has dominated it.

Until now.

An elite German raiding party is passing through No Man's Land every night, attacking the British trenches at will. The Oxfordshire and Buckinghamshire Light Infantry need to reassert control over their front lines.

So the exhausted men of Company E decide to set a trap, a nighttime ambush in the middle of No Man's Land, where any mistake can be fatal. But the few surviving veterans are leading recruits who have only been in the trenches for two weeks. Mistakes are inevitable.

Available in electronic edition.

Christmas Truce

Christmas 1914

In the cold, muddy trenches of the Western Front, there is a strange silence. As the members of a crack English trench raiding team enjoy their first day of peace in months, they call out holiday greetings to the men on the German line. Soon both sides are fraternizing in No Man's Land.

But when the English recognize some enemy raiders who only a few days before launched a deadly attack on their position, can they keep the peace through the Christmas truce?

Available in electronic edition.

The Case of the Purloined Pyramid (The Masked Man of Cairo Book One)

An ancient mystery. A modern murder.

Sir Augustus Wall, a horribly mutilated veteran of the Great War, has left Europe behind to open an antiquities shop in Cairo. But Europe's troubles follow him as a priceless inscription is stolen and those who know its secrets start turning up dead. Teaming up with Egyptology expert Moustafa Ghani, and Faisal, an irritating street urchin he just can't shake, Sir Wall must unravel an ancient secret and face his own dark past.

Available in electronic edition and Print edition!

The Case of the Shifting Sarcophagus (The Masked Man of Cairo Book Two)

An Old Kingdom coffin. A body from yesterday.

Sir Augustus Wall had seen a lot of death. From the fields of Flanders to the alleys of Cairo, he'd solved several murders and sent many men to their grave. But he's never had a body delivered to his antiquities shop encased in a 5,000 year-old coffin.

Soon he finds himself fighting a vicious street gang bent on causing national mayhem while his assistant, Moustafa Ghani, faces his own enemies in the form of colonial powers determined to ruin him. Throughout all this runs the street urchin Faisal. Ignored as usual, dismissed as usual, he has the most important fight of all.

Available in electronic edition and Print edition!

The Case of the Golden Greeks (The Masked Man of Cairo Book Three)

They thought the case was solved.

When an eminent Egyptologist is murdered giving a lecture in front of a packed hall,

Cairo's chief of police quickly rounds up those responsible.

Or at least some of them.

Sir Augustus Wall, antiquities dealer and amateur sleuth, knows there's more to the crime than it seems. With little to go on but an exotic murder weapon, a map of a desert oasis, and some gilded Greek mummies, he sets out across the Sahara with his assistant Moustafa Ghani and the street urchin Faisal, who is the only person to have seen the killer's face. They soon find themselves in the midst of international intrigue on Egypt's remote border with Libya.

Can they discover what mystery lies beneath Bahariya Oasis?

Available in electronic edition and Print edition!

Radio Hope (Toxic World Book One)

In a world shattered by war, pollution, and disease…

A gunslinging mother longs to find a safe refuge for her son.

A frustrated revolutionary delivers water to villagers living on a toxic waste dump.

The assistant mayor of humanity's last city hopes he will never have to take command.

One thing gives them the promise of a better future—Radio Hope, a mysterious station that broadcasts vital information about surviving in a blighted world. But when a mad prophet and his army of fanatics march out of the wildlands on a crusade to purify the land with blood and fire, all three will find their lives intertwining, and changing forever.

Available in electronic edition and Print edition!

Refugees from the Righteous Horde (Toxic World Book Two)

When you only have one shot, you better aim true.

In a ravaged world, civilization's last outpost is reeling after fighting off the fanatical warriors of the Righteous Horde. Sheriff Annette Cruz becomes New City's long arm of vengeance as she sets off across the wildlands to take out the cult's leader. All she has is a sniper's rifle with one bullet and a former cultist with his own agenda. Meanwhile, one of the cult's escaped slaves makes a discovery that could tear New City apart…

Refugees from the Righteous Horde continues the Toxic World series started in Radio Hope, an ongoing narrative of humanity's struggle to rebuild the world it ruined.

Available in electronic edition !

We Had Flags (Toxic World Book Three)

A law doesn't work if everyone breaks it.

For forty years, New City has been a bastion of order in a fallen world. One crucial law has maintained the peace: it is illegal to place responsibility for the collapse of civilization on any one group. Anyone found guilty of Blaming is branded and stripped of citizenship. But when some unwelcome visitors arrive from across the sea, old wounds break open, and no one is safe from Blame.

Available in electronic edition!

Emergency Transmission (Toxic World Book Four)

Trust is the only thing that can save the world.

The problem is, everyone has their own agenda.

When an offshore platform starts emitting toxic fumes that threaten to destroy the last outposts of civilization, the residents of New City have to team up with a foreign freighter to fix it. But a lingering mistrust remains, and neither side has the resources to stop the leak.

That is, until help comes from the least reliable source.

Can old enemies finally set aside their differences for the greater good?

Available in electronic edition!

The Scavenger (A Toxic World Novelette)

In a world shattered by war, pollution, and disease, a lone scavenger discovers a priceless relic from the Old Times.

The problem is, it's stuck in the middle of the worst wasteland he knows—a contaminated city inhabited by insane chem addicts and vengeful villagers. Only his wits, his gun, and an unlikely ally can get him out alive.

Set in the Toxic World series introduced in the novel *Radio Hope*, this 10,000-word story explores more of the dangers and personalities that make up a post-apocalyptic world that's all too possible.

Available in electronic edition!

Warpath into Sonora

Arizona 1846

Nantan, a young Apache warrior, is building a name for himself by leading raids against Mexican ranches to impress his war chief, and the chief's lovely daughter. But there is one thing he and all other Apaches fear—a ruthless band of Mexican scalp hunters who slaughter entire villages.

Nantan and his friends have sworn to fight back, but they are inexperienced, and led by a war chief driven mad with a thirst for revenge. Can they track their tribe's worst enemy into unknown territory and defeat them?

Available in electronic edition!

A Fine Likeness (House Divided Book One)

A Confederate guerrilla and a Union captain discover there's something more dangerous in the woods than each other.

Jimmy Rawlins is a teenage bushwhacker who leads his friends on ambushes of Union patrols. They join infamous guerrilla leader Bloody Bill Anderson on a raid through Missouri, but Jimmy questions his commitment to the cause when he discovers this madman plans to sacrifice a Union prisoner in a hellish ritual to raise the Confederate dead.

Richard Addison is an aging captain of a lackluster Union militia. Depressed over his son's death in battle, a glimpse of Jimmy changes his life. Jimmy and his son look so much alike that Addison becomes obsessed with saving him from Bloody Bill. Captain Addison must wreck his reputation to win this war within a war, while Jimmy must decide whether to betray the Confederacy to stop the evil arising in the woods of Missouri.

Available in electronic edition and Print edition!

The River of Desperation (House Divided Book Two)

In the waning days of the Civil War, a secret conflict still rages...

Lieutenant Allen Addison of the *USS Essex* is looking forward to the South's defeat so he can build the life he's always wanted. Love and a promising business await him in St. Louis, but he is swept up in a primeval war between the forces of Order and Chaos, a struggle he doesn't understand and can barely believe in. Soon he is fighting to keep a grip on his sanity as he tries to save St. Louis from destruction.

The long-awaited sequel to *A Fine Likeness* continues the story of two opposing forces that threaten to tear the world apart.
Available in electronic edition!

The Last Hotel Room

He came to Tangier to die, but life isn't done with him yet.

Tom Miller has lost his job, his wife, and his dreams. Broke and alone, he ends up in a flophouse in Morocco, ready to end it all. But soon he finds himself tangled in a web of danger and duty as he's pulled into scamming tourists for a crooked cop while trying to help a Syrian refugee boy survive life on the streets. Can a lifelong loser do something good for a change?

A portion of my royalties will go to a charity for Syrian refugees.

Available in electronic edition and Print edition!

The Night the Nazis Came to Dinner and Other Dark Tales

A spectral dinner party goes horribly wrong...

An immortal warrior hopes a final battle will set him free...

A big-game hunter preys on endangered species to supply an illicit restaurant...

A new technology soothes First World guilt...

Here are four dark tales that straddle the boundary between reality and speculation. You better hope they don't come true.

Available in electronic edition!

The Quintessence of Absence

Can a drug-addicted sorcerer sober up long enough to save a kidnapped girl and his own duchy?

In an alternate eighteenth-century Germany where magic is real and paganism never died, Lothar is in the bonds of nepenthe, a powerful drug that gives him ecstatic visions. It has also taken his job, his friends, and his self-respect. Now his old employer has rehired Lothar to find the man's daughter, who is in the grip of her own addiction to nepenthe.

As Lothar digs deeper into the girl's disappearance, he uncovers a plot that threatens the entire Duchy of Anhalt, and finds that the only way to stop it is to face his own weakness.

Available in electronic edition !

Writing Books by Sean McLachlan

Writing Secrets of the World's Most Prolific Authors

What does it take to write 100 books? What about 500? Or 1,000?

That may sound like an impossibly high number, but it isn't. Some of the world's most successful authors wrote hundreds of books over the course of highly lucrative careers. Isaac Asimov wrote more than 300 books. Enid Blyton wrote more than 800. Legendary Western writer Lauren Bosworth Paine wrote close to 1,000.

Some wrote even more.

This book examines the techniques and daily habits of more than a dozen of these remarkable writers to show how anyone with the right mindset can massively increase their word count without sacrificing quality. Learn the secrets of working on several projects simultaneously, of reducing the time needed for each book, and how to build the work ethic you need to become more prolific than you ever thought possible.

Available in electronic edition and Print edition!

History Books by Sean McLachlan

Wild West History
Apache Warrior vs. US Cavalryman: 1846-86 (Osprey: 2016)
Tombstone—Wyatt Earp, the O.K. Corral, and the Vendetta Ride (Osprey: 2013)
The Last Ride of the James-Younger Gang (Osprey: 2012)

Civil War History
Ride Around Missouri: Shelby's Great Raid 1863 (Osprey: 2011)
American Civil War Guerrilla Tactics (Osprey: 2009)

Missouri History
Outlaw Tales of Missouri (Globe Pequot: 2009)
Missouri: An Illustrated History (Hippocrene: 2008)
It Happened in Missouri (Globe Pequot: 2007)

Medieval History
Medieval Handgonnes: The First Black Powder Infantry Weapons (Osprey: 2010)
Byzantium: An Illustrated History (Hippocrene: 2004)

African History
Armies of the Adowa Campaign 1896: The Italian Disaster in Ethiopia (Osprey: 2011)

Purchase copies of any of these titles here:
http://www.amazon.com/Sean-McLachlan/e/B001H6MUQI

Printed in Great Britain
by Amazon